Praise for

"A full-bore futuristic sci-fi fantasy, [...] [...] [...] character above techno-wizardry an[...] [...] [...] that comes in handy.... Endlessly su[...] [...]

"[Fforde] writes some of the most wicke[...] [...] ...way-across-the-table funny novels in print. *Shades of Grey* adds a definite edge to the humor with its social and political satire.... His work is rife with wordplay and droll humor, and the more agile-minded and literate the reader, the bigger the comic payoff.... *Shades of Grey* is not to be missed."　　　　　—*The Miami Herald*

"This insanely clever novel from the author of the bestselling Thursday Next series sounds like a cult classic for people who crave a rich brew of dystopic fantasy and deadpan goofiness.... Fforde has now created his most original story, an elaborate social satire about a weird but oddly familiar world almost five hundred years in the future. Every page of this high-concept novel glistens with ingenious details. Fforde is like the stand-up comic in a gulag; his silly but cerebral humor prances through this dreary place without missing a beat."
　　　　　—Ron Charles, *The Washington Post*

"Fforde's premise, a world organized by color, sounds shallow and only capable of furnishing enough material for an episode of *The Twilight Zone*. But in the author's skilled hands, it becomes a sly way to satirize religion and overbearing government, as well as a constant source of amusement. Color us green with envy."　　　　　—*New York Post*

"Fforde winningly mingles enforced orderliness with a *Brazil*-esque bureaucracy . . . A fancifully satisfying concoction."　　　　　—The Onion AV Club

"Already cult-worshipped for his popular Thursday Next and Nursery Crimes novels (*First Among Sequels*, etc.) Fforde is something like a contemporary Lewis Carroll or Edward Lear.... To dispel a black mood and chase away the blues, this witty novel offers an eye-popping spectrum of remedies."
　　　　　—*Kirkus Reviews* (starred review)

"This series starter combines the dire warnings of *Brave New World* and *1984* with the deevolutionary visions of *A Canticle for Leibowitz* and *Riddley Walker*, but, Fforde being Fforde, his dystopia includes an abundance of tea shops and a severe shortage of jam varieties. It's all brilliantly original."
　　　　　—*Booklist* (starred review)

"[An] inventive fantasy . . . Eddie navigates a vividly imagined landscape whose every facet is steeped in the author's remarkably detailed color scheme."
　　　　　—*Publishers Weekly*

Praise for Jasper Fforde and his work

"It's easy to be delighted by a writer who loves books so madly."
—Janet Maslin, *The New York Times*

"Like the creators of . . . *The Simpsons* and *South Park,* Mr. Fforde uses fantasy to dissect real life. . . . He is our best thinking person's genre writer."
—*The Washington Times*

"What captivates here is something that will appeal to any reader—and that's the feeling that there's something at stake in fiction, that characters created in books are every bit as real as the memory of a person."   —John Freeman, *Newsday*

"Fforde's inventiveness remains a bookworm's delight."   —*Entertainment Weekly*

"Mr. Fforde manages to bombard the reader with more bizarre detail than most writers would dare to fit in their entire oeuvre, yet he does so with . . . light prose and easy, confident wit."   —*The Wall Street Journal*

"Like the best novels of Douglas Adams or Terry Pratchett, Fforde goes beyond his genre."   —*Los Angeles Times Book Review*

"Fforde [has a] head-spinning narrative ability."
—Lloyd Rose, *The Washington Post*

"Jasper Fforde's mind-blowing books consistently defy—nay, mock—easy description. Are they fantasy? Mystery? Espionage? Science fiction? Absurdist humor? Shaggy, gleeful, scrambled combinations of the above? Answer: yup."
—*The Seattle Times*

"If you're done with Harry Potter, you'll need some books to fill the empty space. My suggestion? Anything by Jasper Fforde."   —*Richmond Times-Dispatch*

"What is most enjoyable about Jasper Fforde's work is not its silliness—though there is plenty of that. It is admiring the skill that keeps all of those silly balls in the air."   —*The Denver Post*

"The pleasure in reading Fforde is immersing yourself into a satiric, literary world rich in characters, setting, and language."   —*Portland Oregonian*

"Fforde's wicked sense of humor and wide-ranging intelligence make every page a joy."   —*The New Orleans Times-Picayune*

"The well of Fforde's imagination is bottomless."   —*People*

"Jasper Fforde is able to write diabolically. . . . Outrageous satirical agility is his stock in trade."   —*The New York Times*

PENGUIN BOOKS

SHADES OF GREY

Jasper Fforde was an enthusiastic member of the film industry for nineteen years before being published. Author of the *New York Times* bestselling Thursday Next and Nursery Crime series, he says that writing is the same as filmmaking—only you do all the jobs, not just one. He currently works and lives in Wales. *Shades of Grey* is his eighth novel.

SHADES OF GREY

The Road to High Saffron

Jasper Fforde

PENGUIN BOOKS

PENGUIN BOOKS

Published by the Penguin Group

Penguin Group (USA) Inc., 375 Hudson Street, New York, New York 10014, U.S.A. ● Penguin Group (Canada), 90 Eglinton Avenue East, Suite 700, Toronto, Ontario, Canada M4P 2Y3 (a division of Pearson Penguin Canada Inc.) ● Penguin Books Ltd, 80 Strand, London WC2R 0RL, England ● Penguin Ireland, 25 St. Stephen's Green, Dublin 2, Ireland (a division of Penguin Books Ltd) ● Penguin Books Australia Ltd, 250 Camberwell Road, Camberwell, Victoria 3124, Australia (a division of Pearson Australia Group Pty Ltd) ● Penguin Books India Pvt Ltd, 11 Community Centre, Panchsheel Park, New Delhi–110 017, India ● Penguin Group (NZ), 67 Apollo Drive, Rosedale, North Shore 0632, New Zealand (a division of Pearson New Zealand Ltd) ● Penguin Books (South Africa) (Pty) Ltd, 24 Sturdee Avenue, Rosebank, Johannesburg 2196, South Africa

Penguin Books Ltd, Registered Offices:
80 Strand, London WC2R 0RL, England

First published in the United States of America by Viking Penguin,
a member of Penguin Group (USA) Inc. 2009
Published in Penguin Books 2011

THE LIBRARY OF CONGRESS HAS CATALOGED THE HARDCOVER EDITION AS FOLLOWS:

Fforde, Jasper.
Shades of grey : the road to High Saffron / Jasper Fforde.
     p.   cm.
ISBN 978-0-670-01963-2 (hc.)
ISBN 978-0-14-311858-9 (pbk.)
1. Color blindness—Fiction. I. Title.

PR6106.F67S53 2010
823'.92—dc22   2009030813

Printed in the United States of America
Set in Berkeley Oldstyle with Berlinsans
Designed by Daniel Lagin

Tabitha
Welcoming you to the undeniably
enjoyable and generally underrated
sense of being known as existence

There is no light or colour as a fact in external nature. There is merely motion of material. . . . When the light enters your eyes and falls on the retina, there is motion of material. Then your nerves are affected and your brain is affected, and again this is merely motion of material. . . . The mind in apprehending experiences sensations which, properly speaking, are qualities of the mind alone.

—Alfred North Whitehead

A Morning in Vermillion

2.4.16.55.021: Males are to wear dress code #6 during inter-Collective travel. Hats are encouraged but not mandatory.

I t began with my father not wanting to see the Last Rabbit and ended up with my being eaten by a carnivorous plant. It wasn't really what I'd planned for myself—I'd hoped to marry into the Oxbloods and join their dynastic string empire. But that was four days ago, before I met Jane, retrieved the Caravaggio and explored High Saffron. So instead of enjoying aspirations of Chromatic advancement, I was wholly immersed within the digestive soup of a yateveo tree. It was all frightfully inconvenient.

But it wasn't *all* bad, for the following reasons: First, I was lucky to have landed upside down. I would drown in under a minute, which was far, far preferable to being dissolved alive over the space of a few weeks. Second, and more important, I wasn't going to die ignorant. I had discovered something that no amount of merits can buy you: the truth. Not the *whole* truth, but a pretty big part of it. And that was why this was all frightfully inconvenient. I wouldn't get to do anything with it. And this truth was too big and too terrible to ignore. Still, at least I'd held it in my hands for a full hour and understood what it meant.

I didn't set out to discover a truth. I was actually sent to the Outer Fringes to conduct a chair census and learn some humility. But the truth inevitably found me, as important truths often do, like a lost thought in need of a mind.

I found Jane, too, or perhaps she found me. It doesn't really matter. We found each other. And although she was Grey and I was Red, we shared a common thirst for justice that transcended Chromatic politics. I loved her, and what's more, I was beginning to think that she loved me. After all, she did apologize before she pushed me into the leafless expanse below the spread of the yateveo, and she wouldn't have done that if she'd felt nothing.

So that's why we're back here, four days earlier, in the town of Vermillion, the regional hub of Red Sector West. My father and I had arrived by train the day before and overnighted at the Green Dragon. We had attended Morning Chant and were now seated for breakfast, disheartened but not surprised that the early Greys had already taken the bacon, and it remained only in exquisite odor. We had a few hours before our train and had decided to squeeze in some sightseeing.

"We could always go and see the Last Rabbit," I suggested. "I'm told it's unmissable."

But Dad was not to be easily swayed by the rabbit's uniqueness. He said we'd never see the Badly Drawn Map, the Oz Memorial, the color garden *and* the rabbit before our train departed. He also pointed out that not only did Vermillion's museum have the best collection of Vimto bottles anywhere in the Collective, but on Mondays and Thursdays they demonstrated a gramophone.

"A fourteen-second clip of 'Something Got Me Started,'" he said, as if something vaguely Red-related would swing it.

But I wasn't quite ready to concede my choice.

"The rabbit's getting pretty old," I persisted, having read the safety briefing in the "How Best to Enjoy Your Rabbit Experience" leaflet, "and petting is no longer mandatory."

"It's not the petting," said Dad with a shudder, "it's the ears. In any event," he continued with an air of finality, "I can have a productive and fulfilling life having never seen a rabbit."

This was true, and so could I. It was just that I'd promised my best friend, Fenton, and five others that I would log the lonely bun's Taxa number on their behalf and thus allow them to note it as "proxy seen" in their animal-spotter books. I'd even charged them twenty-five cents each for the privilege—then blew the lot on licorice for Constance and a new pair of synthetic red shoelaces for me.

Dad and I bartered like this for a while, and he eventually agreed to visit all of the town's attractions but in a circular manner, to save on shoe leather. The rabbit came last, after the color garden.

So, having conceded to at least *include* the rabbit in the morning's enter-tainment, Dad returned to his toast, tea and copy of *Spectrum* as I looked idly about the shabby breakfast room, seeking inspiration for the postcard I was writing. The Green Dragon dated from before the Epiphany and, like much of the Collective, had seen many moments, each of them slightly more timeworn than the one before. The paint in the room was peeling, the plaster molding was dry and crumbly, the linoleum tabletops were worn to the canvas and the cutlery was either bent, broken or missing. But the hot smell of toast, coffee and bacon, the flippant affability of the staff and the noisy chatter of strangers enjoying transient acquaintance gave the establishment a peculiar charm that the reserved, eminently respectable tearooms back home in Jade-under-Lime could never match. I noticed also that despite the lack of any Rules regarding seat plans in "non-hue-specific" venues, the guests had unconsciously divided the room along strictly Chromatic lines. The one Ultraviolet was respectfully given a table all to himself, and several Greys stood at the door waiting patiently for an empty table even though there were places available.

We were sharing our table with a Green couple. They were of mature years and wealthy enough to wear artificially green clothes so that all could witness their enthusiastic devotion to their hue, a proud-fully expensive and tastelessly ostentatious display that was doubtless financed by the sale of their child allocation. Our clothes were dyed in a conventional shade visible only to other Reds, so to the Greens sitting opposite we had only our Red Spots to set us apart from the Greys, and were equally despised. When they say red and green are complementary, it doesn't mean we like each other. In fact, the only thing that Reds and Greens can truly agree on is that we dislike Yellows more.

"You," said the Green woman, pointing her spoon at me in an excep-tionally rude manner, "fetch me some marmalade."

I dutifully complied. The Green woman's bossy attitude was not atypi-cal. We were three notches lower in the Chromatic scale, which officially meant we were subservient. But although lower in the Order, we were still Prime within the long-established Red-Yellow-Blue Color Model, and a Red would always have a place in the village Council, something the Greens, with their bastard Blue-Yellow status could never do. It irri-tated them wonderfully. Unlike the dopey Oranges, who accepted their lot with a cheery, self-effacing good humor, Greens never managed to rise above the feeling that no one took them seriously enough. The rea-son for this was simple: They had the color of the natural world almost exclusively to themselves, and felt that the scope of their sight-gift should reflect their importance within the Collective. Only the Blues could even *begin* to compete with this uneven share of the Spectrum, as they owned the sky, but this was a claim based mainly on surface area rather than a variety of shades, and when it was overcast, they didn't even have that.

But if I thought she was ordering me about solely due to my hue, I was mistaken. I was wearing a NEEDS HUMILITY badge below my Red Spot. It related to an incident with the head prefect's son, and I was compelled to wear it for a week. If the Green woman had been more reasonable, she would have excused me the errand due to the prestigious 1,000 MERITS badge that I also wore. Perhaps she didn't care. Perhaps she just wanted the marmalade.

I fetched the jar from the sideboard, gave it to the Green, nodded respectfully, then returned to the postcard I was writing. It was of Vermillion's old stone bridge and had been given a light blue wash in the sky for five cents extra. I could have paid ten and had one with greened grass, too, but this was for my potential fiancée, Constance Oxblood, and she considered overcolorization somewhat vulgar. The Oxbloods were strictly old-color and preferred muted tones of paint wherever possible, even though they could have afforded to decorate their house to the highest chroma. Actually, much to them was vulgar, and that included the Russetts, whom they regarded as *nouveau couleur*. Hence my status as "potential fiancé." Dad had negotiated what we called a "half promise," which meant I was first-optioned to Constance. The agreement fell short of being reciprocal, but it was a good deal—a concession that, despite being a Russett and three generations from Grey, I *might* be able to see a goodly amount of red, so couldn't be ignored completely.

"Writing to Fish-face already?" asked my father with a smile. "Her memory's not *that* bad."

"True," I conceded, "but despite her name, constancy is possibly her least well-defined attribute."

"Ah. Roger Maroon still sniffing about?"

"As flies to stinkwort. And you mustn't call her Fish-face."

"More butter," remarked the Green woman, "and don't dawdle this time."

We finished breakfast and, after some last-minute packing, descended to the reception desk, where Dad instructed the porter to have our suitcases delivered to the station.

"Beautiful day," said the manager as we paid the bill. He was a thin man

4

with a finely shaped nose and one ear. The loss of an ear was not unusual, as they could be torn off annoyingly easily, but what *was* unusual was that he'd not troubled to have it stitched back on, a relatively straightforward procedure. More interesting, he wore his Blue Spot high up on his lapel. It was an unofficial but broadly accepted signal that he knew how to "fix" things, for a fee. We'd had crayfish for dinner the night before, and he hadn't punched it out of ration books. It had cost us an extra half merit, covertly wrapped in a napkin.

"Every day is a beautiful day," replied my father in a cheery manner.

"Indeed they are," the manager countered genially. After we had exchanged feedback—on the hotel for being clean and moderately comfortable, and on us, for not bringing shame to the establishment by poor table manners or talking loudly in public areas—he asked, "Do you travel far this morning?"

"We're going to East Carmine."

The Blue's manner changed abruptly. He gave us an odd look, handed back our merit books and wished us a joyously uneventful future before swiftly moving to attend someone else. So we tipped the porter, reiterated the time of our train and headed off to the first item on our itinerary.

"Hmm," said my father, staring at the Badly Drawn Map once we had donated our ten cents and shuffled inside the shabby yet clean maphouse, "I can't make head nor tail of this."

The Badly Drawn Map might not have been very exciting, but it was very well named. "That's probably why it survived the deFacting," I suggested, for the map was not only mystifying but mind-numbingly rare. Aside from the Parker Brothers' celebrated geochromatic view of the Previous World, it was the only pre-Epiphanic map known. But somehow its rarity wasn't enough to make it interesting, and we stared blankly for some minutes at the faded parchment, hoping to either misunderstand it on a deeper level or at least get our money's worth.

"The longer and harder we look at it, the cheaper the entrance donation becomes," Dad explained.

I thought of asking how long we'd have to stare at it before they owed us money, but didn't.

He put his guidebook away, and we walked back out into the warm sunlight. We felt cheated out of our ten cents but politely left positive feedback, since the drabness of the exhibit was no fault of the curator's.

"Dad?"

"Yes?"

"Why was the hotel manager so dismissive of East Carmine?"

"The Outer Fringes have a reputation for being unsociably *dynamic*," he said after giving my question some thought, "and some consider that eventfulness may lead to progressive thought, with all the attendant risks that might bring to the Stasis."

It was a diplomatically prescient remark, and one that I had cause to consider a lot over the coming days.

"Yes," I said, "but what do *you* think?"

He smiled.

"I think we should go and see the Oz Memorial. Even if it's as dull as magnolia, it will still be a thousand times more interesting than the Badly Drawn Map."

We walked along the noisy streets toward the museum and soaked in the hustle, bustle, dust and heat of Vermillion. All about us were the traders who dealt with daily requisites: livestock herders, barrow boys, water sellers, pie-men, storytellers and weight guessers. Catering for more long-term needs were the small shops, such as repairers, artifact dealers, spoon traders and calculating shops that offered addition and subtraction while you waited. Moderators and loopholists were hirable by the minute to advise on matters regarding the Rules, and there was even a shop that traded solely in floaties, and another that specialized in postcode genealogy. Amid it all I noticed a stronger-than-usual presence of Yellows, presumably to keep an eye out for illegal color exchange, seed trading or running with a sharp implement.

Unusually for a regional hub, Vermillion was positioned pretty much on the edge of the civilized world. Beyond it to the west were only the Redstone Mountains and isolated outposts like East Carmine. In the uninhabited zone there would be wild outland, megafauna, lost villages of untapped scrap color and quite possibly bands of nomadic Riffraff. It was exciting and worrying all in one, and until the week before, I hadn't even *heard* of East Carmine, let alone thought I would be spending a month there on Humility Realignment. My friends were horrified, expressed low-to-moderate outrage that I should be treated this way and proclaimed that they would have started a petition if they could have troubled themselves to look for a pencil.

"The Fringes are the place of the slack-willed, slack-jawed and slack-hued," remarked Floyd Pinken, who could comfortably boast all three of those attributes, if truth be known.

"And be wary of losers, self-abusers, fence leapers and fornicators," added Tarquin, who, given his family history, would not have seemed out of place there either.

They then informed me that I would be demonstrably insane to leave the safety of the village boundary for even one second, and that a trip to the Fringes would have me eating with my fingers, slouching and with hair below the collar in under a week. I almost decided to buy my way out of the assignment with a loan from my twice-widowed aunt Beryl, but Constance Oxblood thought otherwise.

"You're doing a *what?*" she asked when I mentioned the reason I was going to East Carmine.

"A chair census, my poppet," I explained. "Head Office is worried that the chair density might have dropped below the prescribed 1.8 per person."

"How absolutely *thrilling.* Does an ottoman count as a chair or a very stiff cushion?"

She went on to say that I would be showing significant daring and commendable bravery if I went, so I changed my mind. With the prospect of joining the family of Oxblood and of myself as potential prefect material, I was going to need the broadening that travel and furniture counting would doubtless bring, and a month in the intolerably unsophisticated Outer Fringes might well supply that for me.

The Oz Memorial trumped the Badly Drawn Map in that it was baffling in three dimensions rather than just two. It was a partial bronze of a group of oddly shaped animals, the whole about six feet high and four feet across. According to the museum guide, it had been cut into pieces and dumped in the river three centuries before as part of the deFacting, so only two figures remained of a possible five. The best preserved was that of a pig in a dress and a wig, and next to her stood a bulbous-bodied bear in a necktie. Of the third and fourth figures there remained almost nothing, and of the fifth, only two claw-shaped feet truncated at the ankles, modeled on no creature living today.

"The eyes are very large and humanlike for a pig," said my father, peering closer. "And I've seen a number of bears in my life, but none of them wore a hat."

"They were very big on anthropomorphism," I ventured, which was pretty much accepted fact. The Previous had many other customs that were inexplicable, none more so than their propensity to intermingle

7

fact with fiction, which made it very hard to figure out what had happened and what hadn't. Although we knew that this bronze had been cast in honor of Oz, the full dedication on the plinth was badly eroded, so it remained tantalizingly unconnected to any of the other Oz references that had trickled down through the centuries. Debating societies had pondered long and hard over the "Oz Question," and published many scholarly tracts within the pages of *Spectrum*. But while remnants of Tin Men had been unearthed by salvage teams, and Emerald City still existed as the center of learning and administration, no physical evidence of brick roads had ever been found anywhere in the Collective, either of natural or synthetic yellow—and naturalists had long ago rejected the possibility that monkeys could fly. Oz, it was generally agreed, had been a fiction, and a fairly odd one. But in spite of that, the bronze remained. It was all a bit of a puzzle.

After that, we paused only briefly to look at the exhibits in the museum, and only those of more than passing interest. We stopped and stared at the collection of Vimto bottles, the preserved Ford Fiesta with its obscene level of intentional obsolescence, then at the Turner, which Dad thought "wasn't his best." After that, we made our way to the floor below, where we marveled at the realistic poses in the life-size Riffraff diorama, which depicted a typical *Homo feralensis* encampment. It was all disturbingly lifelike and full of savagery and unbridled lust, and was for the most part based upon Alfred Peabody's seminal work, *Seven Minutes among the Riffraff*. We stared at the lifeless mannequins with a small crowd of schoolchildren, who were doubtless studying the lower order of Human as part of a Historical Conjecture project.

"Do they really eat their own babies?" asked one of the pupils as she stared with horrified fascination at the tableau.

"Absolutely," replied the teacher, an elderly Blue who should have known better, "and you, too, if you don't respect your parents, observe the Rules and finish up your vegetables."

Personally, I had doubts about some of the more ridiculous claims regarding Riffraff. But I kept them to myself. Conjecture was a dish mostly served up wild.

As it turned out, the phonograph would *not* be demonstrated, because both it and the music disc had been put "beyond use" with a very large hammer. This wasn't a result of mischief, but a necessary outcome of Leapback Compliance issues, as some fool hadn't listed the device on this year's exemption certificate. The staff at the museum seemed a trifle annoyed about this, as the destruction of the artifact reduced the Collective's demonstrable phonographs to a solitary machine in Cobalt's Museum of the Something That Happened.

"But it wasn't all bad," added the curator, a Red with very bushy eyebrows. "At least I can lay claim to being the last person ever to hear Mr. Simply Red."

After giving detailed feedback, we left the museum and headed off toward the Municipal Gardens.

We paused on the way to admire an impressive wall painting of great antiquity that was emblazoned across the gable end of a brick house. It invited a long-vanished audience to "Drink Ovaltine for Health and Vitality," and there was an image of a mug and two odd-looking but happy children, their football-sized eyes staring blankly out at the world with obvious satisfaction and longing. Although faded, the red components in the lips and script were still visible. Pre-Epiphanic wall paintings were rare and, when they depicted the Previous, *creepy*. It was the eyes. Their pupils, far from being the fine, neat dot of normal people's, were unnaturally wide and dark and empty—as though their heads were somehow hollow—and this gave their look of happiness a peculiar and contrived demeanor. We stood and stared at it for a moment, then moved on.

Any colorized park was a must-see for visitors, and Vermillion's offering certainly didn't disappoint. The color garden, laid out within the city walls, was a leafy enclave of dappled shade, fountains, pergolas, gravel paths, statuary and flowerbeds. It also had a bandstand and an ice cream stall, even if there was no band, nor any ice cream. But what made Vermillion's park *really* special was that it was supplied by color piped direct from the grid, so it was impressively bright. We walked up to the main grassed area, just past the picturesque, ivy-gripped Rodin, and stared at the expanse of synthetic green. It was a major improvement on the park back home, because the overall scheme was tuned for the predominance of Red eyes. In Jade-under-Lime the bias was more toward those who could see green, which meant that the grass was hardly colored at all and everything red was turned up far too bright. Here the color balance was pretty much perfect, and we stood in silence, contemplating the subtle Chromatic symphony laid out in front of us.

"I'd give my left plum to move to a Red sector," murmured Dad in a rare display of crudeness.

"You already pledged the left one," I pointed out, "in the vague hope that Old Man Magenta would retire early."

"Did I?"

"Last autumn, after the incident with the rhinosaurus."

"What a dope that man is," said Dad, shaking his head sadly. Old Man Magenta was our head prefect and, like many Purples, would have trouble recognizing himself in a mirror.

"Do you think that's really the color of grass?" asked Dad after a pause.

I shrugged. There was no real way of telling. The most we could say was that this was what National Color *felt* the color of grass should be. Ask a Green how green grass was and they'd ask you how red was an apple. But interestingly, the grass wasn't *uniformly* green. An area the size of a tennis court in the far corner of the lawn had changed to an unpleasant bluey-green. The discordancy was spreading like a water stain, and the off-color area had also taken in a tree and several beds of flowers, which now displayed unusual hues quite outside Standard Botanical Gamut. Intrigued, we noticed there was someone staring into an access hatch close to the anomaly, so we wandered over to have a look.

We expected him to be a National Color engineer working on the problem, but he wasn't. He was a Red park keeper, and he glanced at our spots, then hailed us in a friendly manner.

"Problems?" asked Dad.

"Of the worst sort," replied the park keeper wearily. "Another blockage. The Council are always promising to have the park repiped, but whenever they get any money, they spend it on swan early-warning systems, lightning protection or something equally daft."

It was unguarded talk, but we were Reds, too, so he knew he was safe.

We peered curiously into the access hatch where the cyan, yellow and magenta color pipes fed into one of the many carefully calibrated mixers in order to achieve the various hues required for the grass, shrubs and flowers. From there they would feed the network of capillaries that had been laid beneath the park. Colorizing gardens was a complex task that involved matching the osmotic coefficients of the different plants with the specific gravities of the dyes—and that was before you got started on pressure density evaporation rates and seasonal hue variation. Colorists earned their perks and bonuses.

I had a pretty good idea what the problem was, even without looking at the flow meters. The bluey-green cast of the lawn, the grey appearance of the celandines and the purplish poppies suggested localized yellow deficiency, and this was indeed the case—the yellow flow meter was firmly stuck on zero. But the viewing port was full of yellow, so it wasn't a supply issue from the park substation.

"I think I know what the problem is," I said quietly, knowing full well that unlicensed tampering with National Color property carried a five-hundred-merit fine.

The park keeper looked at me, then at Dad, then back to me. He bit his lip and scratched his chin, looked around and then lowered his voice.

"Can it be easily fixed?" he asked. "We have a wedding at three. They're only Grey, but we try to make an effort."

I looked at Dad, who nodded his assent. I pointed at the pipe.

"The yellow flow meter's jammed, and the lawn's receiving only the cyan component of the grass-green. Although I would never condone Rule breaking of any sort," I added, making sure I had deniability if everything turned brown, "I believe a sharp rap with the heel of a shoe would probably free it."

The park keeper looked around, took off his shoe and did what I suggested. Almost instantly there was an audible gurgling noise.

"Well, I'll be jaundiced," he said. "As easy as that? Here."

And he handed me a half merit, thanked us and went off to package up the grass clippings for cyan-yellow retrieval.

"How did you know about that?" said Dad as soon as we were out of earshot.

"Overheard stuff, mostly," I replied.

We'd had a burst magenta feed a few years back, which was exciting and dramatic all at the same time—a cascading fountain of purple all over the main street. National Color was all over us in an instant, and I volunteered myself as tea wallah just to get close. The technical language of the colorists was fairly obfuscating, but I'd picked up a bit. It was every resident's dream to work at National Color, but not a realistic prospect: Your eyes, feedback, merits and sycophancy had to be beyond exemplary, and only one in a thousand of those who qualified to take the entrance exam.

We ambled around the garden for as long as time would permit, soaking in the synthetic color and feeling a lot better for it. Unusually, they had hydrangeas in both colors, and delicately hand-tinted azaleas that looked outside of the CYM gamut: a rare luxury, and apparently a bequest from a wealthy Lilac. We noted that there wasn't much pure yellow in the

11

garden, which was probably a sop to the Yellows in the town. They liked their flowers natural, and since they could cause trouble if not acceded to, they were generally given their own way. When we passed the lawn on our way out, the grass in the anomaly was beginning to turn back to fresh lawn green, more technically known as 102-100-64. It would be back to full chroma in time for the wedding.

We stepped out of the color garden, and walked back toward the main square. On the way we passed a Leaper who was seated by the side of the road, covered entirely in a coarse blanket except for his alms arm. I put my recently acquired half merit in his open palm, and the figure nodded in appreciation. Dad looked at his watch.

"I suppose," he said with little enthusiasm, "we should go and have the rabbit experience."

Paint and Purple

> 2.6.19.03.951: A resident shall be deemed Purple if his or her
> individual red and blue perception values are within 30
> points of each other. Outside of this, the individual shall be
> defined as the stronger of the two colors. Marital conversion
> rules apply as normal.

The route to the rabbit we would never see took us past Vermillion's Paint Shop, something we hadn't considered when we planned our itinerary. If I'd known National Color had a regional outlet, I would have insisted on at least five slow walk-pasts. The storefront was decorated in docile shades of synthetic olive and primrose, with the National Color lettering a mid-blue that was how I imagined the sky might appear. On display inside the window were paint cans arranged seductively in rows, along with small, garden-sized tubes of plant color-izers for those unable to afford connection to the grid. There were also tins of clothes dye for those eager to flaunt their color, and racks of glass ampules containing food coloring to add that extra I-don't-know-what to otherwise boring dinner parties.

I slackened my pace as I walked past the Paint Shop since it was considered exceptionally low-hued to gawp, and stepping inside was almost taboo, as I had no business to be there. Some of the hues in the window display I recognized, such as the single shade of yellow that often graced daffodils, lemons, bananas and gorse, but there were others, too—wild and sultry shades of blue that I'd never seen before, a cheeky pale yellow that might color who-knows-what and a wanton mauve that gave me a fizzy feeling down below. On the cans I noted familiar terms like umber, chartreuse, gordini, dead salmon, lilac, blouse, turquoise and aquamarine, and others that I hadn't heard before, such as cornsilk, rectory, jaguar, old string, chiffon and suffield. It was all very eye-worthy. I slowed my pace even more when we passed the door, for the interior was as brightly decorated as the exterior, with chatty and hue-savvy National Color salespeople helping prefects from the outlying villages with their choices for communal glory. Our prefects would have come to a place very like this to negotiate a price for the *terre verte* that now graced our town hall, and so would have Mr. Oxblood. Constance's family was wealthy enough to have its own bespoke colors mixed— wild, crowd-pleasing shades of etruscan and klein to free the spirit and tremble the cortex during the Oxbloods' annual panchromatic garden parties.

And then we were past the open door and the color and the wonder; and the rabbit, which had earlier seemed such a fantastically attractive idea, somehow seemed dull and pointless. The train station was also in this direction, and we would not pass this way again today, if ever.

But something happened. There was a scuffle and a thump and several shouts, and a few seconds later, a National Color employee rushed into the street.

"You!" he said, pointing to the first Grey he saw. "Fetch a swatchman and be quick about it!"

It was one of those moments when you are suddenly glad someone might be unwell, or even dead. For Dad *was* a swatchman, and someone else's misfortune might just get me inside a Paint Shop, even if only for a few minutes. I tapped him on the arm.

"Dad—?"

He shook his head. It wasn't his responsibility. There would be plenty of health practitioners in Vermillion, and if the situation turned brown, he'd be the one shouldering the bad feedback. I had to think fast. I tapped my wrist where I would have worn a watch, then made a rabbit-ears signal with my fingers. Dad understood instantly, turned on his heel and made straight for the door of the Paint Shop. As far as he was concerned, a choice between negative feedback and avoiding the rabbit was no choice at all. And that was it. We didn't see the Last Rabbit, and I was on my way to being eaten by a yateveo.

The sweet smell of synthetic color tweaked my nostrils the moment we stepped into the shop. It was an instantly recognizable odor, a curious mixture of scorched toffee apples, rice pudding and mothballs that put me in mind of the annual repaintings I witnessed as a child. We'd all stand downwind of the painters, breathing in deeply. The smell of fresh paint was inextricably linked to preparations for Foundation Day, and to renewal.

"Who are you?" demanded the Blue colorist who had instructed the Grey, eyeing Dad's Red Spot suspiciously.

"Holden Russett," said Dad, "holiday relief swatchman class II."

"Right," was the gruff reply. "Do your thing, then."

While Dad knelt to attend to his patient, I looked about curiously. On the walls were samples of National Color's full range of universally viewable hues, a guide to colorizing your garden "on a budget" and a poster advertising an all-new color that had just been added to the Long Swatch: a shade of yellow that would give bananas Chromatic independence from lemons and custard. There were also full-sized tissue paper outlines for murals, with numbers for easy reference printed on the blocked panels; and next to the counter were displays of mixing kettles, maulsticks, thinners, reabsorbers, every sort of brush imaginable and, for the prestigiously large jobs, rollers. Beyond the stored cans of paint I could also see the entrance to the Magnolia Room, where customers cleared their visual palette before savoring a particularly fine hue.

Dad nudged me, and I knelt next to him on the floor. The patient was a mature, well-dressed man of perhaps sixty and was lying prone, head on one side, with eyes staring blankly into the middle distance. He had upset a pot of blue on the way down, and the staff were busily scraping the floor with scoops and trowels to get the valuable pigment back into the can.

Dad asked the man his name and, when there was no answer, swiftly opened his leather traveling swatch case and clipped a monitor to the patient's earlobe.

"Hold his hand and keep an eye on his vitals."

The monitor took a moment to read his internal music, and the middle light glowed without flashing, which was a good sign. Steady amber—it might be something as simple as the summer vapors.

Dad dug his hand into the man's breast pocket, pulled out his patient's merit book, then flipped to the back page to read his Chromatic rating.

"Oh, flip," he said, in the way that meant only one thing.

"Purple?" I asked.

"Red 68, Blue 81," he affirmed, and I obediently wrote the rating on the man's forearm while Dad dialed the correct offset into the spectacles. I hadn't planned on following him into the profession but had been around him long enough to know the drill. Although many of the broad-effect healing hues used in Chromaticology worked irrespective of one's color perception, the more subtle shades needed Standard Vision to have an effect on the cortex—hence the color offset on the spectacles.

"He's a Purple?" echoed one of the salespeople in a worried tone. Purples looked after their own, and if anyone had slacked in his attempt to maintain this man's continuance of life, there could be severe repercussions.

"Seventy-four percent," I remarked after doing some impressive head math, then added, perhaps unnecessarily, "almost certainly a prefect."

We rolled the man over so he was on his side, and as soon as the staff and the customers saw the Purple Spot pinned to his lapel, they all went quiet. Only an Ultraviolet having an inconvenient dying event right here in their store would cause more headaches. But this placed Dad under pressure, too. If he tauped this, he'd have not only negative feedback, but some serious explaining to do. Little wonder swatchmen generally stayed away from passing shouts.

"We should have gone to see the rabbit," he murmured, placing the offset spectacles over the man's eyes. "Give me a 35-89-96."

I ran my fingers down the small glass discs in his traveling swatch case, selected the glass he wanted and handed it over.

I repeated "35-89-96" in a professional tone.

"Sixty-eight point two foot-candles left eye," said Dad as he slipped the disc into the appropriate side of the spectacles. He set the light value into his flasher, and a high-pitched whine told us the device was charging. I dutifully wrote the time, code, dosage and eye on the Purple's forehead so follow-on practitioners would know what had been given, and as soon as the flasher was ready, Dad called out, "Cover!" and all those in the shop closed their eyes tightly. I heard a high-pitched squeak as the flasher discharged the light through the colored glass and the offset, and from there to the retina and the man's visual cortex. It was an odd feeling that you never really became used to. My first flash had been for my combined Ebola-Measles-H6N14 inoculation at age six, and for a brief exciting moment I could see music and hear colors—or at least, that's what it felt like. I also salivated for the rest of the day, which was usual, and could smell bread for a week, which wasn't.

I felt the Purple patient tense as the color seeped into his visual cortex. The disc was a light orange, and enough to bring the Purple back into consciousness. Quite *how* it did this, no one knew. For all its extraordinary benefits to the Collective's health, Chromaticology remained a poorly understood science. For Dad, it wasn't important. He didn't mix or research the necessary hues; he just diagnosed the problem and administered the required shade. When Dad was in a self-effacing mood, he called it "healing by numbers."

But aside from laughing out loud without regaining consciousness— an uncommon but not unheard-of reaction—the Purple actually got *worse*.

"Flashing amber," I noted from the monitor.

"We're losing him," breathed Dad, handing back the 35-89-96. "Give me a 116-37-97."

I selected the light green disc and handed it over. Dad swapped to the other eye, yelled "Cover!" again and flashed. The Purple's left leg contracted violently, and his vitals dropped to flashing red and amber. Dad quickly requested a 342-94-98 to bring the Purple back onto an even keel and reverse the effects of the 35-89-96. This *did* have a radical effect—in the wrong direction. For with a shudder, all vital signs vanished completely and the ear monitor flicked to steady red.

"He's gone," I said, to a rapid intake of breath from everyone watching.

"With just a 342-94-98?" repeated Dad, incredulous. "That's just not possible!"

Dad checked the disc I had handed him, but there was no mistake. He wiped his forehead, took the ninety-second sandglass from his pack and placed it on the floor next to us. With the heart stopped, ninety seconds was the time it took for the blood to drain away from the retina. Once eye death had occurred, there would be no way to get any more color into the patient's body, and it would all be over. And that was bad. Not just because he was a Purple, but because his full functionality hadn't been fulfilled. And anyone who didn't make target expectancy was communal investment wasted.

Dad flashed him several other hues but without success, then stopped, thinking hard while the sand slowly trickled through the glass.

"Everything I've tried has failed," he said to me in a whisper. "I'm seriously missing something here."

Everyone in the shop was silent. No one even dared breathe. I looked up at the customers and staff, and they stared back blankly, unable to assist. After all, National Color took care of *decorative* hues, not healing ones. It was true that they mixed euphoric shades to aid in maintaining a good humor among the residents, but it was always in consultation with the swatchman general.

I suddenly had a daring thought. "The hues are having no effect," I whispered, "*because he's not Purple!*"

Dad frowned. Wrongspotting was so rare as to be almost unheard of. It carried a thirty-thousand-merit fine—effective Reboot. You might as well put yourself on the Night Train and have done with it.

"Even if that's true, it's no help at all," he whispered back. "Red, Blue, Yellow? And how much? We'd need six months to go through every possible combination!"

I looked down to where I was still holding the man's hand and noticed for the first time that his palms were rough, the top of one finger was missing and his nails were ragged and unkempt.

"He's Grey."

"Grey?"

I nodded and Dad stared at me, then at the patient, then at the timer. The last few grains were beginning to dribble through, and with no plan except the default "do nothing and hope," Dad removed the offset spectacles, selected a glass disc and, after shouting "Cover!" again, flashed the color into the man's eye. The effect was instantaneous and dramatic. The Grey convulsed as his heart restarted and the ear monitor flicked back to steady amber. After a few minutes of carefully selected swatches, to which the patient responded successfully and, more important, *predictably*, he was soon back to flashing green, and everyone in the shop began to chatter in relieved tones about how Dad would be up for some serious A++ feedback *and* an extra cake chit for saving the life of—they thought—such an eminent resident. We exchanged glances as they said this, but for the moment Dad wasn't letting on. There was no point in ruining the chances of a full recovery. Besides, the Collective needed every Grey there was—more than we needed Purples, in fact, but no one would ever say so.

Someone entered the shop in a hurry and knelt down next to us. She introduced herself as Miss Pink, a junior swatchwoman in Vermillion's practice. She looked at Dad quizzically when she saw just how many hues were written on the Grey's forehead, and he explained in a hushed tone about the wrongspottedness.

"You're kidding?" she said, suddenly looking nervous, as though simply being *near* such a grevious infractor made her guilty by association.

"I've never been more serious. Do you recognize him?"

"Not one of ours," she replied after peering closer, "probably a Grey with nothing to lose on his way to Reboot. Let's take a look."

She unbuttoned the Grey's shirt to reveal his postcode, but the neatly scarred number was partially obscured by a livid sweep of extra scar tissue. Not content with wrongspotting, the wretched infractor had also tried to hide his identity.

"It looks like an LD2," said Dad, staring at the mottled flesh carefully, "but I can't read the rest."

Miss Pink took the Grey's left hand and stared at it. The second fingertip had been neatly cut above the first joint, rendering his nailbed identification worthless. Whoever he was, he didn't want us to find out.

"Why do you think he collapsed?" asked Miss Pink, filling out a feedback slip so we could be on our way.

Dad shrugged.

"Mildew, probably."

"The Rot?!"

She said it too loud, and there was an undignified rush for the door as the grim possibility of catching the Mildew overcame natural curiosity and good manners. I'd never seen eight people try to get out a door at the same time, but they managed it. Within twenty seconds we were alone.

"Actually," said Dad, who had an impish sense of humor, "I don't know what he's got, but it's not the Mildew. I would hazard a guess that he may have suffered an aneurism. I would recommend a palette of light yellows somewhere around gervais to promote healing, but you should probably keep him unconscious while you do it. Unless, that is," he added, "the Mildew does come for him."

"Yes," said Miss Pink thoughtfully, "we must always consider that possibility."

She fell silent. No one liked talking about the Mildew.

The Word

Miss Pink gave Dad positive feedback, we bade her good day
and then stepped out of the shop and back into the close
summer heat. We loosened our ties no more than the prescribed amount, and looked about. The square, which before
had been busy and noisy, was now deathly quiet. The townspeople had
organized a voluntary fifty-yard exclusion zone—not unusual, but
pretty pointless. A Mildew sufferer only becomes dangerously infectious an hour *after* death, when the skin is covered in fine grey tendrils
and the victim, whose lungs are now under pressure from the rapidly
multiplying moldy growth, will involuntarily expel the spores in a single
explosive death cough. *That* is the moment to panic and leap out of the
nearest window—irrespective of which floor you're on, or whether it is
open or not.

Barring industrial accidents, sudden body failure, angry megafauna,
Riffraff and—most relevant to me—the occasional yateveo, the Mildew got everyone in the end. It steadfastly ignored the barriers of hue
and took the strongest Violet with the feeblest Achromatic. One morning you'd wake up with long nails and numb elbows, and by teatime

you'd be good for nothing but tallow and bonemeal. But paradoxically, although the Mildew was the number one killer by a long stretch, very few people actually died of it. As soon as a victim had been diagnosed and murmured a rasped good-bye to tear-brimmed loved ones, they would be wheeled into the nearest Green Room, where they would drift into a highly pleasurable reverie and, from there, to death. It was safer that way—a corpse could be bagged and safely in the icehouse when it coughed.

When we reached the small crowd of onlookers at the edge of the exclusion zone, they parted to let us through, but not without a barrage of questions. Dad answered as ambiguously as he could. No, he didn't know if a Mildew had been confirmed, and yes, Miss Pink had taken control of the situation. He was then asked by a reporter for the *Vermillion Chronicle* for an interview. He initially refused until the reporter mentioned he was also a newsfeed for *Spectrum,* so Dad agreed to say a few words. While he was thus engaged, I looked idly about at the gathered townsfolk and made a note of the time. We had thirty-one minutes to catch our train, and if a slowpoke Yellow was on verification duty today and we missed our connection, we might very well be here another day.

And that was when I saw Jane. I didn't know it was Jane, of course. I wouldn't find out her name until that afternoon, after she had done her impossible conjuring trick. I didn't usually stare at girls—less so when Constance was around. But on this occasion I just gaped. I was struck, poleaxed, smitten—whatever you want to call it. I don't know why I felt that way. Even now, if you took me half drowned out of the yateveo, sat me on a log and said, "Listen here, Eddie old chap, what *exactly* was it that you found so attractive?" I would simply waffle about her small, almost perfectly upswept, retroussé nose, and you'd consider me insane and put me back. Perhaps I was struck by not what she was, but what she *wasn't*. She was neither tall nor willowy, nor had any poise or bearing. Her hair was of medium length and had been tied back in a manner that fell just nine-tenths within permissibility. She had large, questioning eyes that seemed to draw me in, and a sense of quiet outrage that simmered just beneath the surface. More than anything, within her features there was a streak of wild quirkiness that made her dazzlingly attractive. In an instant, Constance and her privileged position vanished from my mind, and for the moment at least, I could think of nothing but the plain Grey in the dungarees.

I tried to think of a reasonable opening line, as I had several things to say that could be variously described as witty *or* intelligent, but not both. Quite *why* I needed to talk to her I had no idea. In half an hour I would be gone from this place, and likely never to return. But a few words with her might brighten my day, and a smile last me a week.

But my thoughts were interrupted. The crowd had given out a Collective murmur. It appeared that the Purple Pretender was being carried from the shop on a stretcher rather than a seamless polymer bag, which confirmed to everyone's huge relief that it was *not* the Mildew. But Jane's reaction was quite different. It was one not of relief but of *concern,* and my heart beat faster. *She knew who he was*—and probably what he was doing there. I took a pace forward and laid my hand on her forearm. But my touch, although innocent of meaning elicited a furious response. She gave me a look of cold hatred and growled in a menacing voice, "Touch me again and I'll break your fucking jaw."

I was momentarily stunned—not just by the fact that she had used one of the Very Bad Words, but because she had threatened physical violence to someone up-Spectrum, and seemingly without the slightest provocation. I handled it badly, and defaulted to blustered outrage.

"You can't talk to me like that!"

"Why not?"

It was so obvious a question that it barely needed answering, but I tried nonetheless.

"Because you're Grey and I'm Red, for one thing!"

She reached forward, plucked the Red Spot from my lapel, dropped it onto the cobblestones and remarked sarcastically, "Can I threaten to break your jaw now?"

The impertinence was astonishing, and my as-yet-unbroken jaw may have dropped open. I should have asked her who the Purple Pretender was and put *her* on the back foot, but at that moment Dad called my name, and I turned away. By the time I looked back, the Grey had slipped away into the crowd.

"What are you looking for?"

"A girl."

"With a train leaving in half an hour? Eddie, you really are the most hopeless optimist."

They didn't verify our postcodes down at the station. The Duty Yellow had found a dress-code infraction to deal with—something about work boots with a Travel Casual #3—so after we'd had our tickets checked and claimed our luggage, we settled into seats near the rear of the carriage, with me staring out the window, deep in thought.

"I've got something for you," said Dad, and he handed me a dented soupspoon that had become thinned with centuries of use.

"Where did you get that?"

"The Grey wrongspot's waistcoat pocket. I took it in lieu of payment."

"*Dad!*"

He shrugged. "You saved his life. And besides, you don't have one."

Acceptable rules of conduct were suspended when it came to the spoon shortage. The deficit had gotten so bad that prices were all but unaffordable, and dynastic spoon succession had become a matter of considerable interest. Spoons were even postcode engraved and carried on one's person to eliminate theft, and good table manners, one of the eight pillars upon which the Collective was built, had been relaxed to allow tea to be stirred—shockingly—with the handle of a fork.

I pocketed the spoon without further comment, as the wrongspot most certainly *did* owe me, and we waited for the other passengers to board.

"Dad," I said, "what would a Grey posing as a Purple be doing in a National Color Paint Shop in Vermillion?"

"Steady," said Dad with a smile. "*Curiosity is a descending stair—*"

I finished the oft-spoken rhyme with him: "—*that leads to only who-knows-where.*" Then I added, "but inquisitiveness will pay dividends when I'm a senior monitor."

"*If* you become a senior monitor," he corrected. "We don't know whether you've got the Red—and Constance's hand is not yet won. And remember: The inquisitive have a nasty habit of ending up in Reboot. Like that Carrot fellow—what was his name again?"

"Dwayne."

"Right. Dwayne Carrot. Too many silly questions. So be careful."

And after this sweepingly general piece of advice, he unfolded his copy of *Spectrum* and started to read. Despite our closeness, I had never told Dad that I could actually see a lot more red than I let on. The question was not whether I had the 50 percent needed to be Chromogentsia and senior monitor, but whether I had the 70 percent required to become a potential Red *prefect*. I was quietly confident that I could, but I wasn't certain. Color perception was notoriously subjective, and the very human vagaries of deceit, hyperbole and self-delusion all conspired to make pre-test claims pretty much worthless. But all doubts came to nought the morning of your Ishihara. No one could cheat the Colorman and the color test. *What you got was what you were, forever.* Your life, career and social standing decided right there and then, and all worrisome life uncertainties eradicated forever. You knew who you were, what you would do, where you would go and what was expected of you. In return, you simply accepted your position within the Colortocracy, and assiduously followed the Rulebook. Your life was mapped. And all in the time it takes to bake a tray of scones.

Travel to East Carmine

3.9.34.59.667: In order to maintain the quality of breeding stock and to maintain public decency, complementary colors are *absolutely forbidden* to marry. (Examples: Orange/Blue, Red/Green, Yellow/Purple.)

A few minutes later, and with the shiny steam locomotive huffing out large clouds of white vapor with a rhythmic, hissy thump, the train moved slowly out of Vermillion. I could hear the gyros whining softly, and the air was full of the hot odor of oil and coal smoke. We gathered speed, and then gently banked as we curved past sidings full of twin-rail locomotives, abandoned since the last Great Leap Backward almost a century before.

There was only one passenger carriage, and it was relatively empty. A couple of Blue factory managers were talking loudly about the fact that employment had once more increased, and how they were thus compelled to extend the Greys' working week. It was a worrying development. Once all Greys were overemployed, the next highest on the scale—Reds—would be expected to make up the shortfall. Luckily, it would be the lower-perceptor Reds first, so overemployment would have to reach dangerously high levels before I would be expected to pick up a hoe or stand on a production line.

Across from the worried Blues was a Yellow senior monitor who did nothing but study *The Pocket Guide to Your Civil Obligations,* and right at the front of the carriage were two overdressed Oranges who looked as though they were traveling players. They had been tutted at by the

Blues, who considered that *they* should be at the front of the carriage, then by the Yellows and Greens for the same reason. The Oranges had merely nodded in a friendly manner, and compelled the other passengers to take up seats in no particular order, which made everyone visibly agitated. The downside of this was that the bossy Greens we had met earlier perched themselves opposite us, and we continued the mutual disdain begun at breakfast.

I sat and stared out at the countryside, mostly to avoid the baleful glare of the Green woman, who was no doubt trying to devise an errand for me. My mind, however, was full of the quirky Grey girl who had threatened to break my jaw. She had, in a few short words, utterly defiled, defamed and defaced the finely tuned social order that was the bedrock of the Collective. But what was strangest was this: that anyone *capable* of such rudeness could have survived her youth. The disruptive were always flagged early by six-monthly reviews of merit tally and feedback. If the system was working, she would long ago have been spirited away to Reboot to learn some manners. The fact that she hadn't intrigued me, and her glaring antisocial defects made her not only interesting but curiously *attractive*.

"I think I need a cup of tea," said the Green woman, who was no doubt of the opinion that a lower color sitting idle was a lower color on his way to a lifetime of indolence. I ignored her, since it was not yet an order, but that soon changed. She jabbed me with the point of her umbrella and repeated her request.

"Boy? Fetch me a tea. No sugar, and lemon if they have it."

I looked at her and took a deep breath.

"Of course, madam."

"And a biscuit. Anything with chocolate on it, and failing that, anything without chocolate on it."

The guard's van was stacked high with boxes of fresh fruit, crates of chickens and personal luggage that couldn't go in the boxcars. The train was too small to waste a Grey on manning a buffet, so there was a small serve-yourself kitchenette. I wasn't the only one in the guard's van. Sitting on a pile of leather suitcases was a shabby-looking man in early middle age, who was attired with great incongruity in Standard Social #4: a casual sport jacket with a striped shirt and a loosely knotted, plain tie. *Quite* unsuitable for travel. He had a faded Yellow Spot on his grubby lapel, and his hair was not only without a neat parting, but without *any* sort of parting. I should have disliked him upon first noting his hue, but there is always something ineffably sad about a Fallen Yellow—perhaps because Yellows hated them more than they hated us. I lit the spirit stove and set the copper kettle to boil.

"Where are you headed?" I asked.

"Emerald City," he said in a soft voice, "on the Night Train."

He meant Reboot. The arrival at Reform College at first light was meant to signify a new dawn and a fresh beginning.

"You're on the wrong train for that," I observed. "Green Sector North is on the other side of the Collective."

"The farther, the better. I was expected there a week ago. You don't have any grub on you, do you?"

I gave him a slice of seedcake from the kitchenette, and popped a ten-cent piece in the jar. He consumed the cake hungrily, then told me his name was Travis Canary, from Cobalt City.

"Eddie Russett," I said, "from Jade-under-Lime, Green Sector West."

"Friend?"

It was unusual to be offered friendship from a Yellow, and ordinarily I would have refused. But I quite liked him.

"Friend."

We shook hands.

"So where are you going?" he asked.

"East Carmine. Their swatchman retired unexpectedly, and Dad is to fill in for a couple of weeks until they find someone permanent."

"I wanted to be a swatchman," said Travis thoughtfully, playing with the label on a consignment of cocoa beans, "healing people, y'know. But I'm third-generation sorting office manager, so I didn't have much choice. Why are you with your father? Apprentice?"

"No," I replied. "I made Bertie Magenta do the elephant trick at lunch. Two jets of milk shot out of his nostrils and went all over Miss Bluebird. I successfully pleaded Prank status, but the head prefect thought a bit of humility reassignment in the Outer Fringes might be good for me. Bertie is his son, you see."

"Did they set you a Pointless Task?"

"I'm conducting a chair census."

"It might have been worse," he remarked with a grin.

This was true. I could have been checking the Collective's stool firmness for Head Office's dietary research facility or something. Mind you, that was a worst-case scenario.

I found some tea and placed a measure into the house-shaped infuser, then searched in vain for some lemon. Travis looked around for a moment, reached into his pocket and pulled out a silver swatch case. He snapped open the compact, took a deep gaze at the color hidden inside, then said, "Lime?"

I considered for a moment that he might be trying to trick me into an infraction so he could steam me for some merits, but he looked so lost and beaten and hungry that I decided he was genuine. Besides, I hadn't green-peeked for months. Dad was quite strict about it, because he thought lime could lead to harder colors, but was realistic. "As soon as you've taken your Ishihara," he had told me, "you can look at whatever you beigeing well please."

"Go on, then."

Travis turned the compact toward me, and as my eyes fell upon the calming shade I felt my muscles relax and my anxieties about traveling to East Carmine fade away. Everything about the world suddenly seemed rather jolly—even the crummy bits, of which there were many. Constance's inconstancy, for one, and the fact that I wouldn't see the quirky rude girl with the retroussé nose again. But I was unused to peeking, and my head was suddenly full of Handel's *Messiah*.

"Steady, tiger," he said, and snapped the compact shut.

"Sorry?" I asked, momentarily deafened by the music.

He laughed and asked me if it was Schubert.

"Handel. So, listen," I said, my inhibitions lowered by the lime, "what did you do to get sent off to Reboot?"

He thought for a moment before answering.

"Do you know *why* residents are discouraged from relocating within the Collective?"

I knew that travel was limited, but I had never thought to question the reason.

"To stop the spread of Mildew and disrespectful jokes about Purples, I should imagine."

"It's to save the postal service from descending into chaos."

"That's a nonsensical suggestion," I retorted.

"Is it? Centuries of unregulated relocation have created a terrible burden. A letter might have to be redirected any number of times, as its mail route would have to follow not only your own but all your *ancestors'* meanderings around the Collective."

This was true. The Russetts had moved only twice since we were downgraded, so we could receive mail in two days. By contrast, the ancient and well-traveled Oxbloods, with their prestigious SW3 postcode, were on an eighty-seven-point redirection service, and would be lucky to receive mail in nine weeks, if at all.

"A bit nutty," I conceded, "but it works, doesn't it?"

"On the contrary. If you, or an ancestor of yours, had lived *in the same place more than once,* the mail redirection service defaults to the *earlier* redirection and goes around again. Three-quarters of the postal service does nothing but move post that is stuck in perpetual redirection loops and is never delivered at all. But here's the really stupid bit: The postal service's operating parameters are enshrined in the Rules and can't be changed, so Head Office reduced personal relocation in order to impose a lesser burden on the postal service."

"That's insane," I said, my tongue still loosened by the lime.

"That's the Rules," said the Yellow, "and the Rules are infallible, remember?"

This was true, too. The Word of Munsell was the Rules, and the Rules were the Word of Munsell. They regulated everything we did, and had brought peace to the Collective for nearly four centuries. They were sometimes very odd indeed: The banning of the number that lay between 72 and 74 was a case in point, and no one had ever fully explained why it was forbidden to count sheep, make any new spoons or use acronyms. But they *were* the Rules—and presumably for some very good reason, although what that might be was not entirely obvious.

"So where do you come into this?" I asked.

"I used to work in the main sorting office in Cobalt. I attempted to circumvent the Rules with a loophole to stop redirections for long-deceased recipients. When that failed, I wrote to Head Office to complain. I got one of their 'your request is being considered' form letters. Then another. After the sixth I gave up and set fire to three tons of undeliverable mail outside the post office."

"That must have been quite a blaze."

"We cooked spuds in the embers."

"I suggested a better way to queue once," I said in a lame attempt to show Travis he wasn't the only one with radical tendencies, "a single line feeding multiple servers at lunch."

"How did that go down?"

"Not very well. I was fined thirty merits for 'insulting the simple purity of the queue.'"

"You should have registered it as a Standard Variable."

"Does that work?"

Travis said that it did. The Standard Variable procedure was in place to allow very minor changes of the Rules. The most obvious example was the "Children under ten are to be given a glass of milk and a smack at 11:00 a.m." Rule, which for almost two hundred years was interpreted as the literal Word of Munsell, and children were given the glass of milk and then clipped around the ear. It took a brave prefect to point out—tactfully, of course—that this was doubtless a spelling mistake, and should have read "snack." It was blamed on a scribe's error rather than Rule fallibility, and the Variable was adopted. Most loopholes and Leapback circumvention were based on Standard Variables. Another good example would be the train we were riding on now. Although "The Railways" had been banned during Leapback III, a wily travel officer had postulated that a singular rail*way* was still allowable—hence the gyro-stabilized inverted monorail in current usage. It was loopholery at its very best.

"It's not generally known, but anyone can apply for a Standard Variable," explained Travis, "and all the Council can say is no."

"Which they will."

"Sure, but at least you're covered."

I finished making the tea, and then looked for some biscuits, without success.

"Hey," said Travis, as he had an idea, "what's this East Carmine place like?"

"I don't know. It's Outer Fringes—so pretty wild, I should imagine."

"Sounds perfect. Who knows? A fellow Yellow may take pity on me and negotiate a pardon. Do you have five merits on you?"

"Yes, thank you."

"I'll buy them off you for ten."

"What's the point in that?"

"You're going to have to trust me."

Intrigued, I handed over a five-merit note.

"Thanks. Now snitch on me to the Duty Yellow when we arrive at East Carmine."

I agreed to this, then thought for a moment. "Can I have another peek of your lime?"

"Okay."

So I did, and I felt all peculiar again, and told Travis rather gushingly that I was going to marry an Oxblood.

"Which one?"

"Constance."

"Never heard of her."

"About time!" scolded the Green woman when I finally returned, tea in hand. "What were you doing? Gossiping like the worst sort of Grey?"

"No, ma'am."

"And my biscuit? Where is my biscuit?"

"There were no biscuits, ma'am—not even nasty ones."

"Humph," she said, in the manner of someone horribly aggrieved. "Then another tea, boy, for my husband."

I looked at the Green man, who until his wife had mentioned it had not considered that he wanted a cup.

"Oh!" he said, "What a good idea. Milk with one—"

"He's not going," said my father without looking up from his copy of *Spectrum*.

"It's all right," I said, thinking about Travis and his lime, "I'll go."

"No," said Dad more firmly, "you *won't*."

The Green couple stared at us, incredulous.

"I'm sorry," said the Green man with a nervous laugh. "For a moment there I thought you said he wasn't going."

"That's precisely what I said," repeated Dad in an even tone, still not looking up.

"And why would that be?" demanded the Green woman in a voice shrill with self-righteous indignation.

"Because you didn't use the magic word."

"We don't *have* to use the magic word."

Living in a Green sector as a Red had never endeared the hue to my father. Although the Spectrum was well represented in Jade-under-Lime, there was a predominance of Greens, which tended to push a pro-Green agenda, and Dad was only a holiday relief swatchman because he'd been pushed from a permanent position by a Green swatchman. In any event, Dad had seen enough not to be pushed around. I'd never traveled with him before, but it was rather exciting to see him defy those further up in the Spectrum.

"If your son is unwilling or unable to do a simple chore, I'm sure we can ask the Yellow to conciliate on the matter," continued the Green man in a threatening manner, nodding his head in the direction of the Yellow passenger. "Unless," he added, suddenly thinking that he might have made a terrible mistake, "I have the honor of addressing a prefect?"

But Dad wasn't a prefect. Indeed, his senior monitor status was mostly honorary and carried little authority. But he had something they'd never have: letters. He fixed the Greens with a glare and said, "Allow me to more fully introduce myself: Holden Russett, GoC (Hons)."

Only members of the Guild of Chromaticologists or the National Color Guild and Emerald City University graduates had letters after their names. They were the only permitted acronyms. The Greens looked at each other nervously. It wasn't what Dad's letters *stood for*, but the inferred threat of mischief that went with them. There was a fear—enthusiastically stoked by other Chromaticologists, I believe—that if you annoy a swatchman, he'd flash you a peek of 332-26-85, which dropped an instantaneous hemorrhoid. Doing so was strictly forbidden, of course, but the *perception* of a threat was eight times as good as a real one.

"I see," gulped the Green man as he engineered a rapid about-face, "perhaps we have been overhasty in our demands. Good day to you."

And they moved swiftly off up the carriage. I stared at Dad, impressed by his ability to punch above his hue. I'd not seen him do anything like that before, and was interested to see what else I would learn about him in our stay together in East Carmine. But he was unconcerned by it all, and had closed his eyes in anticipation of a nap.

"Do you do that a lot?" I asked, rubbing my temples. The lime was beginning to get its own back, as small bursts of pink had started to appear on the periphery of my vision.

He gave an imperceptible shrug. "Now and again. Good residency is about having the power to ask someone to do something, but not necessarily exercising it. Impoliteness is the Mildew of mankind, Eddie."

It was one of Munsell's truisms, and unlike most of Munsell's truisms, actually true.

We stopped at Persimmon-on-River, where the Oranges alighted, a couple of Blues got on and a piano was delicately manhandled from one of the boxcars while freight was checked and loaded. We steamed out of there and ten minutes later passed Three Combs Junction, where we clattered over some points, banked to the right and then rumbled across a wooden trestle bridge to steam up a broad treeless valley. Scattered herds of ground sloths, giraffes, kudus and bouncing goats were grazing but paid us little attention. The line shifted direction to the north and plunged into a steep valley of almost indescribable loveliness. The track ran alongside a cascading, rock-strewn river, and steep hills laced with oak and silver birch rose on either side, with kites wheeling over the limestone crags high above.

I stared out the window, my eyes searching for red as a ratfink stalks a squarriel. It was midsummer; we were past the welcome cascade of early orchids, and it was now the time of the poppies, sorrel and pink campions. Once they were done, the snapdragons and maiden pinks would sustain us until the end of the season, and it was in this manner that we Reds leapfrogged through the spring and summer on a frugal diet of seasonal blooms. Mind you, the cooler weather at year's end didn't completely dull our senses. Although better suited to Orange and Yellow eyes than ours, autumn was quite often a rapturous explosion of delights, if the leaves lingered on the branches long enough to be reddened by a fortuitous warm spell. It was the same story for the other colors, to a greater or lesser degree. The Yellows had more seasonal bloom, Blues and Oranges had less. Greens, as they constantly reminded us, had only two Chromatic seasons: the abundant muted and the abundant vibrant. Growing bored, I turned my attention to Dad's copy of *Spectrum*.

The magazine contained pretty much the same articles that it always did. There was an editorial extolling the functional simplicity of the color-based economy, and then, on pages two and three, graphically illustrated accounts of recent swan attacks and lightning deaths. Following this were some "Top Tips" on what you could do to increase your survival chances if caught out after dark, and the weekly Very Racy Story. There were stoppage listings on the rail network and the Science Wild Conjecture page, which this week had an article that linked sunspot activity to the increased fade-rate. There were amusing anecdotes sent in by readers, a comic strip, Gus Honeybun's Birthdays, a preview of what to expect this year at Jollity Fair and the likely contenders for the Fourth Great Leap Backward in three years' time.

But the first thing I read was always Spouse Mart—not because I was looking for a partner away from home, but because it gave a rough scale of prices in the the complex issue of the Chromatic marriage market, a subject pertinent to me, as Dad would have to cough up a fair bit of cash to see me married into the Oxbloods.

There were two types of ads. Some were from parents eager to offer a shedload of merits to marry off their children up-color, such as this one:

21-yr female (R: 32.2%, Y: 12%), strong virtues. Handsome and helpful, with impressive feedback rating. Seeks Chromogentsia-plus family. Brings 4,125 merits and 47 sheep. Delivery negotiable, option to refuse retained. Viewing at Ochre-in-the-Vale, PO6 5AD.

On the other side of the coin were parents willing to trade down-Spectrum in order to *receive* a shedload of merits, like this dodgy chap:

Yellow Beta male (Y: 54.9%, R: 22%), 26 yrs. Feedback generally positive, healthy but not great looker. Mildly slovenly. List of virtues on application. Seeking 8,000 merits or nearest offer. Any family considered. Furniture included. Partial refund if infertile. Viewing at Great Celandine, CA4 6HA.

Coincidentally, I even found one from East Carmine, where we were now headed:

18-yr female with strong Purpleness, 75 genuine virtues, hard-working and eager to please, Egg chit and excellent feedback. Offers invited above 6,000. Available soon. Option to refuse waived. Husband collects. Viewing strongly advised. East Carmine LD3 6KC.

The ad was steeped in code, as the Rules were quite strict as to what could and could not be said. "Available soon" meant she was not yet tested for her perception, but "strong Purpleness" meant she was *expected* to hit the 50 percent mark, which made the six thousand asking price about right, since she already had an egg chit. Reading between the lines, it looked as though her parents were hoping for a wealthy Purple family who had recently lost hue but retained hopes of dynastic recovery, and wanted someone who could child pretty soon. The amount of virtues listed meant little, but the "Option to refuse waived" spoke volumes: Whichever Purple came along with the largest wad won the young lady. Either she was very compliant, or her parents were tyrants. Most parents these days at least *consulted* with their children before negotiating dowries on their behalf, and some forward-thinking parents even allowed them a veto.

As we emerged from the valley, a recently abandoned town appeared on our left, just on the other side of the river. I caught the name of the station as we clanked past without stopping: Rusty Hill. The platform was liberally sprinkled with animal droppings and windblown soil. Grass and weeds grew in happy profusion from the paving-slab cracks, but nothing had been touched since abandonment. Cups and plates still sat on the station canteen's tables, and in the waiting room I could even see a pile of leather suitcases slowly turning to blackened mulch beneath a leaking roof. I looked across at the town, and noted a few missing slates and broken windows. It looked as though it had been lived in as little as five years ago.

We moved through Rusty Hill's abandoned farmland, past a Faraday cage or two and fields that were now covered in tall grasses, low shrubs, brambles and saplings. Wildstock had broken in long ago, and the stone walls had been breached by wandering megafauna. Even the iron-framed glasshouse was slowly succumbing to a dual assault of external weather and rampant growth within—the branch of an unpruned apple had pushed out several panes of glass. Without intervention in the next twenty years, the village would be irrecoverable. We left Rusty Hill's boundary by way of an unattended railgate, and then skirted along one side of a broad valley that was an empty wilderness punctuated by mature woodland and the troublesome rhododendron, which was growing out here in even greater quantities. I noted a few subtle markers of the Previous as we rolled past: a long stretch of perfectly smooth roadway; a few dilapidated buildings that had somehow resisted collapse; the remains of a steel bridge, now marooned in empty grassland by a river that had long since meandered elsewhere; and most spectacularly, a cast-iron phone box eroded by wind and rain to the delicateness of filigree.

Twenty minutes later we entered another steep valley, crossed the river and passed through a V-shaped gap in the hills. Then, as the trees thinned and the smoke and steam momentarily cleared, I had my first glimpse of East Carmine: the twin redbrick chimneys of what I would later learn was the linoleum factory. The train passed through the Outer Markers, crossed the river, slowed for the stockwall railgate, then entered the neatly tilled land of the sub-Collective. East Carmine's patch must have been perhaps thirty miles by ten at its widest part and occupied the middle section of a wide, fertile valley, with low hills to the east and mountains to the north and west. I could see now why there was a settlement here. It was quite lovely in a quaint, uncomplicated sort of way and, despite being on the weather side of the country, warmer and lusher than I had imagined. The railway station was a half mile or so from the village, which was fairly low-lying—except for the omnipresent flak tower, which, along with the Perpetulite roadways, was probably the most visible evidence of the Previous, and no less strange. Quite why anyone would build stark, windowless towers all over the country was never fully explained, nor was how they came by their name. But oddly, East Carmine's flak tower seemed to have a nonstandard domed construction on top of it.

"Already?" grunted my father when I nudged him awake. He got up, pulled our bags from the luggage rack and laid them in the corridor before turning to me. "Eddie, how long have we been father and son?"

"As long as I can remember."

"Exactly. Now, remember: Best behavior, and keep your wits about you. The towns in the Outer Fringes sometimes interpret the Rulebook a bit *differently* than we might be used to, and are awash with the potential for embarrassing faux pas."

I nodded my agreement, and we watched as the tall chimneys grew larger and larger until, with a squealing of brakes, a hissing of steam and a cloud of water vapor that dispersed rapidly in the warm air, we arrived at East Carmine.

East Carmine

2.4.01.03.002: Feedback may not be modified once given.

Waiting to greet the train were a stationmaster, a freight dispatcher, a postman and a Yellow arrivals monitor, whose job it was to log in the arrivals. The youthful stationmaster wore a Blue Spot on his uniform and remonstrated with the driver that the train was a minute late, and that he would have to file a report. The driver retorted that since there could be no material difference between a train that arrived at a station and a station that arrived at a train, it was equally the stationmaster's fault. The stationmaster replied that he could not be blamed, because he had no control over the speed of the station; to which the engine driver replied that the stationmaster could control its *placement,* and that if it were only a thousand yards *closer* to Vermillion, the problem would be solved. To this the stationmaster replied that if the driver didn't accept the lateness as his fault, he would move the station a thousand yards *farther* from Vermillion and make him not just late, but *demeritably* overdue.

The postman watched the argument with a bemused grin, then swapped the outgoing mail package with the incoming before setting off back to the village without a word. The freight dispatcher ignored everyone and walked to the flatbeds at the rear to oversee the loading of linoleum and the unloading of raw materials.

We were the only ones to alight, so the Yellow had little to do.

"Codes and point of departure?" she said without preamble, or even a welcome.

Dad gave her our postcodes and the name of our home village, and she wrote them in her logbook. She was in her mid-twenties, had rounded features and wore a long dress that reached to her ankles. Of the twenty-six permitted modes of dress for girls, it was the one that spent the least time in fashion. It was less of a dress and more of a bell-tent with ankles. And as usual for the sort of Yellow who wore his or her blighted shade with an almost obscene pride, the dress was enriched with synthetic yellow. There was no mistaking the adherence to her hue, and equally, she wanted you to know it.

"I'm the holiday relief swatchman for Robin Ochre," said Dad, looking around. "I was expecting him to be here to meet us."

She looked at him suspiciously. "Did you know him?"

"We were at Chromaticology school together."

"Ah," replied the Yellow, and lapsed into silence.

"So," said Dad to fill the embarrassing silence, "is there *anyone* here to meet us?"

"Sort of," she replied, without giving any further information. Her attitude would have been considered outrageously rude in any other hue; with Yellows it was pretty much standard operating procedure.

"There's a Rebootee hiding on the train," I said, recalling that Travis Canary owed me ten merits.

The Yellow looked at me, then the train, then marched off without a word.

"That was a rotten thing to do," whispered Dad. "I thought I told you Russetts never snitched?"

"He paid me to. We each get five merits out of it. His name's Travis Canary. He set fire to three tons of undelivered mail, then cooked spuds in the embers."

"Life was a lot less complex *before* you tried to explain."

We both jumped as a chirpy voice rang out behind us, "Welcome to East Carmine!"

We had expected Robin Ochre or a prefect to greet us, but we got neither. The man addressing us was a *porter*. Despite the implied insult that we were little better than Grey ourselves, he was well turned out. He wore an immaculately pressed uniform, was just touching middle age and had a friendly demeanor about him, as though he had just been told a very funny joke not half a minute ago.

"Mr. Russett and son?" he inquired, looking at us both in turn. Dad said that we were, and the porter responded with a polite bow, "I'm Stafford G-8. The head prefect asked me to take you to your quarters."

"They are busy, then?"

"Oh, lumme," he muttered, suddenly realizing that a prefectless welcome might seem a mite insulting. "Please don't read anything into it. The prefects always play mixed doubles on Tuesday afternoons."

"Croquet or tennis?"

"Scrabble."

Dad and I exchanged glances. It perhaps confirmed what we had already suspected—that a streak of discourtesy had corrupted the Outer Fringes. While we thought about this, the porter noticed the Yellow woman approaching with Travis.

"Who's that?" he asked, already infringing protocol by initiating a conversation.

"He set fire to some potatoes," confided Dad, "then cooked some undelivered post in the embers."

"Did he, now?" said Stafford. "What a strange fellow. I would have done it the other way around."

"With respect, ma'am," we heard Travis say as they drew closer, "I'm not sure I fully understand how a poorly knotted tie can undermine the Collective."

It was said in a sarcastic tone that the Yellow woman missed.

"A sloppy half-Windsor is the first symptom of serial indolence," she replied in the patronizing voice that Yellows reserved for Rule-breakers, "and ignoring the infraction gives the impression that it is acceptable to be inappropriately attired. The next day it might be badly polished shoes, then uncouth language, showing off and impoliteness. Before one knows it, the rot of disharmony would start to disassemble everything that we know and cherish."

She then said something about how he was a "disgrace to his hue," and they took a footpath toward the village.

"Who was the Yellow?" asked my father.

"Miss Bunty McMustard," explained Stafford, picking up our cases, "deputy snitch and unwavering supporter of Sally Gamboge, the Yellow prefect. Bunty's a nasty piece of work, and totally untrustworthy. If I tell you she's the nicest Yellow in authority, it will give you an idea of how bad the others are."

"The least bitey piranha?"

"Got it in one. Speaking of piranhas, watch out for Mrs. Gamboge's son. His name's Courtland, and he's the best."

"The best what?"

"The best avoided. He and Bunty are due to be married, as soon as Courtland gets around to asking her."

The porter picked up our cases and placed them in the back of his cycle-taxi. We settled ourselves in the front, and he pedaled off at a brisk pace on the smooth Perpetulite roadway.

As we neared the factory I could hear the clanking and grinding of industry from deep within, while on the air there was a sharp taste like burned cooking oil.

"Every square yard of linoleum you've ever walked on would have been produced here," Stafford announced proudly. "Back in 00427, East Carmine hosted Jollity Fair. The 'House of Linoleum' was the focal point—a building made *entirely* from linoleum. They even developed a new foodstuff especially for the occasion: Bisquitoleum. It's still a local delicacy, even today."

"Any good?"

"What it lacks in taste, it makes up for in longevity. We have a linoleum museum, too. Would you like a quick visit? I do the guided tours."

"Perhaps later."

"Everyone says that," replied the porter, crestfallen. "Do you mind if I loosen my tie? The day is hot."

Dad gave his permission, and we pedaled on. The going was easy on the smooth roadway, and after a few minutes we came to a stone-arch bridge that had a weathered WELCOME TO EAST CARMINE notice next to it. As we passed the sign, I saw a young woman with long dark hair standing by the side of the road. She was holding a swinging pendulum in the air above her palm, and next to her on the parapet was an open notebook. She stared at us in a strange, off-kilter manner.

"That was Lucy Ochre," said the porter as soon as we had passed, "Mr. Ochre's daughter. A bit of an oddball."

"What's with the pendulum?"

"She's searching for *harmonic pathways*—a musical energy that runs through the Collective, she calls it."

"What do the prefects think?"

"They think she's a bit odd," he replied with a shrug, "but belief in odd things isn't against the Rules, as long as it's done on your own time, and you don't try to convince anyone else."

Dad turned to look at her as we cycled on, but the girl had returned her attention to her pendulum.

Soon after the bridge we crested a rise and found ourselves within sight of the village. It was a low-lying, highly fenestrated conurbation with whitewashed walls and a roofline bewhiskered with heliostats, chimney pots and water heaters. Between us and the village was an empty landscape of low, grassy mounds interspersed with occasional stacks of standing masonry, weathered concrete and the odd finger of rusty iron. East Carmine, despite being on the very Outer Fringes of the Collective, had once been big. Back at Jade-under-Lime we had barely five streets of abandoned housing, but here the rough landscape continued for almost a half mile in every direction.

"East Carmine is only a fraction of the size it once was," remarked Stafford. "The deFacting wasn't quite as severe over this way, and one can still find artifacture that's almost perfect. I restore vintage office equipment in my spare time. I have six working staplers and a Gestetner stencil duplicator. I can punch holes at competitive rates—and my recipe for black ink is famous all over the sector."

We continued past the undulating grassland, the ancient layout of the old town easily discerned from a crisscrossing of smooth, grassed-over roads dotted with eroded mailboxes and streetlamps. There was little in the way of trees or low shrubs, as this was an area traditionally kept for pasture and reserved to accommodate any of the Previous who might return. Once, it was presumed, the houses had simply stood empty, waiting. But time, weather and neglect had taken their toll, and all that remained was these soft grassy mounds and an inviolable Rule that they be kept that way. No one seriously considered that the once-numerous Previous *would* come back, but Rules are rules.

"What do you think of our crackletrap?" asked Stafford, indicating the large structure that had been placed atop the flak tower.

"Impressive," I murmured.

"The prefects—Mrs. Gamboge in particular—are very big on the dangers of lightning," explained the porter. "It's been finished only since Winternox, and has already been struck over a hundred times."

The lightning lure was a wooden latticework affair topped with a domed bronze attractor about thirty feet in diameter. Since every house in the Collective had a metallic daylight-collection device on its roof, homes were highly susceptible to a wayward bolt, which would course down the steel adjustment rods and cause electrical mayhem within the house. The luckless were sometimes fused to anything metallic, sometimes half vaporized and at other times simply dead in their beds, their eyeballs and internal organs boiled to something closely resembling minestrone soup. Lurid accounts and photographs were published every week in *Spectrum*.

"I expect you take lightning-avoidance issues seriously where you come from?" asked Stafford.

"Our Council are more concerned about swan attack, but lightning isn't ignored," replied my father. "We have a fleet of a half-dozen specially adapted Fords, each with a bronze attractor mounted on a pylon in the flatbed. They're driven in to intercept a storm when the direction and severity are known."

"We have an anomaly ten miles or so upwind," said Stafford, "so ball lightning can be a problem in these parts. There are plans to erect a steel catch-net on the Western Hills, but it's mostly talk."

Fork lightning could be easily lured from areas of habitation, but ball lightning was a law unto itself. It drifted along with the breeze, became caught in eddies and sometimes entered houses. It was sticky, too, and would attach itself to anything organic. A bad ball strike could leave the victim almost completely incinerated; nervous residents who were unspooned etched their names on steel plates to keep in their pockets, just in case.

We continued on the road down to the village itself, a knot of houses on a raised hillock. The dwellings were built in the Salvagesque style, a hodgepodge of construction methods using a wide variety of materials ranging from the deeply ancient carved stone to reused timber, rubber roof tiles, brick, adobe and, in some places, the more modern oak-framed wattle and daub. As we moved off the Perpetulite and onto the cobbled street, Dad asked the porter about Robin Ochre, the previous swatchman.

"Mr. Ochre's absence is deeply regretted," he remarked. "He left a wife and daughter."

"He will send for them in due course, I suppose?" I asked, wholly misunderstanding the comment.

"I'm not sure he's in much of a condition to do anything."

"I was led to believe," said Dad slowly, "that Mr. Ochre had retired from the profession."

"Ah!" said Stafford. "While euphemistically true, the phrase is also potentially misleading. I can only repeat the Council's own findings: that Mr. Ochre was . . . *fatally self-misdiagnosed*."

"Robin is dead?" asked my father.

"I'm no medical expert, of course," replied the porter thoughtfully, "but yes, that's precisely what he is. Four weeks ago to the day."

Dad and I glanced at each other. For some unknown reason we hadn't been told, and as I was trying to figure out what "fatally self-misdiagnosed" might mean, we arrived at a red door set into an unbroken terrace that made up the south end of the town square. That is to say, we arrived at the rear, tradesman's entrance. The façade with the front door would face the town square. If we hadn't just received the disturbing news about Robin Ochre, I daresay my father would have insisted on being taken to the front entrance. As it was, he said nothing.

The porter opened the door, bid us enter and then placed our bags in the scullery hall as we stood, blinking, in the gloom.

"My goodness," he said, "it's as dark as the belly of a frog in here."

He walked past us and into the kitchen, where by the dim glow of the windows I could faintly see him turn the winding crank and then fiddle with the two manual-override rods that dangled from the ceiling. High above us the roof mirror rotated toward the afternoon sun; catching the rays, it then beamed them down the light well and onto a frosted-glass panel set into the ceiling.

"Whoops," said Stafford as the light swept the muddy gloom from the house. "I should have wound the heliostat spring before you arrived. No one's lived in this house for a while. Will there be anything else?"

"How on earth can one be 'fatally self-misdiagnosed'?" asked Dad, who was still not over the news that his former colleague was dead. The porter thought for a moment.

"The Council decided at the inquest that he must have *thought* he had the Mildew and consigned himself to the Green Room to be hastened. As it turned out, he didn't."

"A shocking mistake to make."

"It was, sir, yes. Fine man, Mr. Ochre. We haven't lost a single resident to the Mildew for seven years. And he wasn't *hue-specific,* if you know what I mean."

"Munsell stated that health care is universal," remarked my father, but we knew what Stafford meant. Some swatchmen favored those only of a similar hue.

Dad gave a shiny half merit to Stafford, who tipped his hat and told us he hoped our stay in East Carmine would be happily uneventful. I saw him to the back door, then asked him if the prefects read outgoing telegrams.

"Mrs. Blood is the communications clerk," he said, "and is well known for her discretion—as long as an extra twenty cents is added to the fee. But," he added, "even Yvonne might balk at sending a message of improper raciness or anything against the best interests of the Collective."

"It's poetry," I confessed, "to a sweetheart."

Stafford smiled. "I understand. Mrs. Blood would have no problem with that. She's something of a romantic herself."

This was good news, albeit expensive. But with the Oxbloods on a nine-week redirection service and me away for only a month, there was little choice.

"Excellent!" I remarked. "I suppose—" Suddenly my eye was caught by the figure of a man in his early thirties, standing in the shadows of the alleyway opposite. He was grimy and unshaven and had NS-B4 carved rather clumsily below his left clavicle—most scars were neat affairs, but his looked like a bad weld. He was also inappropriately *naked* and, while staring vacantly up at the sky, was actually peeing on his left foot.

"Stafford?" I whispered, a tremor of fear sounding in my voice.

"Yes, Master Edward?"

"There's a naked man in the alleyway behind us. I think it might be . . . *Riffraff*."

Stafford turned around, looked at the man and said, "I don't see anyone."

"How can you not see him? He's peeing on his own foot."

"Master Edward, *you* can't see him."

"I can."

"You can't. He doesn't *exist*, Master Edward—take Our Munsell's word for it."

I suddenly understood. The Rules, despite their vast complexity and extensive range, had no way of dealing with anything that had no explainable position within a world of ordered absolutes. So instead of attempting to understand or explain them, they were simply awarded the status of *Apocrypha* and stridently ignored lest they raise questions of fallibility.

"He's Apocryphal?" I asked.

"He would be if he were there—which he isn't."

44

I understood Stafford's reticence. Admitting that Apocrypha actually existed was a grave impiety punishable by a five-hundred-merit fine. A whole range of euphemistic language had developed to refer to them, but generally no one did—a slip of tense could leave your hard-won merit score in tatters.

"I've never actually *seen* an Apocryphal man," I noted, unable to stop staring, "and, um, still haven't. Do you think they might all look the same—*if* they existed?"

"I've only not seen one," said Stafford, following my gaze to where the unseeable man was now pouring cooling water over himself from a water butt, "so I've no idea what one shouldn't look like. Would you excuse me? I promised to go and search for Mr. Yewberry's second-best hat. It'll be on his head as usual, but he tips well."

He gave another short bow, and I quietly closed the door before rejoining my father in the kitchen. "That was very strange."

"I know," he agreed, looking up from where he had been searching the cupboards out of curiosity. "You can't misdiagnose the Mildew. *Especially* on yourself. It's just too obvious."

"No," I said, "there was an Apocryphal man peeing on his foot in the alleyway opposite."

"*As I was going down the stair, I saw a man who wasn't there,*" replied Dad with a smile. "That's the Outer Fringes for you. I pity the poor clucks he's not lodging with."

The House

9.3.88.32.025: The cucumber and the tomato are both
fruit; the avocado is a nut. To assist with the dietary
requirements of vegetarians, on the first Tuesday of the
month a chicken is officially a vegetable.

e began by exploring the house. It was a timber-framed
affair that looked as though it dated from the first century
after the Something That Happened and, while in good
order, was showing its age. The floor was tiled to keep the
house cool in summer, and I noted that the mullioned windows were
doubled up with shutters and drapes. The walls were rough-plastered
and whitewashed to maximize natural light, and the faint smell of borax
told me the cavities had been recently rewooled.

There were three floors. The well-appointed kitchen had a gas range,
along with a stained ceramic sink, a table, a clock and a glass-fronted
dresser full of Linotableware. A goodly quantity of pots and pans hung
from the beams, all as clean as new pins, and in the cutlery drawer were
knives and forks but, predictably enough, no spoons.

I put the kettle on in case the prefects arrived without warning, found
the tea caddy and the least-chipped bone china and swiftly set a tray.

"Better not put out saucers with the cups," said Dad. "We don't want
to be seen to be putting on airs."

"Unless they drink from them," I pointed out.

"Good point. Better lay them out as usual."

The kitchen door opened into a corridor that gave access to a small wood-paneled study, with a walnut desk, a chair and a highly polished Bakelite telephone—presumably linked to the village's internal network and not like Old Man Magenta's instrument back home, which was connected only to itself. Farther on, the corridor led to a tiled main entrance hall, with the front door directly ahead. To the left and right were two reception rooms. In each was a large bay window facing the town square, the top third of each fitted with Luxfer prisms to increase the natural light. The rooms were delightfully paneled in various shades of wood-effect linoleum, the furniture was worn but usable, and in the drawing room hung a pair of Vettrianos. Below this was a sealed glass case that held a few Articles of Interest that would have been dispersed out here as part of the Localization. Among the assorted bric-a-brac were three chess pieces crudely carved from ivory, an ornate ceremonial sword, a finely decorated egg and several unusual medals marked "XCIV Olympiad." It was an impressive collection, especially this far from the hub. But then, as we had already seen, East Carmine was once much larger and presumably more important than it was now. The only house I'd visited that was this opulent was the Oxbloods'. It was on the occasion when Constance presented me to her parents, an event made very uncomfortable when she left to inform the butler there was one more to supper and Mr. Oxblood forgot what I was doing there and mistook me for a footman. I didn't know what to say, and if Constance hadn't returned when she did, I probably would have served them tea and filed his corns.

The staircase was circular and faced the front door. It was not just a stairwell but a light well, with the polished heliostat easily discernible through the glazed octagonal skylight high above.

We climbed the creaking treads and discovered three bedrooms on the second floor, which were comfortable, if austere. Each had a bed, a bureau, a chair, a trouser press and a writing table with notepaper inscribed EAST CARMINE—GATEWAY TO THE REDSTONES. There were also a couple of brass angle-poise reflectors to beam light where required.

"I'll take the bedroom at the front," said Dad, exploring his chosen room. After a brief recce, I took the room at the back. It was lighter and faced the setting sun. I was about to carry on up to the third floor when I stopped. It appeared that someone was in residence. Cardboard boxes were stacked up on the stairs in a haphazard manner, and there was a pungent smell in the air. Most of all, I could hear music.

"Goodness," said my father, who had arrived by my side. "That's *Ochrlahoma*!"

It was, although not from any libretto I knew. Hearing the show *itself* was not so strange, as it was mandatory for all villages to put on at least two musicals per year, but hearing a phonograph *was* unusual. Wax cylinder was the last of the replay methods allowable, and ownership could be undertaken only with a yearly exemption, approved by the Council. It made up for the disappointment of the one we hadn't heard at Vermillion's museum, but it was still very odd.

"Hello?" I called, but there was no answer.

"I'll leave this in your capable hands," muttered Dad nervously. "I have our postal redirection forms to complete before the head prefect arrives. Why not invite our lodger for supper this evening?" And without waiting for a reply, he swiftly made his way downstairs.

I hailed our unseen lodger again, then, not receiving any answer, slowly began to climb the stairs. I got to just within sight of the top corridor when my eyes started to water, and I sneezed. By the tenth step I was sneezing almost continuously, aggressive, painful explosions that welled up spontaneously and caused my eyes to water so badly my vision blurred. I beat a hasty retreat to the second-floor landing, where the fit ceased as quickly as it had begun. I wiped my eyes with my handkerchief, and tried again. On the ninth step and sixth sneeze, I gave up and returned to the landing, mildly confused and with a runny nose. Just then, the music stopped. Not at the end of the recording or when the motor had wound down, but as though the needle had been lifted from the cylinder. I heard the sound of a chair being pushed out. Our lodger was in residence.

"Hello?" I said in my most polite voice, "My name is Eddie Russett and my father and I were wondering if you'd take supper with us this evening?"

I was greeted with silence.

"Hello?" I said again.

A creak on the staircase below made me turn. I had expected it to be my father, so was surprised to see the naked figure of the Apocryphal man climbing the stairs. He didn't acknowledge my presence. In fact, I had to step back, as he would almost certainly have bumped into me. It was only as he headed up the stairwell that I realized what he was doing here. He was the *lodger*—or at least, he and whoever had pushed out the chair upstairs.

48

"The ex-presidents are surfers," he said as he walked past, "and don't you yell at *me*, Mr. Warwick."

I ignored him, as protocol dictated, noted that he didn't sneeze as he mounted the stairs, then walked slowly to my room to unpack.

I placed my clothes neatly in the single chest of drawers in case of an inspection, but kept all my private stuff in my overnight valise. I had brought it with me, as the valise was the only private place that we had—two cubic feet that we could call our own. The Rule was so inviolably sacrosanct that without the next of kin's agreement, a valise couldn't even be opened after death. But there was a downside: Anything I had left behind at home would not be covered by the 1.1.01.02.066 Privacy Rule and could be discovered and confiscated, and, if appropriate, I would be punished. So I had to take everything unruleful with me, just in case.

Needless to say, most people's cases held contraband, either surplus-to-requirement spoons, illegally held hue or Leapbacked technology. Most often, though, the valise contained private collections of pre-Epiphanic artifacture, which was regarded as unofficial currency, always useful as a hedge against deflation. A doll's head might be worth a cream tea, and a good piece of jewelry could be exchanged for a week-end in Redpool.

Everyone owned something left behind by the Previous, for the simple reason that they left behind a lot. In my own modest collection I had a mock-tortoiseshell comb with all its teeth, various metal buttons, some coins, half a Bakelite telephone receiver, a Trik Trak car and, best of all, a lemon-sized motor known to the Previous as a PerMoCo, Inc., Mk6b 20W Everspin™, and probably used to power some sort of domestic appliance. I had found it in the river a mile beyond Jade-under-Lime's Outer Markers, the long, slow bend being a good spot for alluvial toshing. I had been up there alone panning for buttons when I came across the Everspin and a lot more besides. I returned to the village that morning with an armful of brightly colored red plastics and a shiny painted-metal toy that turned out to be vivid blue.

The senior toshing monitor immediately organized an expedition upstream, where it was found that a new channel had been cut through the remnants of an old village. Despite being almost three foot-hours into the Outfield and arguably closer to the village of Greenver's Chase, it was claimed by Jade-under-Lime's Council as Color-trove, and yielded several hundred tons of highly colored scrap over the next six years.

The Council were extremely grateful. I was awarded two hundred merits and allowed to keep the Everspin, which was something of a treat: Under Rule 2.1.02.03.047, *all* Leapbacked technology not subject to an exemption was put "beyond use," a term that generally involved several sharp blows with the blacksmith's hammer. My Everspin didn't work, of course. Or at least it didn't when I found it. But after six months of drying out it started to rotate again, albeit slowly, and only when the weather was chilly. But I kept the Everspin's everspinning to myself. Previous agreements notwithstanding, it would have been confiscated.

I returned to the kitchen and found the kettle singing merrily to itself and half boiled out. I was just replenishing the water when there was a soft rap at the back door. I opened it to find a young man with a pale complexion, an almost nonexistent nose and overly large eyes that made him look as though he were constantly surprised. He seemed ill at ease, and wrung his hands nervously.

"Master Edward?" he inquired. "My name is Dorian G-7. I'm the village photographer and editor of the East Carmine *Mercury*. Would you like some shortbread?"

I thanked him and helped myself from the open biscuit tin he was holding.

"What do you think?"

"To be honest, somewhat . . . gritty."

He looked despondent.

"I was afraid you'd say that. I had to use sand instead of sugar. Ingredients are very hard to come by out here. I'm trying to open a supply line for baking requisites. Do you know of anyone who might want to trade?"

By chance, my friend Fenton's father ran the Collective's cake decoration factory, and he'd be the one in the know.

"What are you offering?" I asked, since there was a world of difference between barter, which was legal, and unapproved trading for cash, which was definitely Beigemarket.

"I've got some floaties," he said, and dug into his pocket to produce a small leather pouch. He gave me a grin and emptied the contents into the air. It was a modest collection, to be honest. The half dozen or so scraps of dull metallic material bounced up and down in the air until they settled the usual yard or so above the kitchen floor's lowest point, which was near the broom cupboard. I'd seen bigger lumps pop out of the earth and settle above the ground while I was out on walks, and Old Man Magenta had a section so large it would support his tea, which he used as an occasional table. But this was the Outer Fringes, and I didn't want to hurt Dorian's feelings.

"That's . . . impressive. I'm sure we can do something—do you have much more?"

He explained that the East Field was being plowed, and it was traditionally a place where floaties would rise from the newly turned soil—and his family had the sole collecting rights. I said I would contact Fenton to see if a deal could be made, and then flicked one of the larger floaties with my finger. It shot off to the other side of the kitchen, only to drift languidly back to join the others.

"Weird, aren't they?" remarked Dorian. "Another shortbread?"

"No, thanks."

"Very wise. Could I do an interview with you for the East Carmine *Mercury*? Our readers are very keen on learning about how ridiculously self-obsessed you hub-dwellers are."

I thanked him and told him I was busy right now, but would make time for him in the next few days. He replied that this would be admirable, but seemed reluctant to leave.

"Is there something else I can help you with?"

"Forgive me for being forward, Master Edward, but there is a market for Open Returns in the village, and if—"

"I'm not selling," I said, smiling so he knew I wouldn't report him. "I'll need my ticket to get home."

"Of course. But I could offer, um, two hundred merits. And in cash."

It was a lot of merits for a Grey to have in transferable form, rather than unspendable in the back of his book. Actually, it was a lot for *me* to have. I could buy some serious evenings out with Constance, but if I couldn't get back to Jade-under-Lime, there wouldn't be much point. "Sorry," I said, "I'll need it."

Dorian apologized, said he would be delighted to talk whenever I was free, and departed.

I filled the sugar bowl with our own supply of lumps, then went through to the drawing room.

"Odd," I said to my father, who was sitting in the window seat and fighting a losing battle with the crossword. "I've just had an offer to buy my Open Return."

"The Fringes aren't for everyone," he remarked, not looking up. "You didn't sell it, did you?"

"Of course not."

"Good. Don't hand it to the prefects for safekeeping, either—they'll probably sell it themselves."

I thanked him for this good advice, then asked him if he could guess who our lodger was.

"Three down," he muttered. "*I spy an Equus*. Nine letters, begins and ends in A."

"Apocrypha."

"*Apocrypha?* Jolly good." And he filled it in without thinking.

"No, Dad, our *lodger* is Apocrypha."

"Dangles," he mumbled, rubbing out the answer for perhaps the sixth time. "An Apocryphal man, eh? You didn't ask him for supper, I hope?"

"I didn't ask him anything," I replied, depositing the milk and sugar lumps with the tea things before joining him at the window seat, "and since he doesn't exist, I guess that means he can't be there—even if he is."

"They're never anywhere," replied Dad, "that's the point. *I spy an Equus*. Hmm."

And that was when I heard the doorbell jangle.

"Would you get that?" said Dad, putting down his newspaper, straightening his tie and then adopting a dignified pose by the fireplace. "It'll be the head prefect."

A Grey and Sally Gamboge

1.2.31.01.006: Anyone caught paying underprice or overprice
for goods or services shall be fined.

stood up straight, my heart beating faster. I went to the front door,
pausing only to polish the toes of my shoes on the back of my trouser
legs.

But it wasn't the head prefect.

"You!" I cried, for standing on the doorstep was the quirky rude girl
who had threatened to break my jaw back in Vermillion. I felt a curious
mix of elation and trepidation, which came out as looking startled. And
so was she. A second's worth of doubt crossed her face, then she relaxed
and stared at me impassively.

"You've met?" came a stern voice. Standing behind her was a woman
who I assumed must be Sally Gamboge, the Yellow prefect. She, like
Bunty McMustard at the station, was covered from head to foot in a
well-tailored bright synthetic-yellow skirt and jacket. She even had yellow earrings, headband and watch strap. The color was so bright, in fact,
that my cortex cross-fired, and her clothes became less of a fierce shade
and more the sickly-sweet smell of bananas. But it wasn't actually a smell;
it was only the sense of one.

"Yes," I said without thinking. "She threatened to break my jaw!"

It was a very serious accusation, and I regretted saying it almost
immediately. Russetts don't usually snitch.

"Where was this?" the woman asked.

"Vermillion," I replied in a quiet voice.

"Jane?" said Gamboge sternly. "Is this true?"

"No, ma'am," she replied in an even tone, quite unlike the threatening one I had heard that morning. "I've never even seen this young man before—or been to Vermillion."

"What's going on?" asked my father, who had gotten bored posing with one elbow on the mantelpiece and joined us in the hall.

"Sally Gamboge," said the prefect, putting out a hand for him to shake, "Yellow prefect."

"Holden Russett," returned my father, "holiday relief swatchman. And this is . . . ?"

"Jane G-23," explained Gamboge. "I'm allocating her as your maid. She hasn't gotten much positive feedback, I'm afraid, but she's all I can spare. You can have her for an hour a day. Anything more can be privately negotiated. And I apologize in advance for any impertinence. Jane has . . . issues."

"An hour only?" replied Dad.

"Yes. I'm sorry if you have to sort your own washing and make the bed," said Mrs. Gamboge with a shrug. "Overemployment is particularly bad at present—too many Greys in unproductive retirement, if you ask me."

"You could pay them to do overtime," said Dad.

The Yellow prefect gave out a derisive laugh, not even considering that Dad might have been making a sensible suggestion. The Rules regarding retirement were universal across the Spectrum: As soon as you had discharged your fifty years' obligation to the Collective, you were free to do what you wanted, and extra work would have to be paid for. "The best Greys," our Yellow Prefect had once told me, "are the ones who catch the Mildew the morning of their retirement."

"Hello, Jane," said Dad, realizing he would get no sense from Mrs. Gamboge. His eyes flicked to the TRUCULENT and DECEITFUL badges below her Grey Spot. "Would you make a tray of scones? The other prefects are due shortly."

She bobbed and made to move away, but Gamboge was not yet done.

"Wait until you're dismissed, girl," she said in a curt tone, then added more warmly, "Mr. Russett, your son claims he has met Jane before and that she threatened physical violence. I want to know how that's possible."

Dad looked at me, then at Jane, then at Gamboge. When Yellows start making inquiries, you never really know where it will all end up. *Not* reporting something that had happened was sometimes worse than the infraction itself. But despite the fact that Jane had threatened to break my jaw, I didn't want to get her into trouble. And it would be serious trouble. Threatening to assault was treated the same as assaulting—to the Rules, intent and implementation were pretty much the same thing.

"Well, Eddie?" said Dad. "Where have you seen her before?"

"In Vermillion," I mumbled, wondering how I could back out without a demerit for wasting a prefect's time with a spurious accusation. "This morning—just before we caught the train."

"Then you *are* mistaken," said Gamboge, and I saw a sense of relief cross Jane's face. "Did you see her on the train?"

"No."

"Vermillion is over fifty miles away, and what's more, I saw her doing breakfast Useful Work this morning. There is only one train a day—and it heads north. Could you have been mistaken, Master Russett?"

"Yes," I said, greatly relieved. "It must have been someone else."

"Good," said Gamboge. "You may go, girl." And Jane headed off to the kitchen without another word.

"The head prefect will be attending you soon," said Gamboge, addressing my father, "but in the meantime I was wondering if you could look at some Greys who are claiming to be unwell? If you'd countersign a malingering report, I can dock some merits and knock some sense into the work-shy scalybacks. It'll only take ten minutes."

"I'll, um, do what I can," said my father, mildly perturbed by the Yellow prefect's obvious dislike of her workforce. Yellows were in charge of Grey employment allocation. Some did it well, others badly. Gamboge was clearly one of the latter.

The door closed behind them, and I walked slowly down the corridor to the kitchen, where Jane was busying herself in a halfhearted manner. I stood at the door, but she ignored me. For a moment I thought that perhaps I *was* mistaken—no one could travel over one hundred miles in a single morning without a train. But looking at her, I knew that I wasn't wrong, because when gazing at her, I felt the same odd tautness in my chest. And that nose. It was *quite* unique.

"How did you do it?" I asked. "Commute to Vermillion and back in a morning?"

"Commute?"

"I collect obsolete words," I explained, attempting to impress. "It means to travel a distance to work every day—or something."

"Have you heard of the term *dickhead*?"

"No, I haven't got that one. What does it mean?"

"I don't know," she replied, "but it might describe you. And I didn't 'commute' to Vermillion—you're mistaking me for someone else. Did you just look at my nose?"

"No," I said, which was a lie.

"Yes, you did."

"All right," I replied, feeling brave, "I did. So what? It's actually rather—"

"I would be failing in my duty of care if I didn't warn you."

"Warn me about what?"

"Of what might happen if you were to use the words *nose* and *cute* anywhere near me."

It might have been an odd leg-pull, so I laughed.

"Come on, Jane—!"

She glared at me and I saw that flash of anger again. It was definitely the same person.

"Did I say you could use my name?"

"No."

"Let's get one thing straight, Red. You and I have nothing to say, because we've never met and have nothing in common. So let's just leave it at that, and in a month you can go home to Polyp-on-the-Noze or wherever it is you come from, and carry on your pathetically uninteresting life as far from me as possible. Or farther."

She went back to measuring out the flour as I stood in silence, wondering what to say or do. I'd never quite met anyone so forthright. It was like talking to a Prefect in the body of a twenty-year-old Grey.

"Do you have a preference over the fat I use in the scones?" she asked, holding up two pots. "Pure vegetable is more expensive, but the animal reconstitute might have traces of resident in it. I don't know how qualmy you hub-dwellers are."

"We're not fussed. Who was the wrongspotted Grey in the Paint Shop?"

If I'd known better, I wouldn't have asked. She paused for a moment, then grabbed the nearest utensil from the counter and hurled it in my direction, where it struck the door frame with a *thunk*. It was a carving fork. I stared at the quivering handle barely five inches from my face, then back at Jane, who was glaring at me, so livid with rage that I could see the red in her cheeks. Pretty nose or not, she had a serious temper.

"Okay, okay," I said. "We've never met."

The doorbell rang. Ordinarily, I would have expected Jane as maid to go and answer it, but she didn't.

"I'll, um, get that, shall I?"

She ignored me, so I left the kitchen, then came back, pointed at the fork where it was still stuck in the door frame, and said, "You wouldn't really kill me, would you?"

"No."

"Glad to hear it."

"Not *here*. Too many witnesses."

I must have looked shocked, for she allowed herself a wry smile at my expense.

"Joke, right?" I said.

"Right."

But it wasn't, as it turned out.

I again expected it to be the head prefect at the front door, and again it wasn't. On the step was a wrinkly old woman with two rosy bumps for cheeks and a cheery grin. She wore a dress that was to my eyes a dark burgundy, but it wasn't. It was natural purple—I was just seeing the red component in it. She wore a bright synthetic Purple Spot and, below that, several merit badges and an upside-down head prefect badge—she had once run the village. Instinctively, I stood that much straighter in her presence. She was also carrying a cake: a plain, jamless sponge cake, but with the unusual luxury of a single bright red glacéed cherry atop a sheet of perfect white icing.

"The new swatchman?" she asked in an incredulous tone. "You seem barely out of short pants."

"That would be my father," I replied. "He's with Mrs. Gamboge, sorting out the malingerers. Can I help?"

"I suppose one must get used to the swatchmen getting younger," she said, sighing, as if I'd not spoken. "Welcome to East Carmine."

I thanked her, and she told me that her name was Widow deMauve, that she could see lots of purple and that she was our next-door neighbor. After relating a tedious yet mercifully short story regarding a fatal industrial accident that had left three households struggling to find a cleaner, she finally asked me if I would like the cake.

"That's very kind," I replied, taking the cake from her, "and with a cherry of all things. Would you like to come in?"

"Not particularly."

She paused for a moment, and then leaned closer. "Since you are new here, it would be only fair to warn you of Mrs. Lapis Lazuli."

"Yes?"

"Yes. Despite her honeyed words and faux generosity, she's a thieving, Rot-dodging congenital liar whose contribution to the village would be much improved if she were soap."

"You don't like her?"

"What a suggestion!" replied the Widow deMauve in a shocked tone. "She is one of my closest and dearest friends. She and I log Pooka sightings. Have you seen one recently?"

"Not recently," I replied, not thinking an ex–head prefect would concern herself with something as childish as specters.

"We also run East Carmine's reenactment society—would you care to join?"

"What do you reenact?" I asked, which was a reasonable question, since there wasn't much *to* reenact except scenes from Munsell's *Life*, which was too dreary to even contemplate.

"We reenact the previous Friday every Tuesday, then every Saturday morning is reenacted the following Thursday. It's a lot of fun when the whole village gets involved. At the end of the year we reenact the highlights. Sometimes we even reenact the reenactments. Aren't you forgetting something?"

I made no reply, so she pointed at the cherry cake.

"That will be half a merit, please."

It was a ridiculous price, even from someone who could see a lot of purple.

"However, if you decide not to eat it, I would gladly buy it back at cost—minus the seventy-five percent handling fee."

"The cake?"

"The cherry."

"Can I buy the cake *without* the cherry?" I asked after a moment's thought.

"Really!" she said in an affronted tone. "What point is cherry cake without the cherry?"

"Having trouble, Mother?"

A man had trotted up the three steps to the front door. He was dressed in long prefectural robes that must have been pure magenta. He was undoubtedly the head prefect. He was also middle-aged, tall, and athletic, and he looked vaguely affable. Behind him were two other brightly colored and wholly authoritarian figures, who I assumed were the rest of the prefects. Widow deMauve piped up,

"Mr. Russett is refusing to pay for the cake I made him."

The head prefect looked me up and down. "You seem a bit young for a swatchman."

"Please, sir, I'm not Mr. Russett, I'm his son."

"Then why did you say you were?" asked Widow deMauve suspiciously.

"I didn't."

"Oh," she said in a shocked tone, "so I'm a liar now, am I?"

"But—"

"Are you refusing to pay?" asked the head prefect.

"No, sir." I paid off the old woman, who chuckled to herself and hurried away.

Head Prefect deMauve—I assumed this was he, even though he had not and would not introduce himself to a junior—stepped into the house and looked me up and down as though I were a haunch of beef.

"Hmm," he said at last. "You look healthy enough. Are you bright?"

It was an ambiguous question. *Bright* could mean either "intelligent" or "highly color perceptive." The former question was allowable; the latter was not. I decided to meet ambiguity with ambiguity.

"I believe so, sir. Can I suggest you make yourselves comfortable in the drawing room?"

Along with deMauve were the Blue and Red prefects, who I would soon learn were named Turquoise and Yewberry. Turquoise appeared a decent chap, but Yewberry looked a fool. I saw them to their seats before hurrying back to the kitchen.

"The prefects are here, Ja—" I checked myself just in time, then continued, "Listen, what do I call you if I can't use your name?"

"I'd really prefer it if you didn't speak to me at all. But if you had even an ounce of self-respect, you'd use my name anyway."

It was a challenge. I looked around to see if there were any sharp objects within easy reach, and could see only an egg whisk.

"Right, then," I said. "Jane, the prefects are—"

I hadn't realized that egg whisks could hurt so much, but then I'd never had one chucked at me before. It caught me just above the forehead. That infraction alone—never mind the impertinence, disrespect and poor manners—would have netted her at least fifty demerits if I wanted to make something of it, and a 10 percent bounty to me for reporting it.

"You'll *never* get any merits or positive feedback at this rate," I said, rubbing my head. "How do you expect to get on in life?"

She gave me a weary look.

"Oh," I said, "do you have *any* merits or positive feedback?"

"No."

"And you don't think that's bad?"

She turned and fixed me with her piercingly intelligent eyes.

"There's more to good or bad than what's written in the Rulebook."

"That's just not true," I replied, shocked by the notion that there might be another, *higher* arbiter of social conduct. "The Rulebook tells us *precisely* what is right or wrong—that's the point. The predictability of the Rules and their unquestioning compliance and application is the bedrock of—"

"The scones are not quite done. You take in the tea, and I'll follow."

"Were you listening to a word I said?"

"I kind of switched off when you drew breath."

I gave her one of my most powerful glares, shook my head sorrowfully, gave an audible "tut" and, after picking up the tea tray, left the room in what I hoped was high dudgeon.

The Prefects

1.1.06.01.223: The position of prefect is open only to those with a perception of 70 percent or above. In the event that no one is available, an *acting* prefect with lesser perception may be appointed until a suitable perceptor is found.

When I returned to the drawing room, the prefects were discussing Travis Canary and his burning of the post. I couldn't help thinking that disposing of dead people's mail wasn't actually an offense but a public service. More interestingly, I couldn't help but notice that the Council had purloined all the sugar lumps in my absence. I poured the tea as politely as I could, but my hands were trembling. Prefects made me nervous—*especially* when I hadn't actually done anything wrong.

"So, Master Russett," said Head Prefect deMauve, "what can we expect from you?"

"I will strive to be a worthy and useful member of the Collective during my short stay," I said, defaulting to Standard Response.

"Of course you will," he replied. "East Carmine has no room for skivers, loafers and freeloaders." He said it with a smile, but I took it for what it was: a warning.

"Travel is a very great privilege," he continued, "but can also lead to the spreading of disharmony, not to mention the Mildew. What is the reason *you* travel, Master Russett?"

"Actually, sir, I'm here to conduct a chair census."

They exchanged looks.

"You have orders to this effect?"

"Yes, sir."

"Sally will be interested in helping, I'm sure," murmured Yewberry.

"Was it for Humility Realignment?" asked deMauve, looking at my badge.

"Yes, sir."

"I hope you learn from it, Master Russett. It would be a huge dishonor to your forefathers to waste all the Red they've worked hard to achieve, now wouldn't it?"

"Yes, sir."

The Russett family scandal was annoyingly well known. Three generations ago an eccentric forebear with considerably more Red than sense decided to marry a Grey. He was called Piers Burgundy, was a prefect and distantly related to First Red. His name and hue were lost in the union, and the diluted perception of barely 16 percent that emerged in their son meant a dynastic downgrade to Russett. We'd been attempting to regain our lost social standing ever since. The whole thing had been unthinkably scandalous, even by today's standards, but not against the Rules. Marrying for love was not forbidden; it just didn't make any sense. "If you want your grandchildren to hate you," the saying goes, "marry down-spectrum."

The prefects talked among themselves while I handed around the tea, but they all suddenly fell silent. Jane had just arrived with the scones. Both Yewberry and Turquoise looked vaguely worried, and recoiled a little as she approached. I realized then that Jane's enmity was universal. She didn't just hate me; she hated *everyone* higher up. This meant her dislike of me wasn't personal, which allowed me at least a meager slice of delusive hope—something to build on, at any rate.

"Thank you, Jane," said deMauve, who seemed to be the only person not wary of her.

"Sir," she replied, placing the steaming-hot, sweet-smelling plate of scones on the table while Turquoise and Yewberry watched her carefully.

"Spoon packed and ready to go?" asked Yewberry in a needlessly provocative manner.

She looked at him contemptuously, bobbed out of habit rather than politeness and walked out.

"That's one I won't be sorry to see the back of," murmured Yewberry. "*Quite* out of control."

"A hard worker, despite the antisocialism," remarked deMauve, "and her nose is *very* retroussé."

"Very," agreed Turquoise.

They stopped chatting to help themselves greedily to the scones.

It wouldn't have been considered good manners for me to eat with them unless invited, so I sat quietly, hands neatly folded on my lap. I was thinking about Jane again. Yewberry's comment about whether she had "packed her spoon" could refer only to Reboot. You didn't take much with you, but you always took a spoon. Like Travis Canary, Jane was destined for the Night Train to Emerald City to learn some manners.

"She makes a good scone, though," said Yewberry, helping himself to another.

"Might even be worth a merit," replied Turquoise.

"It won't help her," replied Yewberry, and they all laughed.

"Master Russett," said deMauve, washing his scone down with a mouthful of tea, "I think I should keep your return ticket for safekeeping. There are elements within the village who are eager to attempt an unauthorized relocation. Have you been asked to sell it yet, by the way?"

"No, sir," I replied without a pause. Dorian's secret offer would remain just that—secret.

"We'll give you ten merits if you report to us who asks."

"I'll remember that, sir, thank you."

"Jolly good. Well, hand it over, then."

"I—um—would like to keep it, if that is all right."

"Well, it isn't all right with me one little bit, Russett," replied deMauve sharply. "Perhaps you think we are sloppy with our responsibilities here in the Fringes? If your Open Return were to be stolen, your ability to broaden yourself would be much curtailed."

He was right. Due to a loophole in the Rules, an Open Return could never be questioned or rescinded, and was invaluable to anyone attempting an illegal relocation—hence the two hundred merits Dorian had already offered me.

"No, sir, but—"

"But *nothing*," barked Yewberry. "Do as the head prefect requests, or we will have to consider charges of Gross Impertinence."

They all stared at me, and I caved under their disapproving looks. I handed over my ticket.

DeMauve took it without a word and placed it in his pocket.

And at that precise moment, my father came back in the front door, and we all stood. He seemed to be having some sort of argument with Mrs. Gamboge.

". . . and I say it is malingering," she announced. "Anyone who thinks otherwise is obviously not fully acquainted with the Greys' ceaseless capacity for distortion and untruths."

"You are mistaken," my father replied, maintaining an unraised voice as decorum required. "I contend that it is the sniffles and, as such, Annex III—legitimate work absence."

"A spate of industrial accidents has left us severely lean on the workforce," she retorted, mostly for deMauve's benefit, "and none of the younger Achromatics are even *approaching* their sixteenth. A violent outbreak of the sniffles could spell economic disaster for the village."

"It could spell more than that," replied Dad, this time more firmly. "The sniffles has been known to progress to Variant-P Mildew, and if unchecked, an outbreak could spread far and wide."

He wasn't overcooking the goose. Green Sector South had lost every single resident to the Mildew in an incident many years ago and was only now getting back up to sector strength. Whether it was the sniffles or not was anyone's guess, but outbreaks of the Mildew usually had an annoyingly banal beginning.

Luckily, Dad had the protocol of introductions to take him away from the argument.

"Apologies for my absence," he said as he strode up, hand outstretched. "Senior Monitor Holden Russett, holiday relief swatchman."

"George Stanton deMauve, head prefect."

DeMauve then went on to introduce the prefects to my father, who bowed and shook hands with Turquoise and Yewberry in turn, then asked me to fetch some fresh tea for him and Mrs. Gamboge. I relayed the message to Jane, who put the kettle back on the gas without comment.

"Did you see any sign of Riffraff on the journey in?" I heard Mr. Turquoise ask as I walked back in.

"None at all. Do you have them this far west?"

"One can never be too careful. Two years ago some rail passengers were subjected to an intolerable barrage of jeers and obscene gestures about twenty miles up the line. A posse from Bluetown found an encampment a month later, but happily, they had by then all succumbed to the Rot. Riffraff in these parts seem particularly susceptible to Mildew. I think it's the damp."

"To be honest," remarked Sally Gamboge, "it's the best thing for them."

"We have some monochrome fundamentalists down our way," said Dad, "attacking color feedpipes, that sort of thing. But they haven't been active for a while."

"Killjoys," murmured Yewberry.

"Frightful business," remarked my father, "Ochre's fatal self-misdiagnosis."

"It was indeed," replied deMauve in a sober tone. "The loss of a swatch-man is always regretful, and misdiagnosis is a tragic waste. But it might have been for the best."

The other prefects appeared uneasy, and I frowned. There was something strange going on.

"For the best?" echoed Dad. "How is that possible?"

Turquoise chose his words carefully.

"There were . . . *irregularities* regarding the village's swatch," replied Turquoise, referring to the large quantities of healing colors stored in the Colorium. A Chromaticologist's Long Swatch might hold up to a thousand individual shades—well beyond the small traveling set my father carried.

Dad asked what sort of "irregularities," but deMauve suggested only that they should "meet at the Colorium to discuss it" after tea.

"It's a situation of the utmost delicacy," added Mr. Turquoise.

"Did you see our crackletrap as you came in?" asked Gamboge, expertly changing the subject as deMauve helped himself to his third scone.

"One could hardly miss it," replied my father in a distracted manner. "*Most* impressive."

"We have a lot of lightning down this way," she continued. "Drills are carried out regularly. You'll find full instructions on the back of the kitchen door."

There was a pause.

"I understand," said deMauve, staring at my father intently, "that you were witness to an incident at the National Color outlet this morning?"

"News travels fast."

"We were telegrammed by Vermillion's Yellow prefect."

Dad replied that this was indeed so, and outlined what had happened in the Paint Shop while the prefects listened intently.

"I see," said deMauve as soon as Dad had finished. "It seems the Grey who committed the outrage of wrongspottedness succumbed to the Mildew soon after he was transferred to their Colorium. They wondered if perhaps you knew anything that could shed light on his identity."

Jane had returned with a fresh pot of tea and extra cups, and was doing everything *extra* slowly so she could listen to the conversation.

"He was an LD2," said Dad after thinking for a moment.

"There are eighty-two LD2s on the national register," remarked Gamboge, "and it will take a while to trace them all. None of our twelve match the age and description. Purples are quite rightly not asked for verification, so they don't know when he arrived, or from where."

"Then I'm sorry I can't help you," replied Dad.

"No *other* clues?" asked Gamboge. "Something you might like to volunteer? Either of you?"

"No," said my father.

I glanced at Jane, who was looking at me carefully. She knew I was aware of her connection with the wrongspot, and if she'd been anyone else, I would have told. Despite what Dad said about Russetts not snitching, I needed every merit I could lay my hands on if I was to have a chance with Constance. She liked chocolates, and they were expensive—especially ones with colorized centers. Snitching on Jane would bag me at least fifty merits.

"No, sir."

Jane stopped straightening the tea things and quietly moved off.

"Right, then," said deMauve. "I'll telegram Vermillion and let them know."

They settled down to small talk after that. Dad declined a scone but drank tea, and they talked about unicycle polo, and how the East Carmine team won silver at last year's Jollity Fair.

Jane walked back in. She was carrying a salver with a note on it.

"Excuse me," she said in her most polite manner, "but an urgent message has arrived for Master Edward."

"Me?" I asked, somewhat surprised, but I took the message, thanked her and read it, then placed it in my top pocket. She curtsied and left the room without another word.

"Would you care for a scone, Master Russett?" said deMauve, since they had almost had their fill. "They're actually very good."

"Unusually . . . *piquant*," said Turquoise.

"Tangy," added Yewberry.

"You are most kind," I replied, "but I shan't, thank you."

Usually, I liked scones—but I couldn't help but refuse on this occasion. The note Jane had handed me read: *Don't eat the scones.*

We signed the village register after that. Names, parents, postcode, feedback, merit tally and how much of what color we could see. Dad filled in his as "Red: 50.23%," and I marked mine as "Untested." I noticed that Travis had signed in just above us. He carried a highly influential TO3 4RF postcode, so originally hailed from the traditional Yellow homeland of the Honeybun Peninsula. More interestingly, he carried a 92 percent feedback score. A model resident—right up until the moment he set fire to the post.

"I'm sorry to appear untrusting," said Mr. Yewberry once we had filled in the register, "but would you mind? It's the Rules."

We loosened our shirts and showed him our postcodes, and he compared them to our merit books. As a double check he also looked at the pattern of black and white lines that grew from our left-hand nail beds, and compared these to our record, which took a little longer.

We passed verification, and the prefects had a swift look at our merit status and feedback score, which they seemed to approve of, as no comment was made. My feedback was good, at almost 72 percent, but my merit score less so. Aside from my recent fine for attempting to improve queueing, I generally kept my nose clean, hence my 1,260 merits. Two hundred above the thousand required for full residency wasn't much, but at least I was there. With it I had the right to marry once I'd taken my Ishihara, have seconds at dinner, wear a patterned waistcoat and a whole lot more besides. My father had many more merits, as befit his years, profession and senior monitor status. He would have had more still, but he had been fined a packet when he lost a swatch two years before. Dad had been down to eight thousand the last time we had discussed it, and anything beyond the three thousand earmarked for my dowry would go toward a hardwood conservatory.

"Hmm," murmured deMauve after he had read Dad's total. "Impressive."

"They were my wife's," said Dad simply.

"Indeed?" replied deMauve, no longer so impressed. "She must have been a fine woman. We're sorry for your loss."

"Was it lightning?" asked Mrs. Gamboge in a hopeful sort of voice.

Dad paused, hoping that they wouldn't press him, but these prefects were different from our bunch. Old Man Magenta might have been a fool and a martinet, but he knew when to let personal matters drop.

"Swan attack?" suggested Yewberry.

"It was the Mildew," interjected my father in a quiet yet forceful voice, "and our grief is a private matter."

"We apologize," said deMauve simply. He gave us back our books and rose to his feet. "No more will or should be said."

They made their way to the front door, where they all solemnly shook hands with my father in turn.

"It may take you a few days to understand the peculiarity of village customs," said deMauve, "but I will start you off. Although we're relaxed about dress code, and first names are generally acceptable, we do insist that ties will be half-Windsored, and lateness to mealtimes is not tolerated. Mandatory sports for girls are squash and hockeyball; for boys, cricket and tag-footy. Voluntary sports are tennis, extreme badminton, croquet, fainting in coils and rowing."

"You have a broad enough river?" asked Dad, who used to scull quite a lot back home.

"It's mostly theoretical," replied deMauve. "And we have a ninety-thousand-piece jigsaw puzzle for rainy afternoons."

"But someone lost the picture," grumbled Yewberry, "and there's a lot of sky."

"*Challenging*, we call that, Mr. Yewberry," remarked deMauve. "Master Russett will be rostered Useful Work by Mr. Turquoise tomorrow, and I will have the junior Red monitor show him around the village. As part of this year's Foundation Day celebrations we'll be performing *Red Side Story*. If you want to contribute voice or instrument, my daughter Violet is holding auditions. Do you have any questions?"

"Yes," said Dad. "What's fainting in coils?"

"We have no idea, but the Rules state we have to offer it as a sport."

And that was it. Following the usual courteous farewells, bows, shaken hands and *Apart We Are Together* salutations, the door closed, and we were left alone in the hallway.

"Eddie?"

"Yes, Dad?"

"Keep your eyes and ears open. I've seen a few odd villages in my day, but nothing like this. What was all that about Jane, by the way? The Prefects actually looked frightened of her."

"She doesn't have anything to lose," I replied simply. "She's up for Reboot on Monday."

"Ah," said Dad, "what a waste of a good nose."

The front doorbell rang. Dad opened it to find a junior Grey messenger, who told him that there had been another accident at the linoleum factory.

"But there's no hurry," said the young lad cheekily, "unless you have a swatch that can stitch heads back on."

Dad tipped the messenger, picked up his traveling swatch case and made to leave.

"Keep your eyes open, Eddie. Things here seem a bit rum."

"Robin Ochre and his 'irregularities'?"

"Among others. And one more thing."

"Yes?"

"Don't put so many sugar lumps out next time the Council come around."

I wandered back into the kitchen, where Jane was washing the dishes, and asked her what she had put into the scones.

"You're better off not knowing. And if you think not snitching on me is going to grant you any favors in the youknow department, you've got another think coming."

"You've got me all wrong," I said, trying to sound as though the notion of some illicit youknow hadn't crossed my mind.

"Sure," she said sarcastically, "next you're going to tell me you're saving yourself for your wedding night."

"That's . . . no bad thing," I said slowly, and she laughed. Not with me, but *at* me. It felt humiliating. I tried to get her on the defensive by repeating the awkward question: "How did you get to Vermillion and back this morning?"

"I didn't," she said. "It's not possible. And we've never met before, remember?"

"You don't like me, do you?"

"That would take effort," she replied. "Indifference is much, *much* easier. Listen, you did me a favor, and I did you a favor. So we're quits."

"It was hardly equal," I replied. "I saved you a whole bunch of awkward questions, and all you did was stop me eating scones."

"If you knew what I'd put in the scones, you might think differently."

"What—"

"I'm done," she said, drying her hands on the towel and getting ready to leave, "and what's more important, *we're* done. Speak to me again and I'll break your arm. Make a comment about how cute and retroussé you think my nose is and I'll kill you. Don't think I won't. I've nothing to lose."

"But you're the maid. What if I need extra starch on my collar or something?"

I wished I hadn't said it. I'd wanted to simply keep on engaging with her at any cost, but the comment came out all reedy and needy. She picked up on this right away. It was abundantly clear who had the upper hand. She oozed authority. But it wasn't the sort of authority that comes from a fortuitous birth gift; she had something else—a sense of clear purpose and *strength*.

She took a step closer and stared at me, trying, I think, to figure out if I had any hidden depths. Then, after satisfying herself that I hadn't, she made for the door.

"If you want anything, you can leave me a note."

And she departed, leaving me feeling deflated and somewhat confused. I'd thought Outer Fringes would be uncomplicated and wholly parochial, but in the short time I had been out there, it had begun to seem more subtle and complex than anything my uneventful existence at Jade-under-Lime had thrown at me. There were, however, two things in my favor. First, she had moved from threatening to break my jaw to threatening to break my *arm*, which I think was a step in the right direction. Second, and far more important, *Dad had given me the Grey Purple Pretender's spoon*. And engraved on the back, as with every other personal spoon, was his full postcode: LD2 5TZ. I wish now that I had ignored it, but I didn't. The yateveo's barbed snatch-boughs were already descending.

Tommo Cinnabar

5.3.21.01.002: Once allocated, postcodes are permanent, and for life.

"Hullo!" said a lad who knocked on the door about half an hour later. "Are you the Russett fellow?"

"Eddie."

"I'm Tommo Cinnabar. DeMauve told me to give you the grand tour of East Carmine's glittering highlights. I expect you're almost insane with excitement, eh?"

"It's all I've been thinking of for weeks."

"Actually, it's a dump," he said as we moved off. "Even the cockroaches think it's a toilet. Friend?"

"Friend."

The lightning lure atop the flak tower was easily the most unusually dominant feature as we walked across the square, and I mentioned this to him.

"Did the Yellow Peril tell you the crackletrap was her idea?"

"I think she mentioned something about it."

"The old ratbag bangs on about that to everyone. The lure cost the village more than *three hundred thousand* communal merits, yet we've had only six people zapped in living memory—and five of those were ball lightning, against which a crackletrap is no defense. She makes us drill every week, and insists on a manned watch if there's so much as a single cloud in the sky. I think it's all grade D hogwash. What say you?"

I liked his unruly bluffness almost immediately. He was a stocky lad slightly shorter than myself, with rounded features and a furtive, darting manner that would not have looked out of place on a Yellow. He wore an IMPERTINENT badge below his Red Spot, along with LOW MERIT and HEAD JUNIOR MONITOR badges, which would seem to conflict with each other.

The Cinnabar family were well known. They were big in the crimson pigment trade until a price-fixing scandal led to a massive demerit and forfeiture of assets. Despite this, they still maintained a certain stubborn, tainted pride—and were never averse to bending the Rules when it suited them. But despite Tommo's impressive dynastic lineage and the clan's glamorous FK6 postcode, several ill-advised unions to lesser colors—a clumsy attempt at vanity eugenics, some say—had diluted the line, and now the Cinnabars were generally mid- to low-level perceptors, and heading toward Grey. Russetts were on the way up, Cinnabars on the way down. That's how it worked.

"Can we stop by the post office?" I asked. "I have to send a telegram."

The post office was on the corner, as post offices generally are. There was a board outside with the week's headline from *Spectrum* chalked on it—something to do with Riffraff committing some outrage somewhere. There was also a mailbox, which was a soft, natural shade of red, quite unlike the high-chroma ones in Jade-under-Lime. In fact, it took me a while to realize that the mailbox was a natural red, and deeply faded. In fact, on looking around, I realized that there was very little synthetic color in the village at all.

I sent a telegram to my best friend, Fenton, at Jade-under-Lime to inquire about baking products for Dorian and also to confirm that I had logged the rabbit's Taxa number, as requested. But since I hadn't even seen the rabbit, let alone its bar code, there was a certain amount of fudging to be done. The first twelve digits to *Mammalia* were easy as they were the same as ours, but hazarding a guess as to the code after that was a bit of a puzzle. I eventually plumped on thirteen as the *Order* since there was a Taxa code gap between Rodents and Hedgehogs, then a two and seven for *Genus* and *Species*. I filled in the remaining code with random numbers, making sure I ended with an F, as even Fenton knew the Last Rabbit was female. I felt a bit nervous as it was a bald lie, but they'd never know, and I'd already spent the money they'd given me. I didn't send a poetical telegram to Constance as I still needed to compose something half decent. Constance was used to receiving poetry from me and Roger Maroon, and the bar had been set quite high, since I'd been paying someone else to write it for me, and so had Roger, since neither of us was any good at the rhyming stuff.

Tommo asked me about myself as we left the post office, and I told him about the incident with Bertie Magenta, and the chair census, then about Jade-under-Lime.

"A bit Greencentric," I explained when he asked me what it was like, "but none too bad for that, since the Moldies don't really speak to us."

"Is it on the grid?"

I nodded.

"Full CYM at twenty-six pounds' pressure. We can get most on-gamut colors up around the sixty percent mark, saturation *and* brightness."

Tommo whistled low.

"I wish we could."

"East Carmine doesn't look that bad," I ventured as we walked across the scrubbed pantiles of the town square, past the central lamppost and twice-lifesize bronze of Our Munsell, who glared down at us paternalistically, his heavy eyebrows knitted in eternal deep thought. "At least you are not totally devoid of color."

We had stopped outside the town hall, which was painted in a soothing green. A series of worn stone steps led up to an elevated terrace where six fluted columns supported a flat triangular tympanum high above. Carved into the limestone was the credo of the Collective: APART WE ARE TOGETHER. The massive front doors were twice head height, and on either side of the entrance were faded wooden Departure Boards with names of past residents who had achieved notability in some field: TRACY PEACH, WHO WAS KIND AND THOUGHTFUL AND GONE A LOT TOO SOON—DECEMBER 23, 00207 or OLIVE OLIVE, WHO COULD JUGGLE SIX MELONS AND UNICYCLE AT THE SAME TIME—AUGUST 12, 00450. There was even one for Robin Ochre, and the paint was still fresh: ROBIN OCHRE, A FINE SWATCHMAN WHO KEPT MILDEW AT BAY AND PROTECTED ONE AND ALL—JUNE 16, 00496. The names were graded according to how Worthy they had been—Extremely, Very, Mostly, Partly—something that was determined by the highly unusual procedure of asking residents to mark pieces of paper with their choices.

"It's lucky they repainted it when they did," said Tommo, referring to the color of the town hall. "That stupid crackletrap pretty much cleared us out. It'll be years before we can afford to have it repainted, and as for being on the grid—forget it."

"Really? I heard the Outer Fringes were awash with uncollected scrap."

"Yes," said Tommo sarcastically. "As you can see, the streets here are paved in yellow. It's all complete plums, sorry to tell. The Previous were always more numerous in the south. There are parts around here where I don't think they *ever* lived. Besides, everything local has been pretty much teased out."

It was a problem that was becoming increasingly common. Distribution of synthetic hue was strictly controlled by National Color and could be earned only in a single way: by the collection of scrap color for recycling into raw pigment. It was said that a ton of red tosh might yield about a gallon of univisual pigment—enough to keep three hundred roses at full color for six months or, at halfhue, a year. Some villages spent their every light-hour collecting scrap color, even to the detriment of basic food production. Color, and the enjoyment thereof, was *everything*.

"The linoleum factory must bring in a few merits, surely?" I asked.

"We're selling it at a tenth of the price it was two hundred years ago. The Council has been pleading with Head Office to either cut production or license it for use as roof tiles. It's a little too hard wearing, to be honest."

"I'd heard that about linoleum."

We were still staring at the soothing olive color of the town hall.

"Do you think that's *really* green?" asked Tommo.

"I've no idea," I replied, for no one could explain how we could see a univisual green but not a real one. After all, color in itself has no color—it's simply a construction of the mind: a sensation, like the Humming Chorus from *Madame Butterfly* and the smell of honeysuckle. I knew what a red looked like, but I'd be hard pressed to explain what it actually is.

We had been staring at the town hall for a while now, so decided to move on before a prefect or a monitor walked by.

"So . . . have your family been here long?" I asked.

"I moved here only a year ago. I come from a less well-known strand of the Cinnabars. We're shopkeepers. Good ones, too. Our co-op was the most profitable in Red Sector East."

"So why are you out here?"

"Bog off."

"You bog off."

"No—BOGOF: 'Buy one get one free.' It seems the Council took exception to my aggressive selling techniques. The 'free kettle every morning for a week' didn't go down too well, either."

"You could have covered yourself by logging them as Standard Variables," I said, attempting to sound knowledgeable, even though I'd learned that from Travis on the way in.

"I know that *now*."

I frowned.

"What's the point in 'buy one get one free'? Why not just offer something at half price?"

"Which would you prefer," he retorted, "something at half price or something for free?"

"It's the same thing."

"It is and it isn't," he replied with a smile. "I think there was a whole science involved around selling. The Council said I had shown contempt of the Rules by using arcane knowledge, and I was fined thirty merits and shipped out here to study Floon beetle migrations."

"Did deMauve take your Open Return?"

"Not at all—I lost it on a dead cert at Jollity Fair that came in third. I've been trying to buy my way out, but it's not going too well; in fact, I'm well below zero."

I frowned. Anywhere else, having negative merits would be seen as deeply shameful—Tommo seemed to be wearing his imminent Reboot with *pride*.

"Then Reboot doesn't bother you?"

"Should it?"

"Of course."

He patted me on the shoulder.

"You worry too much, Eddie. I'll figure out something before Monday."

He was taking his Ishihara this Sunday—the same as Jane. Back in Jade-under-Lime, we weren't due to take our Ishihara for another eight weeks. But since we were being so open with each other, I decided to ask an indelicate question.

"Just how many merits below zero are you?"

"Around a hundred, I think," he said with a laugh, "but deMauve said he'd give me five if I showed you around—and as long as I didn't inveigle you into any Tommo-inspired devilry."

"I'm relieved to hear it."

"Don't be. Tommo devilry is of the very highest quality. Do you want to sell your Open Return?"

"With what would you buy it?"

"Don't get me wrong," he said, "it's only book merits I'm short of. Cash is a different bird entirely."

It meant he'd been working the Beigemarket. But if his cash merits were unofficially earned, they wouldn't help him when it came to Reboot. He could be richer than Josiah Oxblood, but it wouldn't matter. You couldn't take cash to Reboot, either—just a spoon. A good one usually, and sometimes two. It was said the remedial teachers liked to exchange them for privileges.

"I couldn't sell it to you even if I wanted to. I gave it to deMauve for safekeeping."

"That's bad."

"It is?"

"Certainly. DeMauve bargains hard. I'd probably have to pay him twice what I'd pay you."

"You're kidding me?"

"Yes, of course I'm kidding you," he said in the manner of someone who probably wasn't. "Come and have a look at what living color we *do* have."

We walked on toward the eastern end of the town square, where there was a sunken garden. About the size of a tennis court, it was enclosed by a low wall that was just the right height for a seat. It was East Carmine's one and only color garden, and it was drab—the grass was a dark shade of green, and the flowers were all in muted versions of blue and yellow. The garden would be run on large toothpaste-tube-shaped pigment refills. Worse, they would be using the outdated Red-Blue-Yellow Color Model, which gave a miserably poor choice of hues.

"The red cartridge ran out last week," said Tommo. "We expect the yellow to dry out any day now, and you know what that means."

"Right," I said, seeing the problem instantly. "Blue grass. That's rotten—no village should be without a color garden."

"We'll still have Mrs. Gamboge's," he said with a sneer. "She spends all her bonuses on nothing else. Even has a gardener employed full-time to tint by hand."

"With the labor shortage as it is?"

"It's not against the Rules. What do you think of that door?"

We were walking past the Prime Residences on the sunny side of the square. The door that Tommo had indicated was painted univisual red, so everyone knew that it was the home of the village Red prefect. The artificial hue made the door almost obscenely bright; all detail and texture were obliterated by an overpowering color that was so strong it cross-fired into my other senses. I could smell burned hair, my ears started ringing and an odd jumble of memories popped into my head. Of my mother, a long-dead family pet and a performance of *South Pacific* I'd seen once.

"Fairly bright," I said, understanding what he was up to in an instant. He was trying to gauge my red perception.

"Hmm," said Tommo, "not *painfully* so, then? Any . . . tinnitus or memory sweeps? Visions of *Repaint Your Wagon,* for example?"

"Not really. How about you?"

"More shades of *Seven Brides for Seven Colors,* really—and Chuckles, our pet badger."

If that was true, he was almost as receptive as me. But from what I knew already of Tommo, bragging up his perception would be pretty much standard operating procedure—and everyone knew an oversaturation of one's own color fired off memories of musicals and family pets.

We walked on. Within a dozen paces we found ourselves outside a large building with LIBRARY written on the front.

"Is that the library?" I asked.

"Your deductive powers are quite extraordinary."

"I need to look something up," I said, ignoring the sarcasm.

"You go ahead," he replied, "but it's not for me. If I wanted to go and look at empty shelves, I'd prefer the supermarket. It smells better, and you don't get pestered."

The unLibrary

Imaginative thought is to be discouraged. No good ever comes of it—don't.

The Munsell Book of Wisdom

I pushed open the doors and walked inside. The library was large and open-plan, with a circular void in the upper floor from where light descended vertically. Dotted around were tables and chairs, and a few mirrors on stands, useful for directing light to study. Or at least, it would have been, had there been any books to look at. As Tommo had already mentioned, the shelves were pretty much empty, and what books remained were so read-worn front and back that barely the middle chapters remained. Reading a book these days was a bit like learning what someone was doing, but never knowing how they got to be there or how it eventually turned out. It hadn't always been like this. Successive Leap-backs had stripped the shelves of science, history, biography, geography, cookery, self-help, poetry, art—and now fiction, genre by genre. There were still books other than the strongly encouraged Very Racy Novels, but they were so few and far between that they were always either being borrowed, in transit or worn out. Not here in the library, anyway.

"Can we help you?" came several hushed voices in unison and I jumped, for seven Blues had all crept silently up behind me and were now peering at me with expressions of wonder. The Rules had decreed that books be part of the successive Great Leap Backward, but due to a poorly drafted Leapback directive, staffing levels had remained unchanged and would remain so forever. The chief librarian was a tall and imperious-looking woman who was covered head to toe in bright synthetic blue and had a large quantity of jewelry draped about her neck and a tiara perched precariously on a large shock of bouffant white hair. She had drawn circles around her eyes, which were joined by a line across the bridge of her nose. It was the traditional mark of her calling, but no one knew why.

"I am Mrs. Lapis Lazuli," she announced in a voice that sounded like rusty wire under tension. "You must be the new swatchman's son. You're here to count chairs, I understand?"

"Among other things."

"Hmm. I heard you fell for the Widow deMauve's cherry cake scam. Watch out for that conniving old hag. The sooner she's carried off by the Mildew, the better. Do you have a name?"

"Edward," I said, meek beneath her baleful stare. "I was actually after the reference section."

"Not fiction, then?" she asked in a hopeful tone of voice.

I waved an arm in the direction of the empty shelves.

"With the greatest of respect, ma'am, I think I'm about three centuries too late."

"Nonsense. I shall give you a personal guided tour. Visitors to the library are almost as rare as books. Indeed, the librarians here outnumber the books seven to one—if you don't count Reference, those frightful Racy Novels or the *Collected Thoughts* of Munsell."

She guided me to the first of the empty shelves, while her assistant librarians all followed close behind.

"I am ninth-generation librarian here in East Carmine," she announced grandly. "Certain information has descended down the years, even if the books have not."

She pointed to a shelf, and I could see that carefully arranged in a row were the much-faded bar codes that had once been affixed upon the departed spines. She tapped a shelf.

"This was where *The Little Engine That Could* once sat."

She lapsed into silence and we all stood there respectfully, staring at an empty space in the air.

"What was it about?" asked one of the junior librarians, as it seemed a tour was an honor not often bestowed.

"It was about an engine," said Mrs. Lapis Lazuli, "that could."

"That could what?"

"Over here," she continued, gripping my elbow and sweeping me to the other side of the corridor, "were the complete works of Beatrice Potter. You may test me if you wish."

She turned her back, and at the other librarians' urging, I picked a bar code at random. "Shout them out!" called Mrs. Lapis Lazuli, back still turned.

"Thin thin, medium, modest," I recited as I read the bar code, "thick, broad, minor, fat, token, token, slim, thin, medi—"

"The Tail of Tom Kitten," she announced happily. "Am I right?"

"I don't know," I said, somewhat confused, since there was no information anywhere, either on the bar code or on the shelf.

"Sixth from the left?"

"Yes."

She turned back to me and beamed.

"You see? I know where every single book used to be in the library." She pointed to the shelf opposite. "Over there was *Catch-22,* which was a hugely popular fishing book and one of a series, I believe."

She moved swiftly to another wholly empty bookcase.

"This used to be the crime section."

She tapped a finger at various points on the shelves and barked out the titles of books, long since extinct.

"The Most Serious Affair at Stiles," she announced, *"Murdoch on the Orientated Ex-Best, The Glass Quay, A Missed Simile's Foaling in Snow, Gawky Park . . ."*

I looked across at the librarians, who were nodding to themselves as they attempted to memorize what she was saying and thus somehow perpetuate the knowledge. It seemed utterly pointless but also, in a curious way, noble.

". . . *The Science of the Slams,"* she continued, her pointing finger moving rapidly around the empty bookcase in a haphazard manner, *"The Pig's Leap, Monday Morning, The Force Bear, The Complete Sheer Luck Homes.* Are you impressed, Master Edward?"

"Very," I replied.

"My father taught me. And his mother before him. And her father before her—and so on. Do you get the picture?"

"I do."

She paused and a sort of lost, dreamy look came over her.

"All those words," she whispered, "so diligently placed together, and so pointlessly torn apart."

She was suddenly overcome by a sadness and paused for several moments, before turning to me with a despondent smile.

"What did you come in here for, anyway?"

I had to think to remember. "The reference section."

"Of course! Hannah will take you to that chair over there, whereupon Gerard will escort you to the stairs. Silas will pick you up there and take you to general fiction, where Nancy will show you to the reference section. Cath will compose the risk assessment."

"What do I do?" asked Terri, as all the others eagerly went to their places to assist me the thirty feet to the reference section.

"You'll be assisting the young man to select the correct book."

She opened her eyes wide and jumped up and down in excitement, while the others grumbled enviously.

Once Mrs. Lapis Lazuli had gone back to pacing the library, mumbling to herself and pointing at the shelves, I was expertly escorted to the reference section. I asked for the local Residents' Manifest, and Terri obliged while the others stared from the doorway.

"What are you looking for?" she asked.

"An old friend asked me to check on some relatives living in the area," I lied, and opened several books at random to disguise my intent. But I found what I was looking for. The postcode on the back of the Grey wrongspot's spoon had been LD2 5TZ, and according to the records, it was in use by a four-year-old Grey living here in East Carmine, which wasn't possible. Codes were only reallocated after death.

"Do you have the historical records?" I asked. This elicited a squeak of pleasure from Terri, who vanished for a moment and then returned with a second volume, even more battered than the first. This was more help, and I found the information I wanted. My tasks complete, I thanked the librarians in turn, filled out their feedback forms and was shown to the door in a similarly labor-intensive manner.

"How did you get along with our resident bookworm?" asked Tommo, who was waiting for me on the library steps.

"She's a bit fierce, isn't she?"

"Her bark is worse than her bite. Despite her position as deputy Blue prefect, she's not averse to bending the Rules when it comes to story time."

"How do you mean?"

"You'll see—as long as your Morse is up to scratch." He nodded toward the library. "Did you find what you were looking for?"

"Not really."

That wasn't strictly true—or indeed, true at all. The holder of LD2 5TZ *before* the four-year-old had been a man who lived in Rusty Hill, the abandoned town we had rattled past on the way in. He would be sixty-eight by now, which fitted the Grey wrongspot perfectly. His name had been Zane G-49, and according to the records, he'd died four years ago in Rusty Hill's Mildew outbreak. *Two people had shared the same code.* Such a concept was unthinkable. The finite quantity of postcodes kept the Collective's population at sustainable levels. One in, one out—that's how it worked. With two sharing one, the Collective was technically overpopulated—an abomination in the eye of the Rules. But it didn't tell me what he was doing in the Paint Shop, or even what Jane had to do with it. I was as ignorant now as I had been when I awoke this morning.

We walked on for a few moments in silence until Tommo looked at his watch, shook it and adjusted the hands so they matched the town clock.

"Right," he said enigmatically. "We're off to the Sorting Pavilion. It's time you met the Big Banana."

Courtland Gamboge

> **5.2.02.02.018:** Yellows are permitted to break Rules in the pursuit of Rule-breakers, but all Rules to be broken must be logged beforehand, and countersigned by the Yellow prefect.

The Big Banana, I discovered, was the name given to Courtland Gamboge, the Yellow prefect's son. I asked Tommo why Courtland wanted to meet me, and Tommo explained that Gamboge-the-younger liked to meet *everyone*. He had apparently topped eighty points in his Ishihara two years before and was certain to take over from his mother when she retired.

"Not that she will anytime soon," Tommo added, "but Courtland has to go some way to fill her shoes with the same level of ruthless unpleasantness."

"All Yellows are ruthless. It's what they do."

"Not like these. Prefect Sally Gamboge has refused the Greyforce a holiday for seventeen years and has had them on sixty-eight-hour weeks for as long as anyone can remember. She treats them like dirt and is always drumming up bogus infractions. Even *I* think it's out of order, and I'm grotesquely indifferent to the Greys."

"Is there a reason she's so particularly unpleasant?"

"The Gamboges think they should be players on a bigger stage. Lots of Yellow, all the overzealous ruthlessness—but a hopelessly provincial CV37 postcode. Transfer requests are simply ignored."

It was a familiar story. Despite being officially only used for addresses, the right code meant a lot, and snubbing was common, if illegal. I was glad that I had an RG6.

"But she has to pay them overtime," I pointed out, still thinking about the Greys. "That's a compensation, at least."

"It would be if there was anything they could spend it on."

"Or even share, pool or bequeath their merits," I said, pointing out one of the more iniquitous regulations regarding Grey wealth.

"Serves them right for always eating the bacon," said Tommo, whose outrage at the Greys' treatment was lamentably short lived, "*Apart We Are Together,* and all that guff."

"If the Gamboges are so frightful," I said, "I'm surprised you have anything to do with them."

"That's *precisely* the reason I do. If there's a tiger in the room, I want to be the one that combs its whiskers. Besides, Courtland has an Open Return, and he might just sell it to me."

We had been walking in the direction of the river.

"That's where the Greys live, over there."

He was pointing at a huddle of terraced houses set apart from the rest of the town. The twin rows of dwellings faced each other, with a road-way between them. Behind the houses were small gardens, tidy masses of runner-bean canes, fruit bushes and garden sheds, and clean laundry fluttering in the breeze. The homes must have numbered a hundred or more. I had never entered a Greyzone alone or known anyone who had. Even the Yellows thought twice about a visit. But rather than admit they were nervous, they simply said the place was unhygienic, which was patently untrue. Greys just didn't like us there, in the same way that they weren't permitted in the village unless on business. The big difference was, Chromatics were *allowed* in the Greyzone—but thought it wiser to stay away.

"We have a Grey named Jane as our maid," I said, attempting to glean some information. "She seems a trifle . . . volatile."

"We call her Crazy Jane, but *never* to her face. She's broken more bones than almost anyone else in the village."

"Accident-prone?"

"Not hers. *Ours.* She'll punch anyone who mentions her nose, and once fractured Jim-Bob's arm because she *thought* he was looking at her whatnots."

"Was he?"

"Not on that particular occasion. But she won't bother us for much longer. We're not sure how deep into negative merits she is, but it's rumored five hundred or so."

I whistled low. "But she's pretty, don't you think?"

"I'll concede that her nose is *definitely* the cutest and most retroussé in the village," said Tommo, "but as for pretty—so is a viper. If you tried to kiss either, you'd get bitten on the face."

The well-worn path through the lumpy grasslands took us past one of the many ancient streetlamps still standing.

"Repainted every year without fail," said Tommo proudly, pausing for a moment to admire the cast-iron lampposts. "The janitor had to take the Ford into Vermillion to have the bands relined, so he took Jabez and me. On the outskirts you drive through a town that is long gone, but the streetlamps are still there, running in great rows upon the land, and standing in the middle of open pasture like stunted oaks."

"Could one get to Vermillion and back in a morning?" I asked, Jane's apparently impossible trip to Vermillion and back still on my mind.

"You could do it in the Ford."

"Is that a practical proposition?"

"No. For a start, Carlos—he's our janitor—treats the Model T better than his own daughter, and every drop of fuel oil has to be logged and accounted for. You *might* get in by Penny-Farthing, but you'd have to push it across the six miles of rutted track between Rusty Hill and Persimmon. *Plus* you'd have to find a way across the ferry without any transit papers. Believe me, if there *was* a way, I'd be the first person to try it. There are a hundred reasons for me to get to Vermillion, all of them highly profitable."

He stared at me for a moment, then cocked his head to one side.

"Do you have some sort of scam cooking—or are you just thinking of a Plan B if you don't get your Open Return back?"

"The latter," I replied, and he nodded knowingly.

The Sorting Pavilion was like a miniature version of the town hall, with four shorter and narrower columns supporting the roof over the main entrance. It looked a good deal older than the buildings I had seen so far. The brickwork was crumbling, and years of hard winter rain had washed the mortar from the walls. The tympanum above the door held a sculpture of a reclining woman, carved in marble. She must have been earth salvage: From the navel upward the weather had scrubbed away the subtlety of the craftsman's hand, but below this every muscle and sinew was finely detailed. The woman's features had vanished almost entirely, but she would once have been beautiful. No one would have expended so much time and effort on such a monument if she wasn't.

The Pavilion had a curved glass roof that boasted no less than three heliostats, and parked outside was a small handcart for moving the sorted sacks of scrap to the railway station nearby. We sat on the oak bench outside and took off our shoes. I knew the protocol, even though we didn't have a Pavilion in Jade-under-Lime; all our scrap color was sorted at Viridian, one stop down the line.

"Ever been in a Pavilion before?" asked Tommo.

I shook my head.

"So who's the hick now?" he said, and pushed open the doors.

The Pavilion's sorting room was long, high and so well lit it was actually *brighter* than the outdoors, which was the point. It takes a lot of light to see color well, and I suspect that work stopped when the weather was overcast. Tommo directed my gaze toward a man a few years older than myself who was dressed head to toe in a yellow outfit, and apart from two Grey orderlies who were transporting sacks of unsorted tosh to the washing room suspended beneath a silk canopy full of floaties, he was the only person there.

"That's Courtland," murmured Tommo in a respectful whisper. "I know you claim to be leaving in a month, but for all our sakes, don't annoy him or anything, okay?"

"Tommo, I have no reason to make enemies of the buttercup persuasion. And *certainly* not one with a mother on the Council."

"Just checking. If Courtland says 'Jump,' you just ask 'How high and in what direction?'"

Tommo waved at Courtland, and he gestured with a lazy jerk of his head for us to enter the work area, where he was sitting at one of the three sorting tables. I looked around curiously. Etched onto the surface of each table were three large intersecting circles representing the traditional primary colors, the intersections denoting the secondary hues. Sorting was a simple enough process. Each sorter was responsible for one of the three colors. Courtland, for example, would pick any yellow items from the tosh pile and place them in the pure yellow section of his intersecting circles, with the brightest shade at the top and the dullest at the bottom. At the same time, he would pick out any yellow-value object he could see from the red section, say, and place it in the intersecting area that belonged to both red and yellow, and from that it could be deduced that the object was orange. It was the same with the rest of the sorting table: Anything in the intersection of yellow and blue would have to be green; and anything in red and blue, purple. In this way, thanks to the talents of those highly perceptive in red, yellow and blue, the entire unseeable Spectrum of color could be laid upon the table. After sorting, the objects would then be bagged and sent off to the pigment plant to be milled, squeezed and enriched—and from there to communal enjoyment.

I noticed that the blue table seemed neat and orderly, as was Courtland's. The red table less so. Untidy, to be truthful. In fact, I could see red items in the reject tosh pile that *should* have been placed, but had been missed.

"Who sorts your red?" I asked.

"Dullard Yewberry," said Tommo, staring at the misplaced red tosh without a flicker. "He's only *acting* prefect, so his perception is not first-rate. Why?"

"No reason."

"Hello, Court," said Tommo in a servile tone. "This is Eddie Russett. Eddie, this is Courtland Gamboge, son of the Yellow prefect and next one up."

Courtland was tall, handsome and well dressed. He had a large jaw, strong eyebrows and odd, unblinking eyes that seemed to stare. Upon his lapel was a parade of badges awarded for meritorious work, and on his cheek a recent scar.

"How much red you got?" he asked.

"Enough," I replied.

"Keeping your cards close to your chest, eh? Good idea. And what's your HUMILITY badge for?"

I told him about Bertie Magenta and the elephant trick, and all that hoo-ha.

"They've given him a chair census to conduct," said Tommo with a smirk.

Courtland sniggered. "It gets less imaginative each time. Now, Master Russett, do you need anything?"

"Not that I can think of right now."

"Bear it in mind. Tommo and I like to think we can fix most things around here. If you want a good job or need to borrow a few extra merits until payday or are in the poo with the prefects, we can . . . make things happen."

There was a pause.

"This is where you say 'Wow' or 'Gosh' or 'Terrific,'" Tommo prompted.

"Gosh," I said.

"Gosh indeed, Russett," said Courtland. "But it's very much quid pro quo. We do things for you, and you do things for us—to the mutual benefit of all. No point in living the Grey life just because the Rules have so little room for maneuver, hey?

"But before we get too embroiled in complexities, you will need to do something for us. Something to prove your mettle." He leaned closer and whispered in my ear, "*We want some Lincoln.* You have access to your father's swatch safe. Do that for us and we'll be the best of friends."

I frowned. This was a new one. Most bullies were uncomplicated characters who simply wanted unearned respect and cash. Stealing swatches was on another level entirely. Lincoln, or 125-66-53, was a chromatropic painkiller ten times more powerful than lime. Even a *glimpse* was enough to lower the heart rate, and a good ten-second stare would bring on a sense of dreamy otherworldliness and hallucinations. Some maintained that greening was a harmless indulgence, but heavy greeners risked damaging their visual cortex. Too much Lincoln and you could lose all sense of color—natural *and* univisual. Peddling Lincoln was peddling misery. I stared at them both in turn.

"I'm afraid I might have to pass on your request."

Courtland looked back at me, unblinking, then put his hand on my shoulder in a friendly but firm gesture and said in a low voice, "What's your first name again?"

"Eddie."

"What you must realize, Eddie, is that I'm the highest Yellow you're ever likely to be able to count as a friend. Friendship, I'm sure you will agree, is a very useful commodity if you're going to spend the rest of your life in this backwater."

"I'm only here for a month."

"Were you fool enough to give deMauve your ticket?"

"Yes."

"Then you could be here for longer. But here's the bottom line: Defrauding the village out of some Lincoln might *seem* something of a Rule dilemma right here and now, but actually it's a very wise long-term investment, wouldn't you agree?"

He said it in a serious, businesslike manner, but with a strong undercurrent of menace. I'd seen Alpha Primes throwing their weight around, but never so blatantly. I looked across at Tommo, who was at the window, checking for prefects.

"I think that's pretty reasonable, don't you?" he said.

"Listen," I said, "I'm not going to steal any Lincoln from my father."

"Hoo," said Tommo, "*scruples*."

"I wasn't for one moment suggesting you *steal* anything," murmured Courtland with a smile. "A missing swatch of Lincoln would have the prefects all in a lather. No. Tommo has a *much* better idea."

"Here's how it works," said Tommo, picking up his cue. "When your father comes to reorder the swatches, all you do is sneak into his office and write a 'two' in the ordering column next to *Lincoln*. He won't notice, and it's not likely deMauve will either. All you do then is 'liberate' the extra swatch when it arrives from National Color. Simple, hey?"

"What if my father doesn't order any Lincoln?"

"Haven't you heard? Robin Ochre was selling off the village swatches on the Beigemarket. The mutual auditor from Bluetown told me he sold almost the entire stock."

Those were the "irregularities" surrounding Ochre that deMauve had been speaking of. It went against *everything* a swatchman had sworn to uphold. DeMauve was right: A fatal self-misdiagnosis may have been the best thing for him.

"It's a brilliant plan," I concurred.

"Splendid! And remember: If you need anything, *anything at all*, you only have to ask. We can fix pretty much anything, can't we, Tommo?"

"Indeed we can," he replied, "except get your Open Return back—or wangle you a date with Crazy Jane."

Courtland laughed out loud.

"Do you remember when Jabez asked her to go to a tea dance with him?"

"Yes," mused Tommo. "I hadn't realized you could actually tear an eyebrow *off*."

"So," said Courtland, "we're all agreed about the Lincoln."

He gave me another smile, patted me on the shoulder and returned to his work. Tommo took my arm and steered me firmly toward the door.

"I think that went pretty well," said Tommo as we walked back toward the village, "although you might have been a *tad* more obsequious."

"I'll try to remember that for next time."

"Stout fellow. You won't regret helping us out, you know. Doors can really open to anyone willing to play the system."

"Oh," said Tommo as he snapped his fingers, "once you've got your paws on your dad's swatch safe, would you let me borrow some 7-85-57?"

He was referring to Redlax, a cross-spectral laxative of instantaneous and unprecedented violence. Even a glimpse would have someone running for the thunderbox as if his life depended on it.

"If you're having problems with your number twos," I confided, "perhaps you might speak to my father."

"It's not for me," said Tommo with a laugh. "I was thinking of using it to play a prank on deMauve—put it into his copy of *Harmony* just as he's about to bore our chops off at assembly."

I was struck speechless. He *had* to be pulling my leg. No one would try something like that.

"It, er, wouldn't take a genius to figure out where the Redlax came from."

"I'm not too concerned over the *consequences* of the prank," replied Tommo, summing up his worldview in one swift statement, "more the prank itself."

We took a path back toward the town, and on the way encountered a group of a half-dozen girls who had just come off their shift at the linoleum factory. They were all dressed in dungarees with their hair tied up in printed gingham head scarves, and were giggling and chatting in an exuberant manner.

"Good evening, ladies," said Tommo politely.

"Good evening, Master Thomas," said the tallest of the group, an attractive willow of a girl who was shaking out her long tresses as she removed her headscarf. "Who's the newbie?"

"This is Master Edward Russett, Melanie. All the way from some dreadful dump near the inner boundary. He has scruples, counts chairs and has seen the Last Rabbit."

"What's it like?" piped up the youngest of the group, a short girl with pigtails and a birthmark on her cheek.

"Well, y'know, kind of . . . rabbitlike."

"Will you draw me a picture?"

"I could do you a shadow puppet."

"Chairs, rabbits and scruples, eh?" cooed the tall one, taking a step closer and tugging at my tie in a playful manner. "That sounds like a *combustible* mix."

She was being almost intolerably forward. The girls in Jade-under-Lime were all demure and polite, and I felt myself grow hot.

"Tommo is wholly mistaken," I said, trying to sound sophisticated.

"Then you have *no* scruples?" asked the girl called Melanie in a low voice as she touched my cheek with the back of her hand. Her companions let loose a volley of sniggering. It was embarrassing, but not without a tinge of pleasure—Melanie's touch was warm and almost tender. Constance had held my hand six and a half times, if you don't count the tea dancing, but never once touched me on the cheek—unless you include the time she slapped me for suggesting that her mother "had politeness issues."

"Yes," I stammered, feeling awkward and seriously out of my depth, "that is to say—"

"Let us know when he makes up his mind as to whether he has scruples or not, Tommo," sang Melanie as she stepped back, my humiliation complete, and they all dissolved into peals of laughter.

Although I felt hopelessly ill at ease, the girls' free and easy laughter was one of the most wonderful sounds I had ever heard. But I was no longer of interest, and they all started to chatter again and moved off toward the Greyzone.

"If you want to meet any of those delightful ladies in private, I can arrange things for a five percent fixer's fee," said Tommo as we watched them walk off. "Do you want to see their *unofficial* feedback ratings?"

I stared at him, unsure of what to do or say. That an illicit market in youknow existed in Jade-under-Lime, despite Old Man Magenta's watchful eye, I was pretty sure. In fact, it was entirely possible that everyone indulged quite happily. But I'd been unprepared for the fact that someone like Tommo—it would *have* to be someone like Tommo—would not only be able to arrange things but do it so openly, and seemingly without fear of punishment. It explained his cash merits, too.

"But *not* to a complementary color," he added, in case I was a deviant or something. "I may live in a partial Rule vacuum, but even I have standards of decency. If you're not up for a bit of youknow," he continued, doubtless reading the look of shocked disapproval that had crossed my face, "they're all game for a cheeky bundle or a lambada in private. But," he added after a moment's thought, "I can't help you with Jane. And don't even *think* of tall Melanie—she's on a promise from Courtland."

"Courtland doesn't strike me as the sort of Yellow to do such a decent thing—bring a Grey up—what with Bunty McMustard waiting in the wings."

Tommo laughed.

"He's not going to actually go through with it, dummy. Courtland tells me Melanie will do anything for him. *Anything*. And it doesn't cost him a bean. He knows Bunty will hang on for him indefinitely, so he'll just dump Mel when the Council decides they need some more Yellows."

"No!" I muttered.

"Daring, isn't it?" Tommo agreed. "Thinking of trying it yourself?"

"Never! I mean, that's the most dishonest and cruel thing anyone can do to someone, not to mention contravening at least eight Rules—including Fundamental Number One. What's he going to say when this gets out?"

Tommo shrugged. "Deny it, I guess. Who are they going to believe? Melanie-Nobody-at-All or Alpha-Yellow-Prefect-in-Waiting Courtland 'Big Banana' Gamboge?"

"*I'll* tell them."

"You heard him promise her?"

"No—"

"Then wake up, pinhead. Forget fundamentals. Rule one as far as Courtland is concerned is Don't get involved. *Courtland will one day be the Yellow prefect*. Just keep that in your mind and fix on it. It will make your life a lot easier, I can tell you. Now, can I fix you up with someone?"

"No, thanks."

"If you change your—"

"I won't. What would the prefects say if they knew you were brokering youknow?"

Tommo stared at me, oblivious to the implied threat. He leaned closer and whispered, "I simply bring the buyer to the market, and I have a broad client base. A *very* broad client base. Why do you think a loser like me is the junior Red monitor? You need to loosen up. If you can get the poker out of your hoo-ha, you're going to enjoy it here."

"But what about the Rules?"

He leaned closer and smiled. "You're living in the Fringes now, Eddie. Out here, the Rulebook is printed on rubber paper. Will you excuse me until later? I have to fetch some sandwiches for Ulrika."

"Ulrika?"

"Of the flak," he replied, as though it were obvious.

The Colorium

2.1.03.01.115: All trips beyond the Outer Markers have to be
approved by a prefect or a senior monitor.

It was half past five by then, and most Chromatics were either returning
home, about to indulge in hobbies or just socializing. For the Greys, it
was time to move on to their third job. I wouldn't be able to try to quiz
Jane any more until she came around to make supper, and I was still
intrigued about her. But try as I might, I couldn't help thinking about Jabez
asking her for a date, and how painful it must be to lose an eyebrow.

Dad's Colorium was two doors down from the town hall, sandwiched
between the post office and the co-op. The bell tinkled as I opened the
door. I found myself in a largish waiting room full of villagers who were
either reading well-thumbed back issues of *Spectrum* or staring vacantly
at the posters on the walls, which were mostly public information ban-
ners. One explained how malingering was a waste of one's Civil Obligation, and was also village time theft. Another suggested that you wash
your hands after touching something that Riffraff might have touched,
and a third explained how premarital youknow might lead to a fall in
personal standards that would lead ultimately to disharmony and, with
continued persistence, Reboot.

My father's consulting room was partitioned by frosted-glass panels,
through which I could see the vague outlines of people moving. I waited
until a patient walked out, and before Dad could call "Next!" I knocked
on his door and entered.

The consulting room was pretty much the same as at Jade-under-Lime, only larger. There was a couch under a glazed ceiling, and to one side an X-ray machine, the swatch safe and several glass-fronted cupboards packed with bandages and a few instruments. I noticed that there was even an arc light, on a wheeled stand, that was plugged into the wall.

"What a relief!" he said as I entered. "It's only you."

He got up and walked across to the filing cabinet, placed a file back into its slot and then closed the drawer.

"I can give you five minutes," he said, rummaging through a mountain of treatment-request forms that all needed his backdated signature. "Ochre has left the practice in an appalling state. I've got five women to time correctly for Chromovulation by the end of the month, the sniffles is definitely getting worse and get this: Ochre's been stealing and selling the village's swatches!"

"The village is buzzing with it," I replied, giving the impression of a lad with his finger on the pulse. "How many have gone?"

He sat back in his swivel chair and shook his head sadly.

"I haven't inventoried them all, but certainly five hundred or so, stolen over a period of several years—in clear contravention of about twenty-seven different Rules *and* the Chromaticologist's oath!"

"Wow," I exclaimed, overwhelmed by Ochre's audacity. Adherence to the strict rule of Rule was maintained not just by the severity of the punishment, but by the certainty of being caught.

"We've still got a few hundred," said Dad, walking across to the swatch safe and flicking through the six-inch-square envelopes that protected the hues, "but mostly the ones he couldn't sell on the Beigemarket. The sort that deal with athlete's foot, male-pattern baldness and excessive wrinkling of the scrotum."

"It wasn't a fatal self-misdiagnosis, was it?"

"I think not. DeMauve believes he'd been indulging in the palette rather heavily. *Beyond* lime—perhaps even beyond Lincoln."

"You think he was Chasing the Frog?"

Dad shrugged. "I don't know. If he *was*, then it's little wonder the Council returned an accidental-death verdict at the inquest. They were doing Ochre's family and the rest of the village a favor."

It explained the "misdiagnosis." "Chasing the Frog" was what hardened greeners did when their cortex was too burned for even Lincoln to have an effect. They would go into the Green Room and partake of the color painted within—the shade of green that you saw only once in your life, when it was time to go. The color painted within the Green Room was known as "sweetdream" and would render you unconscious in twelve minutes and dead in sixteen, but during those twelve minutes every synapse in your brain would fire in a sparkling fountain of pleasure. The cries from the Green Room were never of pain or fear. They were of ecstasy. Chasing the Frog was a dangerous game. Time it right and you were sitting on a cloud. Time it wrong and you'd be good only for the renderers.

"Falsifying a cause of death?" I muttered. "That's got to be five thousand demerits there and then."

Dad shrugged and I thought for a moment. "The Rules are pretty malleable out here, aren't they?"

"In most places, Eddie, if you look—which I don't recommend."

"You're right," I said, thinking of Jane, and how I should really just drop the whole wrongspot issue.

"Ochre's wife and daughter can't be having a great time of it," he added. "The Council exonerated them of all wrongdoing as regards the swatch theft, but even so—guilt by association and whatnot. Next!"

The door opened, and a Grey man walked in. He was a senior, and bent double by either toil in the fields or toil in the factory—toil, anyway. He had a runny nose and watery eyes. It didn't take a six-year Chromaticologist's training to see what the problem was.

"It's the sniffles, Mr. G-67," said Dad kindly. "There's a lot of it about. Unfortunately, we have problems with the Long Swatch, so I don't have anything I can show you for it—it'll be a week's bed rest."

The Grey seemed very pleased with the outcome, and handed my father his merit book.

"Ah," said Dad as he flicked through the pages of the man's employment record and feedback score. "Tell me, Mr. G-67, have you been suffering from heavy legs recently?"

"No, sir."

"I would strongly suggest that you have."

"Yes, sir," replied the Grey obediently. "Awful they've been these past few years. So heavy I sometimes can't get out of bed."

"Exactly as I thought," replied my father. "I am giving you three weeks and four days' additional bed rest. We'll also remove this."

Dad took the MALINGERER badge off the Grey's lapel, doubtless placed there by Sally Gamboge.

The man's worn features cracked into a smile. He thanked Dad profusely and tottered out of the room.

"Heavy legs?" I asked.

"He's got less than half a percent of his Civil Obligation to complete before retirement," murmured Dad, filling in a treatment form, "and he looks like he deserves to finish early."

"That's not really allowed, is it?"

Dad shrugged. "Not really. But the Greys have been worked half to death by the Gamboges, and if it's in my power to afford them a break, I'll do so."

"Are you giving everyone with the sniffles time off work?"

"No. I'm going to get hold of some 196-34-44 tomorrow—it'll have the outbreak cured in a twinkling."

Dad explained that Robin Ochre had been the swatchman for *two* villages and kept a satellite Colorium equipped with a short swatch of about two hundred color-cards. It was in Rusty Hill.

"Next!"

A young Blue girl walked in, holding a bloodied towel to her hand. In the colorless village, the blood looked inordinately bright.

"Hello!" she said brightly. "I seem to have cut my finger off."

"Actually, you've cut two off," said Dad, examining the wound. "You should be more careful."

But I wasn't interested in the Blue's propensity for clumsiness. I was thinking about Robin Ochre's second practice. Rusty Hill was firmly etched in my mind, because it was where the Grey wrongspot had lived.

"You're going to Rusty Hill?" I asked, intrigued by the sudden possibility that had just opened up.

"Yes," he said, selecting some very fine thread and a needle.

"Wouldn't Ochre have swiped the swatches from there, too?"

"DeMauve thinks not," said Dad, placing the offset glasses on the Blue's nose and showing her some 100-83-71 out of his traveling swatch case to slow the bleeding. "Ochre said Rusty Hill spooked him. In any event, Carlos Fandango is taking me over there early tomorrow morning. I'm going to have to sew these back on," he remarked to the Blue, who was staring absently out the window.

"I don't use the pinky," she said, "and there are a lot of people waiting to see you."

"They can wait."

"Dad," I said, "I'd like to go to Rusty Hill, too."

"Out of the question," he replied immediately. "The Council were reluctant to sign a travel order to even allow *me* over there. But they reasoned that if the workforce is laid up with the sniffles, the village will grind to a halt. Fandango is driving me, but he's under strict instructions not to enter the village."

"It's only been four years since the Mildew swept through the village," added the Blue girl, who had been listening to the conversation with interest. "By rights, no one should go there for at least another sixteen."

"Another excellent reason," remarked Dad. "Would you call the nurse? I'm going to need a second pair of hands if I want to see even a handful more patients before supper."

I pressed the NURSE CALL button. She came in, nodded me a greeting, looked at the Blue's hand with a reproachful "Tut" and expertly threaded a needle.

"I'll do the arteries," Dad said to the nurse, "if you tackle the tendons. Oh, Eddie, jot down 37-78-81 on my blotter—nerves always rejoin better when encouraged by a dull orange. Close the door on the way out, will you?"

I walked back into the waiting room, where a sense of daring suddenly gripped me. Not everyone would be seen by my father today, so rather than have everyone queue for hours tomorrow morning to be first in, I thought I'd help out.

I found some paper, made up thirty playing-card-sized squares, wrote a number on each and then went around the waiting room, handing them out to everyone and explaining how the system worked: A number would be displayed as soon as my father was seeing patients again, and when your number came up, you would be seen. "But be warned," I added. "Miss your turn and you'll have to take a new number."

I had to run over the details several times as the concept was somewhat novel, but after a good deal of mumbling and consternation over this, the principle was at last imparted to the villagers. Pretty soon half the room filed off to do other things, or simply go home. I made a sign asking new patients to take a number from a small stainless-steel kidney bowl, and as an afterthought I set aside a box for the tickets that had been used.

Happy that the first practical test of my Russett Mk II Numbered Queuing System was under way, I walked out of the Colorium with a bounce in my step. I stopped at the suggestion box to apply for retrospective permission to use the system under the Standard Variable procedure that Travis had told me about. I was in no doubt that the council would reject it, but at least it covered my hoo-ha against infraction.

One Eyebrow

2.8.02.03.031: Bicycles shall not be used beyond the Outer Markers lest the steel frames attract lightning.

took a deep breath, and sat on a nearby bench to gather my thoughts. I needed to get to Zane G-49's old address in Rusty Hill if I was to have a chance of figuring out what he was doing in the Paint Shop, but Dad was right: I would have to have a very good reason to go with him. Rusty Hill was just close enough to walk in a day, and if I took the ten-merit fine for lunch nonattendance, it could be a possibility. I just didn't fancy walking twenty-eight miles, especially in this heat. I was just wondering if there was a Penny-Farthing in the village that I could borrow, when I heard a voice.

"Do you have any hobbies?"

I looked up. The Widow deMauve was sitting at the other end of the bench, and she was staring at me. It was a rhetorical question, as a minimum of one hobby was mandatory, even for the many Greys who didn't have the time. The theory was that a hobby "drove idle thoughts from the mind," but the Rules weren't specific over what that hobby might be. Trainspotting and collecting coins, stamps, bottles, buttons or pebbles were pretty much the default options, but needlework, painting, guinea-pig breeding and violin making had their adherents. Some collected artifacts from before the Something That Happened, such as super-rare bar codes, teeth, money cards or keyboard letters, all of which came in a bewildering variety of shapes and sizes. There were also those who made up silly hobbies to annoy the prefects, such as belly-button casting, hopping and extreme counting. For myself, I favored the abstract. I collected not just obsolete terms and words, but *ideas*.

"I'm currently devising improved methods for queuing," I said in a grand manner, but she wasn't the slightest bit interested.

"I like to put holes in things," she announced, showing me a piece of paper with a hole in it.

"That must take a considerable amount of skill."

"It does. I put holes in wood, cardboard, leaves—even string."

"How do you put a hole in string?"

"I tie it in a loop," she said, with dazzling simplicity, "and there you go: hole. I thought I was the only one. But look what I found in the co-op this morning."

She showed me a ring doughnut. "Well!" she exclaimed, much aggrieved. "It's as though no one can think of an original hobby these days without some copycat jumping on the bandwagon."

"It's probably Mrs. Lapis Lazuli," I whispered mischievously, and Widow deMauve's eyes opened wide.

"I knew it!"

"Would you excuse me?" I said. "I've just seen someone I must talk to."

I got up and trotted after a Green who had just walked past, carrying a trombone. It wasn't an excuse to get away; I'd noticed that he had only one eyebrow.

"Pardon me?"

He stopped and stared at me for a moment, then a look of recognition came over his face. "You're the new swatchman's son, aren't you?" he asked. "The one who's seen the Last Rabbit?"

"Y-es."

"What was it like?"

"Furry . . . mostly." I introduced myself before he could quiz me too carefully over the rabbit, but it felt uncomfortable and a bit odd talking to him—I hadn't really held a friendly conversation with a Green before. Back in Jade-under-Lime we kept ourselves very much to ourselves. Jabez was not far short of his quarter-century and, by his dress code, looked as though he were a farmer.

"Your eyebrow," I said, pointing to where it wasn't. "Tommo told me Jane pulled it off. Is that true?"

"Oh, yes," he replied with a grin as he touched the scarred area with a fingertip, "but she did it quickly so it wouldn't hurt too much. If she'd hated me, she could really have drawn it out."

"She seems generous in that respect," I said slowly.

"I was thinking of having a donor eyebrow sewn on," said Jabez, "but if they attached it badly I'd look quizzical for the rest of my life. Are you thinking of asking her out on a date?"

"Not anymore."

"I don't know why I did," said Jabez with a frown, "probably that nose of hers. It's quite something, don't you think?"

"Yes," I admitted, "it certainly is."

"Just don't tell her. She . . . doesn't like it."

"Hullo!" said Tommo, who had just reappeared. "Eddie, this is Jabez Lemon-Skye. He's first-generation Green, so hardly objectionable at all. What's going on?"

"Eddie and I were just discussing how to get a date with the Nose."

Tommo raised his eyebrows. "So you *are* interested in Jane?"

"Just making conversation."

"Sure you are. I'd leave her well alone, if you want my advice." He gave out a conspiratorial chuckle. "And if we're talking about guilty secrets, Jabez is a *love child*. His parents married because—get this—*they couldn't bear not to!* Weird, huh?"

"I'll not be made ashamed of it," remarked Jabez with great dignity, "but muse on this: When you meet an Orange or a Green, you're not looking at wasted primal hue, but the product of a couple motivated by something more noble than the headlong rush for Chromatic supremacy."

Up until that point, I hadn't really thought about it that way. The Russetts had been trying to make up our lost hue for over a century. Marrying into the Oxbloods would finally take us back to where we were before my great-grandfather married the Grey. Red was my destiny, if you like—the hue I was born to.

"If we're being so open with one another," declared Jabez with a smile, "perhaps you can tell Eddie how you like to stare at naked bathers."

"That's a scurrilous untruth!" declared Tommo. "I wasn't staring—I was simply asleep with my eyes open, and they happened to walk past."

There was a pause. I didn't really know what to say to make conversation with a Green, so said the first thing that came into my head. "What's it like seeing green?"

Jabez lowered his voice. "It's quite simply . . . the *best*. The grass, the leaves, the shoots, the trees—all ours. And do you know, the subtle variations in shades are almost without number—in leaves, from the brightest, freshest hue when unfurling, to the dark green in late summer before they turn and we lose them. Thousands of shades, if not *millions*. Sometimes I just sit in the forest and stare."

"He does, you know," Tommo put in. "I've seen him. But I'd not swap my reds for his greens if you paid me a thousand merits—Tommo's not going to be taken by the Rot fully conscious, no, sir."

It was one of the downsides of being the Color of Nature: When the Mildew came for you, the Green Room had no effect—even with offset spectacles. If Green, you had to go the hard way. Fully conscious, and slowly asphyxiated as the spores inexorably clogged up your airways. Some Greens took the matter into their own hands to effect a quick way out, and others joined a self-help syndicate, much against the Rules.

"That's the difference between you and me," replied Jabez, staring at Tommo with a smile. "A lifetime of nature's rich and bounteous color in exchange for five hours of suffering? The forest wins hands down every time."

"Not for me," Tommo replied cheerfully. "As soon as the spores start sprouting, I'm diving headfirst into the endorphin soup without so much as a 'Thanks, guys, it's been a heap of number twos.'"

Jabez considered it time to go before Tommo became too insulting.

"Welcome to the village, Eddie—and listen to one word in eight from walking Reboot here. Friend?"

I paused for a millisecond. I'd never accepted a friendship from a Green before. In fact, aside from twelve Oranges, six Blues, Bertie Magenta and just recently Travis, all of my 436 friends were Red.

"Friend."

He gave Tommo a friendly shove, and departed.

We walked along a cobbled street lined with shops of varying description and usefulness. I noticed a tailor, a hardware store, a mender, Dorian's photographic studio, a combination wool shop and haberdasher's and a Head Office–approved forksmith. Tommo pointed out people of interest, and introduced me if he thought it appropriate.

"That's Bunty McMustard. The most poisonous woman in the village."

"We've met already."

"Then you'll know. When she succeeds in prizing Courtland out of Melanie, the offspring will be so devious they'll spontaneously combust—but you didn't hear me say that."

"Of course not." But I was thinking about Rusty Hill. "You said you could fix things, Tommo."

"*Most* things. Courtland was overplaying it when he said 'anything.'"

"My dad's going to Rusty Hill tomorrow, and I need a reason to go there with him."

He bit his lip. "Do you know how many people died in the Mildew outbreak? Eighteen hundred. If I was *truly* without respect for the Rules—which I'm not, by the way—I'd be over there like a shot. There have to be at least a hundred spoons kicking around—and if I can find one with a postcode that is unregistered, it means we can add another worker to the Collective, and any village will pay handsomely to boost their population. Pots of cash, see—but I still wouldn't go."

"Why?"

He looked around and lowered his voice. "Pookas!"

"There's no such thing as Pookas. It says so in the Rules."

"That's what everyone at Rusty Hill thought. But there were *stories*. So are you sure you want to go?"

"Are you sure you want the Lincoln?"

"Leave it with me," he said, thinking hard. "I might be able to come up with something."

We passed the janitor's workshop, where a battered Ford Model T was being judiciously oiled by a man in coveralls.

"Hello, Spoonpacker," he said, addressing Tommo. "Is that Master Russett you have with you?"

"That's me," I answered.

"Welcome to East Carmine," he said with a mildly superior air. "I'm Carlos Fandango, the janitor. Is Tommo here giving you the grand tour?"

I nodded.

"Good show. Fine fellow, but don't lend him any money."

"Sell his own granny, would he?"

"You heard about that? Terrible business."

"At least I can tell when a tomato is ripe," retorted Tommo, who didn't much care for having his besmirched family name besmirched even further. The tomato comment was a demeritable breach of protocol, not to mention downright rude. Fandango, however, simply ignored him, and told me that he would be taking my father to Rusty Hill tomorrow, and would be outside the house at eight o'clock sharp.

I said I'd relay the message. Tommo, hot with indignation that his insult had had no effect, tugged on my sleeve and said we had to move on.

"Fandango is only fourteen percent Purple," said Tommo as we walked away. "He puts on all the airs and graces, but before his Ishihara he was a Grey. Four points lower and he'd be out in the fields or laying burlap in the factory. He has high hopes for cashing in on his daughter Imogen, though, who they think will turn out to be a fifty-percenter."

"He married a strong Purple?"

"*Quite* the reverse."

He pulled a faux-shocked face, indicating that the Chromatic disparity between parent and offspring might suggest a bit of fence leaping. And on this occasion, for profit.

"The Fandangos went to Vermillion to celebrate at the Green Dragon after being allocated an egg chit," he explained. "The bridal suite there is known as the Rainbow Room—for a price, you can have whatever color child you want."

"A Purple flogging their hard-won heredity?" I replied with an incredulous sniff. "Ridiculous. Besides, they'd never do anything to risk losing authority."

"Do they *really* bring you up so naive in the hub?" he said. "There's a whole world out there behind the Rules, if only you look. In any event, Carlos will bend your ear about any suitably rich Purples you might know. If you want to drive the Ford or be shown around the gyrobike, play along."

It would take me a while to get used to how rude Tommo could be—not just his flippancy, but divulging other people's perceptions. It was the height of bad manners.

"How did you know I sold my own granny?"

"I didn't. I was trying to be funny."

"Ah. Listen, when you get to Rusty Hill, will you bring me back a pair of Male Outdoor Casuals?" He showed me his shoes, which were actually not shoes at all, but scraps of well-shined leather tied to the top of his feet.

"Okay."

"Size nines."

"Size nines it is."

"See that guy over there?" He was indicating a handsome man, probably in his early thirties. "Ben Azzuro. Nice guy and a fine all-arounder, but nearly caused a riot in the henhouse by declaring himself. Personally, I'd like to see more like him in the village."

"You'll be declaring?"

"No. It would just tip the marriage market more in my favor. The way I figure it, if six more moved across, I might actually end up with someone quite pleasant. This might come as a huge surprise to you, but I'm not considered much of a catch."

"Whyever not?"

"Careful of the sarcasm, sunshine. That's the local salt lick over there. The woman behind the counter is Mrs. Crimson."

He was pointing at the tearoom, always the busiest establishment in any village. It was called the Fallen Man, which was an unusual name, given that most tearooms were called Mrs. Cranston's. I looked at the faded-to-monochrome painting on the board above the front door. It depicted a man sitting in a leather armchair while plummeting past some fluffy clouds, his tie flapping upward.

"Odd name," I said, indicating the sign.

"Not for here," he said cheerfully. "The other tearoom is called the Singing Coathanger. They both refer to local legends: the Fallen Man to someone who fell to earth quite near here, and the Singing Coathanger to a, well, a coathanger that started to sing."

I'd heard about pieces of metal giving off a tinny noise that sounded like speech or song, but had never witnessed the phenomenon myself.

"Singing bits of wire and fallen men are all we've got in the legend department," added Tommo. "What about you?"

"We have the Lapper Venus," I explained, "though it's more unexplained artifacture than folklore, to be honest. But," I added, "there *was* the Night of the Great Noise. The elderly still talk about how in the morning everything was covered with something resembling cobwebs, and all the ladders were missing."

"I'm almost sorry I asked. That's Daisy Crimson," he added, indicating a young woman who was walking past. "Nice girl and from a good family, if a little low-hued. Her father runs the village's heat exchangers. Some say Daisy giggles too much and her nose is a little *too* pointy, but it's never troubled me—or her, come to that."

We had arrived at the flak tower, which was entirely typical in its construction. Square in plan but with a slight taper to the apex, where flat-lobed projections stuck out on all corners. The bronze doors had been removed long ago for scrap, and the unchecked Perpetulite had grown across the aperture, so all that remained was a vertical scar and a rough dimpling, like on unbaked bread. Another couple of hundred years and there wouldn't even be that.

Tommo walked to the side where a series of bronze pitons was clear evidence of how the crackletrap builders had managed to get to the top. At chest height someone had left a length of steel piping no thicker than a man's fist in what had once been a window. Tommo placed sandwiches in the pipe, followed by an apple, while I stared at him, confused.

"Sandwiches," he explained, "for Ulrika of the Flak. I think she's Riffraff."

"You mean there's—"

"Shh!" he said. "You don't want to frighten her."

When he was done, he beckoned me away, and in answer to my doubtless quizzical expression, said, "What's your problem?"

"How did she get in there?"

He shrugged.

"Then how do you know she's Ulrika? Or a woman? Or even Riffraff, for that matter?"

"Eddie," he said, pulling me closer, "if I want to have a pet Riffraff called Ulrika who lives in the flak tower and gets fed through a pipe, then I will, and no low-end, slow-end rabbit watcher is going to tell me otherwise. Do you understand?"

I said that I totally understood—now—but didn't mention that I too had an imaginary friend who needed feeding. I called him Perkins Muffleberry, and he lived in a hollow beech at the edge of the village. I know it sounds childish, but the food was always gone by morning.

Pickled Onions and Custard

> 2.6.21.01.066: Dinner may be taken privately, but shall also
> be available from the communal kitchens, as long as Head
> Cook is informed before 4:00 p.m., and an attendance chit
> is obtained.

We were supposed to have dinner at seven. Dad hadn't appeared by the time the meal was ready, so Jane threatened to throw the supper out the window if he wasn't at the table in five minutes flat.

"Really?" he said when I dashed over to the Colorium to inform him of this, and I assured him she probably meant it, too.

His work could just as easily be done at home, so he locked the swatch safe and we walked back across the square together.

"I'll need to fill out the order to National Color," he said. "You can help me."

This wasn't good news. I had been hoping Dad would fill out the requisition on his own so I'd have a very good reason *not* to double-order the Lincoln for Tommo and Courtland.

"Right," I replied uneasily, "love to."

I had earlier received an assurance from Jane that nothing unpleasant had been added to the food. In fact, although a bit sharp, this evening she seemed vaguely pleasant. I asked her why, and she replied with a shrug that my father had "shown compassion," which I took to mean his stance on bed rest for the sniffles and Mr. G-67's early retirement. To somehow ingratiate myself into her confidence, I almost asked her out for tea at the Fallen Man, but my nerve failed me, and the moment passed.

"Why don't you join us?" Dad asked Jane as soon as she had laid the dinner out on the sideboard.

She looked around to see whom he was talking to, then realized it was her. I don't think she'd supped at a Chromatic table before. "Thank you, sir, but there's not enough."

"Not enough?" he exclaimed, pointing to the steaming pot of broth. "There's enough here for four people!"

Before Jane could answer, the door swung open, and the Apocryphal man walked in. He was wearing nothing but a grubby string vest.

"I could have been a contender," he mumbled to himself, "and before this decade is out, we aim to land a man and open the box or take the money."

He then picked up the tureen and was out again before we could blink. We wouldn't have minded so much, except that we hadn't helped ourselves yet.

"No one just ate our dinner," said Dad with a sigh. "Is there anything else in the house?"

Jane bobbed and went to have a look while I answered the doorbell. It was Red Prefect Yewberry.

"We were just sitting down to dinner," I explained, and Yewberry, mistaking my comment for an invitation to a free meal, gratefully accepted.

"Smells excellent," he said, for the aroma of the broth had lingered, even if the broth itself hadn't.

I laid him a place, and he looked around expectantly. "Broth, is it?" he asked.

"It *was*," replied my father. "How are we honored by your presence?"

"Two things. First, the Caravaggio." Yewberry explained that it had been brought to the Council's attention that *Frowny Girl Removing Beardy's Head* was still at Rusty Hill. It was unusual that the village had a Caravaggio; Red Sector residents generally looked after the Turners and Kandinskys.

"No one's seen it for over four years," continued Yewberry, "and it should really be taken into protective custody before it falls prey to poor weather, or the Riffraff. You know how they like old paintings."

Dad told the prefect he didn't have time to search for Baroque master-pieces, but Yewberry had other ideas.

"The Council has decided to extend the movement order to include your son."

Tommo had come up with the goods after all. Dad asked me if I was willing to go, and I said that I was. I looked up to find Jane staring at me.

"I can make pickled onions and custard," she announced, still staring at me. "It's all we have left in the house."

"Perhaps I won't stay," said Yewberry, getting up to leave.

"You said there were two things?" said Dad.

Yewberry snapped his fingers and looked at me.

"The Colorman arrives on Saturday, and he's showing the spots on Sunday at noon. The Council wants to know if you'd like to take your Ishihara here, or wait until you get home?"

I felt a flush of excitement run through me. Having my Ishihara results three weeks *before* Roger Maroon had a serious advantage: If I scored well, it might push Constance to agreement before Roger's results were known. Even if she initially deferred me, I could probably force her hand by feigning interest in Charlotte de Burgundy, whom she loathed. If I scored badly, then it wouldn't matter much knowing now or later. I nodded enthusiastically.

"I'll put your name on the list," replied Yewberry. "Good luck tomorrow, and if you see a pencil sharpener at Rusty Hill, would you do the decent thing? Cheerio."

And he was gone.

"You got your own way after all," said Dad, handing me the order form for the replacement swatches. "Looks like Roger Maroon will be searching elsewhere for his wife."

"I almost feel sorry for him," I said with a smile. "Almost."

Jane, meanwhile, had vanished into the kitchen, where we heard some crockery being dropped.

For the next twenty minutes Dad dictated the order while I jotted his instructions down. I am glad to say that when it came to ordering the Lincoln, I resisted the pressure of Courtland and Tommo, and wrote in a "1" as instructed. I would have to find another way of paying Tommo back for the Rusty Hill gig. Like some shoes.

"I'll also need some 293-66-49 for general inflammation usage," Dad continued as he consulted his handbook, "and a 206-66-45 for controlling overproduction of earwax."

I wrote down the numbers.

Jane came back in with the pickled onions and custard, which tasted a lot better than I'd imagined, but then I'd imagined they were inedible, so anything was an improvement.

The meal didn't take long, and Dad adjourned to his office to complete the death and postcode-reallocation paperwork for the Grey who had been caught up in the power guillotine down at the linoleum factory.

I left Dad and went to watch the sunset in case it decided to show some red. I tried to avoid Jane, but she was waiting for me in the kitchen. I decided to say something first, to keep her from getting the upper hand. I wanted to say something intelligent, but it didn't come out that way at all.

"I'm going to take my Ishihara on Sunday."

"That's a weight off my mind."

"Is it?"

"No."

The failed intelligent approach hadn't worked, but I wasn't out of ideas.

"Courtland has no intention of marrying Melanie."

I had thought the information might be welcome, or of use, but I had thought wrong.

"Information as currency? For what? To make me like you?"

It wasn't the reaction I had expected, but she was right—I was trying to curry favor. She didn't strike me as the sort of person you could woolpull, or even try. I decided to be truthful. "I thought it was a toxic thing to do and that she should know about it, that's all."

"That's very caring and sweet of you," she said, "but are you so unutterably stupid as to suppose that Melanie isn't smart enough to realize this?"

"She . . . *knows* the promise is a lie?"

"Of course. If you were Achromatic, you'd see it all a bit differently. In the seething pit of sewage that is East Carmine, being the second pillow to the Yellow prefect-in-waiting is something of a coup. We have high hopes for what Mel might achieve."

"He won't be the prefect for years," I pointed out.

"It's a long-term strategy, Red. Have *you* ever made a sacrifice for the good of the many?"

"I once went without dessert for three months so we could afford some 259-26-86 to color the hydrangeas."

"Well, then," she said, "you must know *precisely* what Melanie's going through."

"You're very sarcastic."

"I know. Now: Why are you going to Rusty Hill?"

"To pick up the Caravaggio."

"No other reason?"

I decided to meet like with like, and question for question.

"What other reason could I have for going there?"

She narrowed her eyes and stared at me, trying to figure out how much I knew, if anything. "Do you want some advice? Go home. You're far too inquisitive, and here in East Carmine curiosity only ends one way."

"Death?"

"Worse—*enlightenment*."

"I like the sound of that."

"No, you don't. Believe me, cozy ignorance is the best place for people like you."

"And who are people like me?"

"Unquestioning drones of the Collective."

Usually, such a comment would be regarded as a compliment, but from her it sounded somehow *undesirable*.

"Are you threatening me?"

"I'm warning you. As a *courtesy* to your father," she added, lest I get the fanciful notion that she found me faintly tolerable.

"Would you extend that courtesy to having tea with me tomorrow afternoon?"

I don't know what possessed me to ask her. To inveigle myself into her confidence, probably. In any event, her answer put paid to any thoughts of tea and Chelsea buns anytime soon.

"I would sooner stick needles in my eyes. And why are you holding on to your eyebrows?"

"No reason. Anyhow, I can't go home—deMauve's got my return ticket."

"You gave it up?" she said with incredulity. "I was wrong—you're not as stupid as you look."

"Thank you."

"It wasn't a compliment. You're far, far stupider."

"Please," I said, "keep on insulting me—I hope to develop an immunity. What have you got against the Order, anyway? In five generations your family might be prefects. Will they be complaining about the Order then?"

The directness of my question caught her off guard, but she soon recovered.

"Probably not, but I should hope the Greys under them will—and that my descendents will have the wisdom to listen."

"The sheep needs the shepherd, and the shepherd needs the sheep," I replied, slipping into the Word of Munsell almost without thinking. "Apart We Are Together. There has to be some kind of hierarchy. The Purples aren't lofty and superior because they're Purple; it's because they're in power. You think Greys would be any different if the roles were reversed?"

"I don't want Greys in power any more than I want the Yellows. I just think that everyone should be equal. Equal merits, equal Rules, equal standing within the village. Purple head prefect one year, Grey head prefect the next—or even no head prefect at all."

"Equality is a proven myth," I remarked, the well-worn arguments tripping off my tongue. "Do you favor a return to the ways of the Previous with their destructive myopia and Worship of the Me? Or simply a descent into the anarchic savagery of the Riffraff?"

"Despite what you read in *Munsell*, those aren't the only choices. We deserve better than this. *All of us*. We could run the village like we run the Greyzone. No spots, no rankings, just people. Why do I have to prove myself an upright member of society and deserving of full residency before being allowed to marry? Why do I have to apply for an egg chit? Why can't I move to Cobalt if I wish? Why do I have to submit myself to any of the Rules?"

"Because *Something Happened*."

"What?"

There was no clear or easy answer to this.

"Something . . . best forgotten. You may hate living under Munsell, but it has sustained for almost five centuries. Besides, your wholly demeritable thoughts and conduct place you firmly in the minority."

She leaned closer.

"You say that, but am I *really* in the minority?"

I opened my mouth to answer, but couldn't. Since visiting the library I had pondered upon the usually unassailable wisdom of the Leapbacks. What was in *The Little Engine That Could* that might cause a damaging rift in society? What was so wrong with the telephone that it had to be withdrawn? Why was Mr. Simply Red no longer listened to? Why no more crinkle-cut chips, bicycles, kites, zips, yo-yos, banjos and marzipan? But I had paused, and that was enough for her.

"I don't need you to agree with me," she said quietly. "I'll go away happy with a little bit of doubt. Doubt is good. It's an emotion we can build on. Perhaps if we feed it with curiosity it will blossom into something useful, like suspicion—and action."

She stared at me for a moment.

"But that's not really your thing, is it?"

And she left me alone in the kitchen with my thoughts. They were confused mostly, but I was at least glad my long-held doubts finally had a use—it made Jane happy.

The East Carmine
Marriage Market

1.1.2.02.03.15: Marriage is an honorable estate and should
not be used simply as an excuse for legal intercourse.

followed the rays of the setting sun out of the village along West
Street, and sat on a bench to draft my telegram to Constance. Neither
the nonadventure with the Last Rabbit nor the Oz Memorial nor the
disgraced Yellow postman would actually impress, and mentioning
Jane's odd view of the Collective would be anathema. Constance had
confided before I left that the things she looked for most in a husband
were "incurious unambition" and "an ability to follow orders," so I composed the telegram along the lines of how much I wanted to discharge
my Civil Obligation to the Collective in the most productive manner, and
how I thought of her all the time. I tried a poem:

> *Oh, Constance Oxblood, my heart in full flood*
> *gushes, torrentlike, over rainburst stream and scrub.*
> ~~*Prove that I'm no dud.*~~ *Prove to you that I'm no dud.*
> *dud? Bud*
> *cud*
> ~~*stud*~~

It wasn't working. I was going to have to outsource my romantic
thoughts to someone who could actually write poetry. I put my notebook away and gazed at the sun, which had just begun to dip below the

Western Hills. The light was dropping fast, and the slopes were now black and shapeless in the lee of the daylight. It was the start of the gloaming, the transitional period between seen and unseen.

It was about the time, in fact, that the janitor would strike the arc. As if on cue, there was a bright flicker from behind me as the streetlamp burst into life, bathing the center of the town in strong artificial light. It was not just a way of extending the day but also a signal that any residents still out and about should think about returning. I could see the roof mirrors of the village swing around to pick up the light so that the beam splitters, Luxfer prisms and intensifiers that brought interior light during the day could service the village at night.

When I was a kid, we used to play dusk running, where the last one back to the safety of the streetlight was the winner. It was usually either Richard or Lizzie, but one evening it was decided that a champion dusk runner must be established, so they both went and stood in the center of the playing field and waited for the night to roll in. The rest of us stood expectantly in the town square, exchanging wagers and giggling. The first to funk out was the loser, the last one back the winner. Lizzie was first in, but Richard wasn't the winner. He was found eight months later a mile beyond the Outer Markers by Greys on coppicing duty. He was identified only by his spoon; his postcode was reallocated a day later. No one tried dusk running after that.

Within a few minutes the river, stockwall and linoleum factory had all vanished, swallowed up in the rolling wall of darkness that was sweeping across the land. I abandoned my seat when the shadows became empty holes in my vision and retreated to the safety of the town square. The streetlamp was now burning brightly, the low hiss of the arc and the occasional squeak and flicker working to dispel the fear of the night. Behind me, only the crackletrap atop the flak tower could still be seen, and that only as a silhouette against the rapidly darkening sky.

"Hello!" said Tommo as he walked up. "I've been looking for you."

I returned his salutation and thanked him for fixing up the Rusty Hill gig.

"Not a problem. Did you double-order the Lincoln for us, by the way?"

"A bit of a snag, I'm afraid."

"Don't be afraid," said Tommo, "or at least, not of *me*. Courtland once beat Jim-Bob so hard he had blood in his wee."

"I'll get the Lincoln for you somehow."

114

"I know you will. More important, are you going to marry my sister?"

I would have to get used to how quickly Tommo could change the subject.

"I didn't even know you *had* a sister."

"A state of affairs I am at efforts to maintain."

"You've lost me."

"It's pretty simple. You're a Red of moderate perception and the son of a swatchman. The fine, upstanding Red womenfolk of this cesspool will be fighting over your plums like dogs about a freshly dead carcass."

"Graphically put, if also a little disgusting. But I'm sorry, I'm on a half promise to an Oxblood."

Tommo raised his eyebrows. Not much impressed him, but this did. I explained about how my potential union to the Oxblood family would be my ticket to the easy life. We would be jointly running the family stringworks come Josiah Oxblood's retirement, and it was well known that the Oxbloods were pretty much rolling in moolah.

"They have three permanent servants and a Leapback-compliant gyrocar," I boasted, "and eat colorized food as a matter of course."

"They're also *notoriously* Redcentric," he murmured.

This was true, too. Countless generations of Oxbloods had been choosing their mates wisely, and it was rumored that, paired with a suitably high-Redceptor husband, Constance might produce offspring who would surpass the Redness of the Crimsons, and topple them from the Red prefecture.

"Are you anywhere near the front of the queue," asked Tommo, "or just a sad wannabe? Put it this way: Do you have pet names for each other?"

"We've shortlisted a few possibilities, but nothing's fixed."

Constance's opinions on the matter, sadly, were entirely conservative. She had thought my suggestion of "snootchy bear" as an endearment a tad risqué, was tempted with a more traditional "dear" or "honey" and had conceded to a tentative "honey bear" as a compromise, but only in private.

"The union is not *quite* as inevitable as I make out," I confessed. "Standing between me and a supremely rosy future is a po-faced slack-jaw named Roger Maroon."

"A Maroon?" said Tommo. "I'd duck out now while you still have your dignity."

"Don't get me wrong," I said quickly. "She's quite affable in spite of her choosy Redcentric fickleness, and our courting has not been without a few moments. She has allowed me on several occasions to take her to a tea dance."

"How scandalously forward of you. Have you tangoed?"

"Not *yet*," I said slowly, "but we're almost there."

Actually, Constance had refused me a tango on the grounds that it was a "gateway dance" to something bolder, such as a lambada. If we'd done that, Old Man Magenta would have *insisted* we marry in order not to further offend public decency.

"Sadly," I continued, "she's also danced with Roger."

"Looks like she's hedging her ballroom bets as wisely as her bedroom ones."

"I suppose so."

"It's all academic anyway," said Tommo with a laugh. "Once you get to know the fillies in this village, all notions of running the family stringworks will vanish like thistledown in a nor'easter."

"I'm not staying, Tommo."

"Well, let's just *pretend* you decide to take up residence. C'mon, Eddie, run with me on this one."

"Okay," I said with a sigh. "Let's hear it."

"Excellent!" he cried, clapping his hands together. "Here's how I see your wedding prospects in this glorious sinkhole of ours: Since you look like too bright a fellow to dilute your color with anything other than the good old House of R., your choices among the Red crumpet in the village are, to say the least, limited. Once you subtract all the Greys, men and other hues from the three thousand or so people living here, there are one hundred and twenty-five potential Red womenfolk. You do the sums. Thirty-nine are already married, fourteen are widowed and nineteen have partners off at Reboot. Seventeen are spinsters over the age of fifty, and twenty-eight are under sixteen. How many left?"

"Nine."

"Right. Up for their Ishihara this year and thus available for nuptials are my sister Francesca, Daisy Crimson, Lisa Scarlet and Lucy Ochre. If those don't suit, Rose Madder, Cassie Flamingo and Jennifer Cochineal will be up for their Ishihara *next* year. If you feel like putting a spinster out of her misery, still on the prowl are Tabitha Auburn and Simone Russo."

"Hmm," I mused, half in jest, "no Blues you can think of for me to start a Purple dynasty with?"

He shook his head.

"DeMauve and the Council would never allow it. But if you're *considering* abandoning your birth hue, Violet deMauve is still available. She's in need of some Red seed to bring the deMauves back to mid-Purple rather than the Bluey-Red they are at present. But you'd have to be so utterly, *utterly* desperate for social advancement you'd be willing to ignore the fact that she's the most poisonous female in the village."

"I thought you said that accolade belonged to Bunty McMustard?"

"I think they're on some sort of rotation. In any event, I decided in your best interests to leave Violet deMauve out of the equation. Unless, of course, you want to spend the rest of your life being told what to do and when to do it?"

I thought about Constance. There was, I had to admit, something of a similarity. "In your own stupid pretend world, no, I wouldn't fancy that."

"I agree. You'd have to be insane to marry into the nest of vipers. The only other girl off-limits is Lucy Ochre. She's reserved."

"Reserved?"

"For me. So paws off."

"Does she know this?"

Tommo shrugged. "Not really."

"Eight is still a pretty good choice."

"Not *quite* right," he replied, counting off my potential choices on his fingers. "Simone Russo is the low-percepting product of the head plumber and a Grey—*quite* unsuitable. Rose Madder is on a promise, and Lisa as good as. Tabitha is on a half promise to Lloyd Bluto. Lisa Scarlet is a bit low on the social scale, what with her father being sent off to Reboot. Cassie is hideously weird, and Jennifer declared herself last week with a Grey named Chloe."

"Ah."

"So that leaves my sister Fran and Daisy Crimson."

"Choice of two? Generous of you, Tommo."

"Not so fast. Since I'll thump you painfully between the eyes if you even *think* about placing any part of your grubby person on my dear Francesca, whom I've sworn to protect from all life's unpleasantness, I'm afraid that leaves only Daisy Crimson. I hope you're very happy together."

"You've got this all worked out, haven't you?"

"I think of little else."

While we had been talking, every last vestige of natural light had vanished. The sky was like ebony, and the only illumination was the harsh white light of the central streetlamp, which cast shadows so hard it seemed you might cut yourself on them. Just as I was telling Tommo what complete rubbish his fantasy marriage league was, a figure dressed in an overcoat and carrying a valise walked out of a nearby house. I didn't realize the figure was Travis Canary until he was quite close.

"Hullo!" he said when he saw me. "How are you settling in?"

"Pretty well," I replied. "Have you met Tommo?"

They shook hands, and Tommo looked at the Yellow suspiciously.

"You're not wearing your spot," he said.

"I'm not going to need one where I'm going."

I thought he meant Reboot, but he didn't. Before we could say anything more, he tipped his hat and walked into the night. In a few seconds the darkness had swallowed him up, and he was gone.

Tommo and I could hardly believe what we had just witnessed, and stared at each other in astonishment. I looked around, but though the square still had a dozen or so people out for a nighttime perambulation, no one else had noticed.

I walked across to press the Nightloss alarm, but Tommo stopped me.

"Wait, wait, Eddie. He's a *Yellow*—one less is no big deal. Besides, he's up for Reboot, and more important, it's nothing to do with us."

"You *never* leave anyone out at night," I retorted pompously, "not even a Yellow."

I pressed the Nightloss alarm, and the klaxon sounded three shrill blasts.

The square was suddenly deathly quiet, and within a few seconds, empty. When there was a shout on, most people found something else to do and somewhere else to be. Nightloss was a sorry, tragic affair, and trying to rescue someone could have doubly tragic consequences. The custom was to not get involved—or at least, not until the morning, when the search took place. We walked to the limit of the falloff and peered into the darkness, which swirled like an angry black fog. We were right on the edge of the village. Beyond the houses to our left and right was only the lumpy grassland.

"Who's out there?" came a voice.

It was Prefect Sally Gamboge, and she looked as though I had interrupted her dinner. I explained that it was Travis Canary who had just walked out, and she looked at me with an expression of supreme indifference. "Reboot or Nightloss," she said, "it's all the same to us. Isn't that right, Tommo?"

"Yes, ma'am."

"But he's *Yellow*," I persisted.

"In color, but not in spirit," she replied. "His selflessness just saved us a train fare out of here, so in that respect we should be grateful."

"So you're not going to do anything?"

She looked at me, and her eyes flashed dangerously. "No."

And without giving me another look, she walked back toward her house.

I stood there, staring into the darkness. He had been Rebooted only for his attempt to *improve* things, and despite Travis' flawed hue, he had offered a friendship, and I had accepted it.

I opened the cabinet below the Nightloss button. The reel of string and the belt clips were there, but the emergency Daylighter magnesium flare was missing. I looked into the darkness and tried to visualize where Travis might be. Although I couldn't see anything, the road in front of me led past the flak tower, through the empty grassland, past the bridge and, beyond that, to the linoleum factory.

And then I heard him. A series of short cries as the night terrors began to take hold. No one was immune, not even the wisest prefect or sagest Colorman. We all knew what it was like—even indoors the absence of light has an effect upon the senses that brought forth a multitude of terrifying apparitions. But only if you panicked, and let the terror get a hold. Once you were in the grip of a night terror, it would take nerves of steel to get you out.

Without thinking, I slipped off my shoes and socks and felt the warmth of the Perpetulite on my feet. If I didn't stray from the roadway, I would have nothing to fear.

"What are you doing?" asked Tommo, as surprised as I was by my actions.

"He sounds like he's at the Faraday cage," I replied, attaching the clip to my belt, looping the string around it and handing him the reel. "I'll be back in a jiffy."

"Without a flare? Wait—"

But I ignored him and stepped forward into the wall of darkness. Although I was initially without panic, after thirty paces or so the enormity of what I was doing caught up with me, and I suddenly felt my chest tighten and my mouth go dry as the swirling darkness started to heap into shapes. I could tell the onset of a night terror, and from long practice simply closed my eyes and breathed deeply until the panic subsided. It didn't help that Travis gave out the occasional cry. Annoyingly, though, he hadn't stopped walking, and his cries were becoming fainter by the minute. After I had walked fifty yards or so and kept to the road by the feeling of the smoother and colder central white line beneath my feet, I heard the Nightloss siren sound again, which was unusual in the extreme—some other fool must have gotten himself lost on the other side of the village.

I walked on for another ten paces, but slower this time, as I was beginning to feel disoriented, and the excited chatter of fresh observers reached my ears, doubtless drawn from their houses by the news of a double Nightloss. It was only when the string went tight, stopping me from going farther, that I realized that the second Nightloss alarm had been for *me*.

"Eddie!"

It was my father, far behind me. I shouted back that all was well, but my voice, which I had intended to be deep and full of confidence, came out sounding weedy and fearful. He told me to turn around and they'd reel me in. I did actually turn, and far away, wrapped in a dark tunnel, was a small village entirely adrift in the night. It didn't stay in one place, either, but seemed to move around as my unpracticed eyes darted back and forth, trying to make sense of the unusual surroundings. For a moment I thought I would do as he asked, but I'd be an even bigger fool if I didn't actually accomplish anything, so I once again told my father that I was fine and asked for more string.

I moved on, despite his admonishments, and all of a sudden something hard struck me on the shin. I fell forward, collapsing onto a painfully angular object, and felt a sharp blow to my face, followed by a salty taste of blood in my mouth.

If there was a time for panic, then this was assuredly it. The swirling darkness suddenly seemed to gain shape and bear down upon me. I felt a cold hand grasp my heart and a sweat prickle my back. I bit my hand to stop myself from screaming, then sat down on the roadway, stared into the inky darkness and took deep breaths. All around me the night seemed to fall ever tighter and closer, in an embrace that made me feel as though I were being smothered; as if the darkness would close over me like a millpond, and I would gratefully pass into unconsciousness and death.

But it didn't happen that way. I fought back the panic, discovered that the object I had fallen on was nothing more nor less than a wheelbarrow and allowed myself to be ignominiously reeled back into the village by none other than the head prefect himself. The feeling of a safe return was short-lived, as the flagrant irresponsibility of my actions were made abundantly clear to me. DeMauve explained in strident terms that I had just recklessly gambled the twenty years of investment that the Collective had placed on my person.

"If you want to attempt such foolhardy stunts," he said, "you should conduct them in your retirement when your Civil Obligation is at an end."

In short, I was subjected to an ear bashing of momentous proportions. But it was without demerit as I had done nothing against the Rules.

By way of consolation, my excursion had convinced the prefects that an effort should be made to look for Travis, "fallen Yellow or not," and Mr. Fandango was dispatched to fetch some Daylighters. Mrs. Gamboge, doubly furious not only that I had disobeyed her but that my actions had required her to do the right thing, insisted that she and Courtland look for Travis. When it was pointed out that this placed not only the Yellow prefect but also her successor in unnecessary danger, Mrs. Gamboge laughed it off and indicated that they would go as far as the boundary and no farther.

The Daylighters were soon produced, and after Gamboge senior and junior had donned walking boots, they pulled the firing cord of the first magnesium flare. The lamp fizzed for a moment before bursting into a flaming white light that pulsed and crackled as it burned, and it gave off an acrid white smoke that made us cough.

They wasted no time, and both hurried off into the night. We watched them beneath their umbrella of flickering light until they were lost from view in a dip.

"Three months' flare allocation gone in a single evening," grumbled Fandango, and the small crowd slowly dispersed.

Dad just shook his head sadly and told me I'd better go to my room and "consider my position," which in Dad-speak meant that he was sorely hacked off, but that it would all be forgotten by the morning.

I went upstairs to my room and sat cross-legged on my bed. My muscles were still twitching from the night panic, but I didn't feel half as bad as I thought I would. I could hear the Apocryphal man moving about upstairs, and the lighter footfalls of a second person, who moved slower. Despite Travis, I still had important matters to attend to, so after pushing the night's events to the back of my mind, I took out my notebook, adjusted the angle-poise mirror to maximize the light that streamed across the landing and in my open door, thought for a moment and composed my telegram to Constance.

> TO CONSTANCE OXBLOOD SW3 6ZH ++ JADE UNDER LIME GSW ++
> FRM E RUSSETT RG6 7GD ++ EAST CARMINE RSW ++ MSGE BEGINS ++
> JOURNEY WITHOUT SERIOUS INCIDENT ++ ARRIVED SAFE AND WELL
> ++ SAW RABBIT IN VERMILLION V INTERESTING ++ EAST CARMINE
> DELIGHTFUL ++ TWICE AS BIG AS JADE RIVER FRONTAGE AND LINOLEUM
> FACTORY ++ CAKE V EXPENSIVE AND LITTLE SYNTHETIC COLOR ++
> SEND BEST WISHES TO YR CHARMING MOTHER ++ MY QUEUING SYSTEMS
> WORKING WELL ++ YR EDWARD XXX POEM FOLLOWS ++ O THAT I MIGHT
> RUN THE STORMY BOUNDARY MARKERS WITH YOU ++ TAKE YOU IN MY
> HEART AND SQUEEZE YOU ALTHOUGH NOT TOO TIGHT ++ AN ANGRY
> SWAN OR MARAUDING RIFFRAFF WOULD NOT STOP ME ++ MY COLOR
> IS YOURS COMMA THE LIGHT OF MY LIFE ++ MSGE ENDS

I decided for strategic reasons *not* to tell Constance of my early Ishihara. In fact, I thought I might surprise her with it on my return, and force her into a decision under Roger Maroon's upswept nose. I was rereading the missive for the fourth time and wondering whether actually *receiving* the poem would make up for its lamentable lack of quality when I heard the Gamboges' return. I moved to the spare room and looked out into the town square, where a small group were welcoming the Gamboges back with hot cups of cocoa and blankets. They were quite alone; Travis was now officially Nightloss.

Only twenty minutes later, the first bell sounded, and exactly ten minutes after that the light abruptly went out, and the world was plunged into an inky blackness without depth, shape or form. Across the gulf of hollow emptiness I could hear the sounds of settling that a village makes when bedding down. The odd cry as someone was caught out and stubbed a toe on a bed leg, the bark of a dog and the wail of a child who'd not yet come to terms with nightfear.

Within a few seconds of lights-out, the first sound of the evening's Radtalk began. It was quiet, as from a distant originator somewhere at the other end of the village, and I strained to hear the metallic Morse code strikes on the radiator. It wasn't anything particularly inappropriate, just sounded like banal gossip among juniors—who fancied who, that sort of thing. They used call signs, as the centralized heating system was an open circuit, so I didn't know who was being talked about, and wouldn't have known them if I had. After a few minutes of this another stream started off, but this one used a wooden striker for separation. This Morse code was faster and harder to keep up with, but it turned out to be chapter eight of a serialized book titled *Renfrew of the Mounties*—likely as not, on the Leapback list. Tommo had hinted that Mrs. Lapis Lazuli might attempt something at story time, so I had to assume that this was she. And indeed, my Morse would have to be up to scratch, for the code was tapped out at a phenomenal rate.

I listened for a bit, until a *third* stream started up, this one below the other two, slower and more considered. It was also tapped out with a lead bar, again for easier separation of the streams. This one was directed to me, and after I had found a piece of metal and wrapped it in a pair of underpants to tap out an acknowledgment, I was asked by someone named "Fifi23" about news from the outside. I signed myself in as "Nik" and tapped out the broadest possible news that I had from the Green sectors. As soon as I strayed onto anything remotely sensitive, the duty radiator monitor would jam my stream with a series of fast random strikes that drowned out all the channels. The jam soon stopped, however, and I resumed, this time watching what I said more carefully. I tapped away for half an hour until my wrist grew tired, and after receiving thanks from "Fifi23" and quite a few others, I listened to Mrs. Lapis Lazuli's serialization, which was enjoyable, despite making little sense—many of the words and idioms were obsolete, and it took me a while to figure out that a "Mountie" was some sort of Red Rule enforcer, but on horseback.

As I listened to the story I stared out of the window. I could just make out the faint disc of a full moon rising through the trees of a distant hilltop. I shivered and pulled the covers over my head.

Breakfast

6.1.02.03.012: The annual thousand-hour lamp-burn
allocation may be discharged however the Council sees fit.
Multiple lamp heads are allowed, but the total allocation
time remains unchanged. Unused time may be carried over.

was awake before dawn. Unable to sleep, I leaned on an elbow and
stared into the darkness. I couldn't even tell if my eyes were open or
shut. The darkness swirled about me like charcoal maggots in a coal
cellar. I touched the hands on the bedside clock to confirm that it was
near dawn, then heard the faint buzz of the first heliostat on auto-align
toward the rising sun. Another started up, and then a third, and soon
the air was filled with the cheery buzz of the clockwork chorus. This
was joined by the birds whistling and chirruping the new day, and before
long, as I stared into the inky blackness, the faintest glimmer of red
punctured the curtain of darkness. It soon became a distinctive thin
crescent, then a semicircle and very slowly sightfulness returned to my
room. First the door frame bathed in the dim glow of deep red, then the
room itself, slowly reassembling itself as the rays of the new day slowly
crept about my small chamber, banishing the blackness.

I arose, washed my face and dressed in my Outdoor Adventure #9s,
which consisted of long shorts, a safari shirt and stout footwear. I then
trod carefully downstairs to make some tea. I hadn't even gotten as far as
the kitchen before the sun vanished behind heavy clouds and the room
dropped to barely a single foot-candle above threshold. After bumping

into the furniture several times in an effort to set breakfast, I gave up and fumbled my way to the settee in the corner of the kitchen.

I awoke to find that the day had brightened. Dad was dressed, and doing some work at the kitchen table.

"Good morning," he said with a smile. "Who's Rude Girl? You were mumbling in your sleep."

"Did I mention any names?"

"No."

"Then I'm not sure."

I had been dreaming. Jane and I were swimming together in a millpond-still lake at dawn. Water vapor had been rising off the surface, obscuring the shore and isolating us from the world. I had been telling jokes, and she had been laughing, even at the bad ones. We had been about to kiss when Constance had arrived, standing up in the prow of a rowboat, dressed in flowing red robes. She opened her mouth to say something when I woke up.

"You also mentioned something about a rabbit," Dad added.

"It had gills and was nibbling our toes," I said with a frown.

He laughed and asked me how I was. I touched the cut on my mouth where I had fallen on the wheelbarrow the night before. It was still sore, but a lot better, and I told him so.

"They didn't find Travis," he remarked.

"No," I replied. "They rarely do."

"You showed some grit," he added, "and that's a good thing—but don't do it too near the prefects. You'll only draw attention to yourself."

I asked him what he meant by this but he simply shrugged, and I headed off to the town hall, as I still had time to grab some cooked breakfast.

I stopped at the post office on the way, and since shop hours were extended to make full use of seasonal daylight, it had been open for half an hour by the time I got there. It was tidy yet immeasurably ancient, but despite this, the original red paintwork was still tolerably bright.

"Are you *sure* you're happy with this?" asked the telegram clerk as she stared at my poetical efforts. "It seems a bit, well, *rubbish* to me."

She was a late-middle-aged woman who reminded me of my twice-widowed aunt Beryl. Very kind, but annoyingly straight talking.

"Constance isn't looking for a husband who's intellectually challenging," I explained, trying to pretend that I had deliberately downplayed my skills.

"Just as well," she replied, then, once she had counted up the words, added, "You could add three more Xs and it wouldn't cost you any more."

I thought for a moment and then declined, as I didn't want Constance to think me too forward. Mrs. Blood then asked me to confirm line breaks before charging me an outrageous thirty-two cents. I suggested that this might be somewhat exorbitant, and she informed me that she'd waive the fee if I brought back a set of sugar tongs from Rusty Hill. I said I'd do my best, and she smiled sweetly and told me she'd tap my message down the line right away.

The town hall was as town halls generally are: spacious, and smelling of boiled cabbage and floor polish. I walked carefully around the prefect carpet that was set near the entrance, nodded respectfully to where the *Book of the Gone* was sited, then blinked in the relative gloom. Far away at the opposite end was the stage, framed rather delightfully by ornate plaster moldings. To one side were the kitchens, and to the other were large oak double doors, which would be the Council Chamber. This was strictly out-of-bounds, except for twenty minutes in a resident's life: This was where they held the Ishihara.

I helped myself to some porridge and a bread roll with a regulation scoop of marmalade, then sat down opposite Tommo at one of the red-hued tables. The room was relatively empty as the early shift Greys would already have eaten, and most Chromatics rarely bothered to get out of bed unless it was their turn to do Boundary Patrol or something. I noticed Jane finishing her breakfast, but she didn't look in my direction. Tommo was there, he told me, to keep me from falling into good company.

"Travis wasn't found," I said.

"He will be. Listen, are you going to pull a night stunt like that again? It makes the rest of us look bad when someone does something pointlessly worthy."

"What if it had been you?" I returned, and Tommo simply shrugged.

"Tell me," I said, "is there anyone living in our house except us? On the top floor, I mean."

Tommo looked at me and raised an eyebrow.

"You mean aside from the one we can't talk about?"

I nodded.

"Not that I know of. Why?"

"I thought I heard noises."

But Tommo was no longer paying attention. He had pulled out a comb with lamentably few teeth and was hurriedly making himself look presentable.

"Spot check?" I asked.

"More important than that. Do me a favor, would you? Try to make yourself as unattractive as possible. It won't be hard, I know—but do your best, hey?"

"What?"

"That," he said, indicating a girl who had just walked in, "is the Lucy Ochre I was telling you about. Each time I see her she's more gorgeous. But you know what I like most?"

"Her sense of humor in agreeing to see you?"

"No. Despite her father's wholesale theft of village property, no charges were ever brought. She must be sitting on a fortune. And when you're married, it's share and share alike."

"You're just a huge romantic at heart, aren't you?"

"If there's cash involved, I'm anything you want me to be."

I shook my head sadly, and switched my attention to Lucy, the daughter of the previous swatchman. She had long, wavy hair, was petite and pale and was looking around in a mildly confused manner. Dad and I had seen her the day before holding a pendulum down by the bridge. As soon as she looked in our direction Tommo waved, and she walked over in an unsteady manner.

"Hello, Timmo," she said, sitting down.

"It's *Tommo*, actually," he corrected. "I thought you might like to sit with us, my dove."

She stared at me for a moment.

"I could kill for a cup of tea."

Tommo took the hint and dashed off.

"He wants to marry me," she said, leaning on the tabletop for support and looking not *at* me, but just above my left eyebrow, "and Mother's given me a free choice in the matter. Do you think I should?"

"He thinks you have money."

She gave out a snort.

"We don't have a bean."

"Then probably not. I'm Eddie Russett, by the way."

"The swatchman's son?"

"That's me."

"You're quite handsome—I like your nose especially."

"It.was a birthday present."

"What else of interest did they give you?"

I decided to change the subject as she was being a little too forward.

"Tommo said you were searching for harmonic pathways."

"The earth is *awash* with silent musical energy," she replied in a dramatic tone, "in the rocks and ground, heath and fields. E-flat, if you're interested, but high up the scale, so impossible to hear. It's like an energy-bearing harmonic zephyr that channels along certain pathways, moving my pendulum as a breeze stirs wind chimes—an energy that binds all things together as one—a Harmony of the Spheres."

I said nothing, which was probably quite revealing.

"I know," she said with a sigh, running a hand through her hair. "That's what everyone thinks. Would you like to give me a spoon?"

I started, taken aback at her forthright suggestion.

"Well, no, yes, I mean, that is to say—I'm sorry, what did you say?"

"Dessert, soup, bouillon or tea—I don't care which. From Rusty Hill. You are going there, I think?"

"Oh, a *spoon*. I thought you meant—"

"That I wanted to buy some youknow? Come on, Eddie, you're not *that* handsome. But while we're on the subject, are you any good at kissing? I need someone to practice with, and you look like you could do with the cash. If we cut Tommo out of the equation, we can save a small fortune."

"How much kissing were you planning on doing?" I asked, thinking that a "small fortune" from 5 percent saved could mean enough to wear my lips out—and my tongue, too, if that's what she had in mind.

She shrugged. "It depends on how good you are at it, I suppose. Friend?"

"Friend."

"*Special* friend?"

"Let's just stick to 'friend' for the time being."

"Here's your tea," said Tommo, glaring at me since Lucy was almost sitting in my lap.

"No tea for me," she said, eyelids drooping. "In fact, I could do with forty winks." And as if to affirm this, she slumped onto the table and started snoring.

"Is she usually like this?" I asked, and Tommo shook his head sadly. The penny dropped. She was well and truly greened. And if the prefects got wind that Lucy had been seen limed in public, there would be serious trouble—not to mention all the wagging tongues.

"Hey, Lucy," I said, shaking her shoulder, "it's time for a walk."

I instructed Tommo to grab an arm, and we heaved her to her feet. With much moaning and complaining, we escorted her from the hall.

"We need deMauve's front door," I said. "The lime that Lucy's been peeking is the yellow side of green, so we need the red side of violet to counteract what's charging around her noggin at present."

"Does that work?"

"You don't grow up in a swatcher's house without learning a few tricks."

Tommo needed no more persuasion, and we walked the increasingly unsteady Lucy toward the Prime Residences.

"Look at the door, Lucy," I told her. "It'll make you feel better."

"I don't want to feel better," she moaned. "They did him in, you know."

"Pardon?"

"No one did anyone in," explained Tommo. "It's the color talking."

This was very possible. On the occasions when I'd arrived home to find Dad a bit limed, he'd spoken complete drivel, often without trousers, from atop the sideboard.

She stared at the door for a full minute, but we couldn't see any improvement. I cursed as I realized *why* this wasn't working—she'd had an eyeful of the hard stuff.

"She's got hold of some Lincoln," I said. "Red door—and hurry!"

We dragged her across to Yewberry's painfully bright front door, and told her to open her eyes. The effect was instantaneous, and dramatic. She gave a sharp cry, winced and held the back of her head as the pain of reverse discordance kicked in.

"Munsell's *hoo-ha*!" she cried.

"Not so loud," I said, "and give me one more look—of a count of at least five elephants."

"Crud," groaned Lucy as soon as she had counted off the elephants, "are you usually bright yellow?"

"It's just your visual cortex reconfiguring," I explained. "It will soon clear."

We took her home, and I let her flop in the window seat while Tommo went to fetch a glass of water.

"Ooh," she mumbled, "my *head*."

"Where's the Lincoln?" I asked.

She stared at me unsteadily. Her eyes seemed to flick around my features before staring at me intently, but in a queer manner that brought disturbing memories of my mother, who'd had the same habit. I'd never thought of it before, but it was possible that my mother had *also* been something of a greener. Lucy closed her eyes and started to sob silently. I passed her my handkerchief, and she wiped away her tears.

"Where's the Lincoln?" I asked again.

She thought for a moment, blew her nose and pointed to a copy of *Old Yeller* lying on a table nearby. I flicked through the pages and soon found what I was looking for. A blazingly bright swatch about the size of a picture postcard and of a green so powerful it seemed to fill the room with an infectious aura of dreamy happiness. I glanced at it and a warm sense of welcome torpidity momentarily washed over me.

"Five hundred demerits if you'd been caught with this," I murmured, folding the swatch color side in. But instead of showing any remorse, she grabbed my wrist and stared at me intensely.

"*They killed my father!*"

"Lucy," I said, "no one does the murder anymore. There's no need. There are *procedures.*"

"Then why—"

But she never got to finish. Tommo walked back in, and Lucy, who had been looking more and more unwell, promptly threw up all over the floor.

We found a mop and cleaned up while Lucy decided to sleep it off.

"Thanks for that," whispered Tommo as we walked out of her house a few minutes later. "We can't have the future Mrs. Cinnabar up on a charge of being saturated in public, now can we?"

"Lucy told me someone did the murder on her father."

"As I said, it was the Green talking. Everyone knows he was Chasing the Frog; the prefects decided to lie for the good of the village. The communal fine would have been pretty swingeing—even more so for the prefects."

This was true; with spectral rank came privilege, but also greater punishment when something went wrong. A prefect could be sent to Reboot for something a Grey would be fined fifty merits.

"Did Lucy say why she thought he was done in?"

I had to admit that she didn't.

"Well and truly greened," repeated Tommo, "and in an exciting way, a bit Lulu. Probably a tiger at youknow. Did I hear her offering you a friendship just now?"

"Yes."

"Blast! She's always turned me down when I've asked. In fact, I'm the only Red *not* on her list of friends."

I decided to be diplomatic. "Perhaps she thinks of you as *more* than a friend."

"That must be it," he replied, much relieved. "Now, Rusty Hill—you won't forget my shoes, will you?"

"Lucy wanted a spoon—and Mrs. Blood a pair of sugar tongs. Perhaps I should write a shopping list."

"No need," said Tommo. "I've got you one here."

I looked at his list, which seemed to have everything on it: doorknobs, a pram, nail scissors, a trifle bowl, a butter dish, a unicycle tire, any shoelaces at all and a mackintosh, preferably in blue, which was silly, as I wouldn't be able to tell. Tommo, it seemed, saw my excursion as a good marketing opportunity.

"I can't get all this!"

"Just the size nines, then—and a spoon, of course, for Lucy."

The Ford Model T

> 1.5.01.01.029: Abuse of medicinal hue is strictly forbidden.
> See Annex IV-B for list of banned shades.

C arlos Fandango arrived punctually with the Ford as promised, and *ahoogah*ed twice. He warmly shook hands with Dad and me, generously expressed his belief that we might one day be friends, then told me to ignore anything scurrilous that Tommo had said. Before I could even deny that he had told me anything, Yewberry arrived with a carpenter and two journeymen carrying a hastily made crate in which to transport the Caravaggio. Yewberry then showed me a street map with the house where I would find the painting marked, and told me not to drop it or anything.

"And if anyone sees, hears or *feels* anything peculiar," he added, "he *must* report it back to the Council."

"How peculiar does something have to be before it's worth reporting?" asked my father.

"*Unprecedentedly* so," Yewberry replied. "I know it sounds stupid, but there were stories of Pookas just before the outbreak. Glimpses of travelers appearing here and there, now and then, to this one and that one. And keep an extra special eye out for swans. A *Cygnus giganticus carnivorum* can carry off a man—and at this time of year, a cygnet can eat eight times its own body weight per day."

Dad and I looked at each other. Not because of the warning about swans, which were a well-known hazard—but about Pookas, which were not only of dubious existence but were listed as so in the Rules. Even if you saw one, it was better not to report it. People often laughed.

Dorian G-7, photographer and editor of the *Mercury,* was waiting for us with his camera. He nodded me a greeting and had us all pose near the Ford. Fandango remained disagreeable during the photoshoot, and I saw him move his head just as the shutter was fired, ruining the shot. Dorian saw it, too, but didn't say anything and didn't retake the picture. Photographic materials were strictly rationed.

"Here," he said, handing us a small package. "It's a snack for the journey. Sponge cake with bonemeal instead of flour. Tell me what you think."

We climbed aboard, Fandango cranked the engine into life and we moved off with a judder. Luckily for me, Dad said I could sit up front, as he'd been in a Model T many times, so I sat there in silence while Fandango skillfully negotiated a route out of town. The Ford was a four-seater sedan that smelled of oil, leather and burned vegetable oil and, despite continual maintenance over the years, was definitely showing its age. Quite what that was remained a matter of conjecture, as even though the numerical date of the Ford's pre-Epiphanic manufacture *was* known, the time between that and the Epiphany wasn't. Conservative estimates had them seven hundred years apart, but they could be double that—there was really no way of telling.

We took the Perpetulite roadway that snaked off to the south, and passed the lumber store, twenty-six-acre glasshouse, hay barns and Waste Farm. After a brief pause to open the steel gate in the stockwall and place our spot-badges in a cubbyhole designed expressly for that purpose, Fandango shifted the Ford into top gear, and we were soon past the Outer Markers and thundering along at a terrific pace. Rusty Hill was about fourteen miles away, and at this speed we'd be there in half an hour.

Unlike all the other pre-Epiphanic roadways, which had long ago been rendered nearly invisible by centuries of natural reclamation, the Perpetulite's powerful memory ensured that the road remained in almost pristine condition: smooth, well drained and clear of obstacles as close to forever as made no difference. But although it was clear of detritus, *images* of organic debris still remained in the dark grey covering—spidery imprints of fallen trees that had been absorbed to feed the organoplastoid's self-maintaining agenda. At the *edge* of the Perpetulite it was a different matter, for the undergrowth grew unchecked right up to the bronze curb rail. The trees arched in above the road and entwined above our heads, which gave me the feeling that we were in a long and perfectly realized arboreal tunnel.

I wanted to ask Fandango a million questions, ranging from the Ford to the gyrobike of which I had heard much, but since he was a Purple—albeit a very light one—protocol demanded that I wait until he spoke first. So I sat on my hands in silence.

Traditionally, the profession of janitor was reserved for the lowest Purple in the village. The reason was probably because the job involved using Leapbacked technology on a Head Office exemption, and the Council wanted someone they felt they could trust. Janitors fell sharply into two categories: those on their way *up* the Spectrum, who embraced the job as a wonderful opportunity and a showcase for their responsibilities; and those on their way *down*, who lamented their lost status, and regarded the calling as nothing more than manual labor more suited to Greys. Carlos Fandango was apparently one of the former.

"Do you have a Ford in your village?" he said at last.

I told him that we had eight, although six were permanent members of our Mobile Lightning Fast Response Group. He said that Carmine had a second Model T, a flatbed that was used to hunt for ball lightning, then asked me how my village could possibly have amassed so many Fords in a time of great shortage.

"We had a very forward-thinking Council at the time of the last Great Leap Backward," I explained, "and guessing the future, they secured eight Model Ts in the days when flatheads and Heavy Austins were still in widespread use. This year we acquired a pair of Darracqs and a DeDion Bouton, ready and waiting to take over when the Fords are put beyond use."

"They won't Leapback the Fords," he said. "They're just too useful."

He said it without conviction. The external telephone network had been about as useful as anything could be, and that had gone. He asked me where I was from and, when I told him, asked if I knew his cousin Elwood.

Few in the region didn't. Elwood Fandango had been head accountant in the village, but had gone somewhat irresponsible in his senior years. During a Mutual Audit he had been found illegally mixing pigment in order to make a potent swatch of Erectile Blue, something that showed a considerable level of skill and experimentation, especially as he had mixed a fan of twenty-two different shades, to cover almost every level of perception in the village. Despite the severity of the crime, it didn't surprise the auditor that Elwood had been leasing out the swatch for over ten years without anyone snitching. Unusually, Elwood survived being sent to Reboot due to his having amassed a huge amount of merits in a lifetime of unimpeachably high social conduct.

"I bet your head prefect was peeved," mused Fandango as he slowed to negotiate a low branch that had grown across the road.

"Incandescent," I replied, "partly because illegal home blending had been going on right under his nose, partly because he'd never been offered a peek but mostly because Elwood had used up his merits to offset mischief rather than for the betterment of the Collective, such as dedicating a park bench or contributing to the bandstand reroofing fund."

Fandango looked at me and raised his eyebrows. "So we have Jade-under-Lime to blame for senior delinquency?"

I had to admit that this was true. The concept of blowing a lifetime's good deeds on a flagrant breach of harmony had spread like all good loopholery to outlying villages, the region and finally the whole Collective. Head Office dealt with the problem with a hard-hitting training play that reminded seniors of their responsibilities.

"Is Elwood still with us?" asked Fandango. "News travels so slow these days."

"He succumbed last year at the age of eighty-eight," I explained. "The whole village turned out to cheer him off as he was wheeled into the Green Room."

We had driven out of the arboreal tunnel by now, and aside from the invasive rhododendrons, which Fandango explained were due "for a burn" quite soon now, the countryside was more open. The river was to our right and on the opposite bank was the railway we had traveled the day before. To our left was a steep, rocky slope, and as we swept around a corner, Fandango stamped on the brakes. Lying in the middle of the road were several large boulders, one the size of a garden shed. There was space to drive around them, but we were in no particular hurry, and stopped to watch. The rockfall was recent, and already the roadway was working to dispel the intruders. With a series of sinuous, wavelike movements, the Perpetulite gently shifted the broken rock toward the side of the road. As kids, we'd sat on baking trays and planted ourselves in the middle of the road, then raced one another to the curb.

"How long have you been janitoring?" I asked as we watched the largest boulder being moved as easily as if it were a feather.

"Thirty-one years, give or take," he replied. "Seen three Leapbacks in that time, each one worse than the one before. I dread to see what they'll ban next. I suppose you're too young to remember tractors?"

We felt the Ford start to move as it too was recognized as useless debris to be rejected, and Fandango reversed gently back and forth to fool the Perpetulite.

"Not quite," I replied, as the Leapback in question occurred when I was five. Horses did the plowing and drilling these days, and any devices that needed static power, such as threshing machines, were run off agri-exempted Everspins, each one about forty times the size of the one I had in my valise.

"I'd been more annoyed by the loss of gearing on bicycles," I said as the larger of the boulders was successfully toppled onto the verge, and we moved off. "Direct drive doesn't really excite, to be honest."

We drove on in silence for a few minutes, which allowed me to enjoy the untouched countryside, and after negotiating a long, unbroken stretch, we drove past the remains of an old town, reduced to little more than tussocky rubble by a series of aggressive excavations.

"This was Little Carmine," said Fandango, slowing so we could see, "picked clean of all hue in 00453. Great Auburn is about six miles to the east. It's been our principal source of scrap color for almost three decades, but even that's nearly exhausted. Most of our toshing parties these days concentrate on rediscovering individual villas or hamlets. It's quite a skill, you know, reading a soft lump in the ground."

We continued the journey, and Fandango and I chatted some more, mostly about the maintenance difficulties of the carbon-arc mechanism that lay at the heart of the central streetlamp—something that seemed to sap a disproportionate amount of his time. And it was in this manner that we passed the time until we arrived at the deserted railway station. Across the river was Rusty Hill, untouched and unvisited since the Mildew took everyone in it four years before.

Rusty Hill

1.1.01.01.001: Everyone is expected to act with all due regard for the well-being of others.

D ad and I climbed out of the car, and Fandango told us he would wait at the top of a nearby hill in case the Ford "proved difficult to start." He wished us good luck, told us to signal when we wanted to be picked up and that he would *ahoogah* twice if he saw any swans. He then departed with almost unnatural haste in a cloud of white smoke.

Dad sat on a low wall and examined the town through his binoculars. Although unlikely this far west, it wasn't unknown for Nomadic Riffraff to use abandoned settlements as homesteads, and neither Dad nor I had the slightest wish to bump into a grunge of well-established and dangerously territorial wildmen. There were gruesome stories that related to well-hued men being kidnapped, with the threat of plum removal if ransom wasn't paid. I knew of no one who wore their spot beyond the boundaries.

"Dad?"

"Yes?" he replied, still studying the deserted buildings.

"I learned something interesting this morning. Lucy Ochre's been hitting the Lincoln pretty badly. She thinks her father was given the murder."

I had thought Dad might reject the notion as quickly as I had, but he momentarily appeared ill at ease. He put down the binoculars and looked at me. "What's given her that idea?"

I shrugged. "Not sure. Why, *could* he have been?"

"Technically, it's possible. He could have been tied to the Departure Lounger and had his eyes taped open."

"They would have seen evidence of that on the body."

"Agreed. Here's another scenario: Let's say he was *planning* to Chase the Frog. He would have controlled the light coming into the room with the lever next to the Lounger. He'd rotate the shutters open to get the full effect of Sweetdream, then close them when he'd had enough, recover in the dark and creep out."

"There's another lever," I said, understanding where he was going with this, "outside."

"Right," he said, "and they're linked. Someone might have just held the lever in the open position."

I shivered. "Is that likely?"

"No. All he'd have to do is close his eyes. Besides, what possible motive could there have been? He was a healer—and a very good one at that. Seven years without a single Mildew. I think it was just a tragic mistake in pursuit of the frog. But it would be interesting to see if Lucy has any more information. By the way," he added, "deMauve bent my ear this morning."

"Oh."

"He said that if you ignored a Direct Order of a prefect again, he'd be down on both of us like a ton of bricks."

"Right," I said. "Sorry."

He carried on studying the town.

"Dad?"

"What?"

"How likely is it that there are Mildew spores still kicking around?"

"Almost nil," he replied. "A twenty-year quarantine is needlessly long, but those are the Rules."

Satisfied that the town was empty, he placed the binoculars back in his bag, and we walked past the faded quarantine board and across the stone-arched bridge. The Perpetulite spalled at the center of the bridge, where the organoplastoid had been cut and bronze spikes driven in to stop self-repair. The method was crude but effective, and the roadway had sent off only a few dark grey tendrils before giving up. We stepped off the smooth roadway and trod the well-worn cobbles into the village. It was unnaturally quiet, and evidence of rapid abandonment was everywhere: Discarded possessions lay scattered in the street and the shops were still open, tattered curtains blowing from windows. Between the paving slabs, grass had once more gained a toehold. Occasionally we came across the remains of the departed, their bleached bones lying within weathered remnants of clothing. I'd been told eighteen hundred had been lost, and all in the space of forty-eight hours.

We stopped by the village color hydrant, which looked relatively new and not at all like the unit back home, which was a fir tree of multiple connections to all points of the village. This one was not connected to anything at all—the color feeds were simply four-inch pipes with threaded caps and a couple of pressure valves, with the stopcock wheels removed to prevent mischief. Grid color had reached Rusty Hill not long before the outbreak. The village must have worked and saved and sorted scrap color for years to obtain the spur line, but ultimately, for nothing.

"Stay on your toes, and meet me back here in twenty minutes."

I nodded agreement, and we split up, he toward the Colorium, me toward the main square. It was only a hundred yards or so down the street and was equally desolate. The awnings in front of the shops were shabby and faded, and bones were strewn upon the floor tiles in the arcades, some even at the feet of the twice-lifesize bronze of Our Munsell. There was no color garden in the square, but there was a fountain, now choked with weeds, and I noted that the last vestiges of faded color could still be seen on the outside of the town hall. The doors were open, so I trod silently up the stone steps and looked inside. The hall was perhaps even bigger than the one at East Carmine, but a good deal gloomier. The clockwork motors on the heliostats had long since run down, but by chance one was at rest in a vaguely correct position, and a slanting shaft of light was shining down onto a scene of such utter desolation that I felt my eyes moisten. The wooden parquet flooring was covered with dust, twigs, bird droppings, windblown detritus, scraps of clothing, wristwatches, hairbands, shoes, jewelry, the odd spoon, coins, a buckle or two and, most of all, *bones*. Thousands of them, all human, all sorts and all sizes. Most had been scattered by animals, but some were still vaguely complete, and the musty smell of ancient decomposition lifted from the floor as I walked among the Mildew dead. There was no sign of panic, simply a sense of resignation. The residents of Rusty Hill had known they were doomed and had sought solace in the center of their world as they waited for the end. Scattered about among the bones were faded sheets of stretched canvas, which would have been hastily painted green and handed around among the residents to dull the pain.

I shivered and turned from the hall to finish my task so I could leave the town. It now felt oppressive, even though I knew from Munsell's *Quietus* that death was just a natural part of the cycle of renewal, and that life should be seen not as a two-hundred-yard hurdle with a tape to reach before anyone else, but more like a relay race without end, and only one team.

But as I turned to leave I looked up and there, painted upon the curved plaster ceiling was a vast mural that told me in pictorial terms the story of Munsell's Epiphany and the Founding of the Collective. Although there was much that I didn't understand, there were sections that were instantly recognizable, such as *The Dispersal of the Treasures, The Expulsion of the Experts* and *The Closing of the Networks*. I had never seen anything quite like it, but unlike the less complex version at home that had been overpainted several times, this ceiling had never been completed. About a third of it was still uncolored, the many shaped blocks that made up the picture empty, the color reference numbers still easily visible. The village had made a start but were unable to finish it. Most of the mid-blues had been filled in, some of the red and nearly all the green. Most attractive of all were the folds of Munsell's cloak, and the forty or so different shades of rich univisual violet made me feel a heightened sense of anticipation, as though something truly wonderful was just about to be revealed. I knew it was only a feeling brought forth by the combination of violets, but it wasn't a feeling I'd ever felt from a color before.

My mentor, Greg Scarlet, had explained that in the early days of the Collective a huge effort had been made to try to bypass the conscious mind and take emotions straight to the core—that the essence of a great novel, a rich symphony and a restful garden might all be combined to give one truly extraordinary sensation that was the abstract product of the mind alone. Although we still had the Green Room to show for it and Chromaticology, National Color had explained that further research into "direct feed" had been abandoned in favor of more pressing problems—such as maintaining the supply of hue and the National Colorization Project.

But looking up, I felt how the painting *might* have worked. The story of Munsell and his Epiphany was apparently a dramatic tale, full of great deeds and personal sacrifice. No one knew the full details, but it wasn't important. A viewing of the ceiling would bring out that same emotional response—the joy, loss, defeat and eventual triumph—without ever having to know the story at all.

I jumped, for a movement in the chamber had caught my eye. Beyond the tables still laid with the remnants of the last dinner was a woman, faded—she was insubstantial and little more than an *impression* that she was there, a glitter in the air. I blinked, but she didn't leave, and although I should have been terrified at the appearance of a Pooka, I wasn't. I was intrigued. I blinked again, then noticed something odd. She didn't vanish with the close of my eyes; in fact, she was almost more substantial with my eyelids firmly shut. She wasn't actually in the room at all—*she was in my head*.

I opened my eyes again to at least give her context and saw her diaphanous form move expertly among the detritus, staring at me all the time. Then she opened her mouth to speak and abruptly faded from view, and I was alone once more. I quickly departed the hall, thoroughly confused but not worryingly so; the known had been so long dwarfed by the unknown that confusion was an easy bedfellow.

I returned to the square, keen to finish my task and leave. I took a left out of the main square and then a right, and soon found the house I was looking for; a large modern building of oak-framed construction. The front door was locked, so I climbed in a broken window and fumbled my way to the kitchen, found the stat-crank and gave it ten or twenty turns. I then dialed in the time, date and year to manually reset the mirror. There was a buzzing from the roof, and a moment later light burst upon the interior of the house. I could see then that this was the dwelling of a well-to-do merchant, although art custodianship wasn't hue-dependent; you would be as likely to find a Caravaggio or a Williams in the home of a Grey as you would a Purple. I unbolted the front door to allow easy escape in case of a nesting swan or something, then walked into the kitchen.

I searched the drawers until I found some sugar tongs for Mrs. Blood, then climbed the stairs. Once on the top landing, I pulled the brass knob to swing the mirror across to illuminate the upper floors. I checked the front rooms first and found only bedrooms; one was occupied, one not. The last place to explore was at the end of a short corridor, and the door swung open when I touched the handle.

The room was large and unfurnished aside from a single armchair and a plain oblong carpet on the oak floorboards. As in most galleries, a large oval skylight covered in linen filled the room with an agreeable soft light, perfectly tuned for viewing. On the wall opposite me hung the Caravaggio, and it was every bit as spectacular as the pictures I had seen.

But those images had been monochrome, and here for the first time was something I had not suspected: The drapes above the scene of *Frowny Girl Removing Beardy's Head* were in a most spectacular shade of crimson, which counterpointed the spurt of arterial blood, also a vivid red. I stared at the large canvas for a few minutes, breathless with the consummate skill of the painter, the fine subtlety of light and shade, and wishing that for just a few minutes I could see more than just red.

I wasn't the only one staring at the painting, just the only one breathing. Sitting in the armchair was the previous custodian. Though the carpet below him had been stained black with the liquids of putrefaction, he hadn't rotted to nothing in the closeness of the room, but still had dark skin stretched taut across his bones. His hands were resting on the arms of the chair, and even though his chin had fallen to his chest, I think he would have been looking at the painting as the Mildew overcame him. He was wearing a Red Spot and a prefect's badge, and poking out from where his clothes had rotted away, a shiny spoon was clearly visible. It proved that no one had been here since the outbreak, and as he had no use for a spoon any longer, I slipped it out of his pocket and into mine.

Mindful of my father's wish for me to be as quick as possible, and with the possibility of still-active Mildew spores, I quickly opened the climate case, released the painting from its heavy ornate frame and rested it on the floor. It was large—almost six feet by four—and I had to carry the stretched canvas very carefully to get it down the narrow stairs without bumping into anything.

I placed the painting against the wall outside and quickly consulted the street map, then set off. The address of the Purple wrongspot was three streets away, and this would be the only opportunity for me to investigate.

I walked down the main street, past more scattered detritus, empty shops and the remnants of a population who looked as though they had attempted to leave, then given up. Grasses and wildflowers had germinated in pockets of windblown soil, and brambles snaked and coiled without encumbrance. After a few minutes' searching I found the last known address of the wrongspot. The front door looked shabby and unused, and the windows were boarded up. I was disappointed, but also hugely relieved. I had taken this issue as far as I could and now could quite happily let it go to concentrate on more socially responsible matters. I was about to hurry back to the Caravaggio, and thence to the bridge to meet my father, when I noticed that although *appearing* unused, the cobbles outside the door were clear of weeds. I paused, my heart beating fast, and without thinking, knocked politely. There was no answer, so I pushed open the door and was met by a sight of such extraordinary magnificence that it quite took my breath away.

Zane G-49

6.1.02.11.235: Artifacture from before the Something That Happened may be collected, so long as it does not appear on the Leapback list or possess color above 23 percent saturation.

was looking into the front parlor of a house that until recently had been very much in use, as the smell of food and soap lingered in the air. The room was large, and cluttered with bric-a-brac, tools, pots of paint, a Racy Novel or two and random items of scrap artifacture. There was a bowl of apples on the sideboard, and several smoked eels hung from the ceiling. All this, while unusual, was not the most magnificent thing in the room. For placed about the shelves, sideboard and picture rail and hung from the walls were perhaps a hundred or more lightglobes, all shining brightly and raising the level of illuminance of the interior to that of daylight. At night it would hardly be night, and fear would be banished. Zane would have found them in the Chapter House's "forbidden cupboard," because unlike most Leapback, lightglobes were too volatile to be placed beyond use by the blacksmith's hammer, so were either stored by the prefects, thrown in deep lakes or buried.

But the globes weren't the only Leapback in the room, nor the most remarkable. Propped against a pile of books was a reconstructed remote viewer in a bespoke wooden frame. It was made up of about fifteen parts, the largest of which was the size of my fist and the smallest barely bigger than a one-merit piece. Unlike the small shards that we uncovered from time to time, and upon which the smallest and most inconsequential images flicked and jiggled, the fifteen component parts of this viewer produced a single, vaguely coherent moving picture that could be followed with relative ease, and I leaned closer to stare at the fine detail. Even though the picture jumped from viewpoint to viewpoint with bewildering rapidity, it seemed to be a dramatic play of some sort, with a couple in a bedroom somewhere. That they were Previous was in no doubt, as the difference between the sexes was comically exaggerated, and they had subtle features with eyes that seemed as hollow as the children in the Ovaltine wall painting. I moved closer and realized that I could hear the people in the viewer actually *speak*. They used a dialect that was obviously ancient but understandable. The woman seemed to say something about how the man wasn't the same one she had known ten years before, and he retorted that it wasn't the years but the mileage, which I didn't quite understand. He used the pet name "honey," which would indicate they were married, but I could see no wedding rings, which was confusing. As I watched, the man showed the parts of his body where he *wasn't* hurt, and the woman kissed them in turn. He eventually pointed to his lips and she kissed them, too, which would have been a sneaky trick, had she not realized what he was up to, which I think she did, and I laughed out loud.

"How much do you know?"

By rights I should have jumped a foot in the air, but Jane's presence was somehow oddly inevitable. She was staring at me with a mixture of surprise and suspicion on her face. My first thought was about how she had traveled here. I had last seen her at breakfast—barely ninety minutes ago and fourteen miles away. Without a Ford, an impossible feat—like her journey to Vermillion the day before. It was as though she could leap from place to place, like a Pooka.

"I don't suppose there's any point asking how you got here?"

"None at all. I'll be honest, Red—you had me fooled with that shamefully ludicrous 'I'm an idiot who fancies you' act. And I don't fool easily. But right now, I need to know who you are, how much you know and what you think you'll do with the information."

I blinked twice. I was glad that she seemed to now have *some* respect for me, even if through a misunderstanding, but as long as she kept thinking that I wasn't groping in the dark, perhaps she might reveal just what she and the wrongspot had been doing in the Paint Shop that day. Or better still, start to like me.

"I'm sorry about Zane. It seems he was a friend of yours."

"Two days ago he was a friend. This time next month he'll be tallow, methane and bonemeal. How long have you known about him?"

"Oh, a while."

"What else do you know?"

"About you—but only since Vermillion."

"And who have you told about us?"

"Why don't we discuss this over tea at the Fallen Man?" I asked, attempting to be suave. "I've heard the scones are excellent—or at least, more edible than yours."

But she didn't go for it. "I'd sooner discuss it right here and now."

"Then perhaps," I replied, "you should tell me what you were doing in the Paint Shop?"

She lapsed into silence for a moment, and moved across the room to touch one of the lightglobes. She didn't need to—she was just positioning herself between me and the exit. I'd asked the wrong question. It told her that *I didn't know* what she was doing in the Paint Shop. On reflection, a better question might have been "How long has this been going on?" or even "Tell me the whole story, right from the beginning—and leave nothing out."

"Are you working for Thorny Yellowood?"

"I'm no fan of the Yellows."

"You risked your life to save one last night."

"He was a friend."

"If that's true, then you're a privateer, in it for the merits. Which is arguably worse."

"It is?"

"Of course. Snitching for the good of the Collective is misguided loyalty. Snitching for cash is nothing but personal greed."

"Oh."

"Irrespective of your motivations, I'll take what you're selling," she went on, "but I need to know the quality of the silence I'm buying."

I stared back at her, trying to figure out what I should do, and feeling hopelessly out of my depth.

"Unless," she added, "you really are as dumb as you look and have stumbled onto Zane and myself by accident?"

"I'm here, aren't I?" I blurted in a vain attempt to regain lost ground. "How could I have known Zane lived here?"

This seemed to make sense to her, but at that moment I heard a distant whistle from my father. I was overdue. And if I didn't come back, he'd start to look for me.

"Okay," she said, stepping aside to let me past, "I'll tell you everything."

"Really?"

"Yes. You'll stop to quarantine on the way back. Make an excuse and head toward the river. I'll meet you down there. Understand?"

I told her I understood, and she nodded her head toward the door. I walked slowly out, hoping to impress her with my insouciant manner, an effect that was somewhat dented when I stumbled on the doormat.

I picked up the Caravaggio and returned to where Dad was waiting for me at the color hydrant. He was not alone. There was a man with him, and he was from National Color. I knew this because he had the splashy paint-tin logo embroidered on his breast pocket, and his denim boiler-suit was liberally covered with smudges, drops, splashes and smears of a hundred different synthetic hues that hung to the cloth like jewels. It showed he had been doing the job for a while; the color-soiled coverall was a mark of rank and worn with pride. He had been checking the magenta in the hydrant as a cheery splash of vented hue lay glistening on the ground, and he was just putting away a leather-cased analyzer. Even more exciting was that he had arrived by bicycle—a sleek racing model of considerable vintage with all the gears fully working. It would be too much to hope he would allow me to ride the exempted Leapback, but I stared, nonetheless.

"Where the Ostwald have you been?" asked Dad.

"Exploring," I stammered, my recent conversation with Jane still ringing in my ears. I wasn't going to mention Zane, Jane or the faded Pooka woman in the Colorman's presence—or indeed, at all. Dad didn't like to be told stuff he shouldn't know. Swatchmen could sometimes tread fine lines of conflicted loyalty between Council and family, and deniability helped.

"This is His Colorfulness Matthew Gloss," remarked Dad, turning to the Colorman, "before he was elevated to National Color, he was a Russett—*distantly* related."

I shook hands in something of a daze—I'd not met someone with the title "Colorfulness" before. It was a title rarely bestowed. I couldn't stare openmouthed for long, however, as Dad said we should be leaving.

We crossed the river to the safety of the opposite bank, with myself and Dad carrying the Caravaggio and the Colorman with the stack of swatches Dad had liberated. Once there, we took the time to size each other up more carefully. Matthew Gloss was a relaxed-looking gent of late middle age with a craggy timeworn face. What little hair he did have was wispy and stuck out in many directions, and his ears seemed inordinately large.

"You say you're from East Carmine?" he said, once more fulsome introductions were finally over. "Not on foot, surely?"

Dad explained that we had a Ford and suggested that he join us for the trip back, to which the Colorman readily agreed, as he had just pushed his bicycle across the roadless gap that began at the remote pump station at Yerwood, six miles away, and he could do with a break.

We sat on a wall to wait for Fandango, and the Colorman told us he was doing a pipeline inspection because Camberwick Red had been receiving their grid magentas at greatly reduced chroma, and that suggested a fracture somewhere in the network of feed pipes.

"It's not an easy job, either," he added, "the grid's full of disused spur lines, most of which are unmapped."

Fandango arrived soon after, having fortunately started the Ford without trouble, and after more introductions, we headed back toward East Carmine, complete with sixty-seven swatches, a cure for the sniffles, a Caravaggio, a traveling Colorman with a twenty-one-speed bicycle and the knowledge that Jane would finally tell me what was going on.

Quarantine

5.2.03.01.002: Any resident who has even been indirectly
exposed to Mildew *must* follow quarantine procedures.

The janitor brought the Ford to a stop on a curved bluff next to the weathered WELCOME TO EAST CARMINE sign. We were within easy sight of the village, less than a mile away, and Fandango flashed a Morse code mirror-message that we had returned, were safe and well and had picked up a traveler. The lightning lookout flashed back that the message had been received, and confirmed that our quarantine would end at midday. If we were infected with Mildew, we would certainly show symptoms within two hours.

The morning was hot, so we sat under a nearby tree while Fandango brewed some tea on an oil stove and the Colorman told us about his career, which sounded forty times better than managing a stringworks. I listened with rapt attention as he spoke of the burning and intractable issues of the day with a sense of authority that I'd not heard before.

He told us that the Saturation Dispersion Index—known to all and sundry simply as the Fade—would doubtless continue to rise, which was glum news indeed. Mailboxes that had been typically painted once every half century now needed a new coat *every decade*. It placed an intolerable strain on limited pigment resources, and caused an increased demand for scrap.

"Is there any truth to the rumor that too much viewing accelerates the Fade?" I asked, as much had been written about the subject, and not all of it sensible.

"None at all," said the Colorman. "In fact, I would recommend as much viewing as possible, to get the most out of the synthetic color before it goes."

"Surely," said Dad, "increased yield of the color harvest will take care of the shortfall?"

The Colorman told us that peak production was long past, and unless new toshing fields were opened up within the unspoiled Great Southern Conurbation, synthetic color might be rationed even more than it was.

"What about the Riffraff?" I asked, since if it weren't for their continued occupation within the Inner Boundary and the problems crossing the hundred-yard-wide Zone of Disagreeability, the rich toshing fields of the Great Southern Conurbation would have been open long ago.

"Aggressive use of Variant-R Mildew," said the Colorman in a low voice, "and if what I hear is correct, something like that will be happening quite soon."

"How would such an action be framed?" asked my father, since the Rules *specifically* forbade the harming of any human, no matter how base their personal hygiene, habits or quality of speech. And *Homo feralensis*, although undeniably primitive, were definitely human.

"That's the clever part," said the Colorman. "The depredations they wreak upon the landscape and crops allow them to be reclassified as vermin—and thus within the scope of Rules regarding eradication." He laughed and added, "Loopholery at its finest."

Dad and I exchanged glances but made no comment. I couldn't deny that Riffraff were little more than walking biohazards, but once Mildew touches your family, you never wish it on anyone—not Yellows, not unpopular prefects, not even the Riffraff.

Sensing our nonalignment with his strident views, the Colorman moved his conversation to safer territory and outlined his recent work at East Park, one of the three truly great gardens within the Collective.

"I heard it was spectacular," said Dad, who was something of a Chromobotanist. "I'd like to go and view it one day."

"It's more magnificent than you can possibly imagine," replied the Colorman. "Full CYM feed boosted to eighty pounds' pressure. We can achieve chroma and brightness at almost sixty percent, and anything off-gamut is hand tinted. They don't just stick to the Botanical Swatch, either—intermediaries, secondaries, triadics—an infinite blaze of subtle hues that enliven the spirit and banish greyness from the soul. The lupin beds are particularly fine, and last time I counted, we used eighty-four different shades of pink alone."

For the next hour or so we listened to him talk about the problems with the grid and the color shortage, which was unnerving. He reiterated his opinions about the as-yet-untapped Great Southern Conurbation, but also made comment that there was a huge quantity of undiscovered scrap color under the soil, as the Age of Geniality had laid a blanket of calming soil and leaf mold atop the Age of Intolerance, and it just needed skilled toshers to tease it out. He and Dad then talked about the pros and cons of opencast and drift mining in tosh pits, and how National Color were looking at ways to make univisual hues from natural pigments and had even managed, using a form of Chromosynthesis, to liberate a pale shade of synthetic orange from carrots.

"Eight tons for a spoonful of enriched univisual orange that's barely sixteen percent chroma," said the Colorman. "It's not great, but the tech boys haven't given up."

I didn't get the opportunity to creep away and meet with Jane until Fandango handed me the Ford's water can and told me to get it filled. I set off through a grove of oaks for the river.

I'd liked what I'd heard from the Colorman. Working at National Color was every resident's dream, but few managed to make the grade. Every year they inducted fewer than four out of a thousand candidates. It was a dream, but as dreams go, the best: senior monitor status, unfettered movement around the Collective on an All Stations Super Season Apex, legal use of Leapback, requisition powers over any Ford and—best of all—surrounded by synthetic color at all times. The only snag was that even if you *did* have the qualifications and 60 percent minimum perception, you had to be put forward for selection by a head prefect—and prefects liked to retain the high-receptors to assist with color sorting. I'd not really considered it as a career because it had seemed somewhat distant and impossible, but it was probably worth a try.

"Over here!"

I caught sight of Jane, who gave me a smile and a cheery wave. Delighted that she seemed to have changed her mind about me, I quickened my pace and was not more than twenty feet away when I stopped dead in my tracks.

"You did that on purpose, didn't you?" I said it between gritted teeth, not daring to move. The smile on her face had now gone.

"I did," she replied, "and now perhaps you'll tell me everything I want to know."

I had been lured onto the smooth, grass-covered area that is typical of the space beneath the spread of the yateveo. I looked nervously upward at the sinewy, barb-covered vines and thought of making a dash for it, hoping that the carnivorous tree had caught a deer earlier and was still sluggish, or that I was still "one trip in hand," as it took two triggered sensors to initiate a strike. But since I knew full well that a hungry yateveo could catch an antelope running at full tilt, I decided not to risk it.

"So," said Jane, walking up to the edge of the spread, "it's time to tell me what you know and, more important, who you've told."

"Listen," I said angrily, "don't you think this joke's gone far enough? Besides, you only said you'd kill me if I mentioned your nose, and I haven't mentioned it once."

In answer, she threw a stick at my feet. It hit a root sensor, and the yateveo raised its barbs in readiness to strike. One more hint of movement and I would be exactly where I am now—inside the digesting bulb with an assortment of corroded spoons, slowly losing consciousness and musing upon how I got there.

"Are you mad?" I exclaimed. "You can't kill me!"

"I'm not going to kill you," she replied. "The yateveo is. A tragic, tragic accident. After the mourning is over—perhaps tomorrow at tea time—you'll get your name on the departures board, along with anything notable or worthy you might have done. Have you *actually* done anything noble or worthy, by the way?"

"Given the opportunity of a long life," I answered slowly, "I might."

"Good try, but no deal. Now, tell me what you know."

I took a deep breath. It was time to come clean.

"I don't know anything," I told her, relieved to be able to finally tell the truth. "The 'shamefully ludicrous idiot who fancies you' act *wasn't* an act. Yes, I'm curious about what you and Zane were up to, but it's nothing more. All I really want to do is have tea with you, and perhaps pretend that there is a viable alternative to a life of string manufacture with the Oxbloods."

"No one can be that deluded," she replied, looking around for another stick to trigger the yateveo. "Did you see the unfinished ceiling in the town hall?"

"Yes."

"Did your father?"

"I don't think so."

"Did you see anything else?"

"Somebody faded."

"Did they tell you anything?"

"No—but she wanted to."

"Hmm. And how did you know to visit Zane's place?"

"Dad gave me his spoon," I said with a nervous squeak in my voice. "It had his postcode engraved on the back."

Jane stared at me for a moment, then shook her head sadly. "So you really are as stupid as you look?"

"I'm far more stupid than that," I assured her, "but then curiosity has *always* gotten me into trouble. You should have heard Old Man Magenta sound off when I tried to improve queuing."

"Normally I would tend to look on curiosity with favor," she said, "but I think this time it's far safer to just have you eaten. Unless, of course, you can think of a good reason why I shouldn't?"

The very real possibility of death focuses the mind wonderfully. Chasing an intriguing Grey girl with a retroussé nose was as pointless as her killing me now. But all was not lost. I still had something to barter with. Perhaps the *only* thing I had ever had to barter with—here or anywhere else.

"Listen," I said, "I have no idea what you're up to, and it's none of my business. You can kill me if you want, but it's just possible I might turn out to be useful."

She laughed. "What makes you think you have anything that I could possibly want?"

"Your hair," I said. "It's red."

She stared at me. I had surprised her.

"Who told you that?"

I pointed to my eyes. I could see more red than most, and perhaps as much as any. Everyone would know for sure after my Ishihara on Sunday, but right now Jane needed to understand that I might one day be up the ladder. *I could be of use.* She cocked her head to one side and stared at me. I could see that my plea was having an effect, so I told her I would be *so* unobtrusive from now on that "even the mice wouldn't see me."

"No," she said after a moment's thought, "I think you should carry on being curious. To keep the prefects distracted."

"Did I say unobtrusive? I actually meant annoyingly inquisitive."

"Annoyingly inquisitive is good—just not anywhere near me. Breathe a word about Zane, Rusty Hill or anything else and I'll make good on my promise. If you agree, nod your head."

I nodded my head, and she walked away without another word.

"Hey!" I said, although not *too* loud, as a yateveo can sense vibrations. "What about me?"

But she had gone. I looked nervously around at the barbed vines, which were still poised, ready to strike if I moved even a muscle.

"Plums," I said to myself.

Heading Home

n case you're confused, don't be. This *wasn't* the time that Jane had
me eaten by a yateveo—that comes later. As far as carnivorous trees
go, she and I have some past history, and none of it good. Or at least,
not for me.

It took thirty-eight minutes for Dad and Fandango to finally come and
look for me, and when they found me, I was all sweaty, with tremors in
my leg muscles. They were more amused than concerned.

"Well, well," said Dad with a faint snigger, "outwitted by a tree, Eddie
my lad?" He kept his voice low, and trod carefully.

"Sweet revenge for all those crackling log fires," added Fandango.
"Where's my water can?"

"It's over there. Can you do something? I'm beginning to get cramps."

Dad walked quietly to the other side of the tree, then rolled a log into
the area under the spread. With lightning speed the yateveo's barbed
vines dove down, grabbed the log, whisked it high up into the canopy,
paused for a moment and then flung it off into the forest, where we
heard it land with a distant thump. The tree looked large enough to
multiple-strike, so after waiting a minute or two for the vines to settle,
Dad rolled a second log in, and the branches again descended, but this

155

time slower. By the fourth log the barbs were striking at a decidedly languid pace, and I simply walked out, easily dodging the vines as they made a lazy swipe in my direction.

"I got caught by one once," said the Colorman a few minutes later, once they'd had a good laugh at my expense. "I wouldn't be here now if there hadn't been several people half digested beneath me. Mind you," he added, "if you *do* get eaten, upside down is the way you want to be—it's all over quicker."

"I'll remember that," I said grumpily. "Thank you very much."

"You're welcome. Oh, and you missed a pair of rhinosauruses, by the way. Crossed the road about thirty yards away. I logged their codes if you want them."

Ordinarily, missing megafauna might have been annoying. But I had a lot more on my mind. Most important was how I should leave Jane well alone and concentrate on winning Constance and getting away from East Carmine just as quickly as I could. I'd throw in some misdirected curiosity, too, just to keep Jane happy.

About three-quarters of the way through the quarantine, Dad ran through the list of *specifically* Rot-like symptoms, such as accelerated nail growth, numb elbows and a certain brittleness of the ears. None of us had any of those, so we knew by then that we were clear. Mildew makes itself known within two hours of infection. Sometimes sooner, but never later.

"I understand that you're taking your Ishihara with us?" asked Fandango once the quarantine period was up and we were heading back to East Carmine.

"It's a huge honor," I said, and meant it.

"My daughter Imogen is being shown the spots this year as well," he remarked. "She'll be quite Violet—a recessive throwback to a *very* purple maternal grandmother, you know."

"Is that so?" I said, recalling Tommo's accusation that Imogen was the product of purchased parentage at the Green Dragon. "You must be very proud."

"We are *hugely* proud, and want only the best for her. Speaking of which, you don't know any Purples who are a bit slack-hued but rolling in moolah? I've had a bit of interest, but nothing terribly exciting—mostly Lilac lowbies wanting to pay in bouncing goats."

I thought of Bertie Magenta. His smarter, elder and Purpler sister would inherit Old Man Magenta's Synthetic Pigment Enrichment Plant and the head prefecture. Bertie had scored a dismal 53 percent Purple on his Ishihara last year, and had a brain the size of a broad bean. Despite this and solely due to his hue, he would live a very comfortable life. If his sister married away and no higher Purple arrived, he might even make head prefect—which was a chilling thought right there all on its own.

"Does he have to be at all smart?" I asked.

"If he's got the cash, I'm not bothered."

"I know this fellow," I said, "not the sharpest banana in the bunch. In fact, some might say he has the mind of a clodworm. But his father is the head prefect."

"Totally perfect!" said Carlos with a grin. "Two percent finder's fee, lad."

"How does Imogen feel about it?"

"She'll do what we think is best," replied Fandango in a tone of voice that I didn't much care for. "Besides, an engagement will bring closure to an unsuitable *attachment.* You could compose a telegram to your friend, speaking of Imogen's dazzling attributes. You might like to mention that she's willing to offer any serious purchaser an evening on appro. I'll get a photograph and a list of her virtues to you just as soon as I can."

He took my silence as agreement and patted me on the shoulder. Although I couldn't be sure, I thought he'd just offered to broker his own daughter for some youknow with Bertie, a slack-hued cash machine he knew nothing about. I shook my head. He *couldn't* have. He must have meant a meal or something.

"Twenty-nine miles," Fandango announced sadly as we pulled up outside the stockwall gates to smarten ourselves up and put our spots back on. "If we pile on the mileage at this rate, the Ford will be worn out in less than two centuries."

Lucy, Violet and Daisy

5.1.02.12.023: It is a condition of custodianship that all paintings, sculptures and other works of art must be shown to any resident on demand.

The word that a Colorman had arrived swiftly got about, and by the time I escorted him to our house, a gaggle of inquisitive villagers had collected to stare. Not just at *him*, but the gears on his bicycle and his richly colorful coveralls. In the relative drabness of East Carmine, he shone like a beacon of hope—an example of how colorful the world *could* look, if only we could afford the pigment, and had time and opportunity to collect the scrap.

"You're very popular," I said, showing him upstairs to his room.

"It's National Color they're fascinated by," he replied. "I've seen people commit unspeakable acts simply to secure a colored orchid. Do you have an interest in color, lad?"

"My shade of mustard won best runner-up at Jollity Fair last year," I said, honored to be given the opportunity to boast. "I went for a darker shade than the others: 33-71-67."

"Hmm," said the Colorman, expertly visualizing the color in his head, "not bad. Tell me, what would we use to stain a primrose?"

"62-62-98, sir."

"And a carrot?"

"31-87-97."

He was impressed. "You know your colors."

"My mentor was a retired mixer," I explained. "Greg Scarlet."

"I met him once or twice," replied the Colorman thoughtfully. "Fine chap. Perhaps you and I should speak again. Undo my shoelaces and take off my boots, would you? Let me give you my laundry—and please, call me Matthew."

I delivered the painting as soon as I had dealt with the Colorman's laundry and changed into more appropriate day clothes. Red Prefect Yewberry seemed happier than anyone I'd ever seen before when I handed over the Caravaggio.

"We'll lodge it with the Cochineals," he announced, staring in admiration at the canvas. "They've already got a van Gogh and know how to look after these things. I may have it copied into a painting-by-numbers, and have it painted with synthetics so all may gaze upon its splendor."

"Our Mrs. Alder has *The Shipwreck of the Minotaur* on her upstairs landing," I said, eager not to be outdone, "and Ruth G-9 has a Renoir."

"You should have a look at our Vermeer," replied Yewberry. "It's in the Greyzone, but you might persuade one of them to escort you in and out."

At a few minutes to one I wandered across to the town hall. The Rules didn't state which meal was mandatory, but it was always lunch. Lucy Ochre was one of the few faces I recognized among the many who were milling about outside, chatting cross-hue before we were confined to our tables. Luckily, the presence of the Colorman seemed to have eclipsed the news about my run-in with the yateveo.

"Hullo!" I said, but Lucy looked at me blankly.

"It's Eddie Russett."

"Sorry," she said, "I was miles away. Thanks for your help with the Lincoln this morning. I might have to ask for it back, though. Mummy will notice it's gone."

"I destroyed it." It was a lie, I know, but it was probably for the best. "I'll tell her that Tommo stole it—I need a good reason to keep him out of the house."

I asked her in the most delicate way possible about her father, and she told me that he liked his Lincoln but never abused the Green Room.

"I don't know what he was doing in there," she said, "but he didn't misdiagnose—and he certainly wasn't Chasing the Frog."

She fell into thoughtful silence, so I decided to change the subject. "I brought you this—*as requested*," I remarked, handing her the spoon

I had liberated from Rusty Hill. I'd wrapped it in an odd sock in case anyone saw. Given the value of spoons, an ugly custom had arisen whereby a spoon might be swapped for youknow, tarnishing the once romantic nature of spoon gifting. "Accepting a spoon" was now a pejorative term and an ugly slur on one's integrity, which was why I had prefaced the gift with "as requested."

"Oh!" she said. "Is that what I think it is?"

I nodded, and she told me I was a darling. "What can I do to repay you?"

"*Absolutely* nothing," I assured her in case my intent was misconstrued. "It's simply a gift."

"What's going on here?" asked Tommo, who had suddenly appeared, and seemed to be taking issue with our talking to each other.

"Eddie was giving me a spoon," said Lucy in an innocent fashion.

"*What?!*"

"The *utensil,* Tommo."

"Oh," he said, calming down, "right."

"Silly me," said Lucy. "I must be more careful with my words."

We sat at the same red-hued table we had used at breakfast, and Lucy fell into conversation with a girl at the other end. I couldn't hear what they said, but they pointed at me and giggled.

"Listen here," said Tommo, "you haven't got a thing for Lucy, have you?"

"Absolutely not."

"Hmm," he said, then: "Still got your eyes on Crazy Jane for a bit of slap and tickle?"

"No—I think it would be mostly slap and very little tickle."

"In that I think you might be correct. How was Rusty Hill?"

"Exciting," I told him, and gave him a rundown of everything that had happened in the twenty-eight minutes I had spent there. The legion of the dead, the rotting fabric of the village, the Caravaggio, the color hydrant and the Colorman. I left out the bit about Jane, Zane and the Pooka, but it didn't matter, since none of it interested him anyway.

"Did you get me my size-nine boots?"

"Here," I said, handing him a paper bag that contained the shoes I had pulled from the dead prefect's feet. "Sorry—I didn't realize at the time how stinky they were."

"I see what you mean," replied Tommo as he wrinkled his nose and plucked off a shriveled toe that was stuck to the insole. "Couldn't you have swiped me a pair from his wardrobe?"

"That would be stealing."

He leaned across and dropped the toe into the water jug. "You're a bit odd, Eddie, did you know that?"

Other Reds soon started arriving at the table, and they nodded politely as I was introduced. I didn't know any of them, but they knew me well enough. I would have liked my fame to be somehow related to the retrieval of the Caravaggio or being distantly related to the Color-man—or even to seeing the Last Rabbit. But it wasn't. I was the one who not only had risked my hide to help a Yellow, but was also "so stupid he nearly got himself eaten by a yateveo."

"Who's that?" I asked Tommo as a severe-looking woman entered the room.

"Mrs. deMauve. If I said she was a Pooka in human form, I would be doing all Pookas a grave injustice. Although not part of the village Coun-cil, she still wields a lot of power. But don't let her airs fool you—she was born a Navy and is Purple by marriage only. The odious creature follow-ing her is their daughter, Violet deMauve. A frightful troublemaker, and confidently touted as the next head prefect. Don't catch her eye."

It was too late. Violet saw Tommo and me talking, and she skipped over to us in an affected little-girl manner. She wore her hair in bunches, which made her look younger than she was, and although her face was tolerable, it was tipped into ordinariness by an inconsequential nose—all snub and hardly-there-at-all. Like Courtland, the Yellow prefect's son, she had a large collection of merit badges pinned on her clothes.

"You must be the Russett fellow," she said in an almost accusatory fashion while running an eye down my badges and catching sight of the punishment badge. "You need humility, do you?"

"So my Council believed."

"A thousand merits, eh?" she said, looking at the better half of my badge collection.

"As you see."

"What ho, Violet," Tommo remarked. "Strangled any small, furry woodland creatures recently?"

She stared at him coldly for a moment before turning back to me. "I'm Violet," she said, putting on her best smile and sitting between us, so we both had to shuffle aside to let her in. "Violet *deMauve,* and if you are very, very lucky, I might make you one of my friends—of which I have many. Some say, in fact, that I have more friends than anyone else in the village."

"I'm delighted at your good fortune," I replied.

"How nice of you! Let me see, now . . ." She took a notebook from the pocket in her pinafore, and flicked through the pages. "Since I already have the maximum friends permitted, I'm going to have to lose one to make room for you. Yes, Elizabeth Gold."

She put a line through Elizabeth's name, and wrote mine in above. I hadn't actually agreed to be her friend, and she hadn't asked. Purples generally assumed stuff like that.

"There!" she announced. "I never liked her sniveling anyway. Her feet splay outward, and she can barely tell a buttercup from a clover. Now, is it true you play the cello?"

"Only as far as the third string. I'm due to start mastering the fourth this summer."

"Excellent! You shall be in the orchestra for *Red Side Story*. I shall not be able to play, for I shall be taking the lead role. It means playing a Green, but we dedicated thespians place art above personal ridicule." She narrowed her eyes and stared at me. "*You* will not ridicule me, I trust?"

"Not at all—I once played Nathan in *Greys and Dolls*."

"How hideously embarrassing," she said with a laugh. "You must have felt a complete idiot. Now—do you see much red?"

The question was a predictable one. Tommo had said Mrs. deMauve was a Navy, so Violet would be right at the blue end of purple. For the deMauves to stay at the top of the stack, she needed the reddest husband she could find to get her progeny back on hue.

"Say no," said Tommo in an unsubtle whisper.

"Can it, Cinnabar. Well, Master Edward?"

I thought of lying and telling her I saw very little, but on reflection I didn't really feel I had to tell her simply because she *asked*. "I don't have to answer that question, Miss deMauve."

"You're mistaken," she said in a petulant voice. "You *do*. Now, what about it?"

We stared at each other for a moment or two, until Violet burst into laughter and pushed my shoulder playfully. "You Russetts! Always larking about. Don't forget the orchestra. Wednesday afternoons straight after tea. Oh, and by the by—there seems to be a toe in your water jug."

Another girl had arrived on the scene. She was of slighter build than

Violet, and looked as though she had been practicing hockeyball. I knew this because she was holding a hockeyball stick.

"Well, well," said Violet with a sneer, "Daisy Crimson. I hear you're to audition for the part of Maria—don't feel rejected when you fail to get it."

"I'm sorry," said Daisy, giving Violet a polite smile, "did you say something? I was thinking about sheep."

Violet smiled without any hint of joy and walked off, pushing against Daisy's shoulder as she did so.

"Well," said Daisy, sitting down and, after seeing the toe in the water jug, helping herself to Tommo's glass, "a hideous fate awaits anyone who marries *that*. Who's the favorite at the moment?"

"Your brother," said Tommo, "on even money."

"I'll have to take him to one side and have a word. Violet as my sister-in-law would be an unspeakable horror. Hello. I'm Daisy Crimson. You must be Edward."

Tommo nudged me, and I remembered that she and I were due to be married—according to Tommo's fantasy marriage league, anyway.

"Eddie," I said, shaking her hand. "Friend?"

"Friend."

She was actually rather pretty. She looked older than her years, with shoulder-length hair and a thin dappling of dark freckles across the bridge of her nose, which was, as Tommo had remarked, quite pointy.

"Double hoorah on the Caravaggio retrieval," she said. "Up until now the village has been a bit heavy on the Postimpressionists, and our Picasso is on loan to Yellowopolis, which is having a retrospective. Watch out for the deMauves, by the way—meddling with that bunch would be like eating a scorpion sandwich."

"That's what I like about this village," I observed. "Everybody is so nice to one another."

"She's right about the scorpion sandwich," Tommo put in. "That's why I didn't factor Violet into your marital-prospect rundown. Besides, Doug Crimson is our strongest Red—*he's* the one who's going to pull the short straw and have to slip the ring on her trotter."

"How does Doug feel about marrying into the deMauves?" I asked.

"Fervently hoping he has less red than he thinks," murmured Daisy, who undoubtedly had concerns for her brother.

I knew what she meant. Although no one could cheat the Ishihara, and most people had a *general* idea of what they could see, there were often surprises as recessive bestowals popped to the fore. Even children of longtime Greys could suddenly discover a perception they never knew they had. The yearly Ishihara tipped village politics on its head and kept the prefects on their toes—and relatively free from excess.

"Master Edward?" said a voice nearby. I turned to find a small girl aged no more than twelve holding a clipboard. She was smartly turned out and had a Yellow Spot with several honor badges next to a shiny SENIOR JUNIOR MONITOR badge.

"Hello," I said in a friendly manner. "What can I help you with, little girl?"

"You can help me by canning the patronizing backchat—unless you want my thumb jabbed in your eye."

My face dropped.

"You couldn't reach," Tommo retorted. "We're both here, so why don't you just tick the stupid lunch register and toddle along?"

"You have to say 'Here' *after* I've called your name. It's the Rules. If you don't want to do it my way I'll simply report you for obstructing a monitor, and you can explain yourself to a prefect."

"Bog off, girlie," he growled, "and when you've done that, bog off again—and then a third time, in case the first two were ineffective."

She narrowed her eyes, glowered for a moment and then walked off.

"Penelope is the youngest Gamboge," Tommo explained, "Courtland's niece and the Yellow prefect's granddaughter. She hasn't got as much Yellow as those two, but enough to make her troublesome."

A few minutes later, Penelope returned with her Yellow prefect grandmother in tow.

"What's going on here?" demanded Mrs. Gamboge, and we all dutifully stood.

"Thomas Cinnabar denied the protocol," the odious child gushed self-righteously, "and then told me to bog off—three times."

"I'm proud to plead guilty to the bog-off thing," Tommo said cheerfully, "but I'd like to apologize unreservedly to Miss Penelope under Article Forty-two *and* plead fair comment under Rule 6.3.22.02.044."

"Agreed," replied Gamboge, who must also have thought Penelope something of a pest. "You will be penalized only five merits, for failing to respect the authority of a lunch register monitor. Do you even *have* any merits, Cinnabar?"

"One hundred and eight below zero, ma'am."

"Then you'd better do something to redeem yourself between now and your Ishihara on Sunday, hmm?"

Penelope was grinning broadly, and had brought out her book so she could be awarded the half merit as bounty. Gamboge told Tommo to pull up his socks and departed, with Penelope skipping along at her heels.

"Was that really worth it?" I asked as we sat again.

"Sure," said Tommo with a grin. He handed Penelope's pencil to a nearby confederate, who put it in his pocket and walked briskly away. "Watch our little friend now."

We both turned to look at Penelope Gamboge, just as she realized that she had lost her pencil. She looked in all her pockets, then started searching the floor with increased desperation.

"Two demerits for losing Council property," mused Tommo, "and another demerit for failing to complete the register in time. *Plus* I get fifty cents on the Beigemarket for the pencil."

I laughed.

"So," Daisy resumed, jerking a thumb in my direction, "who's Russett going to marry?"

"Tommo has a vibrant imagination," I said. "As soon as I've counted all the chairs, I'll be off, so it's a bit moot, to be honest."

"Eddie here will be *your* husband, Daze," said Tommo.

She laughed, and I felt uncomfortable. "Don't sweat it," she said, placing a warm hand on the back of mine. "It's only Tommo's bit of fun. Marry who you want—or don't. As you please."

If only it were that simple. She gave me a good-natured wink, thought for a moment and then said, "But just out of curiosity, who do I have to *theoretically* battle for Russett's *conjectural* affections?"

"Tommo's sister," I said.

"Tommo doesn't have a sister," said Daisy.

"I added her for accounting purposes in my fantasy marriage league," he confessed breezily. "Cassie doesn't have a brother either, and Simone, Lisa, Torquil and Geoff all have existence issues. But it increases the size of the marriage market and gives us the illusion of increased choice."

"For which," added Daisy with a smile, "we are all extremely grateful."

"Actually, Daisy dear," said Tommo, "Eddie's turning out surprisingly well. I was going to reserve final judgment on his nuptials until we witness his performance at the boys-versus-girls hockeyball match."

"Pardon?" I asked, this being the first I'd heard of it.

"It's a yearly East Carmine tradition," explained Tommo. "We just let them win, and they go away happy."

Daisy looked at me and raised her eyebrows. "In truth," she said, "we thrash you all to within an inch of your worthless lives—the humiliation is delightful. Excuse me. I need to speak to someone before deMauve starts to bore our chops off."

"What do you think?" asked Tommo as soon as she had left.

"She seems very pleasant."

"You see? I told you I was good at this marriage-guidance lark."

"Hello," said a pale youth as he sat down next to me. "I'm Doug, Daisy's brother. I understand you're going to marry my sister?"

"According to Tommo."

"You won't be disappointed," he assured me. "A fine sense of humor and a terrific kisser—if a little too much tongue for my taste."

I must have looked shocked, for he stifled a laugh and was nudged by the fellow next to him, whereupon they both started shaking with suppressed mirth at the joke. I was going to say something dazzlingly amusing and erudite in reply, but I couldn't think of anything, so instead just grinned with affected good humor.

"Whose toe is this?" asked Doug when a small black object plopped into his glass as he poured himself some water.

"Tommo's."

He picked it out and slipped it into someone else's mug farther down the table.

"Good afternoon, Edward."

Dad had just arrived at the table, and he wasn't alone. He was with a woman about his age, that is to say, in her late forties. She was wearing a dazzlingly bright red dress that sparkled when she moved—she was liberally draped with jewelry, bright red gemstones in silver settings. Her outfit probably contravened several dress codes and anti-showiness directives, but I couldn't see anyone truly complaining, as she looked magnificent.

"Good afternoon, sir," I replied politely, since the prearranged "Edward" code meant he was with a lady he was trying to impress.

"This is Mrs. Ochre," my father explained, "an old friend."

"Good afternoon," I said, thinking her mode of dress was an odd way to show mourning, unless that was what was meant by the black velvet choker around her neck.

"She's asked us to join the Chromogentsia this evening for the Debating Society meeting," continued my father.

Since I wasn't yet Ishiharaed, I didn't officially have the 50 percent-plus perception required to join the Chromogentsia. But children of members

166

were allowed to attend in order to help out, since Greys were barred, lest listening in to the Debating Society's conversations "gave them ideas."

"I accept," I said politely. "Thank you very much."

She seemed pleasant enough, if a mite flirty and not a little over-dressed. I didn't think it would help if I remarked how saturated her daughter had been that morning, so instead I just said I was pleased to make her acquaintance and was sorry for her loss. She thanked me and said the Debating Society would look forward to meeting us—and could I bring a rice pudding?

The conversation ended with the raucous sound of hundreds of chairs being pushed out, as anyone who was sitting down suddenly stood up and shuffled to find the correct place when deMauve and the other Council members filed in. I let myself be guided by the shuffle and ended up at the end of the table with Tommo to one side and Doug on the other.

DeMauve

1.03.02.13.114: Pocket handkerchiefs are to be changed
daily, and are to be kept folded, even when in the pocket.
Handkerchiefs may be patterned.

"Good afternoon to you all," the head prefect began. He was
greeted with a murmured "Good afternoon" in return, the
three thousand or so bored voices a low rumble in the hall. He
was actually a long way away, but a large voice trumpet was
suspended from the ceiling in front of him, and he spoke into that. Old
Man Magenta's voice was so loud, he never needed one.

I'd attended six and a half thousand assemblies in my life, and according to current longevity estimates, I would probably attend twenty-two
thousand more before I was done. They were tedious after the first couple
of hundred, and none but the Yellows really paid any attention past the
thousandth. For the rest of us, assembly was just a hole in your lifetime,
wrapped in boredom. Whispering, dozing, prodding one another and
passing notes were so utterly forbidden that they simply weren't worth
the risk, so the majority of villagers used assembly as a time for silent
contemplation. Fenton claimed to have learned to sleep with his eyes
open, which would have been useful if it were true. I just used the time
for doing mental arithmetic, refining my theories about enhanced queuing or trying to figure out a loophole plausible enough to enable me to go
into the potentially profitable spoon business. It had been tried before,
but never successfully. Randolph Aubergine had attempted to market

"half-scale models" of garden trowels, but the concept didn't pass the strict Rule Compliance Procedures, and the idea was abandoned.

My reverie was interrupted by deMauve, who had announced my name. I looked up guiltily to find everyone staring at me.

". . . the Russetts have come all the way from Jade-under-Lime, in Green Sector West," continued the head prefect. "I'm sure you will join me in welcoming them to our humble community, and offering them assistance in whatever way possible."

He went on to explain how my father and I had ignored the substantial dangers in the trip to Rusty Hill, and how the Caravaggio would be having its official redisplaying celebration on Friday. Those who were still paying attention—quite a few of them, it seemed—applauded dutifully as we stood up to be recognized, and Dad and I nodded politely in return.

I decided it was probably best to listen to what was going on and leave my cutlery-inspired daydreaming for another day. DeMauve ran through news that, while pertinent to the village, was of little interest to me: Linoleum production was being cut due to deflation, and while bad news for the village profit-and-loss sheet—the color garden would be insipid within a month—it was good news for the Greys. Or at least, it would have been if the Council hadn't also decided to cultivate another nine acres of glasshouse. By the mutterings on the Grey tables, it seemed that factory work, despite the industrial accidents, was still preferable to growing pineapples.

DeMauve paused for a moment, then turned over his notepad. As he did so, the door creaked open. The prefects looked up angrily to see who had dared to enter once assembly was in progress, but they all relaxed when they saw it was the Apocryphal man. He was covered in dried mud, was wearing only socks and carried a string bag with apples in it. He meandered over to the serving table, helped himself to a plate of rolls, then walked back out. DeMauve simply ignored him, and carried on as though he weren't there.

"Many of you will know that the Great Western Pipeline was laid as far as Rusty Hill," he continued. "As I have intimated in the past, I have been in correspondence with Head Office to see if the spur line might be continued all the way to East Carmine, and thus bring us within the National Colorization Program."

Excited murmurings followed this statement as the residents mulled over the Chromatic riches this would involve. Not just a small garden, but the whole area surrounding the village—the trees, grass and flowers. It would place East Carmine on the map and possibly, if its luck *really* held, enable it to host another Jollity Fair.

"This very day," deMauve continued, "we have received a visit from a representative of National Color, and although what he has to tell us is not *precisely* what we might have liked, he does offer a possible solution to our request. I will let His Colorfulness fill you in."

The Colorman stood up and joined deMauve at the lectern. His voice was more authoritarian than deMauve's, but it wouldn't have mattered if it had been ridiculously high and squeaky. This was, after all, a man from National Color. He represented freedom from a drab world, and the Word of Munsell personified. Everyone was in awe of National Color— even, it was said, Head Office.

Jade-under-Lime was already on the network, so I remained unexcited by the possibility. I wasn't the only one. I flicked a surreptitious look at Jane, who was staring at the table and scratching a bit of crud off her knife with a fingernail.

"Thank you for affording me the hospitality of your village," the Colorman began. "I am humbled by the kindness you have shown me, and honored to be conducting the Ishihara on Sunday for the eight residents who have reached their twentieth year and are ready to begin discharging their Civil Obligation to society in a productive and meaningful fashion."

It was a good opener, and safe. Nothing controversial. He had everyone's attention, and after outlining how every village was deserving of National Color's fullest consideration in the pursuit of full colorization, he went on to describe the work that was being undertaken on everyone's behalf, and how color was a privilege that had to be earned, not a right to be expected. It sounded like a speech he had given many times, as he doubtless had, since all villages wanted pretty much the same thing—more color. It was only in his final sentence that he got down to realities:

"Crucially, connection to the grid relates to your scrap-color collection numbers, which I am sorry to say have fallen far short of the target." He directed this comment at the prefects, who looked uneasy. "If deliveries to Central Recycling can be stepped up," he carried on, "National Color will happily reevaluate your submission at a later date."

He thanked us for our time, was greeted with applause, then returned to his seat.

"Our thanks go to His Colorfulness for his words and thoughts on the subject," said deMauve, who had retaken his place at the lectern, "and I want to make perfectly clear that our missed targets do not reflect upon the toshers, washers, sorters and packers who have been doing sterling work for many years. No, the problem is twofold: increased Fade, which is out of our hands, and lack of raw material, which we might be able to do something about."

He paused for effect.

"That is why, with Harmony, Little Carmine and Great Auburn all worked out, we have decided to relax the Rules on how far toshing parties may go. As of today, High Saffron is once again within limits."

I wasn't sure what he was talking about, but by the murmuring around the hall, it seemed to be something that generated universal unease. I caught Dad's eye, and he shrugged; he didn't know either. But deMauve hadn't finished. Before toshing parties were consigned to High Saffron, a comprehensive study needed to be carried out of the terrain and scrap-color potential, ease of extraction and so forth—and he needed volunteers to go over there and have an initial look.

"Since the Rules state," he continued, "that full disclosure of the risks must be divulged, I have to report that we have sent eighty-three explorers to High Saffron over the past half century, and all of them failed to return. Obviously," he added, "the village is prepared to be generous in these matters. One hundred merits have been allocated for those who undertake this hazardous duty. *After* they return," he added, in case anyone was thinking of having a splurge on some up-front cash. "So—any takers?"

Unsurprisingly, he wasn't swamped by volunteers. In fact, the room was so quiet you might have heard a drop of paint splash.

"Very well," said deMauve. "I will leave you to muse on it and contact me directly."

He spoke a bit more about auditions for *Red Side Story*, related the news that Travis Canary was missing, presumed Nightloss, then gave the usual warnings about potential swan attack and Lightning Avoidance Drill. After that, he paused briefly to gather his thoughts.

"Today's lesson is from Munsell's *Book of Truth*, chapter nine."

"This is where we'd use the Redlax," whispered Tommo as deMauve opened the heavy book on the lectern. I had to admit that it would be quite a prank, and at least make one of my twenty-eight thousand assemblies truly memorable.

Six thousand eyes began to glaze over as deMauve began, and three thousand heads filled with thoughts regarding other matters—of perhaps one day owning a personal color garden, or maybe a spoon; of the spouses they'd most like to have, then the ones they'd probably end up with. The words had been read so often and so fervently that they'd lost all meaning and were now just an annoying hum.

It was a reading from "Abominations," and after deMauve had droned on about the sin of waste, poor hygiene, bad manners and overpopulation, he got to the nonconjoinment of complementary colors. That was at least amusing, because he referred to youknow by its forbidden name, which always made the juniors giggle.

Fortunately, deMauve read only a short extract. I think that, like us, he was hungry and just wanted to check off all the boxes and get on with it. After we recited *Richly hued be those who are worthy to enjoy the balance of Chromatic Harmony* and murmured *Apart We Are Together,* we sat and waited while the dinner monitors brought tureens of lamb casserole to each table, along with baskets of rolls and dishes of vegetables that had been overcooked perfectly. I have to report that the food was considerably better in East Carmine than in Jade-under-Lime, although table manners were markedly worse.

"I have a toe in my water," said a young lad named Arnold.

"Treat it politely," said Tommo with a smile. "It might be a prefect's."

Talk soon got around to Travis Canary's walkout. The prefects had vetoed a search on the grounds of "wasted effort," but on reflection, I wasn't surprised Canary had done a runner. If he'd wanted to go to Reboot, he would have stayed on the train.

"No one ever gets lost at night and returns," observed Daisy, "except Jane, of course."

I tried not to appear interested.

"Went missing for three days and nights," whispered Doug, "eighteen months ago. She wouldn't say what had happened to her or where she had been—just said she couldn't remember anything until she wandered back into the village." He leaned closer. "Her clothes were torn and she had lost her shoes—feet badly cut."

"She hasn't really been the same since," remarked Daisy. "Before, she was weird but relatively calm. After—well, are you playing in our annual hockeyball thrashing?"

"I guess."

"Then you'll find out. If Jane looks like she's going to tackle you, just let her have the ball and run the other way. Courtland tried to demerit her for a dress code infraction once and she went for him."

"In what way?"

"Attacked," said Cassie, speaking for the first time, "and rightly so. Courtland's a beast and a liar."

"She went for his eyes," added Arnold, "gouged his cheek so hard he needed nine stitches. She's for Reboot the day after her Ishihara, no doubt about it. And if you ask me, the best place for her. If there is anyone who most represents the dis-words, it's her: disruption, disharmony and discourtesy—she's got the lot."

The conversation turned to High Saffron's having been opened to toshing, and how the Council had shown unparalleled optimism in thinking that anyone would risk almost certain death to go there.

"It's a large town to the west of here," Tommo explained, "on the coast. It's been abandoned since the Something That Happened, so is totally ripe for mining—raw scrap lying around in abundance, of a hue so bright even the lowbies can see it. Spoons, too, they say—and parrots of a color that *everyone* can see."

"How is that possible?" asked Daisy, and Tommo shrugged.

Apparently, an attempt to build a road to High Saffron had been abandoned thirty years ago. Of the eighty-three who had been lost to the village's exploration in the past fifty years, half had been overnighters on the way to Reboot, who had undertaken the hazardous duty in return for enough merits to buy themselves out of their below-zero merit status. But those willing to have a crack at High Saffron were fewer and fewer these days. Considering the odds, the Night Train suddenly looked quite attractive.

"I think it was flying monkeys that got them all," said Arnold.

"You're right," said Doug with a sigh, "that's exactly what got them—and they'll get you, too, if you don't hang some spinach in your wardrobe."

Arnold sensed he was being mocked and fell silent. Flying monkeys were like Pookas, Khan, Freddie and the Hairy Irrational—something parents used to frighten small children who weren't yet able to grasp the concept of Rules, Hierarchy or merits.

"Has anyone here actually seen a Pooka?" I asked.

"They say Rusty Hill's full of them," said Doug, pulling a face. "Echoes of the Previous."

"I've heard some good Pooka stories," said Arnold, "I sometimes frighten myself when I'm telling them."

It was as I thought. Pookas were similar to masters and swans—often talked about, seldom seen. But I pushed them to the back of my mind. I was in no doubt that Jane would carry out her threat if I strayed from the path she had given me.

Dessert was prunes and custard. The prunes were as prunes are, but the custard was grey and unappetizing. Old Man Magenta might have been a colossal pain in the hoo-ha, but he always insisted that the custard was a bright synthetic yellow—sometimes paid for out of his own pocket. It was his single redeeming feature.

As it was being served, Bunty McMustard cast an imperious eye in our direction. At her own insistence, she was the permanent manners monitor. As she approached, the others at the table went quiet, sat up straight and tucked in their elbows. Instinctively, I joined them.

"Hair getting a bit long, Cinnabar?" she sneered.

"Bunty," said Tommo in an even tone, "I'm disgusted by your ugly face."

The whole table, and several about, suddenly went deathly quiet.

"*What* did you say?" said Bunty.

"I said, 'This custard, my, has a lovely taste.' Why, what did you think I said?"

She glared at him, then at us. We all looked back with expressions of innocence. She gave out a "harrumph" and walked off.

"You are *so* going to Reboot," muttered Daisy, who could hardly stop herself from giggling.

"Bunty's a hoo-ha," he replied. "Doug, did you manage to slip the toe into her pocket?"

He nodded, and we all burst out laughing.

Around the Village

1.1.01.01.002: The Word of Munsell shall be adhered to at all times.

O nce lunch was over I ambled off toward our house, hoping I might bump into the Colorman when he came home. I'd never met anyone from National Color who had deigned to speak to me before, and I wanted to try to milk the association for all it was worth.

"Master Edward?"

It was Stafford the porter, and he was holding a small envelope. It was a telegram from Constance, and it wasn't good news.

TO EDWARD RUSSETT RG6 7GD ++ EAST CARMINE RSW ++ FROM
CONSTANCE OXBLOOD SW3 6ZH ++ JADE UNDER LIME GSW ++ MSGE
BEGINS ++ ONLY FAIR TO SAY MUMMY AND I BOTH THOUGHT YOUR
POEM UTTER RUBBISH ++ ROGER HAS COMPOSED MUCH BETTER VIZ
OPEN QUOTES GLEEFUL DARTING OF THE HOUSE MARTINS SPREADING
JOY IN THE HEADY RITES OF SPRING CLOSE QUOTES ++ DO TRY HARDER
ANGEL DONT WORRY ABOUT ME ROGER TAKING ME BOATING ++ YRS
CONSTANCE ++ MSGE ENDS

I cursed and scrunched it up.

"Problems?" asked Stafford.

"You could say that. Roger can barely spell his own name, much less write poetry. That 'gleeful darting of the house martins' stuff sounds suspiciously like the work of Jade-under-Lime's resident verse mercenary, Gerald Henna-Rose."

Roger Maroon had decided to up the ante in my absence, so I would have to do likewise. I asked Stafford if there was anyone in the village who could write romantic poetry.

"But," I added, "it's got to be really good, and not too racy—Constance isn't one for overtly rude metaphors, worse luck."

"I think I know someone who might be able to help," returned Stafford, "but it won't come cheap. There are risks involved. You know how the prefects take a dim view of irresponsible levels of creative expression."

"Five percent finder's fee?"

"I'll see what I can do."

I pushed open our front door and checked the hall table to see if there were any messages. There was one from the persistent Dorian G-7 of the *Mercury* inviting me to give my account of the trip to Rusty Hill, several from Reds suggesting we become friends, and one from "the desk of Violet deMauve" reminding me of my obligations to the orchestra. There were several for my father, too, and Imogen Fandango's spousal information pack. The scrapbook contained a studio photograph of Fandango's daughter, who was, I had to admit, not unattractive in an upmarket perky-nose Purplish sort of way. Written testimonials were followed by a long list of her virtues, which numbered seventy-five. They began with a well-worded *implication* of her potentially high Ishihara rating, and ended with her wish to one day help represent East Carmine in the Jollity Fair unicycle relay. I put the details aside, and decided to wire Bertie Magenta first thing tomorrow morning. Fandango had been asking six thousand for Imogen, and a 2 percent finder's fee would be one hundred and twenty—a useful addition to my dowry, in order to sway Constance from Roger and his perfidious use of proxy poets.

I walked upstairs to add Constance's telegram to my collection. It was, in truth, a pretty feeble collection—less one of letters professing undying love than of letters requesting favors for one thing or another, or telling me how I should be more like Roger Maroon. I did actually consider burning it, but I was nothing if not dutiful with my filing, as Our Munsell had once noted that *life* is an anagram of *file*, and the relevance was pretty clear.

As I passed the door of the bathroom I noticed that it was swinging shut. It seemed odd, since there wasn't a breath of wind either within the house or without. I paused in my stride, and the door stopped swinging. I was the only one in the house; I had even seen the Apocryphal man shouting at a drainpipe in the corner of the town square as I came in.

"Hello?"

There was no answer to my call, and I very gently pushed the door. It opened easily for six inches or so, then stopped. But it wasn't as if it were pushing against a chair—it was the soft, yielding sensation of a *hand*. There was someone behind the door. I briefly thought it might be Jane, who had decided to perhaps kill me after all, but on reflection I decided that hiding behind the bathroom door with a hatchet or something was decidedly not her style.

"Who's there?"

There was no answer, and then it struck me: It might be the Apocryphal man's roommate, the one I had heard overhead.

"Do you live upstairs?" I asked, and whoever-it-was knocked once, for yes. I asked, "Can I see you?" and heard two urgent raps, for no. I was just about to frame a more complex question when I heard someone trot up the stairs below. I thought it might be the Colorman or the Apocryphal man, but it wasn't. It was Mr. Turquoise—the Blue prefect.

"Mr. Turquoise!" I said. "How do you do?"

I felt the bathroom door close slowly behind me.

"Good afternoon, Master Russett," he said in a businesslike tone. "The front door was open, so I came straight in. You don't mind, do you?"

"Not at all, sir."

"Good lad. How's the chair census going?"

"I've yet to start."

"Plenty of time. May I use the bathroom?"

He moved forward, but I stepped into his path. "No!"

"What?"

I had to think fast. Whatever the truth about our unseen lodger, it was something that would be best learned without any prefects getting involved.

"It's . . . broken. Something to do with the cistern."

He smiled. "I only want to wash my hands."

"That's broken, too."

"*Both* broken?"

"Yes, sir. Must be the cold water supply."

"Then I'll use the hot."

"Are wheelbarrows made of bronze?"

"What?"

"I was just wondering."

He shook his head and pushed past me. The door opened easily, and Turquoise strode to the sink. I looked around the bathroom. The shower curtain, usually open, was drawn all around the bath, and I could see the faint outline of a figure within. Turquoise, however, didn't.

"The cold is working, Russett."

"Must have been a blockage."

"Must have," he said, drying his hands. "Now, then, I'm responsible for career advice, organized glee, employment rosters and allocation of Useful Work. Can we walk and talk? I've got to check the inertia racer for Leapback Compliance. Fandango wants to run it at the Red Sector Jollity Fair next month at Vermillion, and it reflects badly on the village if he turns up with something that gets busted by the scrutineers."

I readily agreed, and we walked downstairs, out the front door and across the square.

"Here," said Turquoise, showing me my carefully prepared timetable.

"Sally Gamboge has raised the Grey retirement age to the maximum allowable, and is currently running sixteen-hour days, but we're still short a thousand person-hours a week, so the demands on Chromatic time are perhaps a little more than you might be used to. I daresay, in fact, that you might have to give up tennis or croquet, as there won't be time enough to do both."

"I quite understand the need for sacrifices, sir."

"Good fellow. I've got you down for Boundary Patrol first thing tomorrow, lightning watch on Saturday, anti-drowning supervision Mondays and Wednesdays and a turn teaching the juniors—this afternoon, in fact. Can you do that?"

"I've not much experience of teaching, sir."

"I shouldn't worry—there isn't much left to teach. Talk to them about the different sorts of chairs or something. By the way," he added, "top marks on the Rusty Hill expedition. If you enjoyed laughing in the face of death, you might like to have a crack at High Saffron. One hundred merits, and all you have to do is take a look."

"I understand there's a one hundred percent fatality rate?"

"True. But up until the moment of death there was a one hundred percent *survival* rate. Really, I shouldn't let anything as meaningless as statistics put you off."

"I think I may have to pass."

"Well," he replied, mildly irked, "if you're going to *insist* on being so negative, I suppose we could raise the consideration to two hundred."

"No, thank you."

"I'll put you down as a 'maybe.'"

We had reached the racetrack, which was a large oval of perhaps a mile in length. Because horses were too valuable to risk on the track, the Collective had found alternatives to race at Jollity Fair race day. Ostriches had been briefly fashionable, as had kudu and large dogs ridden by infants. Bicycles had been popular until the single-gearing Leapback had made the races considerably less than exciting. To circumvent this, some bright spark had resurrected the notion of the pre-Epiphanic "Penny Farthing," no doubt named after its inventor. The direct pedal drive on the outsize front wheel gave the cycles a healthy top speed but also made them dangerously top-heavy. With Mildew the most prevalent cause of death by a long shot, someone dying on the racetrack was of considerable novelty, and much applauded.

One sport, however, had dominated the Jollity Fair race day for more years than anyone could remember, and despite prefectural disapproval and a series of Leapbacks that required a great deal of ingenuity to circumvent, the sport had yet to be banned entirely. It was Stored Energy Racing, and East Carmine's entry was called the *Redstone Flyer*.

Like most inertia racers, it was configured with two wheels, similar to a bicycle only sturdier. Because it was driven by gyros and they were all powered up, the *Flyer* was balancing on its own two wheels, much like a train. The gyrobike had been elegantly streamlined within tightly faired bodywork that put me in mind of a salmon, and as I stared at the machine, it gave out a shudder that started small, escalated, then rattled the bike quite violently before calming down again.

"The gyros are going in and out of phase," Carlos explained when Turquoise asked him what was wrong, "and when they do, they tussle with one another. Hello, Eddie. Did you get Imogen's information pack?"

I told him I had, and he nodded agreeably, then placed a tuning fork on top of the gyro housings, presumably to gauge which one was out of kilter.

"So listen," said Turquoise, squatting down to have a closer look at the machinery, but from his look of utter bewilderment he might as well have been staring at the entrails of a goat. "Just confirm for me that this whole thing is compliant, will you?"

"Absolutely," said Fandango. "All the Everspins do is charge up the gyros—they're disconnected when it's racing. The farthest it's ever gone on a single charge is four miles."

"Didn't understand a word," he replied, "but if you say so, I'll sign it off."

And he did, appending his signature to a form that Fandango handed him.

"Right," said Turquoise, walking off in the direction of the glass-house, with me trailing behind as I suspected our conversation was not yet over. "Since you'll be with us for your Ishihara, I have to open your employment file. Any particular leaning you have in mind?"

I said the first thing that came into my head.

"Violin making."

"That's for us Blues only, old chap."

"Then how about string?"

"You'd have to marry into the Oxbloods for that," he laughed. "Be serious now. Any other ideas?"

It wasn't worth explaining about Constance, so I thought about the Colorman.

"I'd like to work for National Color, sir."

"Hmm," muttered Turquoise, ignoring me entirely and looking down the list of approved Red-related professions, "how about plumbing? The Collective always need plumbers. I'm sure you'll find the water supply business a dynamic and stimulating environment in which to work."

"With respect, I'd far prefer to have a shot at the National Color entrance exam."

I told him about my shade of mustard winning "best runner-up," but he wasn't listening.

"Heating or water?" said Turquoise, scribbling a note and handing me a pamphlet. "I'll speak to the village plumber for you to have an intro."

By now we had reached the glasshouse, which was situated a little way outside the village. Turquoise pushed the heavy door open and we stepped inside. Outside it had been hot, but inside it was even hotter, and the air was damp and tasted of lily ponds. Like most glasshouses the building was huge—almost twice as big as the town hall and with a gently curved ceiling shaped like a half melon that was about a hundred feet at its highest point. When built, it had been made of glass panels fully ten feet by four, but natural wastage and the inability to build replacements meant the roof was now filled with repaired sections of leaded glass of varying densities and quality. It was quite pretty in a patchwork sort of way, and I suspect multicolored, as I could see a few red panels and I suspected that ours was not the only color used.

"How are the pineapples, Mr. Lime?"

The head gardener was working without his shirt but with a tie and collar, as befits the letter of the Rules. He was stained with earth and had his spot affixed to a large floppy hat that was dark with sweat.

"Doing mighty fine, Mr. Turquoise," replied the gardener affably. "The surplus will be colorized and shipped to Blue Sector North—you know how they go bananas over pineapples."

Turquoise was taken on a brief tour of inspection, and I tagged along behind as we walked past rows and rows of fresh fruit and veg, all being attended by Greys, shiny with sweat in the heat. There had been an outbreak of clutching brambles that required prefectural approval to destroy, as any prehensile plants were classified as "partly animal" and thus subject to the Biodiversity Continuance Directive of the *Munsell Bestiary*.

"Absolute pests, they are," said the head gardener. "I know they can be taught simple tricks, but cleaning glass or weeding has always evaded them."

Turquoise filled out the extermination order and gave it to Mr. Lime, who thanked him and said he needed to show him something else.

We walked down the central aisle toward the unused fallow section of the glasshouse, which had turned into a jungle of date palms and a small grove of bamboo, from which several marmosets stared at us cheekily, munching on fruit.

"We've had a bit of a problem with these recently," said the gardener, opening a jam jar and showing us a large white centipede about five inches long and thicker than a man's thumb, "and we have no idea what they are."

I glanced at the Taxa bar code on its back.

"Phylum: Arthropoda. Class: Chilopoda," I murmured, and they both stared at me.

"I can read bar codes," I explained. "I can tell you it's a centipede, female, and about six thousand generations from being Taxa tagged—but nothing more than that."

"A useful skill," said Mr. Lime, who was impressed. "Then you concur it is unknown?"

"I do."

The gardener wiped his brow with a filthy handkerchief.

"Yewberry says the same. But if it's not listed in the *Munsell Bestiary*, it should officially be Apocrypha—but we can't ignore it as it's eating through everything. Any suggestions, Mr. Turquoise?"

The Blue prefect stared at the pest minutely, which squirmed in Mr. Lime's hand and gave out a series of high-pitched squeaks in the key of F.

"Can you eat them?"

"We haven't tried."

"Get a Grey to volunteer. If they're not palatable I can still define them as 'farmed comestibles' under Rule 2.3.23.12.220. We can then simply trap them, fry them and dump them. Or, if they *are* palatable, feed them to the Greys. It might make them leave some bacon for us."

Mr. Lime nodded agreeably at this fine display of loopholery, upon which we said our farewells and passed out of the south side of the glasshouse to walk in the direction of the Waste Farm.

"Now," said Turquoise, wiping his brow with a handkerchief, "activities. Sport and dancing are compulsory, of course—do you favor cricket or soccer?"

I told him I preferred cricket but denied my skill with the bat. Being able to actually see the naturally red ball gave an Alpha Red an edge. If you wanted to hide your bestowal, it was good practice to miss a few.

"And your favorite hoof?"

"We used to dance the lambada quite a lot in Jade-under-Lime."

Turquoise looked shocked, even though it was a leg-pull. I'd never danced the lambada—not even by myself, in secret.

"Quite inappropriate, Master Russett. We are fox-trot and rhumba people in East Carmine. Tango is permitted on occasion, but only for approved couples and well out of sight of the juniors. How about pastimes? Beekeeping? Photography? Reenactment societies? Slug racing?"

"You can race slugs?"

"It's quite popular out here in the Redstones. Since slugs are hardwired for strict territorial limitations accurate enough to keep them out of gardens, all you need do is log the bar code on a local slug and then release it outside Vermillion. First one back wins the pot."

"That must take a while."

"Decades, sometimes. A champion my father released eighteen years ago should be hitting the home stretch in about two years."

"I had no idea slugs were so long-lived."

"It's not the original slug," he explained. "The command string for territoriality descends through the offspring, so all we need do is read the Taxa numbers on the slugs as they come in—their heredity can be quickly established. It takes about four generations per mile, Mrs. Lapis Lazuli tells me. It could be done faster, but slugs are easily distracted. So, what shall I put you down for?"

"None of them hugely appeal, sir."

"Listen here, Russett, I have to put you down for *something*."

"The Photography Society, then. But under Rule 1.1.01.23.555 I'd like to form my own association for the social advancement of the Collective."

"I see," Turquoise said suspiciously. He knew 1.1.01.23.555 well enough. It was one of the loopholes that had been serially abused over the years. "And just what would this association do?"

I thought of Jane wanting me to remain curious as a smokescreen for her own activities. "A Question Club."

He breathed a sigh of relief. "Horses? No problem. Everyone likes horses. Especially horses. Horses like horses most of all."

"No, no, not *Equestrian* Club—a *Question* Club."

"There's already a Question Club," he said. "It's called the Debating Society. There's a meeting this evening, isn't there?"

"Yes, sir."

"Frightful waste of time. An hour spent on the jigsaw puzzle would be an hour much better spent. If we don't get a move on, we'll not see the puzzle finished in our lifetime, and I must confess I'd rather like to know what the puzzle actually *depicts* before they wheel me into the Green Room."

We had arrived at the Waste Farm, which for drainage purposes was always lower than the rest of the village. We found the chief-of-works next to one of the off-rotation settling tanks that was being scraped clean. He was a middle-aged man who was short, had a weather-worn face and whistled when he spoke, owing to a missing tooth that for some reason had failed to grow back. Like most of those versed in the arcane recycling arts, he was highly eccentric. He wore a bowler hat and insisted on a three-piece suit with a gardenia in his buttonhole. He wore no spot or gave any hint of Chromatic Hierarchy, which didn't help me know whether I should talk up or down to him.

"Hullo!" said the chief-of-works, who gave his name only as Nigel. "I heard you had a spot of bother with a tree this morning."

"You could say that."

"Don't feel bad by being outsmarted by a vegetable. You're not anyone until you've been wandering in the forest whistling a merry tune, only to find yourself suddenly hauled in the air by your ankle and dumped in ninety gallons of partially digested kudu. I know I have."

I looked around.

"The farm doesn't smell half as bad as I thought it would."

"The very idea!" exclaimed Nigel. "All the pits are sealed. If you can smell something it means we're not doing our jobs properly. But listen, if you want to know how bad it *can* smell, come and poke your nose in the rendering sheds."

Turquoise stayed in the office to check that the 87.2 percent recycling target was being met, and Nigel escorted me past the methane solidifiers to a brick building where the hot air was heavy with the pungent smell of heated offal. Despite the rudimentary exterior of the shed, the interior was scrubbed and tidy, the steel equipment all polished to a high shine. The concrete floor looked as though it was frequently hosed, and two of the plant's workers were feeding chunks of animal waste into a shredder that was driven by an Everspin. The combined kettle and press were to one side, and a gloopy substance—yellow, apparently—was slowly dripping into a bucket as the machine heated and folded the waste to remove the fat.

I covered my mouth and nose with my handkerchief.

"It's actually more skilled than you think," said Nigel with a smile. "The renderers get paid extra when they have to deal with a villager— which is stupid, really, since it's only something we walk around in. Mind you, I'm not entirely without feeling. I excuse them rendering duty if it was a friend or family member."

I almost gagged at the foul smell and staggered outside.

"Not for the squeamish, eh?" said Nigel as he followed me out. "We've got a backlog at present—we've been working our way through an elephant that dropped dead fortuitously just *inside* the Outer Markers."

"An elephant? I heard they weren't worth troubling with—low-quality tallow and whatnot."

Nigel leaned closer.

"It's the targets," he said with a grin. "An elephant *really* boosts the figures."

Once Turquoise had signed off on the pachyderm-assisted target and calculated the monthly bonuses, we struck out from the Waste Farm and into the open fields, where expansive fields of wheat were gently rolling in the breeze.

"What were we talking about?" asked Turquoise.

"I was requesting a Question Club, sir."

"Oh, yes. And I was telling you we already have one—the Debating Society."

"The debating society is restricted to the Chromogentsia," I pointed out. "I want a club where anyone can ask questions."

He stared at me suspiciously.

"What sort of questions?"

"*Unanswered* questions."

"Edward, Edward," he said with a patronizing smile, "there are *no* unanswered questions of any relevance. Every question that we need to ask has been answered fully. If you can't find the correct answer, then you are obviously asking the wrong question."

This was an interesting approach, and initially I could think of no good answer. We were walking along a track that was in a slight dip, and all that could be seen of the village was the flak tower with the lightning lure on top of it. It seemed a good point to raise.

"What were flak towers used for?"

"It's a nonquestion. The intractable ways of the Previous are best forgotten. Their ways are not our ways. Before, there was material imbalance and a wholly destructive level of self. Now there is only the simple purity of Chromatic Hierarchy."

"And why does that forbid anyone from making any more spoons?"

Turquoise's face fell. It was a thorny question that had been hotly debated for years. It seemed that spoons had been omitted from the list of approved manufactured goods as prescribed in Annex VI of the Rules, and the more daring debaters had suggested it might be an *error* in the Word of Munsell—proof of fallibility.

"You pseudo-rationalists always drag up the spoon issue, don't you? Our Munsell works in mysterious ways. Top Chromatologians have thought long and hard over the spoon question, and have come to the conclusion that, since the Word of Munsell *is* infallible, there must be some greater plan to which we are not yet privy."

"What plan *could* there be for not having enough spoons?"

"This is *precisely* why the Debating Society is open only to the Chromogentsia," he said in an exasperated tone. "Open discussion leads to the mistaken belief that curiosity is somehow desirable. Munsell tells us over and over again that inquisitiveness is simply the first step on a rocky road that leads to disharmony and ruin. Besides," he added, "asking a poor question gives it undeserved relevance, and attempting to answer a bad question is a waste of spirit. The question you *should* be asking yourself is: How can I discharge my Civil Obligation most efficiently to improve the smooth running of the Collective? And the answer to that is: Not wasting a prefect's valuable time with spurious suggestions for associations."

He stared at me, but not in a bad way—I think he was secretly enjoying the discussion as much as I was.

We had arrived at the circular head of a tosh pit, brick built and protruding three feet from the ground. The wooden cover was off, and two Greys were on duty—one with a polished bronze mirror on a stand to reflect the sun's rays down the mine to the workers below, and another who held a rope, presumably to haul dirt and scrap color to the surface. Beside them was a cart, half-filled with damp black soil, while laid out on trestle tables close by was low-quality rubbish, ready for sorting.

"Good morning, Terry," said Turquoise.

"Sir."

"Anything to report?"

"Not much this morning, sir. Jimmy found what he thought was a car at vector 65-32-420, but it was only a front wing."

"That's annoying," said Turquoise, running an eye over the tosh. I could see that little of it was red, and by the look of the prefect's demeanor, not much blue, either.

"Better get it down to the Pavilion as soon as you can—the Colorman wants to have an inspection tomorrow."

The Grey nodded and we walked away.

"We had a tosh-pit collapse last week that almost cost us a first-class miner," said Turquoise. "We're all about colored out. Another good reason for you to go to High Saffron for a look-see. What about two hundred and fifty merits?"

"I'll consider it," I said, actually meaning I'd do no such thing. "And my Question Club?"

"Very well," replied Turquoise through gritted teeth, since, according to the Rules, he couldn't refuse. "Consider your association formed. We will allocate you a slot within the prescribed time frame."

He stared at me for a moment.

"Just because you can pull wool, Russett, it doesn't follow that you should. With the leadership of an association comes responsibility, something I trust we will not see abused."

I told him I would do no such thing, and asked to be excused if he was done with me, which he was. I'd just noticed a figure a few fields off with a camera on a tripod, and this could only be Dorian—he had requested an interview from me for the *Mercury*.

Dorian and Imogen

1.1.6.23.102: The raising of one's voice is permissible only at sporting events, and only by the spectators. At all other times, speech is to be kept at a polite volume.

Dorian was photographing that year's floatie harvest. I walked past a field where a team of horses was pulling a plow through the harvested wheat field. As I watched, small specks of the floating material rose from the ground as they were unearthed, then started to drift off downhill, where they were channeled by a natural dip into long muslin nets strung a yard above the ground.

"Hello!" said Dorian, who was framing the billowing muslin with an oak tree in the background for his photograph. "Look at this one."

He showed me an exceptional floatie that was the size of a chicken's egg and still had a part number stamped on the side and some wiring attached. It was resting in the net with a lot of smaller sections—fragments, really, and some almost dust—and I tapped a finger on the top to gauge its strength. Ten merits per negative ounce was the usual price, and with the fragments, he might make twenty or thirty merits on this crop alone.

"We got up here late, so missed a few," he said, pointing in the downhill direction that floaties always took. "Redby-on-Sea have a net across the estuary, but only in the past decade or so, and it doesn't catch them all."

I stared at the odd pieces of metal thoughtfully. That they were man-made was without dispute, and also that they were parts of something much larger. Quite what, no one knew, as a floatie's natural propensity for heading off out to sea to seek the lowest point almost guaranteed there would be few around to study. The only pieces we could find these days were either trapped in natural hollows or embedded in the ground because of some past accident or burial.

"Where does it all end up?"

"Rumor speaks of a floating island somewhere on the oceans which is actually lived upon, but you'd need several thousand cubic meters of the stuff to have any chance of supporting a settlement. More than likely it'll be a home for seabirds and the like—until the weight of the guano pushes it beneath the waves."

I switched my attention to his camera, which was a full-plate Linhof. As in most cameras, the shutter had gummed up years ago, but emulsions were slower these days, and exposure was more usually controlled by simply removing the lens cap for the requisite period. I'd often asked for Constance and me to be photographed together, but her mother had forbidden it, lest "we get used to the idea." Dorian let me look at the image formed upside down on the viewing screen, and the framing was actually very good.

"I need some good clouds for it to be perfect," he said, staring up at the sky. "Had you heard that a deep red filter increases the contrast in the sky?"

I *had* heard that but didn't know quite how it worked.

"I heard the trip was a huge success," he added as we walked toward the handcart that held all his photographic gear and some tea-making equipment. "How were the bonemeal cakes I gave you?"

"Inedible."

"I thought so, too. Have a look at this."

He showed me the photograph he had taken of the expedition, which was suitably heroic if you didn't count Carlos Fandango, who had ruined the picture by moving his head. I pointed this out.

"He did it on purpose. Mr. Fandango and I don't agree on several fundamental issues. So," he continued, "tell me about the trip—for the *Mercury,* you understand."

So we sat on the grass and I told him as much as I dared, omitting the bits about Jane, Zane G-49's house with all its treasures and the Pooka.

"Tell me," I said while he was writing down the bit about meeting the Colorman, "how does a Grey get to be the editor of the village news sheet?"

"Before my Ishihara I was Lilac," he said with forced cheerfulness.

"My parents were frightfully disappointed, although not surprised—the family's been going downhill for a while. My great-great-grandmother was head prefect in Wisteria, and Dad was the janitor here in Carmine before he died."

"Oh," I said, "I'm sorry to hear that."

"It was inevitable. In any event, I was doing the editing job *before* my Ishihara, and deMauve took pity on an ex-Purple and allowed me to keep it, although for loophole reasons, I'm officially the assistant typesetter—the highest wage grade I'm permitted to hold."

"That's annoying."

"On the contrary," he said with a smile. "It keeps me from twelve-hour shifts in the factory under the watchful eye of the delightful Mrs. Gamboge."

"You should do an exposé on the way Greys are treated here."

"Yes," he said, "that would be *really* smart. On reflection, it would be better to reserve my ire for more acceptable outrages—such as the scandalous level of sin at the Jollity Fair sideshows."

I couldn't agree, but didn't say so. The unregulated "added attractions" were the best part of the fair.

"Hmm," said Dorian, staring down at his shorthand. "I think I'll leave out the heaps of dried bones and the rotted prefect, and just concentrate on the Caravaggio. I should have given you my Speed Graphic to take a picture."

To Dorian, this was more than his job. He took his interest in photography seriously, and told me that in the past twenty-four hours he had taken the East Carmine Scrabble team's group photograph, a picture of Mr. Eggshell's champion lupin, the Rusty Hill expedition picture, several individual portraits and the inquest photograph of yesterday's power guillotine accident. "Do you want to see?"

"Go on, then."

He opened one of the many bulging portfolios that were lying on the cart. The pictures were of village life, the harvest, fields, residents swimming in the river, that kind of stuff.

"Look," he said, "that's Mr. and Mrs. Beetroot just before they were burned alive in their home, and this is one taken just afterward. The Rules state only that the sprinkler system has to be *fitted*. They don't state that it has to work." He turned over another. "This one is of the village performing *Hamlet, Prince of Tyrian* last year—Violet deMauve played Ophelia, as you can see."

"Was she any good?"

"She was *awful*. Everyone cheered when she drowned."

"How did she take it?"

"She rose from the dead, told us all to go to Beige, then died again."

He showed me another. "This was taken a few minutes after Jerry was dragged screaming into the threshing machine. The largest part we found of him was his leg."

He showed me the picture of the limb, which lay on the ground with a crowd of curious villagers standing around.

"I remember seeing this in the cautionary-photo section of *Spectrum*."

"Thank you," he said modestly. "They pay ten merits and a positive feedback for every one they print. What do you make of this?"

He showed me another photograph, which made me frown. It was taken from an attic window, as the rooftops and the town hall were clearly visible—not so strange in itself, except for the fact that the sky was pitch-black with a series of very fine circular white lines radiating out from a central point.

"Where did you take it?"

"Outside—at *night*. I had set the camera up to try to photograph lightning, but then I fell asleep and left the shutter open. What you see here is a seven-hour exposure."

"And these circles in the night sky?"

"I don't know what they are. It might be some sort of—I don't know—unexplained phenomenon. But here's weird for you: There was no moon that night."

The notion that there was a small amount of light reflected from the moon was pretty much accepted wisdom. Although much too feeble for us to see by, it was enough for some creatures: Tracks of Nocturnal Biting Animals were often found in the morning where none had been the night before, and I had once seen a herd of grazing capybara and a hippo illuminated by a lightning flash. But Dorian's picture posed an entirely new concept: that there was light from *another* source when the moon had waned—enough to illuminate the buildings and hills over seven hours—and that this source might be the curious circles in the night sky that he had photographed.

"Can I have this?" I asked.

"Sure. This is yesterday's accident," he said, handing me another photo. "Look."

The atmosphere of the shot was particularly strident. A shaft of light had shone in from one of the factory windows at precisely the right moment, backlighting the victim's severed head agreeably.

"I like the framing," I said, "especially the windows reflected in the pool of blood."

"Thank you."

At that moment a pretty girl trotted up. I was partially hidden behind Dorian's handcart, and she didn't see me.

"Snookums—!" she said to Dorian with a smile, and my heart fell. The girl was Imogen Fandango, and Dorian was the "unsuitable attachment" the janitor had alluded to.

"Oh!" said Imogen as soon as she saw that Dorian wasn't alone. "Master Russett. I, um, didn't see you there. I actually meant 'Snookums' in a *pejorative* sense—Dorian and I hate each other—don't we, darling?"

She wasn't fooling anyone.

"I'm not going to snitch," I told her.

Acutely embarrassed, Dorian rubbed his forehead, and Imogen shyly clasped his hand after looking around to check that we were unobserved.

"We don't know what to do," she said, glad, I think, to be able to share the problem. "Daddy has been advertising in *Spectrum* and wants six thousand for me. Who's this Purple he's asked you to contact?"

"Just some guy back home," I said awkwardly. "He probably won't be interested."

"That's a relief," replied Imogen, blinking her large eyes. "There's still hope. Perhaps Daddy will get bored and let us marry—he said he loves me, after all."

"The only thing he loves about you is your ability to have Purple children," grumbled Dorian. "If he wants to trade in eggs, he should start a chicken farm. It's not as though you're even his daughter."

They then started to have an argument, right there in front of me. It was all a bit embarrassing. Imogen told Dorian that her father was a good man "compelled by circumstance" to sell her to the highest bidder. Dorian was more the one for action, and hinted darkly at "extreme measures," which I took to mean an escape.

"Don't try anything stupid," I warned. "Elopements always end in failure—and sometimes put you on the Night Train."

"Didn't Munsell say that we should always choose the lesser of two evils?" retorted Imogen. "Besides, it's said that Emerald City is so large a couple might find work without questions being asked."

"That's right," said Dorian. "We can vanish into the city."

I wasn't convinced. "You'd never get farther than Cobalt junction."

"We're going to wrongspot. Not even a Yellow would dare question a Violet."

It was a crazy plan, and they both knew it. Romantic-induced walk-outs were always returned, but wrongspotting was punishable by a ten-thousand demerit. Reboot, effectively. And at Reboot, couples are always separated. It showed how desperate they had become. It also explained why Dorian had wanted to buy my Open Return.

"You're not going anywhere without tickets."

"We've got one," explained Dorian. "The other is . . . under negotiation."

"Courtland says he wants me in the wool store for it," said Imogen, "which is all fine and good, except that he won't hand over the Open Return until he's been paid in full."

"He has no intention of giving up the ticket."

"Yes, we know."

"*Blast!*"

"What?"

I said it was nothing, but it wasn't. Having now met these two, I couldn't introduce Bertie Magenta to Fandango, and in consequence of that, I would not be receiving my one-hundred-fifty-merit commission. And that was almost a year's wages—for one lousy telegram. It was the fastest one-fifty I never made.

"Listen," I said, "my cousin the Colorman goes to Emerald City on a regular basis. Let me make some inquiries, and I'll get back to you. Just don't do anything stupid, and don't take Courtland up on his offer."

They both stared at me.

"Why are you doing this?"

"Perhaps," I said, "I want for you what I can't have for myself. And now, if you'll excuse me, I have to do my Useful Work."

School, Poetry, Co-op

> 2.1.01.05.002: All children are to attend school until the age
> of sixteen or until they have learned everything, whichever
> be the sooner.

The school was situated at the back of the village, two streets behind the town hall and opposite the firehouse. Due to the architectural infallibility of the Rules regarding school design, no better building could or would be thought of, so every school in the Collective was identical. I immediately knew my way around, and the place had an eerie familiarity about it.

I paused in the main hall next to the bronze bust of Munsell and read the school's oft-quoted mission statement: "Every pupil in the Collective will leave school with above-average abilities." It wasn't until I had studied advanced sums that I realized this could not be possible, since by definition not *everyone* could be of above-average ability.

"It's a *historical* average fixed soon after the Something That Happened," my mentor, Greg Scarlet, had explained when I dared broach the subject. "How else would you be able to compare one year with another? Besides, an average pegged to a time when education was considerably worse than it is now ensures that no pupil is ever stigmatized by failure."

This was true, and since one's career path was never decided by ability or intellect, it didn't much matter anyway. Lessons were generally restricted to reading, writing, French, music, geography, sums, cooking and Rule-followment, which meant sitting in a circle and agreeing on how important the Rules were. Most pupils referred to the subject as "nodding."

I made my way to the head teacher's office and tapped nervously on the door.

"Glad you could make it," she said as soon as I had explained who I was and what I was doing there. She introduced herself as Miss Enid Bluebird. She was a slight woman who was dressed in shabby tweeds and carried the benign expression of the inwardly harassed. This was not surprising, as her office was knee-high in stacks of dusty and much-faded examination papers.

"I've managed to bring the backlog down to a mere sixty-eight years," she announced with some small sense of achievement. "I hope to be able to start marking the papers of pupils who are still alive by the end of the decade."

"A very worthy aim," I replied, thinking carefully about how I could apply queuing theory in this instance. "Excuse the impertinence, but wouldn't it be better to reverse the queuing order so that the *oldest* papers were *last* marked? It would allow pupils to know their results sooner, and as far as I can see, would not be against the Rules, since queue direction is not specified."

She stared at me oddly, then smiled kindly after having given the matter no thought at all.

"A fine idea, but since everyone is above average, improvement to the system is really not that important."

"Then why mark them?" I asked, emboldened by the rejection of my suggestion.

"So we can make sure the education system is working, of course," she replied as though I were simple. "If I work really hard I might be able to clear the backlog to the fifty-year mark by the time I retire—and we can know just how well we were doing half a century ago. If we commit ourselves wholly to the task, in twenty years we might know how well we are doing right now."

"You must have very little time for teaching."

"No time at all," she replied airily, "which explains why Useful Workers like you are now essential to the smooth running of the school. Why, we've not had a teacher actually *teaching* for over three centuries.

She introduced me to the class, and I gave the afternoon lesson. Because Munsell had attempted to make the world knowable for everyone by simply reducing the number of facts, there wasn't that much to teach. But I did my best, and after doing some long-division practice and talking a little about my home village, I set them a puzzle in which they had to estimate how many Previous there had once been by using Ovaltine sales projections of the year known as 2083. Following that, we discussed why the Previous might have been as tall as they were, which foodstuffs made it through the Epiphany, then possible reasons why the Previous had apparently denied the future by ranking their year system without a double-zero prefix. After that, we had a general Q&A session, where they asked me stuff about Riffraff eating babies, and why the Previous' tables had four legs rather than the more stable three we used at present. I answered as best as I could, and after giving them a brief introduction to the skill of reading bar codes, we ended up talking about the rabbit. I was very glad that I had earlier found an article in *Spectrum* that described a visit to the rabbit six years ago. I sounded almost expert.

We finished up with a song of praise to Munsell as the clock moved around to four, and as soon as I dismissed them there was a flurry of banged desk lids and they were all gone.

I was rather pleased with myself, and after pushing in the chairs and placing their homework in the waste bin, I went to find Miss Bluebird, who asked me how it went without much interest, and then gave me positive feedback and ten merits.

"Find anything useful to teach them?"

Jane was waiting for me outside the school. She looked almost pleased to see me, and that instantly made me suspicious.

"I . . . like to think so," I replied cautiously, looking around to see if there were witnesses in case she tried something.

She picked up on my nervousness and raised an eyebrow. "What are you so worried about?"

"The last time you smiled at me, I found myself under a yateveo."

She laughed. The sound was lovely—yet quite out of character. It would be like hearing a fish sneeze. "Honestly," she said, "are you going to drag that up every time we meet? So I threatened to kill you. What's the big deal?"

"How can you not think it's a big deal?"

"Okay, I'll demonstrate. You threaten to kill me."

"I'd rather not."

"Come on, Red, don't be such a baby."

"All right: I'll kill you."

"You have to say it like you mean it."

"I'LL KILL YOU!"

And she punched me in the eye.

"Ow! That *hurt*. And how could that possibly demonstrate that it's no big deal?"

"You might have something there," she said thoughtfully. "It *could* have been a bit rude of me. But let's face it, you are a bit pointless, and the world will certainly carry on spinning without you."

I rubbed my eye. "You really have a winning personality, don't you?"

"Steady," she said, again with a slight smile. "I'm supposed to be the sarcastic one."

"What in Munsell's name is going on?" Miss Bluebird had just walked out of the school. She was carrying a huge pile of papers, and had a look of shocked disbelief on her face. "Did I just witness a lethal threat and an up-color assault?"

It was time to think fast, and when it comes to making up lieful deceits on the spot, I soon realized that Jane was even better than Tommo. "Far from it," she replied innocently. "Master Edward and I were discussing the best way to mock-fight in *Red Side Story*."

"We're attending the auditions together," I added, "aren't we, Jane?"

She gave me a brief grimace, but nodded.

"It was *most* convincing," replied Mrs. Bluebird, full of admiration. "I'm adjudicating this evening—perhaps you might demonstrate the technique for us all?"

"As many times as you want," replied Jane happily.

"Splendid!" replied Mrs. Bluebird. "See you there, then."

As soon as she was out of earshot, Jane turned to me and said in a low growl, "We're *not* going to the auditions."

I had to agree, as being punched endlessly wouldn't be much fun. In fact, I'd prefer to just lose an eyebrow and be done with it.

"We should keep moving," said Jane, "before we raise any suspicions. If anyone comes within earshot, talk to me about what you'd like for dinner, and then castigate me about the poor starching of your collar."

We walked off, and after a moment of silence I said, "You were waiting for me. Did you want something?"

"No," she said, "but you do. Word in the Greyzone is that a sad Red wannabe with no imagination and a lump in his trousers needs help to get his leg over some unobtainable Alpha crumpet back home."

"Aside from the subtly imbedded 'I don't like you' message hidden in your statement, what does that mean?"

"It means I heard you wanted some poetry written."

"And you're the best poet in the village?"

"By a long way."

I attempted to take advantage of the narrow window of opportunity that had just opened, and asked if she'd like to discuss it down at the Fallen Man over a d'nish pastry.

"I'd sooner stick a bodkin through my tongue."

"You really don't like me, do you?"

"It's not *just* you. You might say I am impartial in the politics of the Colortocracy—I despise all Chromatics equally."

"Would there be any point in asking what's going on in Rusty Hill, and how Zane and you relate to Ochre and the selling of the village swatches?"

"None whatsoever."

"I thought you might say that . . . and we should have mutton on Wednesday," I said, as Yewberry was walking past, deep in conversation with the Colorman about pipeline routing, "and with salad, not vegetables."

Yewberry acknowledged my presence with a nod of his head, but the Colorman actually greeted me with a polite "Edward." I replied, "Matthew," which I could see impressed Yewberry.

"Right," said Jane as soon as they had passed, "poetry. Who's the bunny?"

I took a deep breath. "The 'bunny,' as you so indecorously call her, is an Oxblood, *Constance* Oxblood, and her father runs the stringworks in Jade-under-Lime. We've been seeing each other for several years, and we've even—"

"Do I look as though I'm interested?"

"Not really."

"You're right. The details of your hopeless quest to sacrifice your individuality on the altar of Chromatic betterment is about as exciting to me as pulling clodworms out of the juniors. Do you love each other?"

"I'm sure that in the fullness of time we will come to regard each other with—"

"That's a no, isn't it?"

"Yes," I replied with a sigh. "She needs the Red, and my family need the social standing."

"How *awesomely* romantic! Have you told her? It would put the union on a business footing, and you'd save a small fortune in flowers, chocolates and poets."

"She knows. It's just a game, really. Besides, the old-color Roger Maroon is the odds-on favorite—despite his lack of Red, intelligence, charm and looks. Here," I said, handing her a letter I had been drafting, "you may like to use this as a basis."

"Drivel," she said, scanning the words quickly. "Were you really going to send that?"

"The bit regarding the Caravaggio was okay," I replied a bit stupidly, "and I thought it important to mention the queuing. Should I scrub the paragraph about the rabbit?"

"It's all sheep and no shepherd," she remarked and started to write on the back of my letter as we walked. She scribbled, crossed out and then wrote again, a bit like an artist trying to capture a likeness. She looked quite lovely, and it wasn't just her nose. The hair that wasn't tucked into her ponytail dropped in front of her eyes several times, and she pushed it out of the way behind her ear, where it would stay for perhaps twenty seconds or so before making its way out again. I could have watched her for several circuits of the village, and fervently hoped she was a slow poet. Unfortunately, she wasn't.

"There," she said a minute later, and handed over the finished product.

> Rouge of my heart, intertwined with double-hued destiny,
> Thread of my thoughts, constant and rubicund legacy,
> Filament of my future, endeared unto my expectation,
> Cord of my emotion, seared with eternal elation.

"That's . . . *beautiful*," I murmured.

Although the meaning wasn't at first obvious, it seemed to have the right sort of words in it. Fairly long and not used that often. It also *sounded* intelligent, and had a lot of string references, which would go down well with Constance's mother. More important still, it was a lot better than I could do. "Should I place it at the beginning or the end of the letter?"

"This *is* the letter, numbskull. You just put Tim or Peter or whatever your name is at the end. No Xs, no kisses and none of that 'My heart yearns for you, poopsie' nonsense."

"It's 'honey bear,' actually."

"I'm sorry?"

"Nothing. What do I owe you for the poetry?"

"You can have Constance on me. All I need is a favor."

I looked across at her. "I have a feeling it's probably not to scratch your back or put up some shelves."

"No. What do you know about this Matthew Gloss character?"

"You mean *His Colorfulness*? Not very much."

"But he's kin, living in your house, and you called him Matthew in public. You wouldn't have done that unless he'd allowed you to."

"We're getting along okay," I conceded.

"I'd like to know what he's doing here."

"A Magenta feed-pipe leakage, he told me."

"I heard that, too. But we're not on the grid. He's been invited to conduct the Ishihara, but that's not for three days. I want to know what he's *really* doing here."

"You want me to spy on a National Color operative? Someone *Colorful*?"

"Wow," she said, "you got it. I thought I was going to have to explain that one for a *lot* longer."

"I can't spy on my fourth cousin!"

"Of course you can. And you will."

"You seem very confident about this."

She leaned forward. "You'll do this for me, Red, because despite Constance, you're in love with me."

And there it was. She'd said it. If I'd wanted to deny it, there was a half-second window in which to do so. But I paused too long, and all hope of believability was gone forever. "Oh, sure," I said in an unconvincing manner, "I'm on a half promise to an Oxblood, and I let myself fall for a Grey girl who not only despises me but is up for Reboot in under a week. Does that sound remotely sensible to you?"

"Love isn't sensible, Red. I think that's the point."

I ran my fingers through my hair and thought hard for a moment. "You want to know what the Colorman is doing here?"

She nodded.

"Okay," I said, "I'll see what I can find out. But you have to stop threatening to kill me and punching me in the eye and stuff."

"This is the new me," she said, and gave me another smile. I was being used, but then I didn't mind—and I didn't actually have to do as she asked. In under a week she'd be pacing the yard at Reboot.

We turned the corner into the main square and came across a small crowd outside the town hall. It looked like an allocation ceremony, so we wandered over to dutifully offer our best wishes.

I had been nine at the time of my own allocating, and up until then I'd carried a nondescript BS3 code from the open pool that was held by the prefects. With the increased importance of family and inheritance, a loophole had been drafted to allow residents to transfer a relative's postcode to a junior member of the same family. The RG6 7GD code that was now scarred into my chest had been my grandfather's. I'd have liked any child of mine to have had my mother's old code, but that had been reallocated to someone named Holland Claret, and I'd never liked him because of it. The Oxbloods had elderly relatives in abundance, so any children of Constance would almost certainly carry an SW3—Oxblood through and through.

We were standing at the back of the crowd of perhaps fifty or so people. DeMauve was conducting the ceremony, and it seemed that young Penelope Gamboge was having her allocation on the last day possible—her twelfth birthday, which lent a double sense of occasion to the proceedings. Old Man Magenta back in Jade-under-Lime treated allocation as the formfillery it was, but at least deMauve was making an effort. The whole Gamboge clan, which numbered eight as far as I could see, were beaming happily and even shedding a tear or two, which I never thought Yellows could do.

"Wonderful, isn't it?" whispered Jane. "A new life to an old postcode. A connection to our past, and to the future."

"You can be quite sarcastic sometimes, can't you?"

"It's more than sometimes."

"How did you get to Rusty Hill this morning?"

It was a daring question, but she had promised not to thump me. As it turned out, her answer was as matter-of-fact as it was impenetrable.

"The highway obeys my every wish."

"What?"

She ignored me, and the ceremony came to an end.

"Aren't you going to give a donation?"

I wasn't planning to, but said I would so as not to appear cheap. I placed the smallest coin I had in the jar marked PENELOPE DAFFODIL GAMBOGE, TO3 4RF, which I noted was already half full of low-denomination coins, and quite a few buttons.

"There," I said, "happy?" But I was talking to myself. Jane had slipped

201

away in the crowd, her job completed. I looked at the poem again. It was the best I'd seen, and I wished she had written it *to* me, and not *for* me.

I stopped off at the telegraph office to send Jane's poem to Constance. Mrs. Blood was impressed and congratulated me on the quality of my words. "You're smarter than you look, young man. While I wouldn't go so far as to say your Constance is a lucky woman, she might conceivably do worse."

"You're very kind," I replied. "I just needed to get into my groove."

And then, despite what Jane had told me, I wrote after the poem: *I take my Ishihara this Sunday. All my very best, Edward.*

"There," I said, handing over the completed telegram form and counting out the money. "That will sort out Roger Maroon once and for all."

I went next door to the Co-op to buy some pudding rice and found Tommo behind the counter, bagging some lentils for Carlos Fandango.

"Hello, Edward," said the janitor, placing a custard powder tin on the counter to be refilled. "What did you think of Imogen's information pack?"

"It was most impressive," I said, "especially the unicycling."

"Then you'll be contacting your friend?"

"It's at the top of my list."

"Excellent."

He turned to Tommo. "Put this on my account, would you, Spoon-packer?"

Tommo said he would, and as soon as Carlos had gone, Tommo opened the accounts ledger and took a pencil from behind his ear.

"One tin of custard powder . . . one hundred twenty pounds of lard . . . a haunch of lamb . . . two licorice sticks."

He snapped the book shut, handed me a licorice stick and took one for himself.

"That should sort him out. Did he offer you a one percent finder's fee?"

"Two percent."

"He must have liked the look of you. If Dorian was still Lilac and had six grand kicking about, there might be a happy ending. He's Grey and has only thirty, so there won't be. Tears all around. Did you have a particular Purple in mind for her?"

"There's only Bertie Magenta back home."

"The elephant trick guy?"

"The same. But I'm not going to help out. Fandango intimated that a prospective purchaser could have her in the wool store on appro."

"What a fantastic sales gimmick," he said in admiration. "When I hear stuff like that it makes me proud to be in retailing."

"I say it's vile odiousness. Would you do that to your daughter?"

"Technically speaking, it's not his daughter. If I'd brought up another man's girl for twenty years, I think I'd be due some sauce for my investment."

I could see I was wasting my time arguing with Tommo over this one.

"Even so, it's just not right."

"There is no right or wrong," said Tommo. "Only the Rulebook makes it so. Do you want a banana?"

"Not really."

"Reserve judgment until you see it."

He reached behind the counter and produced an ordinary-looking banana—but in a beautiful dark yellow shade that was delightfully non-standard. It was one of the new Chromatically Independent bananas I had seen advertised in Vermillion's Paint Shop.

"Wow. Where did that come from?"

"The regional fruit and veg allocations manager owed me a favor. I was going to keep this one for myself but instead thought I'd sell it to some shallow dope who's impressed by this sort of thing."

"Like me?"

"Like you."

I stared at the fruit from several angles and wondered if I could send it to Constance as some sort of love token, then dismissed the idea as quickly—sending bananas to young ladies really only meant one thing, and you could expect a face slap for it. Or in Constance's case, six.

"How much?"

"To you, thirty."

"Come on! An uncolorized one is only five cents."

"That was a special price because I like you—everyone else paid forty."

"Fifteen, then."

"Done."

The shop bell tinkled and Violet deMauve walked in. We both instinctively gave a respectful bow and she returned our greeting with an almost imperceptible inclination of her head.

"Ah!" she said. "The new bananas are in. Just what I was after."

She opened her purse.

"How much, Tommo? If you try to overcharge me I'll poke you painfully in the eye."

"I'm so sorry, Miss Violet," said Tommo, enjoying the pleasure of seeing her disappointed, "I've just sold the banana to Master Edward here."

"Oh," she said, turning to me, "then I will buy it from you. I am prepared to be generous—I will be more than happy to pay two cents over the price charged by Tommo."

"It's not for sale," I said as Tommo moved away to look busy elsewhere.

"How funny!" exclaimed Violet, blinking rapidly. "For a moment there I thought you said it wasn't for sale." She lowered her voice to a growl. "Now—how much?"

"I'm sorry, Miss deMauve, but I'm keeping it."

A look of incredulity seemed to well up inside her; then, after a moment or two, she smiled.

"It's another one of your 'no' jokes isn't it? Like at lunchtime?" She rested a hand on my cheek for a moment. "You're so sweet—but I'm really in a dreadful rush and if I'm not back in a few moments, Papa—Head Prefect Papa—might be miffed. Do you want to see a head prefect miffed?"

"Not really."

"Correct answer. Now, *how much*?"

"It's not—"

"Tommo?" she said, beckoning him over as you would to inform a tea shop attendant that you'd just found a dead mouse in the teapot. "Is there something wrong with Russett? He doesn't seem to quite get it."

Tommo stayed where he was, skulking behind the picture-postcard display rack.

"Russetts are like that, Miss Violet," came Tommo's voice, "contrary."

"A demi," I said.

"What?"

"You heard me."

She stared at me again, took a half-merit coin from her purse, stuffed it in my hand and walked huffily out of the shop. I stood there for a few moments until she returned, took the banana and walked out again.

"Wow," said Tommo, coming out from behind the display, "I like you. You'll suffer for it later, but anyone who tries to annoy the deMauves is a friend of mine. What can I get you?"

"I'm going to need a half pound of pudding rice," I said, "and peaches, boot polish, a quince, one large turnip, a tin of sardines and a bag of sprinkles."

Tommo took out a notebook and scribbled in it.

"Problems?"

"Not at all," he answered, "but with all those ingredients I'm just reminding myself never to dine with you."

I walked back across the square to put on the rice pudding, have a bath and ready myself for the Chromogentsia. I looked into the bathroom on the way past and noticed that the shower curtain had been pulled back. Of our unknown lodger there was no sign. But that wasn't strictly true. Lying on my bed was a pre-Epiphanic snow globe of the sort that might change hands for hundreds of merits. I shook it, and the white flecks floated upon a scene of tall buildings and a woman holding a torch in the air. It wasn't mine, and I'd never seen it before. But I was willing to bet it hadn't been blown there.

"You've stolen my snow globe!" came a voice from the door.

I turned to see the Apocryphal man glaring at me.

"I did not!" I declared indignantly. "I found it on my bed."

The Apocryphal man stared at me for some moments in silence. When he spoke next, it was with a voice tinged with sadness.

"You know what this means, don't you?"

I shook my head.

"It means I'm not invisible!"

Three Questions

1.6.02.13.056: Generally speaking, nudity and unselfconscious regard of the body is to be encouraged. Clothes are required to be worn as and when decorum demands it. (See Annex XVI.)

"You mean," said the Apocryphal man, once I had explained that he had been ignored only because of an arcane rule, "I've been walking around the town naked all these years and people saw?"

"Pretty much. But since you don't technically exist, there can't be any embarrassment, either."

"Oh," he said, much relieved, "thank goodness for that."

I stared at him for a moment. Apocrypha could be anything from the tangible, like that notoriously unlisted big bird with the long neck that was twice the size of an ostrich, to the abstract—such as a forbidden idea or taboo discussion point. But this was the first human Apocrypha I'd encountered. The thing was, he didn't look any different from us—except for his postcode, which was truncated. He had NS-B4 scarred just below his collarbone. I was going to ask him why, but it seemed rude. Besides, he spoke first.

"That broth last night was excellent, wasn't it?" he said.

"I'll have to take your word for it."

"What was for pudding?"

"Pickled onions and custard. Can I ask a question?"

"It depends."

"Depends on what?"

"On whether you have any jam."

"I've got lots," I replied, delighted that the Apocryphal man could be bought so cheaply.

"But not any jam," he added with a mischievous grin. "I want . . . loganberry!"

This was another matter entirely. Jam was expensive, but you could get it. Loganberry, however, was a bit like off-gamut color. It existed, but was almost impossible to get your hands on. It was the preserve of the Ultraviolets, and its manufacture was strictly controlled. The Apocryphal man saw my face fall and giggled.

"Yes, loganberry. My question-to-jam ratio is three to one. One jar, three questions. It's a good deal."

"One jar for five questions," I suggested.

His face fell.

"You have loganberry?"

"Possibly."

"Then . . . two questions and a follow-on."

"You said three just now!"

"That was when I thought you didn't have any."

"Four."

"I respect a hard bargainer," he conceded. "Three questions, a juicy snippet and some wisdom. Final offer."

"Okay."

"You do have some loganberry, I take it?"

As chance would have it, I did. A jar that I'd been given many years before, just after Mother succumbed to the Mildew. I fetched it from my valise and handed it over. The Apocryphal man took the jar gratefully and, using his grubby fingers in a most revolting manner, proceeded to eat the entire pot. I watched in dismay as he devoured in a couple of minutes something that would have taken me at least six months. I stood in silence until he had scraped out the last atom of jam and licked his fingers, which were now a good deal cleaner.

"That was good," he remarked agreeably, handing back the empty jar. "What's the first question?"

I thought for a moment. His demi-postcode was intriguing, but there were bigger questions to ask.

"Why are you Apocryphal?"

"I'm actually a historian. Head Office always felt it would be easier to study society if those doing the studying were invisible, so that's why I am ignored by statute. It's just been a while, and I think I may have become muddled. But then they canceled history during one of those interminable Leapbacks, and here I am, like a cobbler in a world without feet."

"Why did they Leapback history?" I asked.

"It was a logical extension to the deFacting," replied the historian with a sigh, "and in a world devoted to Stasis, there's no real need for it. After all, this week is not substantially different from last week, or next week, or a week I can remember thirty-seven years ago. Oh, no, hang on, I got married that week. Okay, the week *after* that."

"I wasn't in the world thirty-seven years ago," I replied, "so it was substantially different to me."

"What was your grandfather's name?"

"Same as mine: Eddie."

"And his postcode?"

"Same . . . as mine. I see what you mean. But my grandfather wasn't me."

"He might as well have been. In the grand scheme of things, there's no real difference. Not to the Collective as a whole, and certainly not to Head Office."

I pondered on this for a moment. My grandfather would have used the same furniture and lived in the same house. He would have known the same facts and wanted the same things in life. He had even looked like me. The only thing different was that he would have seen less red. I mentioned this last fact to the historian.

"Stasis, but with *circulation*. But color, you recall, has no color. You're not *really* Red—just one soul in transition, making his spiraling way through the hive—part of the Chromatic Circle."

He was right. The circle principle was sound and embodied in Munsell's writings: *"Today a Purple, tomorrow a Grey,"* I quoted. *"Tomorrow a Yellow, a Blue today."*

"Simple, isn't it? It's not by chance the longest time anyone has been Grey is five generations."

"In *theory*," I said, since some families had "ovaled the circle" by being brightly hued for longer than was usual—the Oxbloods and the deMauves, the Cobalts and the Buttercups. In fact, the lack of Grey families was the chief reason for the overemployment problem—that and the lack of postcodes to reallocate.

The Apocryphal man shrugged.

"It's only been going for five hundred years and might need some tweaking. Second question?"

"What happened to Robin Ochre?"

The Apocryphal man stared at me.

"Careful," he said, "information can liberate but also imprisonate. Ochre was skittering right on the edge of the Rules and drew attention to himself."

"You mean he *was* murdered?"

"They wouldn't see it as such, and if it *was* murder, it was committed in a very pleasant way. I've not partaken of green myself, but I understand that if you have to go, the Green Room is an exceptionally agreeable way to do it."

"Who murdered him?"

He shook his head and sighed deeply. "I blame myself. He had questions and I directed him toward the truth. But if you want answers in a world where hiding them is not only desirable but mandated, you have to take risks. I understand Zane is dead as well?"

"Yesterday at Vermillion. The Mildew."

"It was as he expected," he muttered. "Last question?"

"Are wheelbarrows made of bronze?"

The Apocryphal man raised an eyebrow.

"That's it?"

I shrugged.

"Listen," he said, "perhaps you don't get it, but I was once a *historian*. The closest thing you'll ever get to meeting the Oracle. I can remember the days when Ford flatheads were the vehicles of choice, and Model Ts languished in museums. I've seen the advance of the rhododendron and the retreat of general knowledge. I've got more information in my head than you'll forget in twelve lifetimes, and you ask me if wheelbarrows are made of bronze?"

"It's been annoying me since this morning."

The Apocryphal man tilted his head on one side and stared at me.

"Wheelbarrows aren't made of bronze."

"Then how did I fall on it when I trod the roadway last night? Perpetulite automatically *removes* all debris—except bronze, as far as I can see."

"Be careful with all that dangerous *reason*," he said after a pause. "The Collective abhors square pegs."

"Unless the hole is *meant* to be square," I said with a sudden erudition that surprised me, "in which case, all the round pegs are the ones that are wrong, and if the *round* hole is one that is not meant to be square, then the square ones will, no, hang on—"

"Shame," said the historian, "and you were doing so well. Keep your head down, Edward. Those that see too much quickly find themselves seeing nothing at all."

I didn't really understand, but then I don't think I was meant to.

"You've had your three questions. So here's the bonus snippet: Sally Gamboge uses Tommo for carnal relief."

"That . . . explains quite a lot."

"It does, doesn't it? Being the invisible part of the Spectrum can be lonely, but one does get all the best gossip. Okay, this is the wisdom: First, time spent on reconnaissance is never wasted. Second, almost anything can be improved with the addition of bacon. And finally, there is no problem on earth that can't be ameliorated by a hot bath and a cup of tea."

"That's good wisdom."

"It was good jam. And jam is knowledge. Will you be at the Chromogentsia meeting this evening?"

I told him that I would—but as a helper and unlikely to speak.

"I always drop by. It's quite amusing, really—and the food is generally good."

"I'll see you there, then."

"No, you won't. I'm Apocryphal, remember?"

His Colorfulness
Matthew Gloss

3.6.23.05.058: National Color employees are exempt from
daily Useful Work.

I sat cross-legged on the window seat and watched the evening rain.
It was a cloudburst of unusual heaviness, and in the distance peals
of thunder could be heard. I watched as the gutters filled, then over-
flowed, and the path outside turned into a stream.

I picked up a piece of paper in order to write a list of the various puzzles
in the village. I planned to start with the most intractable and work my way
down. I wrote "Wheelbarrow" at the top, then stopped to think. After my
conversation with the Apocryphal man I had returned to where I'd tripped
over the wheelbarrow the previous night. The wheelbarrow was still there,
resting on the grass beside the Perpetulite. I had put it back on the roadway
and timed it. The Perpetulite had taken nine minutes and forty-seven seconds to sense that the wheelbarrow was foreign, and another five minutes
and twenty-two seconds to remove it. Slower than the boulders we'd seen
removed on the way to Rusty Hill, but the principle was the same. The
problem was, it had been dark for over half an hour by the time I walked
out there, so who—or *what* placed the wheelbarrow on the Perpetulite.

"Wheelbarrow?"

It was the Colorman, and he had walked up unnoticed because of
the noise of the rain outside and read over my shoulder. I started to rise,
but he magnanimously indicated for me to stay seated, then asked if he
could join me.

"Of course," I said, shuffling aside to let him sit.

"Writing a list?" he asked in a friendly manner.

"My birthday list," I explained, then started to gabble. "It's unusual, I know, and my birthday isn't until October. We don't have a garden, either—not one big enough to warrant a wheelbarrow, anyway—but I thought I might make a few extra cents by hiring out garden implements—with the prefect's permission, of course."

"A surfeit of information often hides an untruth," he said, with annoying clarity.

"No untruth, sir. I'll freely confess to feeling nervous in your company."

He nodded, and seemed to accept my explanation. "Your father said you were interested in queues."

I told him this was so.

"Then perhaps you can reveal why I never get into the fastest queue at the cafeteria back at National Color?"

"That's easily explained," I replied. "Since only one queue can be the quickest, in a set of five checkouts, eighty percent of the queues will be slower than the fastest. It's not a question of your choosing badly. It's more that the odds are stacked against you."

He thought about this for a moment. "So the more checkouts there are, the less chance I will have of getting into the fastest queue?"

"Absolutely," I replied, "but conversely, if you were to reduce the number of queues to one, you would always be certain of being in the fastest."

"I had no idea queuing could be so interesting," he said, "nor that anyone might have invested so much thought in the matter."

It was an ambiguous remark. It could have been either praise or criticism, but I was unsure which. I had skillfully avoided the wheelbarrow question, and now, as Jane had requested, I had to find out what he was doing here. But he had other things on his mind.

"May I ask an indelicate question?"

"I will answer it as best I can."

"Is there anyone who can fix me up with some youknow? A Colorman's life is a lonely one, and I spend many weeks on the road."

The question placed me in a difficult situation. He may already have known about Tommo from the Council, and if he did, then he was simply testing my loyalty. If he didn't and this was a sting, then I would be as guilty as Tommo. But I needed him to trust me.

"I could make inquiries on your behalf," I replied slowly, "on account of your position, hue and kin. I would be stepping across the line as a favor, and would trust that I would not be compromised on account of it." It had come out better than I'd imagined. It made me sound almost intelligent.

"An answer worthy of a prefect, young man. Neither yes nor no, but somewhere in the middle—and with the ball firmly back in my court."

It was going well, and now it was my turn. "May I ask a *hypothetical* question, Your Colorfulness?" I was using an obsolete term to impress, but annoyingly, the Colorman knew it.

"I positively welcome it, young cousin—and please, call me Matthew."

"Thank you. Just *supposing* there are two people with whom I was vaguely acquainted. One is a mid-Purple and the other an ex–light Purple, now Grey. Let us also suppose they are both young and foolish. They desire to be together, but their parents have other ideas."

"And would these hypothetical young lovers be living, hypothetically speaking, in East Carmine?"

"I couldn't say."

"Ah! Go on."

"They plan on running away, but they have nowhere to go. I was wondering whether a contact might be found in Emerald City who would be willing to employ a hardworking young couple with no questions asked."

He smiled. "I appreciate your hypothetical concern, and give you full marks for compassion, which is certainly a trait worth cultivating. The short answer is that you should report these two for the infraction, pocket the bounty and move on with your life, happy in the knowledge that you have dutifully served the Collective."

"And the long answer?"

The Colorman stared at me, considering the matter. "Let's just *suppose* I have a friend in Emerald City," he said. "Let's also suppose that I decide to put your theoretical couple in touch with her. I should imagine that providing such a contact—hypothetically speaking—would be worth a thousand merits, in cash. Once they are there, they will have to negotiate privately with my contact. Do I make myself clear?"

"Yes, sir, you do."

I blinked. I had been playing with fire, but seemed to have got away with it. I wasn't even sweating. Dorian and Imogen would be pleased, but a thousand merits in cash was a lot of cautionary photos in *Spectrum* and at least half a negative ton of floaties.

The Colorman thought for a moment, then lowered his voice. "Tell me, Edward, have you ever thought of a career at National Color?"

Everyone had, at some point in his life.

"You think I might be up for it?"

"It's possible. Your diplomatic skills impress me, and you have a good knowledge of color. I heard about your escapade beyond the curtain last night. It showed a certain . . . grit."

"I ended up having to be rescued."

"In order to fail, first you have to try. But tell me, why risk your hide for a Yellow?"

"He was my friend."

The Colorman nodded his head slowly. "I admire loyalty in a resident," he said, "as long as it is used correctly. Loyalty misplaced is loyalty wasted."

"I also wanted to see what it was like," I said quietly. "Being Nightloss, I mean."

"And what was it like?"

"I'll be honest: frightening."

He looked at me for a long time, then seemed to come to a decision and took an envelope from his breast pocket. "See this? It's an invitation to sit the National Color entrance exam. You will still need your head prefect's approval, which isn't likely—they generally like to keep even medium receptors for color-sorting duties. But a capacity for ingenuity is looked on favorably by National Color. Wangle a signature on this, and you've got a shot at the color trade."

I thought he was going to give me the letter, but he didn't. He just placed it on a nearby table.

"Can I count on your complete discretion, Edward?"

I told him that he could.

"Then I want you to swear an oath that what I say goes no further than this room."

"On the Word of Munsell."

He looked around, then lowered his voice. "My appearance at East Carmine is not simply about magenta leaks and conducting Ishiharas."

"No?"

"No. National Color takes the illegal sale of hues very seriously, so Robin Ochre's theft is of considerable interest. One of his accomplices was Zane G-49, whom you met. He died before we could ask him to account for his actions. We think he posed as a Purple, selling 'surplus' swatch hues to various Paint Shops around the Collective. Naturally, since he seemed Purple, no one thought to question him or his motives. Conservative estimates place the value of the stolen swatches at twenty thousand merits."

"Goodness," I said, wondering if I could remain convincingly naive until the end of the conversation.

"But that's not the end of it," continued the Colorman. "We think there was *someone else* involved. Someone who may still be hiding here, in East Carmine. Someone who is a very grave danger to the Stasis."

"A fanatic?"

"Of the very worst sort. I don't wish to panic anyone, but once mono-chrome fundamentalism gets a hold, it can be hard to eradicate without harm to other residents."

I wasn't sure what the term meant, but if it was hating the system, then Jane was definitely part of it. I just didn't know if it was a bad thing or not. After all, ignoring the prescribed dress code was also considered "most serious," but I would be hard-pressed to say I felt it actually *was*. The Apocryphal man seemed no worse for wearing no clothes at all, and us for having to see him, even if we pretended we didn't.

"Surely the prefects would be the best people for you to ask?" I said warily. "There are over three thousand people in this village, and I've met barely thirty."

The Colorman shook his head. "Prefects are good people but can only be trusted to maintain themselves and their bonuses. You saw Zane at Vermillion, so are involved in a way, and you have been here two days and have a reputation for curiosity, so can nose about with impunity. Tell me, *have* you seen anything unusual?"

Five things sprang to mind immediately. If I'd been given a little lon-ger, I probably could have made it the round dozen.

"There is little in this village that isn't unusual," I admitted, "but of the matters of which you speak, nothing springs to mind."

He stared at me for a long time, then picked up the envelope from the table. "Don't disappoint me," he said, and handed it over.

He left me sitting at the window seat, my understanding of Jane, while not transformed, at least open to reappraisal. She was involved with the theft of the swatches, along with Ochre and Zane. There were twenty thousand merits kicking around somewhere, and they didn't end up with Ochre—Lucy had told me they didn't have a bean. Three people in on the scam, and only one still living. My mind started to crowd with unwelcome thoughts. I knew from personal experience that Jane was capable of doing the murder and didn't like my asking questions. She was up to something, that was true; but the question was: What? And should I snitch on her and take the buckets of bounty that would come my way?

Meet the Chromogentsia

9.7.12.06.098: Anyone above 50 percent receptive is given the designation "Chromogentsia" and is eligible for such privileges as listed in Appendix D.

My father straightened his bow tie for the tenth time and pressed the doorbell outside Mrs. Ochre's house. I hadn't seen him so fastidious with his appearance for a long time, so presumed he was interested in her. I knew for a fact that he was lonely. He and I never talked about my mother, as it was too painful, but he, like me, carried a picture of her in his valise.

"Speak when spoken to at the Chromogentsia," he said as we heard someone come to the door, "and don't do anything that might jeopardize my chances with Velma."

"Velma?"

"Mrs. Ochre."

"Ah," I said, not realizing this had gone as far as it had, "right."

The door opened.

"So good of you to come!" exclaimed Mrs. Ochre, who was dressed in a particularly stunning red evening dress. It hugged her body tightly, and looked as though it had been adapted from a Standard Strapless #21. I saw Dad's eyes look downward when he thought she wasn't watching, but I think she noticed, and was flattered.

"We wouldn't have missed it for anything, Mrs. Ochre," said my father. "I brought you these."

"Roses!" she exclaimed. "How too, too divine." She turned to her daughter, who was hovering nearby. "Lucy, my dear, would you find a vase and some water? Too wonderful to see you, Edward—is that the rice pudding? How marvelous. Would you put it in the kitchen? Lucy will show you."

I walked into the kitchen with Lucy and watched as she selected a vase, then ran some water into it, making something of a mess.

"Did you hear that my mum and your dad took tea at the Fallen Man?"

"I'd not heard that, no."

"They were even laughing together. Uproariously, some say—and they may even have held hands under the table. Look," she added, "cards on the table and all that. My mother is interested in your father. And not just for the odd cup of tea and a stroll around the Outer Markers. She's vulnerable at present, and I don't want her hurt. If your father thinks he can take advantage of a grief-stricken widow, he'll have me to contend with."

Mrs. Ochre wasn't exactly *acting* like a grief-stricken widow, what with laughing uproariously at the Fallen Man on a date with her dead husband's replacement.

"Likewise," I replied. "I don't want anyone taking advantage of my father's good nature and lonely disposition to effect a union that is not in his best interest."

"Hmm," she said, "I think that makes them both pretty much equal in the parental vulnerability stakes. Perhaps we should just give them free rein and see where it goes. We can meet again to discuss whether to throw a spanner into the works or not."

"I agree. Do you have any loganberry jam, by the way?"

"Ooh!" she murmured, "chasing knowledge, are you?"

"You've spoken to the Apocryphal man, too?"

She smiled. "I managed to reconstitute some loganberry from a dried-out jam pot I found at the back of the cupboard. It wasn't very good, but enough for half a question."

She opened the cooker and checked the chicken vol-au-vents.

"If you find some jam, I'll come in for half the cost in exchange for a question."

"Deal."

There was a pause.

"I'm sorry to bring this up," I said, "but your father—did he have much to do with the Grey, Jane?"

"Whyever do you ask?"

I had to think quick, but couldn't, so said the first thing that came into my head. "It's part of my, um, chair census."

"Oh. Well, no. Not that I know of. But he would have seen everyone at some point—he would have been there when she was born. Unless—"

"What gorgeous flowers!" said Mrs. Ochre as she walked in. "Lucy, would you mind pouring the tea while I greet guests with Holden—I mean, Mr. Russett—at the door? Edward, be a dear and make yourself useful with the coats, and after that you might like to hand the sandwiches around."

I picked up the cucumberesque sandwiches and walked into the large, wood-paneled drawing room. Mrs. Ochre could have used *real* cucumbers, but they don't hold the green dye so well. These were the more dye-absorbent sliced courgettes, and were a bright emerald mock-green. Although the room was half full, the only people I recognized were Mrs. Lapis Lazuli and the Apocryphal man, who had cleaned himself up and was even wearing a suit. Since I would not be able to acknowledge the Apocryphal man in company without heavy demerit, I merely walked past him so he could take some sandwiches off my tray. I nodded a greeting to Mrs. Lapis Lazuli, who inclined her head favorably in return.

The conversation was mostly about the possibility of High Saffron's being open for toshing and how, with full colorization from a pipeline extension, East Carmine might once more host Jollity Fair.

The next guests to arrive were Aubrey and Lisa Lemon-Skye, parents of Jabez.

"You must be Edward," said Aubrey as Lisa chatted with Mrs. Ochre and my father, who had fallen easily into the roles of hostess and host.

"You have a bicolored name," I observed. "I've never heard of that before."

"And not likely to again," mused Aubrey. "Although Ruleful, its use is not encouraged. My wife is Turquoise's cousin, so she managed to swing it for us. Besides, it's not as though we were *complementary* colors."

I gave an involuntary shudder. The notion of a Red-Green, Blue-Orange or Yellow-Purple conjoining was too scandalously degrading even to contemplate.

"Do you enjoy the bedtime story?" came a loud voice. I turned to find Mrs. Lapis Lazuli staring at me.

"Very much, ma'am."

"Splendid. I can't imagine who taps it out—most irresponsible."

And she gave me a broad wink.

"I understand you're thinking of staying with us for good?"

"Not really," I replied. "In fact, not at all."

"Glad to hear it. We are in need of fresh seed to stir up the politics before stagnation. Good gracious!" she exclaimed as an equally wrinkly lady on the other side of the room caught her eye. "It's Granny Crimson. How remarkably Rot-free she looks. I must take a closer look."

And without another word, she moved off.

"One of the stalwarts of the Debating Society," remarked Mr. Lemon-Skye as we watched the old woman move in a sprightly fashion across the floor. "Top hockeyballist in her time; represented the village sixteen times at the Jollity Fair athletics. Her areas of expertise are bar codes, book titles and maps—she has an *original* Parker Brothers map of the world."

This was interesting, since the map represented the only view we had of the world before the Something That Happened. For some reason, its destruction had not been demanded under Annex XXIV.

"Does she adhere to the theory that it represents global Chromatic regions of the pre-Epiphanic world?"

"She does, although I'm doubtful myself. If we *were* regionally blue when Something Happened, there'd be more evidence of it now."

"And the RISK acronym? What does she think that stands for?"

"Regional International Spectral Kolor. Yes, I know," Mr. Lemon-Skye agreed when I looked doubtful, "it must be an archaic spelling. But get her to show you the map. It's almost complete, you know—only the nations of Irkutsk and Kamchatka have been eaten by clodworms."

"I'll be sure to. Thank you."

"My pleasure. What do you think of our crackletrap?"

"It's . . . *impressive*."

"It is, isn't it? Some say it wasn't worth the Greys lost in construction, but scaffolding is so *very* expensive these days. We're lucky to have Prefect Gamboge, don't you think? *Splendid* lady."

I had forgotten that although Aubrey was spotted Green, he was the Lemon in Lemon-Skye. A Yellow through and through.

Another couple had entered the room. I recognized the woman because Tommo had pointed her out at the Fallen Man. They were Doug and Daisy Crimson's parents. The father was a trifle somber-looking and had the unmistakable air of a senior monitor passed over for promotion.

He also had an annoying habit of constantly looking about when being conversed with—as though there might be a more interesting conversation going on elsewhere.

"This is Edward Russett," said Aubrey as they walked over. "I was just telling him how dangerous lightning was."

There was a brief round of hand shaking and pleasantries in which I could sense they were studying me intensely on the off-chance that I stayed. Like their son, I was potentially a strong Red.

"Lightning? I'd be more concerned about swans. And the Riffraff."

"Do you know anything about the Riffraff?" I asked, trying to make it sound like an intelligent question, and not the sarcastic remark I intended it to be.

"I'm not a big fact person," said Mr. Crimson, who was honest, even if a twit. "Unproved speculation is more my thing. But Mrs. Gamboge knows a bit, don't you, ma'am?"

I hadn't noticed that the Yellow prefect had arrived, notebook in hand. It was usual for a prefect to be present to take minutes for the faculty's record, as "great and important thoughts" sometimes emerged from the meetings. Thankfully, Courtland didn't seem to be with her.

Sally Gamboge moved into the center of the room. She seemed marginally less unpleasant than usual, but that wasn't saying much. Although she was not an ugly woman, her demeanor had soured her appearance into one that generated only mistrust. But she had my full attention, and my father's. The rest had heard the story before, but stood in respectful silence regardless.

"I was visiting my sister in Yellopolis last year," she said. "They'd had problems with Riffraff camping close enough to raid crops at dawn and dusk when no one was about, so they set a few snares around the Outer Markers. Astonishingly, they actually caught one."

"What did it look like?"

"Scruffy beast. Unwashed, covered in lice, bad teeth, stained pinafore, torn dress and distinctly unshiny shoes—subhuman, if you ask me."

"Could it have been Nightloss suffering from advanced nyctopsychosis?" asked my father, who, like most people, had seen or personally experienced the effects of a night panic: quivering, palpitations, irrational shouting, dissociation from reality and finally insanity.

"It didn't have a postcode," replied the Yellow prefect, tapping her left clavicle. "I checked when they stripped it off to hose it down."

"Could it talk?" asked Lucy.

"A gutter mix of tongues," replied Gamboge expertly, taking another sip of her yellow-tinged elderflower cordial. "Many of the nouns were slang in origin, with the grammatical construction similar to our modern tongue, but with the sort of frightful mispronunciations one would expect from someone without access to proper schooling. I could understand *part* of what she was saying, but the language was so peppered with obscenities of the worst possible kind that it was barely worth trying to understand her at all."

"A savage," remarked Mr. Lemon-Skye with a shiver.

"Quite so," replied Gamboge, "yet oddly enough, it did repeat a man's name numerous times. If I didn't know any better, I might have thought it capable of a monogamous relationship."

There was polite laughter at the somewhat fanciful notion, although I didn't join in myself.

"But here's the curious part," continued Mrs. Gamboge. "The creature had lost part of its foot in the snare, and within a day infection set in. It grew listless, went pale and moaned in a most pathetic manner until it fell unconscious and died. It was all over in three days."

"You mean," said Lucy, "it didn't catch traumatic Mildew?"

"Not a spore in sight. If any *civilized* person had suffered physical damage as bad as that, he'd have been carried off by Variant-T in a twinkling."

The society went silent as they mused upon the possibility that the Riffraff had immunity from the Rot, excepting Granny Crimson, who told everyone she had just seen a bee fly past the window.

"I understand that some villages actually *trade* with the Riffraff," announced Mrs. Ochre, being the perfect hostess and filling the hole in the conversation. "My sister Betsy lives in Hennarington on the Honeybun Peninsula, and they said the Riffraff leave sacks of sorted blue scrap at the Outer Markers, which they trade for semolina, Ovaltine and gravy granules."

"If that's true," Aubrey replied, "one would have to come to the rather astonishing conclusion that the Riffraff may have a rudimentary understanding of color."

Everyone nodded sagely in agreement.

"I have been studying *Homo feralensis* for many years," remarked Mrs. Gamboge, "and I firmly adhere to the theory that they are Greys who have simply dropped the short distance into savagery. Without the stabilizing hand of Munsell's Chromatic ideology, we would be like them—ignorant, filthy and bestial."

"Is it true they eat their own babies?" asked Mrs. Crimson.

"It is *absolutely* true—and any other babies they can get hold of. Some say they produce babies only to eat."

"How could feral *Greys* have a rudimentary sense of color?" I asked.

Mrs. Gamboge fixed me with an icy stare and announced in a doom-laden voice, "By eating the brains of those they slaughter, in order to inherit their Chromatic cognicity."

"Eat their brains?" echoed Mrs. Ochre in a quavering voice, breaking the stunned silence that followed.

"Without a doubt," murmured Mrs. Gamboge, "and with a spoon—the instrument of the truly barbarous."

"Goodness!" Mrs. Lemon-Skye exclaimed. "Perhaps that's why *Harmony* left spoons off the list of manufactured goods."

"Truly, Munsell works in mysterious ways," announced Mr. Crimson.

"The sooner we deal with the Riffraff problem once and for all," continued Mrs. Gamboge, who was eager to drive her point home, "the sooner we can sleep safe in our beds at night."

A chorus of agreement greeted this sentiment, followed by a long pause as everyone presumably thought about how lucky they were to be living within such a safe, ordered civilization. Except me, who was thinking about how I *already* slept safe in my bed.

"What utter balls!" came a loud and gravelly voice.

"Who dares to use such lang—" Mrs. Gamboge began, but she stopped when she saw it was the Apocryphal man, and changed the comment into a cough, while everyone stared at their drinks, or at the walls, or something.

Mrs. Ochre, attempting some misdirection, decided we should be seated. "Time for dinner," she announced, clapping her hands together. "It's boy-girl-boy-girl-boy-girl."

Arguments over Dinner

9.02.02.22.067: Jam jars and milk and cordial bottles are to be manufactured and supplied in one size only.

W e walked through to the dining room, but the Apocryphal man had beaten us to the table and upset Mrs. Ochre's carefully thought-out place settings. After a few moments of consternation, she announced that the Apocryphal man's place was "to be left empty as a token of respect for lost friends," and pretty soon everyone was rejiggered to Mrs. Ochre's satisfaction.

Naturally enough, Lucy and I were expected to wait table and did not have place settings. Interestingly, I noted, Sally Gamboge had been put next to my father.

"The Rusty Hill expedition was a huge success," she said in a strained manner, "and I believe the sniffles is clearing up. Congratulations."

Dad returned the compliment graciously.

"So!" said Mrs. Ochre. "Before we start our meal, I should first offer a toast to absent friends who are unable to attend this meeting. By this I mean our recently departed father and husband, Robin Ochre, who is missed"—she stopped here as her voice cracked, and I felt Lucy tense—"most terribly. We should also not forget Travis Canary, a member of the Collective lost last night, who will no more enjoy the simple pleasures of relentless toil, nor the buzz of comradeship that makes the Collective so special. On the positive side, I would like to welcome the new swatchman, Mr. Russett, and his son, Edward. We hope and trust they will enjoy their stay here."

She held her glass up, and everyone murmured "*Apart We Are Together*" before Lucy gave a small reading from Munsell's *Harmony*. Once that was done, she and I laid out the first course, which was colorized mock-prawn cocktail.

By the time the food was served and Mrs. Ochre suggested that everyone start, the Apocryphal man had already finished and had made a start on his neighbor's.

"Well," said Mrs. Ochre, once everyone had tried the starter and exclaimed not only how wonderfully average it was, but how delightfully *pink*, "last month we discussed a possible reason why metal corrosion was such a huge problem to the Previous, and a possible theory that might have explained ball lightning, but didn't. For our first talk this evening, Mrs. Crimson will give one entitled—what's the title again, dear?"

Mrs. Crimson stood up. "I call this talk 'Forgotten Eponyms and the Etymology of Capitalized Nouns.'"

Everyone's eyes swiveled to Mrs. Gamboge to gauge her reaction. Discussion was meant to be unfettered, but it was generally best to have prefectural approval. Gamboge, however, said nothing, and simply made a note in what must have been light yellow ink in her notebook—to us, it didn't appear as though she had written anything at all.

"How many of you," began Mrs. Crimson, "have ever wondered why the following words are capitalized: Morse code, eggs Benedict, Ottoman, Faraday cage and fettuccine Alfredo?"

They all shook their heads. They hadn't really thought about it. In fact, *I* hadn't really thought about it.

"I will argue," she continued, "that their origin may be in the person who coined them, or were involved in their discovery."

"How can you discover eggs Benedict?" said Mrs. Gamboge with a snort. "Next you'll be telling me Battenberg was discovered by someone named Battenberg."

"Yes," said Mrs. Crimson, giving her a baleful stare, "that's exactly what I contend."

Mrs. Crimson gave a spirited talk that, while skirting controversy by the avoidance of proof, did offer a tantalizing glimpse of life before the deFacting: a rich world full of interest, and what's more, *meaning*.

The conversation turned to the subject of High Saffron after that, and how the town was wholly untouched since the Something That Happened and would have a rich seam of colored waste just ready to be teased out of the soil. Mrs. Lapis Lazuli contended that there was a library there, too, of great antiquity, stocked with books long since confined to the Leapback list. Mrs. Gamboge replied that this was just the sort of "fanciful nonsense" that librarians are apt to speak, and professed her opinion that if it weren't for the Rules, she would long ago have relocated Lapis Lazuli's band of librarians to "somewhere they might benefit the community," an opinion that caused Mrs. Lapis Lazuli to go so red with anger that I think even the Ochres noticed. Mr. Crimson defused the situation by telling us about the picked-clean village of Great Auburn and how, in order to flush the color from the soil, high-pressure water hoses had been used; although damaging to the ground, the hoses were by far the most time-efficient method of extraction. He was just getting to the difficulties of transportation when the night bell sounded. And with a fizz and a flicker, Fandango struck the arc outside. A fresh white light shone through the large windows, and the Luxfer panels above the sash projected their angular-patterned light upon the ceiling.

Lucy and I cleared the table and returned with the main course. After a discussion regarding the intractability of finding a way around the Spoon Question and a discourse on the unhelpfully random nature of pre-Epiphanic family names, Mrs. Ochre asked if anyone had come across anything "odd" in the past month that they wished to bring to the society's attention.

"May I speak?" I asked, and when no one objected, I produced Dorian's picture of the village taken at night. I passed it to my father, who studied it closely before he passed it on.

"This picture was taken a few weeks ago," I explained. "Dorian G-7 accidentally left the camera shutter open all night and photographed these strange concentric light rings in the sky. Does anyone have any idea what they are?"

Dad passed the photograph to the Widow deMauve, who passed it to Mrs. Gamboge, who made another invisible yellow-ink note before handing it on. Mrs. Lapis Lazuli stared at it for some time and even traced the path of one of the lines with her finger. "They are not full rings," she observed. "They are simply a series of interlocking *arcs*, all moving around a central point."

She gave the photograph to Mrs. Lemon-Skye. "I would suspect that it is either a hoax," she said, passing it on, "or a fault in manufacturing."

"I don't think so," said her husband. "You can clearly see the lines falling *behind* the silhouette of the crackletrap." He looked closer. "There are *other* lines, too—wispy ones, crisscrossing the circles."

"Not circles," corrected Mrs. Lapis Lazuli, "*arcs*."

"Arcs, then—but for what purpose?"

"Circles in the sky we cannot see?" remarked Sally Gamboge, whose eagerness to believe nonsense about Riffraff did not leave much space in her head for objectivity. "I have never heard of anything more ridiculous."

"Cats and Nocturnal Biting Animals can see on a moonless night," observed Lucy, "so there must be *some* light, and from *some*where."

"You are all mistaken," said the Apocryphal man. "They are distant suns."

There was an uncomfortable pause. We all wanted to know what he meant, but no one dared even acknowledge him.

"It's of . . . distant *suns*," said Granny Crimson, who was now staring at the picture intently. Everyone looked at one another, but no one challenged her on the impiety. Not even Sally Gamboge. We were all too curious.

"And could you tell us more?" asked my father.

"I'm not sure," said Mrs. Crimson doubtfully, looking surreptitiously at the Apocryphal man.

"Distant suns," repeated the Apocryphal man, "very like our own, but at such an immeasurable distance from the earth that they appear only as points of light, too dim for the *Homo coloribus* eye to see."

"Suns," repeated Granny Crimson, so all could legally reflect upon the Apocryphal man's words, "too far away to be seen . . . points of light."

"*Stars*?" murmured Lucy. The obsolete word sounded ancient to our ears. But we all murmured our understanding. We'd *heard* about them but hadn't considered that we would ever be able to observe them in any meaningful way. Like the Pyramids, the Great Sweat, Chuck Naurice, Tariq Al-Simpson, M'Donna and the Rainbowsians, we all knew they had once existed, but there was no record, or proof—they were now just labels on lost memories, cascading down the years from resident to resident, echoes of lost knowledge.

"But these are *not* points of light," observed Aubrey. "They're *circles*."

"Arcs," repeated Mrs. Lapis Lazuli. "Let's just stick to the facts, eh?"

"They *move*," said the Apocryphal man, "and describe a circular motion in the night sky. What you see is not a moment in time, but seven hours of time, seen as one."

Granny Crimson repeated what he had said, word for word.

There was another silence as we all took this in, and I felt a thrill of discovery, of gained intelligence. But there was something else, too: an overwhelming sense of inconsolable *loss*. Progressive Leapbacks had stripped so much knowledge from the Collective that we were now not only ignorant, but had no idea *how* ignorant. The moving stars in the night sky were only one small part of a greater understanding that had gone for good. And as I stood there frowning to myself, I had a sense that everything about the Collective was utterly and completely *wrong*. We should be dedicating our lives to *gaining* knowledge, not to losing it.

"But *why* do the stars move?" asked Mrs. Crimson.

"They don't."

"They don't," repeated Granny Crimson.

"But you said—"

"*We* move," remarked Lucy with a flash of understanding. "The earth rotates about its axis once a day. If you think about it, our own sun *also* describes a circle about us."

I saw the Apocryphal man nod his head agreeably, and everyone went silent, pondering the notion carefully.

"I must say I find this extremely far-fetched," said Mrs. Gamboge, who was doubtless miffed that we were debating anything at all. "It is well known that mental incapacity places Granny Crimson not a week from Variant-G. Besides, what you are saying cannot be true, for there is a single point, right in the middle of the rings, which does not move at all."

"Arcs," said Mrs. Lapis Lazuli.

"I suggest," replied Granny Crimson, once the Apocryphal man had spoken, "that it is a distant star perfectly aligned with the rotating axis of the earth."

We all fell into a hushed silence. The Apocryphal man spoke self-evident truths with such clarity that we all felt humbled. But my father put it best. He looked straight at Granny Crimson and said, "I have been to Debating Society meetings for over twenty years. In all that time I have listened to nothing but poorly reasoned theories and weakly argued supposition. Tonight, we have listened to true knowledge."

"I'll get the rice pudding," said Mrs. Ochre, and hurried from the room.

"Perhaps," said Mr. Lemon-Skye, addressing the Apocryphal man but looking at Granny Crimson, "you might bring your keen intellect to bear on another intractable puzzle that has confounded our weekly gathering for some years?"

The Apocryphal man made no sound, but Aubrey didn't get to ask his question, for Lucy interrupted to pose one of her own. "What is the music of the spheres?"

The Apocryphal man stared at her for a long time, then, with great deliberation, said, "Once, music was *everything*. It answered all problems, fulfilled all needs. It powered industry, transport, entertainment. It delivered comfort and light, information, books, communications and death. It could even bring . . . music."

He then yawned as though tired of the proceedings. He took out a pocket handkerchief, filled it with food and walked out of the room.

Before Granny Crimson had even finished repeating his answer, Aubrey Lemon-Skye let his feelings be known. "Well, thank you very much," he said sarcastically to Lucy. "There I am, about to ask the timeless riddle about why apples float and pears sink, and you go and annoy him—sorry, her, with your silly harmonic pathways, which, might I say, are of questionable relevance. Music bringing music? Ridiculous!"

There was a sharp intake of breath at Aubrey's rudeness. He had almost—but not quite—raised his voice.

Lucy stared back at him, hot with indignation. "Their relevance might be in doubt, sir," she replied with a thin veneer of cordiality, "but compared to *your* question, they are raised to a level of unprecedented profundity." She was talking heavily out of hue—Crimson was higher and redder than she—but we were all guests in the Ochre house, so her conduct, while unacceptable, was not technically actionable.

"And I say it is all poppycock and fiddle-faddle," announced Mrs. Gamboge, who obviously felt she didn't have to guard her language at all, an opinion embraced by Granny Crimson, who declared that Lucy's interest in the supernatural was "the milk shake of the indolent." She probably wouldn't have said it if Mrs. Ochre was in the room, and I could sense that Lucy and her talk of harmonic pathways had gotten up everyone's noses several times in the past.

Lucy thought for a moment, took a lead ball and a length of thin steel wire from her pocket and, after fetching a thumbtack from the bureau, attached the pendulum to the middle of the top of the door frame, set it swinging and then stood back respectfully.

"And what is that supposed to prove?" asked Aubrey, just as Mrs. Ochre brought in the rice pudding I had made, plus her own treacle sponge and custard "just in case."

"Have I missed something?" asked Mrs. Ochre, since Aubrey's

rudeness toward Lucy had caused something of a silence to descend on the room, and we were all staring at the pendulum with mild embarrassment, for it would reflect badly on Lucy when it did what pendulums do, which was to stop.

"Your daughter is demonstrating her theory of harmonics," said my father, and after Mrs. Ochre had said, "Fancy that!" we concentrated on the dessert, and the conversation turned to approximating the migration cruising altitude of the species *Cygnus giganticus*, and a reason why they seemed to constantly fly in large figure-eight patterns.

"Sometimes they are so high they barely look like swans at all," remarked Mrs. Crimson.

The talk didn't stay on swans for long, however, as everyone's attention turned back to the lead ball, which had not slowed and stopped, as one would expect from a pendulum of less than a foot in length, but seemed to be *increasing*.

"How curious!" remarked Mr. Crimson, echoing our thoughts perfectly.

As we watched, the pendulum increased its swing until the lead ball came into contact with the underneath of the door frame with a sharp *snock*, swiftly followed by another as the ball struck the other side. From then on the swing increased ever more dramatically, and within a minute the wire was invisible, the lead ball a semicircular blur and the noise a sharp staccato of sound that increased in volume until it was a continuous howl and several of the diners leaned back in alarm.

As the wood on the door frame began to splinter with the constant hammering, the wire suddenly broke and the lead ball shot off, bounced on the sideboard, shattered a tumbler in front of Mrs. Lapis Lazuli and then vanished out the window, leaving an almost perfect hole in the glass.

Lucy said nothing, for there was little to be said. Aubrey gamely said that he would pay for the damage, which was about as good an apology as one might expect from someone born a Yellow.

"Before you ask," said Lucy, "I have no idea why it works. But it *does*."

"It's the motive power behind the Everspins," I mused, building on the Apocryphal man's contention that to the Previous, music was everything, "and probably runs the lightglobes, too."

"How does it do it?" asked Mrs. Crimson, which was a question no one even attempted to answer.

"I think maybe there's a huge tuning fork somewhere," suggested

Lucy, "or a network of them, and they resonate together in harmony, each feeding off the other, sending vibrations through the air around us."

"And still humming after five centuries?" observed my father. "It must be a very large tuning fork indeed."

"Enormous," remarked Lucy in a quiet voice.

The table lapsed into silence as we considered all manner of things that up until now had no simple explanation. The hot-water elements in boilers, for one, which went scaldingly hot twice a day for an hour, and pre-Epiphanic window glass, which buzzed itself clean at midday.

"Furthermore," said Lucy as a final comment, "I've noticed that in an area of strong harmonics, a floatie will rise a good two or three extra inches—thus suggesting a link between music and gravity."

We ate our pudding in silence following these dramatic revelations, and after lemon tea Mrs. Lapis Lazuli gave a talk on her lifetime's research into bar codes, which, although carefully studied and diligently argued, was long on theory and short on facts. She had decoded seven of the known thirty-one variants, yet had been unable to explain exactly what benefit bar codes held over numbers, nor why almost everything tended to have them. Not just all the pre-Epiphanic artifacture but almost every-thing else, too—from Perpetulite to oaks, yateveos, slugs, fruit flies, mice, root vegetables, rhinosauruses—even us, with something similar to a bar code growing out of our left-hand nail beds. Her favored theory was that the Previous performed periodic stock-takes and needed to know not only where all the stuff was but how much there was of it. This seemed likely, as the Previous were renowned for their desire to count things in order to control them. She also noted that some things had partial or "vestigial" codes, like the now-unreadable smudges on the necks of donkeys, and that a few things had no trace of a bar code at all: most notably bats, apples, bar codes themselves and rhododendrons. She was given a round of applause at the end, and she thanked us all modestly, giving credit to her librarians, who had so ably assisted her in the research.

The rest of the meeting was spent less in debating and more in gen-eral chitchat, and by the time the evening was out, and the lime had been passed round and peeked with enthusiasm, everyone was the best of acquaintances. Even Sally Gamboge was faintly acceptable, and she even made a joke about the shriveled toe that Bunty had found in her pinafore pocket.

I got home an hour before lights-out. Dad told me to go ahead, as he would be helping Mrs. Ochre tidy up. The streetlamp went out less than twenty minutes after I had got into bed, and I listened to the Morse chatter on the radiators for a while. It was mostly about the possibility of connection to the grid, the presence of the Colorman and who would be stupid or daring enough to volunteer for the High Saffron expedition. There was even talk about me and my attempt to rescue Travis the previous evening. The opinions ran from "insane" to "brave" to "I think he's got a cute bottom."

Across the top of the chat, the nightly serialized book was being tapped out by Mrs. Lapis Lazuli. And now that I knew it was she, I could hear the mild tremor in her hand. I listened to *Renfrew* for a while before falling asleep, thinking about whether I should tell the Colorman about Jane, or Jane about the Colorman, and whether starting a Question Club was a good idea. I also thought about the wisdom of advanced queuing theory, and, of course, the wheelbarrow.

Boundary Patrol

> **3.2.02.58.624:** Boundary Patrol is to be performed a
> minimum of daily, frequency to be determined by
> requirements. All are to take part.

"Right, then," said Prefect Turquoise. "I want a good Boundary Patrol, but I don't want any silly accidents. No straying beyond the boundary unless absolutely necessary, and *under no circumstances* farther than the Outer Markers. There hasn't been a swan attack for six years, and no one's seen any Riffraff for thirty—but I don't want anyone to think this means we can afford to be complacent. Usual pairings, keep your eyes open, don't startle any megafauna and be sure to check in at every phone booth. Mr. Lime has asked us to keep a careful eye on any rhododendrons creeping over the boundary—if you see any seedlings, pull them up. You know how invasive they are. Those walking Delta and Echo sectors will be dropped at Harmony by Mr. Fandango in the Ford and work their way back. Russett, you'll be with Doug in Foxtrot sector. Any questions?"

"Yes," said a light Yellow. "Will we be back in time for breakfast? You know how the Greys always scoff the bacon in the first five minutes."

"First come, first served," said Turquoise. "That's the Rule, irrespective of hue. If you don't dawdle, perhaps you might finally get to taste bacon."

"I heard it's really good," said someone farther down the line, a sentiment that everyone seemed to agree with.

Sixteen of us were standing outside the town hall. We were dressed in Outdoor Adventure #9s, and carried no spots. I'd had similar duties since I reached eligibility at age thirteen, so was acquainted enough with the procedure to know how boring it could be. Swans rarely came close to settlements, and Riffraff were far too canny to be surprised by a Boundary Patrol. Besides, if you talked loudly enough they'd hide anyway, and would become someone else's problem.

There were no other questions, so each team was handed a copy of a much-thumbed procedures manual, which contained detailed descriptions of the various types of swan, lightning and Riffraff, together with their individual peril ratings and a checklist of what to do if they were spotted. Turquoise wished us all well, told us again not to stray beyond the boundary and to call from *every* checkpoint, then left us to it.

"How are you this morning, Eddie?" asked Doug, who had a ready smile and was significantly more pleasant than Tommo, if a mite less interesting. Doug looked as though he were wired to fit in; Tommo was wired wholly for himself.

I said I was well, even though I wasn't. The Jane/Colorman whom-do-I-tell-on-whom question had not resolved itself. The safest course was actually the simplest—do nothing at all and hope everything turned out for the best. It wasn't a great plan, but it had the benefits of simplicity and a long tradition.

Doug set off and I followed, away from the houses of still-sleeping residents and past the lumpy grasslands in the direction of the linoleum factory. We chatted on the way, mostly about family. The Crimsons were on their way down the Spectrum, but unlike the Russetts, who had fallen dramatically from high perception, the Crimsons seemed to be slowly losing their Redness—about 10 percent a generation.

"Are you seriously going to marry Violet?"

"I guess," he said with a shrug. "I'd sooner not, of course, but Violet's very difficult to refuse. When she suggested a half promise that was binding on me but not on her, I tried to tell her I was going to join the Keepers of the Long Swatch and devote my life to silent devotion of the hue, but it came out as 'Thank you, Violet, that would be very nice.'"

I told him about Constance, and we exchanged views on marrying up-Spectrum. I think I was more optimistic than he was, but then Constance didn't sound quite as bad as Violet, who once screamed so loudly to get her own way that she shattered a trifle bowl *in another room.*

"Mind you," continued Doug, "if I marry into the deMauves, I'll never be short of pocket money and a cushy job at the factory. Perhaps I should just lie back and think of the linoleum."

I would probably do the same thing—only with string.

"Doug," I said, thinking about the Apocryphal man, "do you have any jam?"

"Of course."

"Loganberry?"

He rolled his eyes.

"I wish. There'd be some in the deMauves' cellar."

"Would they sell any to me?"

He laughed, which I took to mean no.

We crossed the river in silence, walked past the factory and railway station and then headed out along the western road. Ahead of us a narrow valley opened up into the wood-covered heights of the Redstone Mountains. In between the hills I could see a large grey structure, and I pointed this out to Doug.

"It's the five-part dam complex left behind by the Previous," he explained. "It rained a lot round here, even then. It still feeds Blue Sector West by way of a seventy-four-mile-long aqueduct. So big you could once walk inside, but the lime scale is about a foot thick these days. You'd pass the dams on the way to High Saffron. Mostly silted up, now."

After an abrupt right turn up a pathway, we arrived at the boundary. It was much like the one at Jade-under-Lime: simply an earthen dike thirty feet high, topped with a partially dilapidated stone wall and a deep ditch filled with clutching brambles. It was enough to halt a rhinosaurus or an elephant but wouldn't stop a ground sloth or bouncing goat.

There was a phone booth on the village side of the boundary, which for sound colornomic reasons was painted grey rather than red. There was no door; only three panes of glass remained and soil creep had buried it to almost a quarter of its height. But the Bakelite telephone was still in good order, kept safe and dry under a domed cloche that would not have appeared out of place covering a cake.

Doug took off the cloche, dialed a number and reported where we were. Turquoise would be underground in the Plotting Room, where, for doubtless sound but unknown reasons, the team's positions and progress could be marked on a large table painted with a map of the sub-Collective.

This done, Doug replaced the receiver and cloche, and we trudged on, the sun still low and the air cool and laden with dew. Occasionally

I caught a glimpse of natural red in the countryside's rich bounty. The birds, roused perhaps by our tramping boots, popped their heads out from under their wings and sang.

"I'd sing, too, if I could fly," said Doug. "See over there? The Fallen Man."

He was pointing at a low-walled enclosure just outside the boundary, on a flat piece of cleared ground overlooked by two large ginkgo trees and several rhododendron bushes that looked as though they were discussing invasion plans. I found a footpath, and trotted down for a closer look. The enclosure was perhaps forty feet in diameter, built to less than waist height. The iron gate had been saved from rusty oblivion by a timely coat of paint, but was no more substantial than a spider's web. The grass within the enclosure was kept short and neat by the industrious work of a team of guinea pigs, which blinked at me from their burrows as I opened the gate. Inside was the Fallen Man: Like our lodger, he was something inexplicable in a world of carefully ordered absolutes, so what remained of him was kept exactly as it was, with nothing taken away and, aside from the wall and the guinea pigs, nothing added.

The chair and the man were lying flat on the ground, having landed sideways. Of the Fallen Man's body, little remained. He had rotted long ago, and the weather had broken down the bones to crumbling white dust wherever they poked out of the finely nibbled grass. His heavy boots were still relatively complete, as were his helmet and other scraps of clothing, some of which were a faded red in color. The chair was not at all like the stuffed-leather variety portrayed in the sign outside the tearoom. It had been beautifully constructed of aluminum, brass and chrome and had once been painted, but the sun and rain had burnished the metal to a dull grey, and even though half-embedded in the soil and badly crumpled from the impact, the chair had not corroded appreciably.

"How long has he been here?"

"I remember being brought up here soon after he landed," replied Doug after a moment's thought. "That would have been about thirteen years ago."

"Where did he come from?"

Doug shrugged and pointed straight upward, which was of little help.

"With all the unanswered questions kicking around," he said, checking the time, "the arrival of a strange man strapped to a metal chair is of little significance."

"Perhaps," I said, "the bigger mystery is that no one seems eager to find out. What do you think?"

"If you're buttering me up to join your Question Club," said Doug with a smile, "you're barking up the wrong tree. Knowing where the Fallen Man came from will not substantially alter our lives—and neither will finding out what the Something That Happened was, or even the name of Munsell's seventh apostle and the Unrevealed Abomination."

"Okay," I said, "that's the last time I mention it."

We climbed back up to the footpath, and carried on in silence for the next half hour, following the contours of the valley until the earthen dike curved around to the south. We intersected the western road where it left the boundary through a large pair of sturdy wooden gates, and stopped to report in. There was another phone booth here, along with a rain shelter and a Faraday cage, conveniently located to protect travelers from lightning.

"You can make the call this time, Eddie."

I removed the cloche, and rang Turquoise. I gave him our code and the number of the phone booth. He told me not to dawdle, and the line went dead.

"We're about halfway around our sector," said Doug, taking a drink of water, "and making good time. Do you want to see something pretty amazing?"

"You're not going to turn blue, are you?"

He laughed. "You saw that sideshow, too, did you? No. It won't take long—just past the markers."

He opened the gate, and we walked on the smooth Perpetulite toward the Outer Markers, which were nothing more than a series of wooden posts running at twenty-yard intervals parallel to the boundary, about five hundred yards farther out. They were decorated with scrap red to mark the village's predominant persuasion, and were freshened every year as part of the Foundation Day celebrations. The Outer Markers were technically the edge of our world, but the strip between the boundary and the posts was traditionally a Tolerance Zone, in which one could disport oneself with a modicum of privacy and freedom. One could amble, think, talk, touch-dance, have an impromptu picnic, shout—even indulge in a cheeky bundle or matters more usually reserved for the wool store, as long as they're conducted with all due discretion.

We arrived at the posts, and Doug pointed at the roadway with a grin. "What do you think of that?"

I'd often seen it happen to foliage, occasionally to small creatures, but never to something so large as a giraffe. The poor creature had chosen to drop dead on the roadway and the organoplastoid compound, rather than move it to one side, had elected to *absorb* it.

"There isn't much tree cover on the road to Bleak Point," explained Doug, "and the anti-rhododendron fires have damaged it quite badly; it'll absorb pretty much anything it can get."

The giraffe had been digested like leaf litter, and all that remained of it was a giraffe-shaped image in the smooth Perpetulite, the skeleton clearly visible with a subtle image of the giraffe's reticulated hide across the top of it. The bones and teeth were breaking down, and the powdered white calcites were forming a sweeping trail toward the road markings.

"Amazing stuff, isn't it?" said Doug. "It's only taken six days. Come on, we'd best be getting on."

We walked back toward the gates, and I told Doug about the Inner Boundary near Viridian, which was another Perpetulite road, only ten times as broad as this one. Since it was hemmed in by concrete and isolated from any easy source of nutrients, the compound would aggressively absorb anything organic that happened to be unlucky enough to tread on the surface. It would take ratfinks, an unwary dog and even a bird with a speed that was quite frightening.

"It sounds really dangerous."

I shrugged. "We've grown up with it. But because of this, the Inner Boundary really *is* a boundary. Only the very stupid or very brave would attempt to dash across, even with bronze-soled running shoes. But it's not all bad," I added, "for what keeps us *out* of the Great Southern Conurbation also keeps the Riffraff *in*. What's that?"

I was pointing at a pair of leather boots sticking out of the grass under a gum tree, about midway between the boundary and the markers. It was unusual, because something so valuable would never be discarded, and it's difficult to lose boots without realizing it. We walked over to investigate, only to discover that the boots were still being worn, and Travis Canary was the person still wearing them. It was not as though he would use them again, for he was quite dead—by lightning. Not by fork lightning, which usually leaves flash burns, but by ball lightning, which disfigures horribly. Most of his head had been burned away. But though partially eaten, he was still recognizable. The flies buzzed merrily about, and already his hands were puffy and shiny. He hadn't even made it past the Outer Markers.

"This will *really* upset Mr. Turquoise," said Doug, wrinkling his nose as the smell of decayed flesh wafted in the air toward us. "He *hates* paperwork."

As soon as Doug had gone to make the call, I squatted down for a closer look. Despite the large quantity of time, energy and resources spent on lightning avoidance, this was the first victim I'd seen—if you don't count the cautionary pictures published weekly in *Spectrum*.

Breathing through my mouth to avoid the smell, I peered into what remained of his head. It was badly burned inside, and looked far more dramatic than any of the lightning strikes I'd read about. Intrigued, I picked up a stick and gently probed the cranial cavity. I leaned closer, then delicately reached in and pulled out a fused lump of metal about the size of a chess piece. I stared at it for a moment, realized what it was and then quickly wrapped it in my pocket handkerchief. I then looked around, for I had seen Travis leaving the village carrying his overnight case. I couldn't see it at first, but the puzzle was soon solved, for the Perpetulite roadway was close by and I found what I was looking for scattered along the bronze curb.

"What have you got?" asked Doug who had just returned.

"Look," I said, pointing at the road, where there was still a case-shaped stain on the Perpetulite. "He must have dropped his valise on the roadway. The leather gets absorbed, but the indigestible stuff is moved to the verge."

Doug bent down and sorted through the small collection. Aside from the case's brass locks, hinges, rivets and name plate, there were several coins, his lime compact, a belt buckle, a can of sardines, part of a remote viewer with images of moving fish on it, several toy cars, a few nuts and bolts and two spoons—one engraved, the other not.

"What a waste," exclaimed Turquoise, who arrived in the Ford with Carlos Fandango twenty minutes later. "If he was going to throw his life away, he might have done it in the name of exploration or achieving color scrap collection targets."

And with a comment about how lethal ball lightning was, he made a few notes, took Travis' boots, spoons, lime compact and cash, told us we could have anything else as a finders-keepers and then climbed back into the Ford.

"What are you waiting for?" remarked Turquoise as Fandango turned the Ford around. "Patrol continues, lads. Consider yourselves lucky I don't demerit you for being outside the boundary."

Luckily for us, Boundary Patrol was completed without further drama. *Unluckily* for us, the delay caused by Travis meant the early land workers ate all the bacon after all. Turquoise was unsympathetic. "If you'd wanted to beat the Greys to the bacon," he said, "you should have just left Travis for tomorrow's patrol." Doug agreed. After all, what was one more day to a dead body?

We divided up Travis' possessions before we parted. Doug took the belt buckle, and I kept the pocketknife. Everything else we agreed to send to his relatives. They would doubtless want to have a few mementos, and to know what had become of him. I was planning to tell them it was a ball-lightning strike, even though it wasn't. Travis had not been denied his full Civil Obligation by chance—it had been taken from him.

Ball Lightning

2.5.03.16.281: Lightning Avoidance Drill is to be practiced at least once a week.

I found Dorian in his photographic studio after breakfast and told him about the Colorman's offer of a safe passage to Emerald City.

"A thousand?"

"That's what he said."

"We might scrape all that together," he said, "but not have enough for an Open Return as well."

"How was the harvest?"

"Negative fifteen ounces all told," he said, "considerably worse than last year."

I told him to stay tuned as the situation might improve, and he thanked me for my time.

Soon after that I bumped into Carlos Fandango, who was cleaning out the mechanism in the village arc light.

"Did you send word to your Purple contact?" he asked, after demonstrating how the mechanism worked and explaining how constant maintenance was required to keep the streetlamp from flickering or, worse, going out altogether—the janitor's worst possible faux pas.

"He's at a leadership convention at Malachite-on-Sea," I lied, reasoning that if Fandango at least *thought* Bertie was in the cards, he'd delay other potential suitors, "but I've requested the name of his hotel. Tomorrow, perhaps."

"Jolly good! Did you see Courtland? He wanted to talk to you about something."

After seeking directions, I walked out of the village to a large open pasture where I found East Carmine's second-best Model T. This was a pickup, and far more battered than the sedan, if such a thing was possible. The bodywork had been dented and hammered out so many times that it resembled the skin of a baked potato, and the tires were homemade from scrap rubber, expertly stitched together with braided nylon. As Fandango had explained, the second T was used to neutralize ball lightning. Mounted on the flatbed was a swivel mount upon which sat a powerful crossbow, tensioned and loaded with a copper spike.

Sitting on a deck chair by the side of the vehicle was Courtland. He was dressed in herringbone tweeds and had a cup of tea and a plate of biscuits on a small table. Just a little way away, a Grey was staring toward the Western Hills through a pair of binoculars. Like Courtland, he would be on triple wages. Fork lightning was fairly predictable, but ball was a law unto itself. Our team back home would lose a ball-trapper a year, almost without fail. Nasty business.

"Glad you could make it," said Courtland. "Tea?"

"No, thanks."

"Suit yourself. My man Preston does a smashing cuppa. Isn't that so, Preston?"

Preston murmured, "Yes, sir," but kept his eyes firmly glued to the horizon.

"Before they Leapbacked riding," continued Courtland, "ball-lightning hunts were conducted on horseback. Fine sport, they say, although I don't believe they neutralized a single one. Tricky business, throwing a harpoon at full gallop—and the earthing wires always ended up tangled in the horse's hooves."

He chortled to himself, then turned to me with a scowl. "Tommo tells me you didn't double-order the Lincoln for us—*despite* his having wangled you a ride to Rusty Hill."

I shrugged. "Double-ordering the Lincoln without Dad noticing was difficult."

"Of course it was difficult," snapped Courtland. "If it was easy, I would have asked Tommo, or done it myself."

"Ball!" announced Preston, swiftly moving from his binoculars to a simple inclinometer mounted on a wooden tripod. We stared toward the horizon and saw a shining white orb slowly wending its way in our

242

direction. Courtland put down his tea and picked up a stopwatch and clipboard.

"Bearing two hundred and sixty-two degrees," recited Preston, "elevation thirty-two."

Courtland wrote the numbers on a pad, then pressed the stopwatch. "Mark!" he called, then turned back to me. "So what are you going to do to make amends? Do you have anything else to bargain with, or will I simply take our favor off your account?"

"I have an account?"

"You most certainly do," asserted Courtland, "and it's already in deficit—by the cost of setting up the account. Mark!"

Ten seconds had ticked past.

"Bearing two hundred and sixty-seven degrees, elevation thirty-six," recited Preston. "High and fast, I think, guv'nor."

"*I'll* be the best judge of that, thank you," said Courtland, consulting a cardboard calculator before announcing, "Fast and high—it will probably land somewhere near Great Auburn, if it doesn't wink out before then. Right, then," he added, turning back to me, "to make amends I have decided you are to return to Rusty Hill and collect up as many spoons as you can. Even a dented teaspoon would be worth a hundred merits on the Beigemarket, and out of the fifty or so spoons kicking around there must be two or three carrying clear title postcodes we can sell to an underpopulated village. Now *that* would be some serious cash—and legal."

But Courtland's avaricious spoon talk had little effect upon me. I had something else on my mind, and I couldn't hold it in any longer.

"We found Travis."

He stared at me intently before replying in a nonchalant manner: "Alive?"

"No."

"Shame. Did you manage to swipe his spoons before anyone arrived?"

"I was more concerned about Travis."

"That's what happens when you accept friendships from other colors," he chided. "It makes one unprofitably sentimental. What happened to him, by the way?"

"His head was half burned away."

"That's good news for the Council. It justifies the hideous cost of the crackletrap."

"But not good news for Travis."

Courtland shrugged, and I showed him the piece of molten metal I'd found in Travis' skull.

"Do you know what this is?"

"Of course," he replied evenly, "it's a section of unburned Daylighter. Tommo could probably get you four merits for it as salvage. He could sell green to an Orange, that boy."

"Do you want to know where I found it?"

"My dear fellow, you might enjoy grubbing around for scrap, but I have greater demands on my time."

"I found it in Travis' head."

He stared at me with a blank expression for several moments, giving nothing away. He and his mother had gone out at night to look for Travis, armed with Daylighters. A magnesium flare would be hot enough when thrust into the head to emulate a ball strike. They said they hadn't found him, but the evidence seemed to indicate otherwise. Courtland tapped his fingers together.

"Something on your mind, Edward?"

"Why?"

"Why what?"

"Why did you kill him?"

He rose to his feet. I thought he was going to violent me, but he didn't. He just laughed out loud and patted me on the shoulder.

"You've been listening to too much *Renfrew,* old chap. There isn't any murder anymore—there's no point to it. Why would we even *consider* such a thing?"

"I don't know."

"Exactly. Besides, what proof do you have? Did anyone see you take that from Travis' head?"

I didn't say anything, which was answer enough.

"You're sharp," he said, "and I respect that. And since they say you've got good red and will be here for a while, I guess you and I will have to get along."

"I'm not staying, Courtland."

He smiled.

"You really don't get it, do you?"

He pointed at my NEEDS HUMILITY badge.

"Do you really think it was Bertie Magenta's elephant trick that got you sent out here?"

244

"Yes."

"You're going to have to guess again. The Outer Fringes have a greater purpose than you credit them. They are a receptacle for those who have done nothing against the Rules but are deemed 'potentially problematical.' When it comes to *Harmony*, it's far better to be safe than sorry. Counting chairs in the Outer Fringes is Reboot with a small *r*."

A sudden thought struck me. Old Man Magenta hadn't been annoyed about the elephant trick perpetrated on his son. In fact, he had laughed for the third time ever, and Mr. Blaupunkt, our Blue prefect, had privately told me that Bertie deserved it, as he was something of a clot, and everyone thought so.

"It was the improved *queuing*, wasn't it?" I said in a quiet voice.

"Now you're getting it. The Collective has a built-in resistance to change. Not just in technology and social mobility but in *ideas*. Queue modification isn't an offense, but it's enough to have you covertly flagged."

"What about 'Buy one get one free' offers? Is that a flag, too?"

"Tommo's out here for the same reason. But it was greed that had him flagged, not seditious thoughts about corrupting the sanctity of the dinner queue. Are you certain you wouldn't like some tea?"

"Certain."

"Designing flyable models, discovering the harmonics, an overly obsessive interest in history, talking about specific ideas at the Debating Society, uncovering certain artifacts—the list is long. You're not leaving."

"But I've an Oxblood to marry."

"Your frustration and anger will become bearable in time. Most people in the Fringes eventually stop struggling and wear their defiance with a certain tattered pride. In a generation or two your descendants will forget why they are here and may once more circulate. Unless—?"

"Unless what?"

He reached into his pocket and pulled out his wallet. He then opened it in a very obvious manner so I could see how many notes were stuffed inside it.

"There is no proof of your ridiculous assertions regarding Travis, but let's just say I am willing to be generous to someone who is perhaps a little too nosy for his own good. What's the going rate for Red silence at the moment? Three hundred?"

I stared back at him.

"I won't be bought off."

He sighed. "Your misplaced scruples are becoming wholly tiresome, Master Russett. Are you going to name a price, or do we have to indulge in a tedious series of negotiations?"

"I just want justice for Travis."

Courtland laughed again.

"Good luck to you. What have you got? A piece of scrap metal and an *outrageous* story. What have *we* got? A prefect and a senior monitor who will swear on the Word of Munsell that we saw and found nothing."

He leaned closer and lowered his voice to a growl.

"You have nothing, Russett. *Nothing.* In fact, since earning the ire of the Gamboges, you have considerably *less* than nothing."

"Low and slow, west by south!" shouted Preston, running toward the Ford. "And it's a binary pair!"

It was indeed. The two football-sized balls were orbiting each other as they moved across the treetops about five hundred yards away, drifting with the breeze. Preston had the Ford started in an instant, and Courtland jumped on the back.

"Come on, Russett," he said heaving the heavy crossbow around on its mount and checking that the copper spike was still seated securely on the string. "Why not make yourself useful?"

After a second's hesitation, I hopped into the cab. I was just in time. With a lurch and a cry of "Tally-ho!" from Courtland, the Ford leaped forward, sped across the grass and drove down an incline toward a spinney.

"Hello," I said to Preston. "Eddie Russett."

"First time to hunt ball?"

I nodded as we bumped over a rut.

"You'll like it. We get plasma storms every thirty-seven days; they're so accurate you could set your calendar by them."

I lowered my voice so Courtland couldn't hear, but I needn't have bothered, as the Ford drowned out everything but a shout anyway.

"Is Courtland a bit . . . you know?"

"Dangerous? Violent? Insane? *Definitely.* And you, sir, are as stupid as a clodworm. Accusing Courtland and his mother of murder? Do you think they're going to take that lying down?"

"In Jade-under-Lime," I said, "everyone *respects* the Rules."

"You're in the Outer Fringes now, Master Edward. *Quite* a different fish kettle."

He steered through an open gate, entered the spinney, swerved around some trees and drove across some brambles before coming to a halt. We were in a small clearing surrounded by silver birches; an old twin-rail locomotive was lying half buried on its side, with the roots of a mature oak embracing it tightly. We expected to see the binary plasma spheres dancing close by, but the air was still, and they were nowhere to be seen.

"Burst?" asked Courtland.

"Nah," replied Preston, licking his lips as he tasted the air. "Somewhere close. Metal's a good attractor," he added, nodding toward the rusty locomotive. "Feel that?"

Now that he mentioned it, I *could* feel something—a faint buzzing in the air and an odd metallic taste in my mouth. I followed Preston out of the cab and joined him at the back of the Ford, where Courtland was waiting silently. Our recent upset was for the moment forgotten. Hunting ball was more important, and besides, we could all sense that our quarry was near.

"There!"

With a rustle and a crackle, the two orbs slowly drifted from behind some foliage. Courtland lined up the sights of the crossbow while Preston jumped into action. He grabbed the drum around which the harpoon's earthing wire was wound, then drove a copper stake into the ground a safe distance from the Ford. He clipped on the wire and yelled, "CLEAR!"

Several things seemed to happen at once. Courtland fired the harpoon, which took off with a *twong*, and the trailing wire ran out from the drum with a buzz. When the harpoon made contact, there was a bright flash as the energy coursed down the copper wire to the earthing stake, and with an ear-popping noise that sounded like a C-minor ninth, a massive hole was blown in the ground where the earthing stake had been. It took me a moment or two to recover, but Preston and Courtland were not yet done. There had been *two* balls, and both of them were potentially destructive. I jumped onto the flatbed as Preston reversed out, and I helped Courtland re-tension the crossbow. Once we were back onto the pasture, it was easier driving, and we soon overtook the ball as it drifted toward the linoleum factory.

We stopped ahead of it, and with the crossbow now at full stretch and the string on the catch, Courtland placed a second copper bolt in the slide while Preston ran out the wire drum.

"*Come on!*" yelled Courtland impatiently as the ball floated overhead with a buzzing that could be felt rather than heard.

But Preston was having difficulties attaching the earthing wire to the stake.

"Quick!" said Courtland. "Help the idiot untangle it!"

I jumped off the flatbed and ran across to where Preston was struggling with the earthing wire. If the sun hadn't been in the position it was, and casting Courtland's shadow to my right, then I would not have lived to be eaten by the yateveo. But there it was, and I saw Courtland's shadow as he swiveled the crossbow in our direction. I didn't even think but moved rapidly to my left. There was a loud *twong* and I suddenly felt a sharp pain in my side as the harpoon buried itself in the grass in front of me.

For a moment, I thought it had gone right through me. I looked at Preston who by his expression, clearly thought the same. I paused for a moment, hardly daring to breathe, then brought up a hand to my midriff and felt around for a wound. I breathed a sigh of relief as I discovered that my swift avoidance movement had spoiled Courtland's aim—the copper spike had merely nicked my side and done no more damage than a nasty cut.

"Oh, my goodness!" cried Courtland with a sense of shock in his voice that would have won a drama prize in any town of the Collective. "Are you okay?"

I stood up and turned to face Courtland. I had been a fool—again. I had so much still to learn.

"You piece of . . . *shit*," I said, using a Very Bad Word for perhaps the third time ever. "You did that on purpose!"

"My dear fellow," exclaimed Courtland with another liberal helping of faux concern, "an accident, nothing more! Ball hunting is a dangerous pursuit. Are you sure you are unhurt? I feel *frightful* about this."

Saying nothing, I took my handkerchief from my pocket and pressed it across the cut, while behind us the missed ball evaporated harmlessly in midair—as they quite often do.

The ball hunt was over, but the Russett hunt had probably only just begun. I mused upon the irony of the situation. Courtland and Jane, poles apart from each other, yet united in their wish to get rid of me. Somehow, it seemed unbelievably unfair.

"Master Edward," whispered Preston, "watch your back. The Gamboges will place everything possible in your path to trip you up."

I stared at him for a moment.

"Trip me up?" I echoed.

"Yes. Are you sure you're all right? You look kind of . . . dreamy."

"Aside from a vexing Yellow problem, I'm okay," I replied, "but thanks—you've just explained the point of the wheelbarrow."

He frowned. "Wheelbarrows don't have points."

"This one did."

Eyes and the Colorman

1.3.02.06.023: There shall be no staring at the sun, however good the reason.

I walked slowly home, all the while cursing myself for my own stupidity. Not just for needlessly putting myself in jeopardy with the most unpleasant family in the village, but also for not taking the opportunity to make a deal when it presented itself. I mused that there might, in fact, be something wrong with me. Something odd in the head that seemed to beg my own destruction. First Jane, now Courtland.

I flushed out the cut with the hottest water I could bear and affixed some newspaper dipped in vinegar over the wound. I then sat on the edge of the bath and considered my position. Sally Gamboge or Courtland—perhaps both—had, for reasons unknown, killed Travis. This in itself was incredible, and aside from keeping it to myself, I didn't see quite what I could do to avoid them. I could only hope that Courtland might consider me so terrified by my near miss that I would be forever silent. In this he was undoubtedly correct—as he so rightly pointed out, I had no proof. Nothing at all. Not even a motive. It didn't make any sense. Yellows don't kill Yellows. They support them, nurture them—and, if necessary, lie for them.

I took a deep breath and stood up to stare at my reflection. I moved the light mirror into position so I could study my own eyes carefully. Preston had warned me about the Gamboges' "putting everything in my path to trip me up," and his comment, while helpful, put me on an entirely different train of thought. I had tripped over the wheelbarrow the night of Travis' loss because *someone had placed it in my path*. And what's more, done so under cover of darkness.

I had heard my mentor, Greg Scarlet, speak of the theoretical *possibility* of being able to see at night, and although it was an interesting concept, I had never given it a huge amount of thought. The night was quite simply the night: an empty time, a hole in your life. Nothing happened, nothing stirred. A time to be safe, the time to be home.

I stared closely at the entrance aperture of my eye. It was, to my best estimation, barely a sixteenth of an inch across. Not much light could enter, which was why we all saw best in bright sunlight. But Greg Scarlet's reasoning was that, since there was a large area surrounding the pupil, it would seem to indicate that a bigger entrance hole would be physically possible. And from what I knew about the basics of photography: bigger hole, more light, see farther into the twilight.

Unusually, this wasn't all conjecture. Many of the Previous who were featured in pre-Epiphanic photographs and paintings were noted for their strange wide-pupil "hollow-eyed" look, and the fact that they could see at least tolerably well at night was pretty much uncontested. But the vast quantity of optical correctives that had been uncovered seemed to suggest that whatever night sight they enjoyed was at huge cost to clarity of vision. Up until now, I had thought seeing in the dark was a lost skill, like speed skating or the cha-cha-cha, but it wasn't: Someone had been out watching me the night I attempted to rescue Travis and had placed the wheelbarrow in my path to see if I would trip over it. *There was someone in the village who could see at night.*

"Eddie?"

It was the Colorman, and I jumped guiltily.

"Oh, I'm sorry," he said. "You should sing 'Misty Blue' if engaged in thingy—you know the convention."

"I wasn't thingying—I was looking at myself in the mirror."

"Vanity is an abomination, Edward."

"I was looking at my eyes."

There must have been something uncertain in my voice, for the Colorman nodded sagely and told me he'd see me in the kitchen if I wanted to talk.

I went downstairs ten minutes later to find that the Colorman had made me a cup of tea. I couldn't even begin to think what an honor that was. Someone titled His Colorfulness making *me* tea. It put my mind at rest almost immediately. At least I had someone on whom to unburden myself, and it also resolved the whole "Do I snitch on Jane?" issue, for with the wheelbarrow mystery finally resolved, I had something positive to give him. He had, after all, showed me considerable kindness regarding the National Color entrance exam.

But the Colorman was surprisingly uninterested in the wheelbarrow.

"That's it?" he said when I'd finished. "You fall over a wheelbarrow, and all of a sudden people are doing things they haven't done for over five centuries? *Nothing* happens at night, Eddie, that's the point."

"The wheelbarrow couldn't have been left there," I explained. "Perpetulite *removes* all debris. I timed it the following morning."

"While fascinating," he said in a voice tinged with displeasure, "I find this wholly far-fetched. Really, Edward, I was hoping for a little more information from you—something about the theft of the swatches."

I had disappointed him. I didn't want to tell him about Jane, so thought I'd give him something he already knew.

"I don't think Robin Ochre misdiagnosed himself."

"I agree," replied the Colorman. "Do you know who his accomplice was yet?"

"No, sir."

He gave me a piercing look. He *knew* I was hiding something. If I told him there was nothing, he'd know I was lying.

"I don't know. Not yet. But there's something else."

"Yes?"

"I believe someone did the murder on Travis Canary."

He raised an eyebrow. "Is this related to the swatches?"

"I don't think so."

"You have proof?"

"Not really."

"What about a motive?"

"I'm still thinking about that."

"A suspect?"

"Someone . . . in the high Yellows."

"Well, now," he murmured in a disparaging tone, "I'm beginning to think you are the sort of person who does a great deal with very little."

He meant a liar.

"Now, listen," he said, "is there anything *else* you want to tell me?"

As bad luck would have it, that was precisely the moment when Jane opened the back door. By the look on her face, she had heard the

Colorman's last sentence. The two cups of tea and the relaxed style of sitting at the kitchen table probably spoke volumes, too.

I looked up, and she blinked twice. If she was surprised or angry, she didn't show it.

"I'm sorry, Your Colorfulness," she remarked in a respectful tone. "I was just collecting the washing. Am I disturbing you?"

The Colorman turned to look at her. I don't think he'd given her much thought before now, and he smiled in a manner that to me looked like politeness, but to Jane would have appeared patronizing.

"What's your name, my dear?"

"Jane, sir."

"Well, Jane, has anyone ever told you that you have a very pretty nose?"

Her eyebrow twitched momentarily. "People tend to avoid mentioning it," she said slowly. "I've no idea why."

The Colorman told her that if he lived here, he would make a point of praising her nose quite often. Jane replied ambiguously that he might "think differently, given time." He told her there were some shirts in his wardrobe that could do with a pressing. She bobbed politely and departed.

I tried to say something within earshot of Jane to at least set her mind at ease, but the Colorman held up a finger to keep me silent until her footsteps had reached the top of the stairs. "Greys are notorious gossips and busybodies," he said. "Now, what else can you tell me?"

"Nothing *positive,* sir. But I'll keep my eyes open."

"Good lad. And please, keep your wild night-vision fantasies to yourself, eh?"

I didn't stay in the house. I didn't want to have to confront Jane if she thought I was snitching on her. Mind you, I didn't want to face the Gamboges either. In fact, being in a crowd or hidden in the broom closet were probably the two safest options for me right now. I packaged up Travis' effects and wrote his postcode on the front, reasoning that he would have relatives living with him at his last address. While I was dispatching this at the post office, I was handed a telegram that had just come down the line. Constance had replied to Jane's poem.

TO EDWARD RUSSETT RG6 7GD ++ EAST CARMINE RSW ++ FROM
CONSTANCE OXBLOOD SW3 6ZH ++ JADE UNDER LIME GSW ++ MSGE
BEGINS ++ MUMMY AND I GREATLY MOVED BY YOUR POETIC WORDS

++ APOLOGIES FOR SUGGESTING ROGER FRONT RUNNER WHEN NO
DECISION MADE ++ ACTUALLY HES DEAD BORING ++ WILDLY EXCITED
AT POSSIBILITY OF YOUR SEEING BUNDLES OF RED ++ DADDY CAGEY ON
HOW MUCH PERCEPTION SECURES ME ISNT HE A TEASE QUESTION MARK
++ LOTS OF LOVE CONSTANCE XXXXXXXXX ++ MSGE ENDS

It was *excellent* news—tantamount to making me the front-runner.
She'd even ended the telegram with "Lots of love" and *nine* kisses, which
bowled me over until Mrs. Blood explained that it would be the same
price for two as for nine.

I returned home, made sure Jane wasn't in the house, carefully filed
the telegram in my valise and then hid under the bed for half an hour,
before making my way down to the sports fields. The news from Constance raised my spirits a little, but probably not as much as I might have
liked. Courtland had intimated that I wouldn't be leaving, but he hadn't
met the Oxbloods—and when they wanted something, they generally
got it.

Hockeyball

1.1.19.02.006: Team sports are mandatory in order to build character. Character is there to give purpose to team sports.

The three playing fields were on a flat piece of land between the village and the river and within sight of the Green Room. There were two wooden pavilions, a changing room, a scoreboard for cricket, tiered seating and several wheeled sight-screens. They had all once been brightly painted, but the colors had long since faded and were now just a series of pastel shades, the paint cracked and shrunken like a dry lake bed.

Of the three pitches, the most perfect was for cricket; for economic reasons it had only had the creases dyed green. The two others were for hockeyball and soccer, and although vaguely flat and clear of sheep droppings, they could have done with a good roll and a sprinkling of grass seed. But the place was cheery enough in an enthusiastically amateur sort of way, and aside from the faint smell of hot oil that was blowing across the fields from the linoleum factory, the setting was almost pleasant.

I was late in arriving for the match, partly because I was hoping to miss selection and be reduced to nothing more than a substitute, and partly to avoid bumping into Jane or Courtland. They were, in fact, already there and glared at me dangerously, leaving me with the odd choice of whom I feared more. In this context, probably Jane, as she was on the other side. On-field fatalities, although rare, were cited as "accidental" and thus carried no demerits—but only if the victim was actually in possession of the ball when the tackle occurred and the game was in play. I could avoid an attack from Jane as long as I never got the ball, but couldn't guarantee that some fool wouldn't give me an easy pass.

As to my hope of being made a substitute, it was not to be. I was handed a striped team jersey by Tommo, then a hockeyball stick by Courtland, who wished me good luck in such a pleasant manner that I could only think he meant entirely the opposite.

Naturally, serial overachiever Violet deMauve was the girls' team captain. She looked me up and down as I arrived, the banana extortion incident doubtless still forefront in her mind.

"Glad you could be troubled to turn up," she said, "not that it will make a scrap of difference to your humiliating defeat."

"What does she mean?" I asked Doug as Violet strode off to give a pep talk to her team.

"The boys have never beaten the girls in the entire history of East Carmine hockeyball," he replied somewhat cheerlessly. "We just run around a lot, try to avoid being hit with those damnable sticks and concede as soon as the score reaches ten-nil."

"Wow," I muttered. "I wouldn't like to be the captain on *this* team." They all stared at me as I said it, then clumped around me in a worrying fashion. "Blast," I said.

"It's me, isn't it?"

"It's traditionally the last person to arrive," said Courtland with an unpleasant leer. With a sudden sinking feeling, I realized I should have avoided the match entirely.

"I'm captain?"

"Yes," replied Courtland. "Looks like you'll be able to dazzle us with your superior Green sector leadership qualities."

"Listen, I've never captained hock—"

"Any strategy for us?" asked Doug. I could see I was wasting my breath. The captaincy decision had been made, and if I complained any further or attempted to back out entirely, I'd be seen as a bad sport.

"Strategy?" I mused. "How about this: Get the ball in between their goalposts, and try not to get too badly clobbered in the process."

This frankly preposterous idea was met with laughter.

"Aren't we a few players short?" I added, looking around. Whereas the girls' team seemed to have a full side plus at least three substitutes, as well as a full complement of supporters and coaches, we were fielding a mere seven players, with no spectators at all except my father and Dorian, who was only there to photograph the girls when they won.

"Some players have unresolved issues with members of the girls' team," Doug explained, "and if there were a choice between a painful whack in the plums and ten demerits for missing the game, I know which one I'd choose."

"Right," said Violet, striding up like a terrier approaching a barnful of frightened rats. "Which of you hopeless losers has been designated captain?"

"That would be me," I said, "and we can't play, because we're understrength."

"Cowardice has its just deserts, now doesn't it?" she answered, and there was a ripple of laughter from the girls. "Does that mean you concede? Or will you stand as men and play understrength?"

I almost agreed to concede, but I needed to explain myself to Jane. "According to the rules, we can take one of yours to make up the numbers."

"Very well," said Violet. "You can have the clumsy cluck." She pointed at the unfortunate Elizabeth Gold, the one who had been recently scrubbed from Violet's friendship book in favor of me. She was sitting on the substitute bench, looking dejected.

"No, I think we'll take her," I said, pointing at Jane. She stared back at me coldly. She'd trusted me, agreed to spare me from the yateveo, and now I'd betrayed her to the Colorman—or so she thought.

"Absolutely not," said Violet. "Jane's our most aggressive—I mean, our *best* attacker. You can have Liz."

"It's my choice, Violet."

I turned to Daisy, who was the referee, and she ruled in my favor.

Violet glared at me, and Jane stepped forward. It was a good move on my part. She wouldn't be able to legally kill me if we were on the same side. In fact, she'd be hard-pressed to explain away a hard tackle.

"Smart," she whispered as she moved past me, "but it won't save you."

The boys all looked away as Jane pulled off her spotted jersey and replaced it with a striped one. Her departure raised concern among the girls, who realized they might actually *receive* a beating this year, and her arrival on our team raised morale. Only Courtland seemed less than happy, and he stared at her with the contemptuous look that high Yellows reserve for those on the very lowest strata.

"Fun's over," said Violet. "Has the swatchman been alerted?"

"He's waiting on the touchline."

I cursed inwardly. Dad wasn't here to support me after all. He was here on a professional basis. Violet jabbed a finger in my direction. "Which end do you want to lose from?"

"We'll play into sun for the first half."

"There won't *be* a second half," remarked Violet to another ripple of laughter. The girls went into a huddle to talk tactics, so we did the same.

"Okay," I said, "who are the best players?"

Jabez, Keith and Courtland put up their hands, as did Jane.

"Right, you're all strikers. I want—"

"Come on, Red," interrupted Jane, "use your brain. No one except Violet is going to dare tackle Gamboge, so he's our only player of relevance."

No one could argue with this logic.

"So if we should ever get the ball, which I doubt," continued Jane, "we pass to Courtland. And since Violet will be their striker, Jabez and Keith should shadow her at every opportunity and foul her when Daisy's not watching. I'm on attack. The rest of you just try to get in the way of the other team." And she walked off up the pitch.

"New plan," I murmured. "We do as Jane suggests. I'm hopeless at this game, so I'm joining Jane upfield. Watch your shins, and do the best that you can. And I don't want any dives or amateur dramatics. We get thrashed, but we put up a fair show for ourselves."

There was a reluctant murmuring of agreement at this, and everyone went to their respective positions. I joined Jane, who simply stared at the ground, saying nothing.

The girls won the toss and bullied off. Within the space of no more than eight seconds, they had scored their first goal.

"Constance sent me a reply," I said. "Your poem went down really well."

"That's a huge weight off my shoulders, Red. I hardly slept a wink last night, worrying whether you two would find the unhappiness you deserve."

Her sarcasm was starting to grow on me in an odd sort of way. But she wasn't so fond of small talk and rounded on me. "What did you tell the Colorman?"

I wasn't quite so fearful this time. Maybe I was beginning to understand her better. "I didn't tell him anything about you—just some daft theories of my own. But I'll confess I'm confused and don't know who to trust."

"You can trust me."

"Can I? Robin and Zane are both dead, and the Colorman tells me there's twenty thousand merits kicking around somewhere. You were involved, and His Colorfulness is looking for you. The question I want to ask is this: Did you have a hand in Ochre's death?"

For the first time since I'd met her, she looked genuinely upset. "Absolutely not. Robin's death benefits no one. It was the worst thing that could have happened to this village and all who live here."

"So who killed him? And don't tell me he was Chasing the Frog or had misdiagnosed himself."

She looked down for a moment, and her voice went quieter.

"I don't know. I wish I did, but I don't. There aren't many things that scare me, but whoever got to Ochre, *they* scare me."

"I didn't have you down as the 'being scared' sort."

"Well, you don't know everything, do you?"

"That's an improvement. Twenty-four hours ago you had me knowing *nothing*."

She recovered her composure, and when she spoke next it was with her usual vigor.

"What have you found out about the Colorman?"

Before I knew what I was doing, I was telling her everything. Consciously, I was in a quandary over loyalties. Unconsciously, I was with Jane all the way. "He knows there was a third person in the swatch scam. It's his only concern. I told him there might be someone in the village who can see at night, and he couldn't have been less interested."

"You told him *what*?"

"That there—"

"I heard. Someone who can see at night? What makes you think that?"

I told her about the wheelbarrow, but she, like the Colorman, wasn't impressed.

"What else did you tell him?"

"Only that there was something hokey about Ochre's death—and Travis was a murder."

She shook her head sadly. "Look here," she said. "You seem like a vaguely okay person—for a Red. Just count your chairs and head home. You'll wangle a ticket somehow. All these questions are not going to make you smart or worldly-wise or any better off. They're going to make you dead."

"That means you kind of care about me, doesn't it?"

"Not at all. I play the long game and I may need a favor from you one day—dead people don't do favors."

"You didn't *have* to tell me that. You could have let me believe you cared."

"You're too old for a nursemaid, Red. Yours."

"What?"

"*YOURS!*"

Strange as it might have seemed, the ball was actually coming our way. I took the shot and whacked it up-pitch, where, as if by magic, Jane was already waiting to receive it. Imogen Fandango was in goal, but she didn't stand a chance, and the ball zipped past her so quick she didn't even see it. The whistle blew and the fighting stopped, except for Tommo, who was tussling with Cassie and seemed to be coming out the loser. Daisy's whistle blowing a quarter inch from their ears made them stop, and they growled and snapped at each other before calming down.

"You've got a new idea for a strategy," said Courtland as we all gathered for a confab. We'd lost Jabez, who was being stitched up by Dad on the touchline, but no one cared about numbers anymore.

"I have?"

"Yes, and here it is: I'm going to be striker and everyone else works my defense. Tommo, you tackle Daisy and pocket her whistle. Once I get the ball, all you have to do is defend me in whatever way you can. The Grey—"

"It's Jane," said Jane.

"Very well. *Jane* takes my right flank, because no one will dare tackle her, and Keith, you take my left, because I know you can soak up a beating without going down."

"Okay," said Keith.

"Right," I said, since it sounded like a good plan, even if illegal. "What do I do?"

"Nothing," growled Courtland. "Your job is to carry the can."

"Come on," said Jane, "is this really necessary? I know Russett's a drip, but he is a guest in the village."

He ignored her, and they all walked off to the bully-point.

"What's going on?" I said to Tommo as he walked past. "My job is to carry the what?"

"The can," repeated Tommo with a snigger. "Surely you know? The team captain has to take full responsibility for his team if they cheat.

And with the amount of merits you've got, we can do a fair amount of cheating. And listen, I think Courtland's seriously browned off with you about something—and I'm not that pleased with you myself. You lied to me. You lied to *all* of us."

I stood there dumbfounded as the clacks from the bully-off started, and play began. Within a second, Courtland was off, Daisy had been parted with her whistle and the violence had begun.

Demerits and Violet

2.3.09.23.061: Slouching is not permitted under any circumstances.

"Two broken collarbones, three twisted ankles, two fractured tibias, bruises without number, a thumb half torn off, two fractured wrists, Gerry Puce with a compound break to the femur and Lucy had to have her ear stitched back on."

"The ear I can explain. She was on the subs bench and—"

"Quiet, Russett." Head Prefect deMauve closed the report and stared at me. "What in Munsell's name did you think you were doing? Leading a legion of first-strike retaliators against a horde of marauding Riffraff?"

It was half an hour after the game ended, and Violet and I were in the prefect's chambers to account for our actions. The game had developed into a violent free-for-all and gone rapidly downhill from there. Daisy had broken Tommo's thumb to retrieve her whistle, then blown it so hard and for so long that she passed out. Dorian had the presence of mind to take a photo, thus preserving the unprecedented event for all time, and the violence only stopped when I whacked the ball into the Green Room's walled enclosure, where no one dared enter. Of the players, only those wise enough to have scattered avoided serious injury, and the damage was pretty evenly distributed between the teams, with Courtland accounting for most of it. He lashed out at anyone with whom he had a score to settle—which was almost everyone, it seemed—safe in the knowledge that I, as captain, would be called to account for his actions.

He could have nobbled me, too, but he didn't; I think he wanted to see me humiliated and demerited before he had his revenge.

I had Violet sitting next to me as codefendant. The girls' team had also decided to ignore the rules and attack anything that moved—which was pretty much what they usually did, only with the legality of a whistle.

DeMauve was sitting on a raised dais, with the Council in a semi-circle in front of and below him. As he spoke, they pulled long faces, shook their heads and gave out accusatory "tuts." We were still muddied and bloody: I had got away with only bruising, and Violet had a hastily stitched gash on the back of her head. Her hair, which this morning had been so perfect, was now matted with blood.

"Puce's femur may take a month to be completely right again," said Turquoise in a sober tone, "and every day away from work is a day lost to the Collective. Finbarr Gardenia's collarbone was pushed through the skin—he may be permanently lopsided. What do you say to that?"

"Pardon me?" I said, for I had been thinking about the wheelbarrow again.

"I was asking," repeated deMauve in a testy manner, "how you felt about all the injuries?"

"It would have been a lot worse if I hadn't introduced my *priority queuing system*," I replied, feeling impulsive.

"We'll get around to your queuing presently," barked Gamboge, who had been glaring at me dangerously since the moment I walked in, "and remember where you are."

"Violet," deMauve continued as he turned to his daughter, "do *you* have anything you'd like to say?"

"The girls' team was merely acting in self-defense," replied Violet innocently. "The boys' team went completely loco—it was all we could do to avoid extreme injury."

"We will take that into account," said her father, "but witnesses attest to *both* teams fighting after the whistle had blown—and your team did almost as much damage as Russett's."

"Nothing out of the ordinary," she pointed out. "It wouldn't be the boys-versus-girls match if we didn't shatter a few shinbones and hand out a concussion or two."

"That's as may be," said Prefect Sally Gamboge, who had been perusing the Rulebook to more fully understand the regulations regarding on-pitch violence, "but only as long as the ball is in play. As soon as you ignored Daisy's whistle, you became *personally* responsible for your teams."

"We are especially disappointed with you, Violet," added Yewberry. "Russett here is clearly an irresponsible, oafish hub-dweller. *You* should have known better."

I saw her fume quietly to herself. Both Violet and I knew who was really to blame, but the Rules were the rules, and Courtland was pretty much untouchable. We'd just have to take what they were handing out. I hadn't fully understood why Jane had joined in the melée, but then I'd realized: Whereas Courtland had caused trouble to punish *me,* Jane had caused mayhem to get at the *prefects.* The incident would affect their end-of-year report and, more important, their Peace Dividend from Head Office. A year without any aggression could be worth ten thousand bonus merits, split on a sliding scale between the prefects and the village.

Turquoise asked us both to wait outside for a moment, and we stood, bowed contritely and trooped out.

"Pea brain," said Violet as soon as the door was closed. "I am *so* going to make you pay for this."

"What are you going to do?" I asked. "Ban me from the orchestra?"

"For starters," she said, annoyed that I had thought of it first. "But I shall also instruct my many close personal friends not to cooperate with your chair census. Your stay here will be an empty, hollow experience without my kind patronage. *And,*" she added, "I am scrubbing you as a friend. I expect you are devastated."

"I can think of at least eighty-seven worse things," I told her, "beginning with yellowless custard."

She narrowed her eyes at me and made a petulant *harrumph* noise. The door opened, and Mrs. Gamboge told us we could return. We filed back in and sat when instructed.

"Do you have anything to say before we prescribe punishment, Master Russett?" asked deMauve.

"No excuses, sir," I murmured. "I will endeavor to improve myself."

"Miss deMauve?"

"It's a plot to discredit me," she blurted, pointing a finger at me. "I'm not a bad person. *Everyone* wants to be my friend. I would never have done anything that—"

But even her father had had enough. He put up a hand to silence her.

"Violet deMauve," he said, "we are deeply disappointed that you failed to control your team as soon as the game had ended. As a respected Purple, you are expected to be an example to others. However, we have also taken into consideration your abundant good works for the community and the pleas for leniency on your behalf by many worthy members of the Collective. You will be fined . . . one hundred merits."

Violet looked shocked. I think she thought she'd get off without a scratch, and in many ways, she had. She must have had twice as many merits as I did, and would doubtless have many opportunities to earn more. Still, dishing out a hundred wasn't so bad—I'd still have enough for residency.

"Edward Russett," said deMauve in the sort of voice one generally uses for announcing the onset of the Mildew, "we hold you chiefly responsible for this farrago. Your poor judgment, failure to properly control your team and inadequate leadership skills have led to the worst case of on-pitch violence this village has ever seen. You are fined . . . two hundred merits."

I breathed a sigh of relief. It was bad, but I had almost thirteen hundred merits, so two hundred still left me eleven hundred—enough for residency. I would still be able to get married, one of the perks afforded those who prove themselves Worthy.

We should have been dismissed then, but we weren't.

"In addition," said Sally Gamboge, "we find your meddling with the gracious clarity of the queue lines here in East Carmine severely disturbing. The Rules often work in mysterious ways, and impetuous acts that *seem* to offer short-term benefit sometimes have unforeseen consequences that bring only disunity."

"Luckily for you," added deMauve, "you applied for a Standard Variable application, and according to the Rules, we cannot demerit you."

I may have smiled at this, which was probably a mistake.

"But now," said Yewberry, "we come to the most serious of the charges laid against you."

I looked at the prefects in turn. I couldn't think of anything that I had done that wasn't somehow deniable or difficult to prove. The prefects could be harsh, but they had to be fair and respect due process. If they didn't, I could make a complaint to the mutual auditor in the next village, and the prefects could be up for a demeriting themselves.

"I regret to inform you," continued Yewberry in a sarcastic manner, "that the Last Rabbit has died. Not of old age, as was predicted, but by choking—on a large dandelion leaf."

"That's too bad," I said in a quiet voice, attempting to fill the unnatural silence that had descended on the room. Then I *understood*, and my heart fell. "When did it die?"

"The day before you got here," intoned deMauve gravely. "If you had visited the rabbit as you'd claimed, you would have found that out for yourself."

"You *lied* to us!" cried Violet. "All that talk of its being furry and the teeth and the little white tail—well! I am *so* disappointed."

"We are all disappointed," said deMauve, "and quite frankly, Edward, your father shares our disappointment. You have boasted of your rabbit connection all around the village and even spoken of it to the juniors during teaching—which is a hideous breach of trust that I hope I never live to see repeated."

I hung my head, for it was all true. I *had* lied. But the crunch came with a copy of the telegram I had sent to my best friend, Fenton, listing the rabbit's bogus Taxa number. Lying was one thing, but Fraudulent Gain was quite another. I was in very serious trouble.

"Do you deny these charges?" asked deMauve.

I couldn't, and said so. In respect of this, I was fined an eye-watering six hundred merits, bringing my total loss to eight hundred. In any less well-merited individual, it would have been Reboot. That wasn't going to happen to me, as I still had just under five hundred left. But crucially, I'd have to be up to the thousand-merit threshold again before I could even *consider* asking Constance to be my wife, and even with extra Useful Work and no hiccups, it would still take me the best part of three years. And Constance wasn't a "waiting" kind of girl. Worse, I had been hoping a positive Ishihara would have her father sending me an Open Return; I needed to get out of here more than ever.

I removed my 1,000 MERIT badge and handed it over.

"You will also be instructed to wear this for a month."

Yewberry handed me a badge that simply read LIAR, and, taking a deep breath, I pinned it on, just below my NEEDS HUMILITY pin. I'd only worn a LIAR badge once before, and hadn't enjoyed it.

My immediate thought was of how to regain the lost merits. I thought of Courtland and his proposal regarding the theft of Lincoln, or even of getting him the spoons from Rusty Hill. But I wasn't going to be bullied into anyone else's Rule-bruising schemes. Besides, those would be cash merits, not the ones that count—the ones in the back of your book. But what I said next surprised even me. "I'll lead the expedition to High Saffron," I said in a loud, assertive voice.

"We accept," said deMauve before I could change my mind. "We will pay one hundred merits, as agreed."

"I'll go for nothing less than six hundred."

There was an outburst of guffawing at my outrageous suggestion.

"The impertinence of the boy!" Turquoise blurted out.

"Such ungratefulness!" said Yewberry.

Loudest of all was Sally Gamboge: "We don't deal with liars!"

DeMauve, however, was more considered in his response. "What makes you think you're worth six hundred merits, Edward?"

Without thinking, I blurted out, "I'm at Alpha threshold. You know as well as I do that sending expendable lowbies on a jaunt like this is a waste of time. Even if there *is* red in abundance, they'd never even see it."

The prefects looked at one another uneasily. If I *was* Alpha threshold, then my offer made excellent sense. Although I could see only the one color, it would at least give an *indication* of the total volume to be found. But more important, High Saffron was the key to East Carmine's fortunes, and they knew it. And if I was the key to High Saffron, I had something to bargain with. It was a brilliant move on my part—if you didn't count the almost-certain-death aspect of the plan.

"You are pre-Ishihara and have no color rating," remarked Gamboge. "How can we be sure this is not a lie as well?"

I looked around the room, which contained not just the seven hundred and eighty-two volumes of *The Word of Munsell* (unabridged) but shelves and shelves of unsurrendered tosh—Previous artifacture that was too brightly colored to keep legally but too perfect, pretty or rare to have scrunched, squeezed, rolled and enriched. That they could keep it at all was thanks to a loophole. The items were simply listed in the Accessions Ledger as "awaiting sorting."

I scanned the items on the shelves and pointed out the one with the subtlest red tone—a small milk jug, which shone out at me from a display of shiny grey pottery. They all looked at Yewberry, who frowned. "I see only the merest *hint* of redness in it," he confessed, "and I am 71 percent."

They all stared at me, and I was surprised myself. If I was more than 71 percent redceptive, then I could be prefect.

"Pay him the six hundred," said Yewberry, "and send him to High Saffron."

Courtland's assertion that the Outer Fringes were Reboot with a small r was true. I was here to stay and Yewberry knew it. Little wonder he was eager for me to go on a trip with a low possibility of survival. There was silence in the room for perhaps half a minute, as the consequences of my potential rating were absorbed. Mrs. Gamboge simply glared at me.

I don't think she liked the idea of a Russett being prefect—my father had shown a sense of fair play that I hardly thought she'd welcome, and Courtland would have told her of my suspicions regarding Travis. Chromatic politics. You couldn't get away from it if you tried.

"You are a very impertinent young man," observed deMauve quietly, "but you have pluck, I'll grant you that. Four hundred."

But I was going to stand firm on this. I *had* to get back above residency.

"Not a cent below six hundred, sir."

"To hear you barter like this is disgraceful," remarked Yewberry with an angry tremor to his voice. "An upright member of the Collective would have *volunteered* his services, happily and without cost."

"As you did, sir?"

He went so red that even the worst lowbie in the village could not have failed to notice.

"Very well," said deMauve, looking ruffled, "six hundred it is."

We were dismissed, and after bowing again, Violet and I left the room. In the corridor outside, I felt Violet clasp my forearm. Half expecting some further admonishment or even a slap, I started to walk faster, but in an instant she had swung me around, placed her hands on my neck and pulled me toward her. Oddly, it took me a moment to realize what she was doing, and despite her offensively brash exterior, her lips were soft and her kiss, while lacking passion, was extremely professional. Since kissing the head prefect's daughter was not something I'd ever thought I'd end up doing, I placed both Constance and Jane at the back of my mind and gave as good as I got. I like to think I did all right with the kiss, despite little experience in these matters beyond what Lizzie the maid had taught me. It would have been unthinkably rude to pull away, so I waited until she relaxed, then gently separated myself.

"You dark red horse, you!" she said, giving me a shy smile and a playful jab on the sternum. "Why didn't you tell me you could see so much red?"

"I didn't want to seem a braggart," I replied, regretting that she had been there to hear me speak of it. She moved to kiss me again, but I didn't want this to get out of hand. "What about Doug? I understand you and he are on a half promise?"

"Doug is very sweet," she conceded, "but he's likely only a fifty-percenter. It wasn't a *true* half promise, anyway—more of a default position on my part. Do you *really* have Alpha Redness?"

"More or less."

"If that is the case," she said with a smile, "I'm going to speak to Mummy and Daddy about altering my marriage plans. If they agree, I'd be more than happy for us to be wed as soon after our Ishihara as possible."

"Violet," I said, beginning to see that this was getting monstrously out of control, if not a little scary, "I'm very flattered by your interest, but I'm on a half promise to an Oxblood back in Jade-under-Lime."

"Tish!" she replied with a smile. "Conjoining with a Purple is *considerably* better than with an Oxblood. How many people get to trade their surname up five steps in one hit? Edward deMauve. Sounds kind of classy, doesn't it? And what's more," she added with a giggle, "my dad's rolling in cash. Your father should demand at least ten grand for you. I'll have my father speak to your father, and we'll announce it just as soon as everything is set."

She leaned over and kissed me again, smiled and whispered in my ear, "There's more where that came from. *Much* more. Did you know that deMauve girls have a reputation for insatiability regarding the procreational arts and a one hundred two percent feedback rating?"

"I wasn't aware of it."

"Well, we do. I've gone to considerable lengths to prepare myself for my wedding night, and in respect of this, I don't mind if you want to practice with a Grey so everything is functioning perfectly. I have an egg chit ready and waiting. You can impregnate me on our wedding night, so I'll be with child by the spring—we can call her Crocus. Won't that be simply glorious?"

"No," I said. "In fact, not at all. Not one little—"

"Hush!" she said, placing a finger over my lips. "You're a passenger now, my dove—no worries from here on in."

She sighed happily, and then a cloud passed over her features. "Oh!" she cried, placing a hand to her mouth as a sudden thought hit her. "We'll have to get a postponement on your High Saffron gig, at least until you've got me pregnant. That way it won't matter so much when you don't come back."

"I can't marry you until I've got residency, Violet, and that's even if I wanted to, which I don't."

"Love will find a way," she said cheerfully, "and what love can't provide, my father's wallet certainly will. We should meet for a romantic walk and discuss my future this evening—shall we say at lamplighting tonight, next to Munsell's twice-lifesize bronze?"

"I'm busy."

"Of course you are—with me." She laid a hand on my cheek. "I'll make a few notes about the guest list and the menu for you to agree with. But to show that you can also bring some input to our relationship, I will permit you to choose our pet names. I'm so happy we were demerited together—otherwise we'd never have met and fallen so wonderfully in love."

She blinked at me and smiled, then asked what was on my mind. I think she wanted me to tell her how ecstatic I was, but all I could think of was how I could use this nightmare to my advantage.

"Do you have any loganberry jam?" I asked, thinking of the Apocryphal man and his gateway to knowledge.

"A jam connoisseur, eh? You and Daddy are going to have so much in common. I'll check the cellar. Do you want a spoon as well?"

"Just the jam."

"Loganberry it is. Until this evening, gorgeous."

She gave me another smile and skipped off down the corridor and out of the Council's Chapter House.

I watched her go with a feeling of dread, and cursed myself for my weakness. I should have just told her to get knotted, but up-color girls seemed to have a tongue-tying effect on me. Besides, Violet was probably not the sort of person to accept a "get knotted" answer to anything she had set her heart on. I walked slowly back out into the daylight. Although I did not know it, the yateveo that would eventually devour me was suddenly three large paces closer.

Tommo and Dad

2.6.03.24.339: Finder's fees are not permitted to be higher than 10 percent.

found Tommo waiting for me outside, sitting on the wall of the village's color garden. The yellow had run out sometime overnight, and the grass was now a sickly shade of blue. The pump would have been switched off, but the remaining color would take a few days to leach through. I wasn't feeling that well disposed toward him, so I just walked off in the direction of home.

"What did you get?" he asked, trotting to catch up.

"I didn't *get* anything," I replied. "I lost eight hundred."

"Wow," said Tommo, visibly impressed. "Not even I've lost that many in one hit. Never had that many to lose, actually."

"And I'm leading the expedition to High Saffron."

"You're insane. And I'm not sure they can do that as a punishment."

"I volunteered—in return for six hundred merits."

"Not *quite* so insane but still amusingly irrational. But with a one hundred percent fatality rate, it will be difficult to draw up odds on this one. Unless . . ."

"Unless what?"

"Never mind. Violet was grinning fit to burst when she came out. What was that all about?"

He'd doubtless hear about it in due course, and I'd rather he had the correct story from me so I explained what had happened.

"Congratulations," he said, "I'm sure you'll be very happy together."

"Happy?"

He shrugged. "It's a relative term. If you've got that much red," he added, "you're going to be prefect."

"Perhaps, but not here. I've got an Oxblood to marry and a string-works to inherit."

"That will all change when Violet gets weaving on her father. You're Chromatically made for each other. Violet is way down the blue end of Purple and your Red plums are just the thing to keep the family at the pointy end of the Chromatic Hierarchy."

He smiled and put a hand on my shoulder. "Eddie, my friend, you are in a uniquely strong bargaining position. Do you want me to negotiate your dowry? The deMauves are pretty oiled. I'll only charge ten percent."

"*No.*"

"You drive a hard bargain—five percent, then."

"No."

"Two?"

"I mean I'm not marrying Violet."

"You'll come around to it."

I accused him of attempting to profit from my enforced marriage, but he didn't even bat an eyelid.

"Listen," he said, as though I were the one being unreasonable, "I need that commission if I'm to avoid Reboot on Monday. Could you have that on your conscience?"

"Easily. I thought you said Violet was 'the most poisonous female in the village.'"

"I must have misspoken. And listen: It wasn't all bad news on the playing field this morning. Lucy let me hold her ear while she waited to have it stitched. Then, rather than telling me to go youknow myself, as she usually does, she thanked me quite sweetly."

He looked at his bloodstained hand reverentially. "It was this hand. I'm never going to wash it."

"I didn't think you ever did."

"Perhaps not, but now at least I have a reason. I'll see you at lunch."

I went and had a bath. Although Violet's unwelcome attentions, the loss of nearly eight years' worth of merits and the lack of a ticket home were matters of some concern, there was still plenty of room in the Eddie

Russett worry pot: There was someone in the village who could see at night, Jane was up to something regarding Ochre and Zane, my father was seeing Mrs. Ochre and, incredibly, the Gamboges had killed Travis. All, however, were eclipsed by the fact that I would be traveling to High Saffron. The survival rate was so poor, in fact, that even Tommo wasn't willing to lay any odds. But I wasn't *that* worried. If Violet had her way—and I think Violet generally got her way—she could have the trip postponed forever.

I climbed out of the bath, dried, dressed, carefully parted my hair, tied my tie in the prescribed half-Windsor, then walked downstairs, where I found Dad waiting for me in the hall.

"Let's walk together," he said, for it was still ten minutes until lunch. I agreed, and we stepped out the door.

"This Tommo Cinnabar fellow," he murmured as we walked across the square, "can we trust him?"

"Not even the tiniest bit," I replied, "but I'll admit he's shrewd. Why?"

"He's offered his services to negotiate the dowry we should charge for you to marry Violet deMauve."

It was lightning-quick work on Tommo's part.

"I don't want to marry Violet, Dad."

"Perfectly understandable," he said. "She's frightful. More important, I've not yet been approached by the head prefect, so nothing's official. I just wanted to make sure we were singing from the same song sheet. Tommo seems to think we can get ten grand for you."

"Dad!" I said, shocked by the notion that he might decide to sell me without consultation. "I'm up on a half promise to Constance, remember?"

"And that would *cost* me three grand," he said. "Children are so ungrateful. Why the puce didn't you tell me you were potential Alpha Red?"

I shrugged. "I wasn't sure—and I didn't want to be a braggart."

"Very noble of you," he replied sarcastically, "but if I'd known, I could have offered you for less or nothing to the Oxbloods, and spent the money on a hardwood conservatory instead."

"Roger's potential Alpha, too," I said a bit uselessly.

Dad shook his head and lowered his voice. "I've seen his parents' charts, and they don't make exciting viewing. Josiah Oxblood is a strictly dynastic man. He'd have Constance marry a can of paint if it would enRedden the line."

"That's not a very good idiom, Dad."

"It was the best I could come up with at short notice." He glared at me and I fell silent.

To be honest, I hadn't really considered the consequences of keeping my bestowal a secret. Usually a Chromatically arranged marriage was simply a source of gossip and a cheap laugh at someone else's expense. When it happened to you, it suddenly seemed, well, a bit *crummy*. The higher-hued you became, the less choice of life partner there was. This kind of garbage never happened to the Greys.

"If this Tommo fellow is correct and the deMauves are both stinking rich *and* hue-desperate, we can probably get a preemptive bid or go to auction. Plus," he added, as though to try to soften the deal, "I'd be happy to split the dowry with you. We'd walk away from the deal with both our pockets comfortably full."

"That's the difference," I said. "I *don't* get to walk away. I get to stay right here. And be married to Violet."

"Is she really so different from Constance?"

"Not at all," I replied. "But at least Constance was *my* decision."

"Choice is overrated," said Dad, quoting Munsell, something he rarely did. "I'm sure you'll warm to her, given time. You'll be Red prefect as soon as you've taken your Ishihara, and with deMauve as father-in-law, you'll eventually run the linoleum factory."

"Dad, we always agreed to talk this through before a decision was made."

"We're talking it through now, aren't we? Besides, you've only yourself to blame, blurting out your bestowal—you see what happens to those who shamelessly boast? Like that Carrot fellow. What was his name again?"

"Dwayne."

"Right. Dwayne Carrot. Exactly."

We stood on the steps in silence as the other residents streamed into the town hall. They were chattering volubly, and paid us little attention.

"How did the hearing go?" he asked at length.

I told him about the eight hundred demerits, which he didn't seem so annoyed about—presumably because it increased the likelihood of my going the deMauve route. He asked me why so many, and I explained about the rabbit. He shook his head sadly, and said that he always knew the rabbit would be trouble. I then took a deep breath and told him I'd offered to go to High Saffron to earn the merits back.

"You did *what*?"

"High Saffron. For six hundred merits."

"What if you don't make it back? What if night falls?"

"Night *always* falls, Dad."

"With you inside it, I mean."

"Dad," I said more forcefully, "I'll be fine, really. All the missing were feckless Rebootees who took the opportunity to leg it and are now probably running around in a loincloth with uncombed hair and poor table manners. I'll be fine."

"You might have consulted me before you took this rash decision. I have a twenty-year stake in you, too, you know."

"In volunteering for tosh squads," I replied, "the Rules do *not* require me to seek your permission."

But he knew this.

"I suppose it *might* improve your leadership skills," he grumbled, "useful if you *do* become a prefect. When is this to be?"

"If the deMauves have their way, not until we're wed and their grandchild is in the bag. Who knows, if Violet gets to like me, she could postpone the trip indefinitely."

"That would suit all concerned."

He was partly right. Dad would get his ten grand, Tommo would get his commission, Violet would get a Purple child and deMauve would secure his dynasty. The only beneficiary missing from the list was me.

But Dad was nothing if not fair, and after thinking for a moment, he relented. He sighed, patted my shoulder and said, "Listen, I can't force you to marry Violet with a half promise to Constance on the table, but as the sole supplier of your dowry, I think my arguments might at least count for something."

Once inside, I sat at the usual Red table and pondered the situation. At least I still had a way out. I could telegraph my Ishihara results to Constance on Sunday afternoon, and she'd agree to our marriage. I could get her to wire me a ticket authorization by return and be gone by Tuesday. Simple . . . except for the ticklish problem of not having enough merits to get married. Still, that was a problem I could deal with back home. It was now Friday, and all I had to do was to keep my nose clean until Sunday, the day of my Ishihara. And avoid Courtland. And Jane. And the Colorman. And Violet. I was just wondering how long I could barricade myself in the broom cupboard with a stack of cheese sandwiches and some water when the prefects walked in.

Lunch

2.3.03.01.006: Juggling shall not be practiced after 4:00 p.m.

"The annual boys-versus-girls hockeyball match was won this year by the boys, despite the disgraceful behavior by all concerned. The two captains have been justly punished, and Miss Ochre's ear was saved, so no more will be said."

DeMauve was giving his prelunch speech. We were all sitting attentively at our places, feeling hungry.

"Due to another highly regrettable but wholly unavoidable accidental death at the factory," he continued, "the average age of the village has risen above safe parameters. Because of this, we have licensed an extra conception certificate to be taken up forthwith. All eligible parties should contact Mr. Turquoise for consideration at tomorrow's Council meeting."

There was a murmuring among the villagers about this, mostly from the Grey end of the room, as a hastened Grey worker usually required a Grey birth to replace it. There was even an audible "Hoorah!"

"Right," said deMauve, consulting a sheet of printed paper. "As of this morning we have a volunteer to lead the High Saffron expedition. His name is Edward Russett, and considering that he is visitor, he has shown considerable pluck and fortitude to have stepped forward, a selfless act that I think should be an example to you all."

He paused, expecting a flurry of voices goaded into action by his words, but there were none. If worse came to worst, I would be on my own.

"Moreover, we have decided to increase the expedition payment to two hundred merits."

Still silence.

"Then I'll leave it up to your own conscience," said deMauve, faintly annoyed. "Now, against my better judgment and well-argued wishes, the High Saffron expedition will take place . . . *tomorrow!*"

He glared at both Gamboge and Yewberry as he said it, and my heart fell. Tomorrow was the day *before* my Ishihara. I should have seen it coming. Yewberry didn't want to lose his position, and Mrs. Gamboge, no fan of Edward Russett, would fondly like to see the back of me long before I even took my seat on the Council. The sooner I was out of the picture, the better for both of them. The implication wasn't missed on Tommo, who gave a low curse over his potential lost commission, and I saw Dad shake his head sadly. Myself, I felt a sudden sinking feeling as the full inevitability of what I had agreed to do settled in my stomach like an anvil.

"So for reasons that I won't trouble you with," added deMauve, "I am personally willing to add three hundred merits to the two hundred already offered—on condition that the team leader is returned safely, alive and in one piece."

"I will add two hundred more to that!" said my father. He was breaching protocol, but no one minded.

Despite the Rules against talk, there was a lot of murmuring. DeMauve, sensing that a fair hand would be better than a firm one, let everyone chatter for a couple of minutes before waving us all to be quiet. Seven hundred merits. *For a single day's work.* It was unprecedented stuff. But not, it seemed, unprecedented enough. The number of arms that shot upward was as close to zero as it could possibly be.

"Very well," said deMauve, visibly angry. "If anyone changes his mind, he can contact me directly."

He looked around before continuing.

"Russett, you are to present yourself for a briefing with Mr. Yewberry straight after lunch. You'll leave with Mr. Fandango at first sight tomorrow morning. Now, today's reading will be from Munsell's . . ."

The talk was fortunately a lot shorter this time, and was mostly about working together in strict harmony, and respecting the Colortocracy that our bestowals had decreed, and how anyone might, through hard work and strict adherence to the Rules, ensure that his future progeny might move up the ladder by using his well-earned merits to ensure a better marriage for his children. And so on and so forth. I wasn't paying much attention. I was thinking about going to High Saffron and cursing my own impetuousness. DeMauve finished his reading, tacked a bit onto the end about how we should be thankful that no one was permanently injured during the boys-versus-girls hockeyball match, and announced that we could all eat.

There was silence at our table, and everyone avoided looking at me.

"Well," said Doug, finally breaking the silence, "you'll come back, Eddie. It'll be fine."

"I agree," said Tommo with a more confident air, "but not from a hopelessly optimistic viewpoint, more simply because you're too valuable for the deMauves to lose."

This was possibly true, but I didn't see how they could guarantee my safety. Once beyond the Outer Markers, I was on my own. The others nodded their heads, but I could see they weren't confident of my chances. But since the matter had been raised and dealt with, the conversation was ready to move on. I was just like one of those people who dropped in on their way to Reboot. There, then not.

"So," remarked Daisy, who was in possession of one of the biggest bruises I had ever seen, "how stuffed did you get over the match?"

I told them the punishments Violet and I had been given.

"She only got a hundred for your two hundred?" said Lucy. "That hardly seems fair."

"She's a deMauve," said Tommo. "I didn't expect her to get *any*. How is your ear, by the way?"

"A bit sore," she replied, touching it gingerly. The offending article was purple and very swollen, but had a fine row of my father's most delicate stitches around it. "Matron told me to listen through the other for a couple of days until it got better."

"Any idea who did it?" asked Doug, who had a split lip to match his bruise.

"It all happened so fast. But we could match the tooth marks, I suppose."

"Hardly worth the trouble, surely?" said Tommo, a little too quickly to make me certain he'd had nothing to do with it. "After all, that's the rough-and-tumble of hockeyball, eh?"

"By the way," said Doug, "I must thank you for getting Violet off my back."

There was sudden silence, and they all stared at me, waiting to see what my comment would be. Gossip travels at the speed of light in any village, and there couldn't have been many people who didn't know of Violet's sudden change of allegiance. My opinion of it was as likely as not the biggest question on everyone's lips.

"It's not going to happen," I said with a dramatic air of finality, "even if I do come back."

"Violet can be very persuasive," remarked Daisy, "and she's used to getting her own way."

"There is a downside to the whole Russett-deMauve marriage," said Tommo, who hadn't spoken for a while.

"You see?" I said.

"It's thrown my entire marriage fantasy league into disarray. With Doug now available for the first time in six years, I'm going to have to completely restructure the league from the bottom up."

It wasn't the sort of "downside" I had in mind.

"Unless," added Tommo, snapping his fingers, "Doug, would you do me a tremendous favor and declare yourself? It would save a huge amount of paperwork."

"I'll second that," said Arnold, giving Doug a wink.

"What's with the LIAR badge?" asked Daisy, who was the first to notice. I had skillfully obscured it behind my Red Spot.

"He may have inadvertently *exaggerated* his viewing of the rabbit," declared Tommo in a voice tinged with glee.

I stared at Tommo. "How did you know about the rabbit?"

"Whoops."

"*You* snitched on me?"

The entire table turned to stare at Tommo. Lying was bad, but snitching on one's own hue was far worse. He seemed somewhat less than contrite.

"I should apologize, really. But your sneaky rabbit subterfuge would have come out sooner or later, so it's far better that a friend and colleague should cop the sixty merits of bounty rather than someone less deserving."

"Less deserving than you?" remarked Lucy. "How is that even *remotely* possible?"

"There's no need to be unpleasant. I'll make it up to him."

"How?"

279

He didn't answer, and instead caught the eye of the dinner monitor and asked to switch tables, which he did. To be honest, his perfidy worked in my favor, for the LIAR badge was not mentioned again.

"Does anyone know anything about High Saffron?" I asked. "I'm not convinced that my briefing from Yewberry will be anything but absolutely useless."

There was silence around the table.

"The, um, lack of eyewitness data makes *facts* thin on the ground," replied Daisy diplomatically, trying not to make me any more worried than I was already, "but there are many half-truths and suppositions."

"Which are?"

They looked at one another, then Lucy spoke. "Legend says High Saffron is where the memories of the Previous have collected. They lament upon their lost lives and vanished histories, and lurk in the shadows, waiting to feed upon the *charisma* of those still living."

"I've changed my mind," I said hurriedly, "I don't want to hear the half-truths. Anyone have any *facts*?"

"Mining speculators arrive in the village every now and again," said Daisy, "lured by stories of unimaginable Chromatic riches. The prefects sell these miners a speculating license," continued Lucy, "and they take the road to High Saffron and do not return. Or at least, not this way."

"I heard that travelers arrived by sea," said Doug, "who came from the same place as the man who fell from the sky. And they take people to work for them somewhere across the ocean."

"I heard that High Saffron is populated entirely by cannibalistic Riffraff," added Arnold in a remark that possibly helped the least, "and they eat the brains of everyone who approaches."

"There are many who blame the Riffraff for the disappearances," said Lucy, giving Arnold a sharp kick under the table, "but if there was a community there, we'd know about it by now. And *someone* would have escaped to tell the tale."

There were other stories, none of them helpful, and all of them unproved.

"I'm on my own, aren't I?" I said in a quiet voice. No one replied, which was answer enough.

Joseph Yewberry

1.2.23.09.022: A unanimous verdict by the primes will countermand the head prefect.

"Good of you to drop around," said the Red prefect as soon as I had settled on the sofa opposite him. He seemed chirpy and friendly, despite our recent enmity—it was probably because he was confident I'd not live long enough to take his job. The front room of his house was what I called "untidy chic." Prefects weren't subject to the same Rules on room tidiness, but since no one really enjoyed clutter, a certain style of ordered untidiness was generally considered *de couleur* for a prefect's room.

"Comfortable?"

"Yes, sir."

"Can't have that. I need you as sharp as a tack. Here, sit on this piece of metal. How's that? Still comfortable?"

"Not in the least."

"Good. Since you'll be off at dawn tomorrow, I wanted to brief you fully over the trip to High Saffron. I'd be joining you myself, but the burden of leadership precludes one from doing one's duty. Since no one else volunteered, you'll be going on your own. Have a look at this."

He laid a hand-drawn map on the coffee table.

"This is us here—and that's your destination. So you have to go from *here*"—he pointed to East Carmine—"and travel all the way to—"

"High Saffron?"

"You've done it before?"

"I understand the theory about traveling—that it involves moving between two points, usually different ones."

"But not *always*," said Yewberry, eager not to give me the intellectual upper hand.

"True," I conceded.

"Excellent. This map is an amalgam of every trip that was aborted in the High Saffron direction, mixed with a few guesses and some unsubstantiated rumor. As you can see, the Perpetulite only goes partway. It spalled at Bleak Point, and after that it's about sixteen miles, all on foot, all trackless. Mr. Fandango will take you to the Bleak Point and drop you there. The track of the abandoned roadway can be clearly seen, and it was worked on up until thirty years ago—you may find some abandoned Leapback on the way and a Faraday or two. In fact, it's all plain sailing until you get to . . . *here*."

He pointed to a spot on the map about five miles beyond Bleak Point, where there was a picture of a flak tower. I leaned forward and studied the map carefully. Beyond this, the detail was worryingly vague. Of High Saffron itself, there was only its position on an estuary. But also marked on the map were Riffraff, man-eating megafauna, an impenetrable grove of yateveos and the Apocryphal bird with the long neck that wasn't an ostrich. I pointed this out.

"Mapmakers can get carried away," he admitted. "The sorry truth is that once past Bleak Point, it's all pretty much guesswork."

"May I take the map?"

"I'd rather you didn't. I wouldn't want anyone to find his way back here."

I knew he meant nomadic Riffraff, but I said, "Like who? Swans?"

"That's not funny, Russett. Any more of that kind of disrespectful backchat and you could find yourself—" He stopped, wondering what he could do to make my life any worse. He couldn't, so instead opened a wooden box and showed me a compass.

"Can I take that with me?"

"Absolutely not!" said Yewberry. "I just thought I'd show it to you—the only one in the village. Beautiful, isn't it? I like this leather bit here especially."

"Very nice. So . . . what can I expect to find in High Saffron?"

"We're not really sure. A detailed study of the Council minutes suggests that the founders of East Carmine first attempted to mine it about three hundred years ago. They described it as about forty square miles in size, with evidence of a bypass, a harbor, a railway station, several thousand domestic dwellings, municipal buildings, something loosely described as 'defensive structures' and *two* temples of commerce. But to be honest, that might describe any one of hundreds of pre-Epiphanic towns, and they saw it only two centuries after the Something That Happened. So aside from the odd cementless building and anything made of Perpetulite, there won't be much left."

"And what do you want me to actually *do*?"

"You're to sketch, observe and describe. Take any pieces of scrap color that you can find for appraisal back here, and keep an eye out for a route that the Ford might take. But most of all, we really want to know if it's safe. No swans or Riffraff, that sort of thing—and what happened to the others, of course."

"How do I report back if it's not safe, sir?"

"Hmm," he said, rubbing his chin thoughtfully. "I think you've got me there. Returning would help, I suppose."

He thought for a moment, then showed me his daylight calculations. "You've got a little over sixteen hours of daylight tomorrow, but I can't give you any accurate journey timings as the precise terrain and distances are unknown. You'll need to time yourself from Bleak Point to the flak tower, and from there to High Saffron. *No matter what happens,* make sure you leave enough time to get back to Fandango an hour before sundown—that's when he'll leave."

"Marvelous," I said, somewhat rattled. A four-hour walk beyond Jade-under-Lime's Outer Markers was the farthest I'd ever gone from the safety of civilization. Even in the long days of high summer, a two-hour margin for safety was the *minimum* during an extended toshing trip— although tough nuts had been known to make it back with only twenty minutes of light left. Mind you, I always suspected that they'd engineered it that way. That they might have got back hours ago and then waited around the corner, for the hero effect.

"Now," said Yewberry, "we want you to complete this mission, but not to throw your life away unnecessarily."

"I'm with you on that one, sir."

"Good man. Is that sofa still uncomfortable?"

"Almost excruciating, sir."

"Excellent. Watch out for eruptives on the summit section, keep a wary eye out for megafauna, clutching brambles and yateveos—and don't keep any metal that is unusually warm to the touch. Oh, yes," he added, "if you you find any toy Dinky cars, bring them back for my collection. I'll give you an extra ten merits for each one you find. Any questions?"

"Yes," I said. "What do I get in my packed lunch?"

"Whatever you decide to put in it, I suppose."

Pepetwlait and Vermeer

1.2.02.03.059: All residents are expected to learn a musical
instrument.

sat on the wall of the color garden for a moment, thinking hard. If
I was to have even a hope of returning from High Saffron, I would
need someone to go with me. Someone motivated, highly adaptable
and capable of violence. Someone like Jane, in fact. I found her pot-
ting tomato seedlings in the glasshouse. I hadn't talked to her since the
hockeyball match, and she had a bruised left eye.

"Hello," she said with a refreshing lack of animosity that made me feel
a great deal better. "How's Violet's new sweetheart?"

"Wishing he was Violet's ex-sweetheart."

"Think how happy you've made Doug. He's had his eyes on Tabitha
Auburn for a while."

"He should get a half promise in before Violet changes her mind. The
carnage at hockeyball was partly your fault, wasn't it?"

She smiled.

"Just trying to even the score. I managed to plant a small one on Violet, but Courtland was just too quick. What made you volunteer for the
High Saffron gig?"

I shrugged. "Getting back up to residency, and Constance, I suppose.
Do you know anything about the town?"

"Enough to know that no one ever comes back."

I wanted to ask her to come, too, but straight out was probably not the best approach. Luckily, I had a host of other questions I wanted to ask her.

"How did you get to Vermillion and back in a morning? Or even to Rusty Hill for that matter?"

I knew she didn't like my asking, but I hoped that her hostility had moved from "naked" to "implied" in the time we'd known each other.

She looked at me and thought for a moment.

"Promise not to tell?"

She punched out on the time clock and we walked out of the glasshouse, past the Waste Farm and through a small spinney to where we came across the Perpetulite roadway. It was a leafy spot, hung about with beech trees whose long boughs trailed ivy against the grass. It was also conveniently deserted. In one direction above the brow of a hill was the village; in the other was the stockgate, and beyond, Rusty Hill. She checked that we were quite alone and then took a small pendant from around her neck.

"Do you know what this is?"

"A really ugly piece of jewelry?"

"It's the key that enabled the Previous to talk to the roads. If you see anyone coming, yell."

She laid the bronze key on the surface of the Perpetulite and almost instantly a rectangular sunken panel about the size of a tea tray appeared in the road. It was barely a half inch deep and, curiously, was still the same color and texture as the roadway, but now had several raised buttons, a few graphs and windows in which figures constantly updated. Across the top on a separate panel were some curious words that looked as though they had been engraved into the surface.

"*Pepetwlait Heol Canolfan Cymru A470 21.321km Secshwn 3B. Wedi codi 11.1.2136,*" I read with a frown. "What does all that mean?"

"I'm not sure. The designation of the road and when it was built, probably. Despite all you've heard, the Previous were quite astonishingly clever. We all know that Perpetulite is a living organoplastoid that is able to self-repair, but what is less well known is that it's possible to access the road's inner workings through this panel. We can monitor the health of the Perpetulite and see what minerals it lacks, and best of all, we can tell it to do things."

She let this sink in before continuing.

"I'm still learning, but I can set the temperature to keep ice off in the winter and illuminate the white lines. I can fine-tune the absorption rate of organic debris and the speed at which water is removed, and display messages on the road itself, presumably intended to assist the travelers who once used it."

"And how did you discover the panel was right here?"

She smiled. "It's not here. It's wherever I place the key."

To demonstrate, she picked up the pendant, and the panel melted back into unblemished roadway. She walked a few yards down the way and laid the key on the road again, and the same panel opened there instead.

"If they could make something as mundane as roads do this," she murmured, "just think what else they must have been able to do."

I thought of harmonics and floaties, remote viewers, lightglobes and Everspins. It was like arriving at a concert just as the orchestra had finished, and all that was hanging in the air was the final chords, fading into nothingness.

"But how did you use this to get you to Vermillion?"

"Ah!" she said with a smile. "Watch this."

She pressed one of the buttons, and the panel changed shape to a *new* set of buttons, each with some similarly unreadable writing above them. She expertly manipulated the controls, and the road began to ripple silently in a curious fashion, much as it does when removing objects. But instead of a localized ripple running *sideways* across the road, the movement ran *laterally* in the direction of Rusty Hill.

I looked at Jane, who seemed uncharacteristically enthusiastic about the whole thing.

"It's a conveyor," she explained, "I think intended for the removal of spoil when the road was built, although its uses could be almost without number. Watch this."

She stepped on to the edge of the Perpetulite and was moved ever so slowly down the road. The center of the roadway rippled faster, however, and by simply walking to the middle of the road, she was moved swiftly off toward Rusty Hill. After thirty yards or so she again moved to the edge, where she once more slowed down; then she stepped off and trotted back to where I was waiting.

"I can make it go forward, backward—even limit the distance of the conveyor. Sit on a chair in the center of the road and you can be in Rusty Hill in twenty minutes. On a trip to Vermillion I'd convey to Rusty Hill, get off, walk the empty section and then rejoin the Perpetulite all the way to Vermillion—leaving out the ferry, of course, and getting off well before anyone sees me."

She switched it off and the road abruptly reverted to its usual state, and when she picked up her pendant, the sunken panel vanished from view.

"It's astonishing."

"It seems astonishing *now*—but it was once so ordinary you'd not have given it a second's thought. And, Red?"

"Yes?"

"You can't tell anyone about this."

I assured her I would add it to the long list of secrets, and she laughed. A sudden thought struck me.

"You're not going to submit to Reboot, are you?"

A look of seriousness came over her face, and she replaced the pendent around her neck.

"No. Monday morning I'm gone. It's not an ideal outcome, but I'm eight hundred merits below zero."

"*Eight hundred?* What did you do?"

"It was what I *didn't* do. When people take a dislike to you, it's amazing how quickly you can become a demerit magnet."

"Where will you go?"

"I have no idea. Rusty Hill, perhaps. It's not an ideal situation, but at least transport isn't a problem. I can ride the conveyor to wherever I want."

I said the first thing that came into my head: "I'll miss you."

"Red," said Jane, placing a hand on my arm with a rare display of tenderness, "you won't be around to."

I fell into silence for a moment. Despite her annoying forthrightness, it was the first vaguely pleasant conversation I'd had with her—she hadn't once threatened to kill me or hit me with a brick or anything, and we'd been talking for nearly twenty minutes. I'd like to think it was because she trusted me, but it was more likely that she, like everyone else, didn't rate my chances at High Saffron very high. But I still didn't feel the moment was right to ask her to come with me. I had an idea.

"Can you accompany me into the zone?"

"Why?"

"I'd like to have a look at the Vermeer."

I'd visited the Greyzone in Jade-under-Lime only a few times, when much younger. It wasn't somewhere Chromatics generally went. Partly because we had little business to be there, partly because the Rules were fairly strict when it came to Grey privacy and partly because we simply weren't welcome.

I looked around curiously as we walked in. The houses were built in the twin-terraced fashion of mostly stone, with a single roadway in between the buildings, which had their doorways facing each other in an unusual fashion. The streets were scrubbed, and everything was as tidy as a new pin. Since almost a third of any town's population was made up of Greys, the zone was a large part of the residential area but always slightly removed from the Chromatic part of the village. *Apart We Are Together.*

I had expected to be stared at when we walked in, but I wasn't—no one took the slightest notice of me.

"It all seems very friendly," I observed.

"You're with me," she said. "I wouldn't attempt this on your own. Don't believe me? Watch." And she told me to wait for her as she ducked into a house.

I suddenly felt very alone and vulnerable. Within a very short time I was being stared at, and after less than a minute, a young man approached and spoke in a voice that, while polite, carried with it a sense of understated menace. "Have you lost your way, sir?"

"I was waiting—"

"He's with me," said Jane, coming out of the house, holding a plate with a slice of cake on it. "Clifton, this is the swatchman's son. Red, this is Clifton, my brother."

"Pleased to meet you," he said, his manner entirely changed. "Jane says you're 'mostly deplorable,' which for her is quite a compliment."

I looked at Jane, who said, "Don't listen to him. It's every bit as insulting as it's intended to be."

"So," continued Clifton, who seemed as gregarious as Jane was serious, "for you it's death or marriage to Violet. You do like difficult choices, don't you?"

"If I get back, she's the last person I'd marry."

He laughed. "So you say. Violet can be very persuasive. She and I have had an *understanding* that goes back a couple of years."

He opened his eyes wide so the meaning was clear. "You won't be disappointed. Mind you," he added, "I upped the feedback score to ensure repeat business." He winked and added, "If you don't use the word *no* in her presence, I daresay you'll be very happy."

"Thanks for the advice," I replied in a humorless tone.

He smiled, said it was nothing and departed.

"Clifton keeps us well fed with Violet's tittle-tattle," said Jane as we walked on, "so his position within the Hierarchy is not totally one sided. In fact, your marriage will cut off a very useful gossip stream."

"I'm not getting back from High Saffron," I said, "remember?"

"Then perhaps we're safe after all. The cash helps, too. Here we are."

We had arrived at a plain front door at the end of the terrace, and Jane knocked twice. The man who answered the door was Graham, the elderly man who'd had the sniffles.

"Enjoying your retirement?" I asked.

"What retirement? Mrs. Gamboge has me on part-time work."

I asked him how this was possible, and he responded that Sally Gamboge was a master at finding ways to extract every last ounce of sweat from the Greyforce.

"We came to look at the Vermeer," said Jane to Graham. "I brought you some cake."

Mr. G-67 thanked her and then showed us upstairs, where the painting was hanging in a room all by itself. There was a linen-covered roof-light and a plain viewing bench to sit on.

"It's quite lovely," I said after a minute's silence.

The canvas was of a woman pouring milk out of a jug and into a bowl. In front of her was a small table with a basket of bread laid upon it, and the whole scene looked as though it had been lit from a window to the left—although of the window itself there was no sign. The canvas had several scorch marks along the bottom of the frame, and the paint had come away in patches, but there was still enough that was wonderful.

"I'm told her tunic is yellow and her dress blue," observed Graham. "The Greens come up here quite a lot to practice their color separation. We had someone around last month who was ticking Vermeers off her I-Spy book. Seen all eight, she said. I'll leave you to it."

I sat down on the viewing bench, leaving ample room for Jane, but she remained standing. I decided to pop the question. "I'd like you to come with me to High Saffron."

"I'm sorry," she said, "I never do death on a first date. Have you found out anything more about the Colorman?"

I shook my head.

"Then perhaps you should start going through his valise. See what you can find out."

"You're joking!"

"Do I look like I'm joking?"

"No. But—"

I stopped because there was a mild commotion outside, and Jane moved to the window.

"What on earth are they doing here?" she murmured, and made her way swiftly out of the door. Intrigued, I followed. But she didn't exit out of the front of the house, where the commotion was; she made for the rear, through Graham's kitchen. When I tried to follow, the elderly Grey stood in my path and looked at me in a way that, while not openly hostile, made me realize that the only way out of the house was the way I came in.

I stepped into the street and was met by a brilliant flash of yellow. It was Sally Gamboge, Courtland, Bunty McMustard and even little Penelope. They were striding down the street and didn't look as though they were here to see the Vermeer.

The Chair Census

3.6.03.12.009: Croquet mallets are not to be used for knocking in the hoops. Fine: one merit.

"Ah!" said Sally Gamboge when she saw me. "We were told you were in the zone. Reason?"

"The Vermeer."

"Of course," she replied, "what other reason *could* you have? We're here to help you conduct your chair census."

"You are?"

"Yes indeed," replied Bunty in a friendly manner that was completely at odds with her hue, "since you have so selflessly committed yourself to the exploration of High Saffron, we thought we would selflessly commit ourselves to helping you finish the task that you were sent here to do."

"You don't mind us helping, do you?" asked Sally Gamboge, who wore a smile wholly alien to her features. "Well—"

She didn't wait for an answer, and instead went to the first door and banged three times in a way that wasn't designed to be friendly. A middle-aged man answered, and started when he saw the unwelcome flash of synthetic yellow on his doorstep.

"Chair census," announced Mrs. Gamboge, "by order of Head Office. You have no objections, I trust?" It wasn't a question she actually wanted or needed an answer for, and she swiftly directed her charges to conduct a "full chair search" while I stood on the step with the resident.

"Hello," I said. "Edward Russett."

"Hello," said the man, glaring at me suspiciously.

"It's a Head Office assignment," I said, feeling a bit stupid.

"And that gives you the freedom to look through my house?"

"Anyone conducting a census is an agent of Head Office, and has right of access."

"Hmm," he said doubtfully. "Aren't you the one starting a Question Club?"

"I hope so."

"Then you can ask this: Why did the Previous insist on separate taps for hot and cold?"

"Why not raise the question yourself at the first meeting? I may not be able to make it."

The Yellows all trooped out a few minutes later, and reported seven chairs, two sofas and a piano stool.

"Thank you for your time," I said as politely as I could, and followed the Gamboges and Bunty as they moved next door. They were already beginning to attract a small group of Greys. It was early afternoon, and the zone was mostly empty—but then I didn't think they would have attempted a census when people were at home.

Mrs. Gamboge knocked at the door of the next house, and it opened to reveal a young woman who stared at the prefect in an insolent manner that, if outside the Greyzone, would have instantly led to a heavy demerit.

"Chair census," announced Sally Gamboge, "by order of Head Office."

The young Grey looked at us all in turn. "Right. And I'm the Colorman."

The impertinence was too much for Courtland. "Are you calling my mother a liar, Wendy?"

"We don't have many Rules in our favor," she retorted, "but privacy of dwelling is one of them."

"Russett," said the prefect, "show Wendy your assignment."

I told her I didn't have it with me, but Bunty produced it like a conjuring trick.

"I took the liberty of fetching it from your bedroom," she said, handing it over.

"That seems to be in order," murmured the Grey after studying my assignment carefully, and the Yellows walked in without another word. They were more cautious this time, as though expecting a Riffraff snare under the hall carpet or something.

"Sorry about this," I said to Wendy as we stood in the hall. She didn't answer, and instead glared at me until the Yellows returned with a list of chairs in their notebooks.

"Listen," I said as Mrs. Gamboge was about to knock on the door of the next dwelling, "this is all a bit awkward—why don't we ask the Greys to do a self-declaration?"

"That would be a waste of time," declared Bunty. "Greys are the most *consummate* of liars."

"You don't actually have to be here at all," added Penelope, who despite being the smallest and youngest, managed to ooze just as much unpleasantness as the rest of them. "Why don't you bog off home and leave the serious census taking to the professionals?"

"I'm staying," I said.

Mrs. Gamboge grunted, and knocked on the next door. She took a step back when the door was answered—by *Jane*.

"Well, well," she said, "you don't see a Yellow in the Greyzone for years, and then four come along together."

"This isn't your house, Jane," observed Mrs. Gamboge suspiciously.

"The Rot take your hue, Gamboge."

They all took a sharp intake of breath, and I could see them rankle at not just the insult, but the supreme lack of respect that accompanied it.

"Three days to go until the Night Train," remarked Sally, "and *still* unrepentant. I pity your poor Reboot mentor. Mind you, there's always the Magnolia Room for hard nuts. Show her your warrant, Russett."

Jane read the assignment, then waved the Yellows past.

"What's going on, Jane?"

"Did I say you could use my name?"

"No."

"Then don't. Now, I want you to stop all this."

"I don't have any control over the Yellows."

"Come on, Red—show some grit for a change. Stand up and be counted."

I took a deep breath. "I want you to come with me to High Saffron."

"And I told you: I don't do death on a first date."

"You could do with the merits. You could buy your way out of Reboot. You said yourself that legging it on the conveyor or staying at Rusty Hill wasn't an ideal situation."

Courtland walked past. Jane put out her foot and he stumbled on it, glared at her and then went into the basement.

"Watch out for that one. The village will go all to Beige in a match pot when his mother retires. You and I are going to have to take care of him."

"What do you mean?"

"Take him out," she said, "you and me. Together. Now *that* would be a first date to remember."

"I'm sorry," I said, hoping she was pulling my leg, "I never do death on a first date."

She laughed. Delightfully so, in fact. But then her attention was taken by the Yellows, who were opening cupboards and drawers to "check for folding chairs," as they put it, and Jane leaned forward and spoke in a urgent voice.

"Fun's over. You have to put a stop to this!"

"But I've got to conduct my chair census. Orders from Head Office."

"Plums to Head Office," she replied. "You think the Yellows are *really* here to count chairs?"

"What else would they be doing?"

She sighed.

"It's a merit sweep, dummy. They're using your chair census as an excuse to go through our stuff and log infractions. The more demerits they find, the harder we have to work to earn them back. But they can only do it during an official Head Office census—it's the Rules."

"I go to High Saffron tomorrow."

"Exactly. The census dies with you, so they're just exploiting the opportunity while they can. The thing is, there is stuff here they shouldn't find. Things that *have* to stay hidden. If they find them, the Yellows can't leave the zone and will end up beneath a patio or something. Perhaps we'll get away with it, but as likely as not we won't. You want the death of four Yellows on your conscience?"

"Is this some sort of prank or something?"

She stared at me. It was clear that it wasn't.

"What secret do you have here that you'd kill for?"

"Stop the search, Red. You can save the lives of four people you don't much like, and who cause us untold misery. Sort of a weird ethical dilemma, isn't it?"

"Will you come with me to High Saffron?"

"Red, you have to do this one for yourself."

At that moment Sally Gamboge returned and barked out her chair tally. Before I could even *think* about Jane's request, Sally Gamboge had moved next door and demanded entry. The Grey homeowner was older and less abrasive than Jane, and he started to panic. I caught Jane's eye and she looked upward, toward the attic.

"I'll do the top floor," I announced. "It's time I did some chair counting myself."

The Yellows looked at one another but could raise no realistic objections, and I mounted the steep, narrow stairs to the third floor while Penelope and Bunty searched the second. The stair twisted back on itself, and by the time I got to the top landing and paused in the dim light from the skylight, my heart was beating fiercely. I grasped the handle and carefully opened the door.

The only light came from a thin, mullioned window at the far end, which afforded the room only meager light. I could just make out a small bed, a table, a bureau and a pitch-pine chest. There was a single chair in the middle of the room, and it was occupied by an old woman. She was dressed in a simple linen smock, had no spot or any merit badges and was knitting a long scarf that lay in an untidy cascade at her feet. Her hands were twisted and gnarled like old roots, and although I could see no detail in her face, her cheekbones were prominent and her slack skin hung in soft folds that jangled when she spoke. If she had not moved, I would have considered her to be sundried Nightloss, such that we find from time to time.

She stopped what she was doing when I walked in but didn't look up—she simply listened in a peculiar manner.

"Jane?"

"No—Edward Russett."

"The new swatchman's son?"

"Yes, ma'am. What are you doing up here?"

"Not much," she replied, "but I have my knitting—and *Renfrew* at bedtimes."

She reached for the glass of water that was next to her, but she didn't look—she just moved her fingertips across the tabletop until they encountered the glass, then grasped it. The hair on the back of my neck stood on end, and I felt myself tremble. This was something I had never before encountered, nor ever thought I would.

"You're . . . *blind!*"

She gave out a short laugh.

"We are *all* blind, Master Edward—just some more than others."

"But you can't be," I blurted out. "As soon as poor sight becomes

296

apparent, then Variant-B kicks in and, and, well—look here, you should be *studied*, not kept in an attic!"

"Hmm," she said, "Jane told me you were a bit foolish. I have to stay hidden for I dispel fear, and fear is a commodity much needed by the Collective."

"Fear of the night?"

"Yes; a couple of sightless people kicking around would really finish off that particular nonsense, now wouldn't it?"

"I don't understand."

"Then you have fulfilled all that is expected of you. What's going on downstairs?"

"A merit sweep by the Gamboges."

"Jane also told me you showed potential," said the old lady. "I suggest you show it. It's time you left."

I closed the attic door and ran downstairs, where I met Jane on the doorstep. A larger crowd of Greys had turned up from the fields, glasshouse and factory. Some even carried tools. The mood had grown darker.

"How did you get along with Mrs. Olive?" asked Jane.

I looked around nervously, and the crowd stared back at me silently.

"How many do you have hidden?" I asked.

"Sixteen in the Greyzone and one living above you. Mostly damaged Nightloss, a few Rebootees. Five are blind and one of them can't move anything from the waist down. To the prefects they're 'unlicensed supernumeraries' and harboring them carries a twenty thousand demerit—applicable to anyone who lives in the house or 'could not have reasonably failed to know.'"

"Unlicensed supernumeraries?" I echoed, having never heard the term.

"I agree it's somewhat dispassionate. We just call them 'the Extras.'"

"Tommo's Ulrika of the Flak," I said, recalling the sandwiches he had left for an imaginary friend in the flak tower. "Does he know about them?"

"Thankfully not. But feeding imaginary friends has a long tradition, and the sandwiches are always welcome. Do you know how hard it is to smuggle food out of the dining room?"

I answered that I did, because the lunch monitors had the power of Stop and Search—eating between meals was *strictly* forbidden.

"So try doing it for sixteen people—even with Apocrypha on your side."

"Perkins Muffleberry back home," I murmured. "I left food for him in the hollow beech. It was always gone by the morning."

She laid a hand on my shoulder.

"Don't sweat it, Red," she said, doubtless reading the despondency in my face. "Few people see anything at all. Everything might look fine and dandy on the outside, but behind the closed door there's a fire raging. Now, will you stop this from getting any worse?"

"Yes," I said quietly, as the full scale of what was going on suddenly became apparent, "I think you're right."

"What did you find up there?" asked Sally Gamboge, stepping out of the house.

"A three-person bench and an armchair," I replied, voice cracking.

"Very well," said the prefect, and she made a move toward the next house.

"Wait!"

She stopped.

"I have decided," I said slowly, "to conduct my chair census in a less . . . intrusive manner."

I started to sweat and swallowed down my nervousness as the Yellows all glared at me.

"No, you haven't," said Little Penelope Gamboge in a belligerent screech. "You'll do this census the Yellow prefect's way, or you won't do it at all!"

"Then I won't do it at all."

"You will," said Sally Gamboge, "and that's a Direct Order."

"I'll be dead on the road to High Saffron in under twenty-four hours," I replied, the apprehension in my voice readily apparent. "I can certainly afford to defy you on this occasion, ma'am."

"Your almost certain death is *precisely* why we need to hurry this along," remarked Bunty with a singular lack of empathy. "If Head Office has entrusted you to conduct this important work, it behooves you to complete it as soon as you can. The Collective expects all residents to act with the highest level of integrity."

"The answer is *NO*."

They stared at me for a moment in astonishment.

"We'll magnanimously let you *reconsider* that last response, Russett," observed Courtland. "Refusing a Direct Order from a prefect carries a maximum five hundred demerit. Haven't you lost enough merits today already?"

I had—and a loss of five hundred more would put me teetering on the edge of Reboot. It was all so hopelessly unfair. I was refusing not just in order to keep the Extras hidden but to save the *Yellows*. The Greys who were standing close by were not just idle onlookers but there to defend the secrets in the attics and their potential twenty thousand demerit for complicity. I looked at Jane, the Greys—and then the Yellows, who were completely oblivious to just how close they were to becoming compost.

But then, just as I was about to confirm my rejection of Gamboge's Direct Order, take the five hundred hit, reduce my merits to zero *and* kiss farewell to an Oxblood marriage this decade, relief came from an unexpected quarter—the *postman*.

He walked into the small knot of people, nodded us all a greeting and gave out the mail. The situation had an odd, even surreal quality about it. If a piano should suddenly have fallen from the sky or a talking bear rode past on a bike, I would not have been unduly surprised. We all stood there, momentarily paused. We said nothing as the mail was handed out and just looked at one another suspiciously.

"Oh, look," said the postman, "there's even a package for you, Penelope."

He handed the youngest Gamboge a parcel, tipped his cap and moved off. And as soon as he had, the balance suddenly tipped in my favor. *I recognized the parcel.*

"Okay," said Courtland, "last chance. Are you refusing a Direct Order?"

I stared back at him. I had been sent to the Fringes to learn a lesson in humility, and I *was*—but not from the prefects or anyone in authority. I was learning it from the *Greys*, who were harboring damaged Nightloss in their attics at huge personal risk to themselves.

"You speak of integrity?" I said, my voice no longer tremulous. "Would that be the same integrity that had you allocate Travis Canary's postcode the day before we even knew he was dead?"

There was a deathly hush. Travis had carried a prestigious TO3 postcode from the traditional Yellow Honeybun Peninsula. It was the sort of postcode that could open yellow doors. The sort of postcode that could get a Yellow away from a Fringes village forever. It was the sort of postcode, in fact, that a pushy grandmother and a murderous uncle might do *anything* to procure, so that their granddaughter and niece would have a better chance in life. Penelope Gamboge. She had been allocated Travis' code on the last day possible—her twelfth birthday.

"I sent Travis' personal effects back to his postcode," I said, "thinking the redirects wouldn't be up yet. I was wrong. The parcel has just been delivered."

Bunty and Penelope looked confused, but Sally Gamboge and Courtland looked at each other, then at the parcel. The arrogant veneer suddenly dropped, and there was silence for almost a full minute.

"He was Nightloss and as good as dead," growled Mrs Gamboge, "so I just preempted the inevitable. I'll take the hit for that."

She stared at me, and I stared back. They might argue their way out of the Daylighter in Travis' head *or* the reallocation, but not both together. But I think the Gamboges knew that.

"This census is henceforth canceled," said Prefect Gamboge quietly. "Bunty, hand Master Russett back his assignment."

"What—?"

"Do as I say, Miss McMustard."

She handed it over, and I considered it was probably time to leave, so I walked quickly away, leaving a foursome of loathing and loathed Yellows within a knot of disgruntled Greyfolk, whose sixteen charges remained unmolested and secret. I also left a Grey with a retroussé nose who was, I hoped, impressed enough to join me on the trip to High Saffron.

Slugs, Jam and Tickets

7.3.12.31.208: Reckless disrespect of the lightless hours will
not be tolerated.

When I got home, there was a note from Violet reminding me
that we had arranged to meet at lamplighting that evening
for a romantic walk, and that I was to brush my teeth and
put some moisturizer on my lips. She had also sent round
some jam. Some *loganberry*. It was a small pot, such as you might find
at a jam-tasting session organized by the sector jam-in-chief. I smiled to
myself but Violet's kindness notwithstanding, I cleared out the broom
cupboard so that I would have a safe retreat if she came calling unexpectedly. I even practiced a form of "Violet escape drill" in which I could
be noiselessly inside the cupboard from anywhere within the house in
under five seconds. I had just completed a front-door-to broom-cupboard
dash in under four seconds, and had emerged from the cupboard much
pleased with myself, when a voice made me jump.

"By all that's navy, young man, what *are* you doing?"

It was Mrs. Lapis Lazuli, and she must have walked in the back door
unannounced.

"I was—um—rehearsing for hide-and-seek."

"Hmm," she replied in her odd, imperious way that I knew was hiding someone deeply devoted to story and librarying, "not some sort of
'hiding from Violet' procedure?"

"Maybe that as well."

A smile cracked upon her austere features.

"I don't blame you. A frightful child is Violet—quite *horribly* spoiled. I hear you're going to High Saffron?"

I told her this was so, and she reiterated her belief that there was a library hidden within the overgrown oak and rhododendron forest, and that she wanted me to keep an eye out for it.

"I'm humbled by your optimism," I told her. "No one else thinks I have even the slightest chance of coming back."

"Ah," she said, faintly embarrassed, "I had—um—made provision for that eventuality. Might I explain?"

I sighed. "Go on, then."

"This box contains two homing slugs," she said, passing me a beautifully crafted wooden container no bigger than a goose egg, "each in its own compartment. The first is marked 'Hoorah, yes, there's a library,' and the second, 'No, worse luck, there isn't.' I've logged the Taxa number on each. All you have to do is release the appropriate slug when you get to High Saffron. Do you want me to run over the details again?"

"I think I've got it. You know that High Saffron is over forty miles away?"

She smiled.

"I won't live to see the return of the slug," she said, "but the next generation of librarians shall. Time is something we *definitely* have on our side. Is there anything I can do for you in return?"

I thought for a moment.

"I'd like to hear the end of *Renfrew of the Mounties* this evening—about whether he catches the train robber or not."

She smiled. "I've no idea who commits that indefensible abuse of the centralized heating system, but I'm sure they can be persuaded."

"I'm very grateful," I told her. "Would you excuse me?"

I had just seen the Apocryphal man enter the front door. I found him in the living room, staring absently at one of the Vettrianos.

"Really?" he said when I told him I had some loganberry. "Show me."

His face fell at the meagerness of my offering, but a promise was a promise, and we sat down on the sofa.

"You told me yesterday you could remember a time before Model Ts—when the Ford flathead was the vehicle of choice."

"Yes?"

"I had a look in the *Leapback Book*. Flatheads were disposed of at the Third Great Leap Backward—one hundred and ninety-six years ago."

"So your question is—?"

"How old are you?"

He thought for a moment and then counted on his fingers

"I'll be four hundred and fifty-two years this August. A card might be nice, but don't worry about a present. Unless it's jam, of course."

"How can you live so long?"

"By not dying. See this?"

He pulled up his shirt to reveal where NS-B4 was scarred into the place his postcode should have been.

"It stands for 'Negligible Senescence—Baxter #4.' That's my name—Mr. Baxter. Now, if you had to devise a historian, what would be your design parameters?"

I had to think about this.

"Intellect, for analysis."

"You're very kind. What else?"

"An excellent memory."

"Flatterer. Anything more?"

"Longevity?"

He smiled. "*Precisely*. Unlike you, I don't have any of that tiresome obsolescence that is both the bane and boon of mankind."

I stared at him for a moment without speaking.

"You must have seen a lot."

He shook his head. "Not a lot—*everything*. You recall I told you I was once a historian? I was lying; I still am. But Baxters don't teach; Baxters *observe*. They note, they file, they compile reports."

"For whom do you do this?"

"Head Office."

"But since no one *studies* history anymore," I pointed out, "what's the point of recording it?"

"You've got it all wrong," he said slowly. "I don't exist to record your history; *you* exist to give *me* something to record."

It was an interesting concept, although quite clearly loopy. One might just as easily suppose that we are here only to give function to houses, or to give a market to Ovaltine and string.

"So let me get this straight," I murmured. "We are here only to give *you* something to study?"

"In one. I'm amazed you've taken so easily to the concept. Those that can be troubled to muse upon the meaning of life are generally disappointed when they figure it out."

"In that case," I said, thinking quickly, "what is the meaning of your life?"

He laughed. "Why, to study all of you, of course. It's the perfect symbiosis. Once my studies are complete, I will be recalled to the faculty at Emerald City to present my findings."

"And when will that be?"

"When the study is complete."

"And how will you know when that is?"

"Because I will be recalled to Emerald City."

"That's insane."

"If you look around, you won't find much that isn't."

I had to agree with this, but the Apocryphal man, perhaps unused to having a chance to explain himself, carried on.

"There were initially ten Baxters, but despair took all but one. The weakest willed was always going to be the last Baxter standing. Sadly, it was me—I will have to shoulder the responsibility on my own."

"What responsibility?"

"Without me, no one's life has any meaning."

"I thought Munsell said that color was here to give our lives meaning?"

"Its function is to give life *apparent* meaning. It is an abstraction, a misdirection—nothing more than a sideshow at Jollity Fair. As long as your minds are full of Chromatic betterment, there can be no room for other, more destructive thoughts. Do you understand?"

"Not really," I said, confused by Mr. Baxter's odd view of the world. "What was the Something That Happened?"

"I was born after the Epiphany. I don't know what happened. But if you want to find out, then you should return to Rusty Hill and finish the work Zane and Ochre started."

"The painting of the ceiling?"

"Everything is there in the ceiling," he said. "All it needs is a key."

I recalled the strong feeling of anticipation I had felt at the appearance of the Pooka. As with the Perpetulite's hidden panel and the harmonics running Everspins, there was far, far more to the world than I supposed, and quite possibly a lot more to us.

"But—"

I was interrupted by three loud raps at the door. Aware that I should not even be acknowledging Mr. Baxter let alone *talking* to him, I went to the door to see the caller away.

It was Courtland Gamboge. He was on his own, and his manner seemed . . . *businesslike.*

"Twenty-two minutes."

"I'm sorry?"

"Twenty-two minutes," he repeated, "until the train departs. You surrendered your Open Return to deMauve, and I've a spare. This time tomorrow you can be back in the arms of your sweetheart. No trip to High Saffron, no chair census, no getting married to Violet, *nothing.* It's life as it was before you came out here to the Fringes."

"I'm still down eight hundred merits."

"You'll have to sort that out for yourself."

"And the catch?"

"No catch," he said with a forced smile. "We give you a ticket, and you get on the train. You don't owe us anything, and we don't owe you anything. Clean slate. It's like you were never here."

"I need to tell my father."

"You can leave a note. He'll understand. Twenty-one minutes. If you're going, you have to go now."

They had timed it well, and the decision was an easy one to make. I took the proffered ticket.

"Good lad," he said, "I'll see you to the railway station."

Open Return

2.6.32.12.269: The Leapback list shall be maintained by the most westerly village in Green Sector East. Fresh Leapback shall be chosen in reverse alphabetical order.

Courtland's timing was indeed perfect: The train had just pulled in when we got to the railway station. Bunty was in her usual place and nodded to Courtland, who turned and walked back toward the village without comment. The day was by now blistering hot, with barely a cloud in the sky, and the trainspotters on the slope above fanned themselves with their notebooks to keep cool.

I opened the carriage door, smiled a greeting to an amiable-looking Blue woman in a hat and veil and sat by myself in the nearly empty carriage. I looked at Bunty, who was still seated on the platform, and she stared at me with as much disdain as she could muster, which was considerable. I took a deep breath and settled back into my seat. The train would leave as soon as the linoleum was loaded, and since I was impatient to be away, time seemed to slow down. I didn't know what the Jade-under-Lime Council would say when I arrived back early, but I didn't really care. I was away, and *alive*.

"Master Edward?" came a voice. "There's a telegram for you."

It was Stafford, who smiled and tipped his cap. I thanked him, and asked him how he knew I was here, to which he replied that he was simply picking up a fare, and always had at least a half-dozen telegrams to deliver.

"Off for long, sir?" he asked.

"For good, Stafford. Thanks for everything."

"Most kind, sir. I hope things turn out delightfully uneventful for you."

"Yes," I said slowly, "I hope so, too."

"Back to the usual routine, then is it, sir?"

"Yes, yes," I replied, "I expect so."

"Master Edward?"

"Yes, Stafford?"

"Never underestimate the capacity for romance, no matter what the circumstance."

"You mean Jane?"

But he didn't answer.

"Pleasant voyage, Master Edward."

He tipped his hat a second time, and was gone. I sat back in my seat again, confused and annoyed. Stafford might have been pulling my leg, of course—or may not have meant Jane at all. I tried not to think about her and instead concentrate on what I had learned: Don't rock the boat, don't stand out, respect the Chromatic scale and, above all, don't try to improve queuing. From what I'd seen in East Carmine, I now had all the tools necessary for a long and prosperous life. With a bit of luck, I would marry Constance, keep the Collective well supplied with string and give the Oxbloods the Reddest son they had ever had. It all seemed so simple, really, and in some respects, I thanked my lucky stars that I had been given the opportunity to allow clarity to be brought to my dangerously unsociable outlook.

I saw the stationmaster ready his flag, and for the first time since I had arrived in East Carmine, I felt myself relax. I smiled and looked out the window. The only alighting passenger looked like Bertie Magenta. Same large ears and mildly dopey demeanor. I looked closer. It *was* Bertie Magenta. He was dressed in a light synthetic-violet three-piece suit with matching hat, and was carrying a small overnight case. He held a perfumed handkerchief to his nose and had wrapped his shoes in newspaper, presumably to avoid soiling them.

"Bertie?" I said, having lowered the carriage window. "Is that you?"

"Hello, Eddie," he replied. "Are you leaving?"

"It's a long story. What in Munsell's name are you doing here?"

"Very droll," he said with a laugh. "Another one of your quippy japes?"

"Not at all," I replied, "I really want to know."

"Because *you* sent for me. Something about a frightfully vivacious sub-Beta gal who would be willing"—he leaned forward and lowered his voice—"to offer *favors* on approval."

"Tommo!" I cried, suddenly realizing what had happened. Foolishly, I had mentioned Bertie's name in his presence.

"No, I think her name's Imogen, and she looks and sounds like just the sort of filly I'm after. If she's half as purplicious as you made out in your telegram, I will *happily* give you the fifty-merit introduction fee you asked for."

"There's been a misunderstanding."

"What?" said Bertie. "You mean she's not available?"

"No. Well, yes, I suppose she is, but—"

"Welcome to East Carmine!" came a voice, and I turned to see Tommo and Fandango walking along the platform. Behind them in the station yard was the village's Ford. Bertie was being given the full treatment, and while Fandango greeted Magenta warmly and led him toward the Ford, Tommo leaned on the window to talk to me.

"What are you doing on the train, Eddie?"

"Something I should have done the moment I got here. And just for the record, you had no right to contact Bertie."

He smiled. "I meant to explain what I was up to, but I couldn't think of a way of doing it without your flying into a rage. So I didn't."

"You forged a telegram from me!"

"Let's just say I might have misrepresented the sendee a little bit. It's no worse than lying about the rabbit. In fact, I'm doing the Magentas a favor—always a good move, if you know what I mean."

"But Bertie's a vacuous oaf. I wouldn't wish him married to my worst enemy!"

"You're *not* wishing him married to your worst enemy. You're wishing him married to the lovely Imogen."

"This will make her and Dorian *miserable*. How can you have a part in that?"

"When I have no cash *I'm* miserable," he said, "so it's either them or me. Good-bye, Eddie."

And he walked off toward the station yard to join Fandango and Bertie.

I sat back in my seat, my relaxed feelings replaced by annoyance and frustration. I felt partially responsible, but there was, in fact, nothing I could do. I'd be overnighting in Cobalt and back in Jade-under-Lime by lunchtime tomorrow. I looked down and opened the telegram. It wasn't perhaps the best thing I could have read.

TO EDWARD RUSSETT RG6 7GD ++ EAST CARMINE RSW ++ FROM
CONSTANCE OXBLOOD SW3 6ZH ++ JADE UNDER LIME GSW ++ MSGE
BEGINS ++ DELIGHTED TO HEAR NEWS OF YOUR GOOD FORTUNE HOPE
YOU AND MISS DEMAUVE VERY HAPPY TOGETHER AND THAT ONE
DAY OUR PATHS MIGHT CROSS AGAIN ++ SINCE YOUR MARRIAGE HAS
REDUCED MY MARRIAGE MARKET I HAVE ACCEPTED ROGERS OFFER
AND WE ARE TO MARRY IN THE SPRING ++ BE WELL CONSTANCE X ++
PS ROGER SENDS REGARDS AND ASKS IF HE CAN HAVE YOUR TENNIS
RACKET ++ MSGE ENDS

I suddenly felt sick, angry, relieved and cheated all at once. I closed my eyes and scrunched up the telegram.

"Bad news?" asked the Blue woman with the veil.

"Ten minutes ago it would have been," I said, thinking of Stafford's words, "but right now it's probably the best news I've had."

I got up and opened the door of the carriage as the stationmaster was putting his whistle to his lips. But before I could climb out and shut the door behind me, Bunty strode up with a look of thunder.

"There was a deal, Russett!"

"The deal is off."

"*We'll* tell you if the deal is off!"

And before I knew it, she had pushed me roughly back inside the carriage. I used my foot to keep her from shutting the door and wormed my way half out again, whereupon Bunty punched me painfully in the midriff, then grabbed my ear. The stationmaster and the Blue woman in the veil looked on, he with the whistle poised in his mouth, and she tutting audibly, shocked and appalled by the unseemly tussle playing out in front of her. Bunty was stronger than I, and the struggle soon descended into her pushing with all her might from *outside* as I tried to keep hold of the varnished door frame on the *inside*. I caught the eye of the stationmaster. I knew he wouldn't risk his job by assisting me, but I also knew that punctuality was of vital importance. So I suddenly let go of the door frame, and Bunty and I both tumbled inside. The stationmaster slammed the door and blew his whistle. By the time we had disentangled ourselves, the door locks had clunked and the train had begun to move off.

"You idiot!" yelled Bunty, her hair unpinned and her pinafore askew. "Just look at me!"

I told her it appeared we were now traveling companions, and she said only for the next forty minutes until Bluetown, where she would alert their departures clerk as to my behavior and use force if necessary to keep me on the train.

"And the next stop after that will be Greenways," she added—"out of Red Sector West and our hair forever."

I didn't reply to this, except to say I had cut my lip, and excused myself to go to the toilet, leaving Bunty apologizing to the woman in the Blue veil and explaining that I was "trouble of the worst kind."

But I didn't go to the toilet. I went to the next carriage, lowered the window and climbed out until I was standing on the step. I timed my moment and jumped. The train was going at a reasonable speed by now, but I wasn't much bothered as I tumbled on the grass and fell into a thorn bush. I sat up, scratched and bleeding, and watched the train until it was out of sight, then walked back down the line to the railway station.

"Changed your mind?" asked the stationmaster as I struggled back onto the platform twenty minutes later.

"The Outer Fringes grow on you."

"So does lichen if you stand still long enough."

My Last Evening Ignorant

4.2.12.34.431: The menu at village tearooms shall not be deviated from.

made my way to the Fallen Man, where long-established custom would find Carlos Fandango offering tea and scones to Bertie, and discussing potential dowries, feedback ratings and virtues. I didn't know what I was going to do, but I knew I needed to do *something*.

Dorian was pacing around on the opposite side of the street, and before I could say anything, he punched me on the nose. It wasn't that hard, but enough to stop me in my tracks.

"That's for betraying my confidence," he said. "I thought you were positive toward our predicament. And now I find you've invited this Magenta idiot to come over and feel the goods before purchase. What is Imogen to you? Ripe fruit?"

"Not my doing," I assured him. "I think you should be looking for someone who would sell their own toes for a couple of extra merits."

"Oh," he replied with a look of sudden contrition, "Tommo."

"In one." I peered into the tearoom, where Fandango seemed to be in heavy conversation with Bertie. Sitting between them was Imogen, who looked very delightful indeed in her Outdoor Informal with Hat #8. She spent her time glaring sullenly at her father and potential husband in turn.

"You can't claim you're totally free of blame," continued Dorian. "I mean, Tommo must have found out about Magenta from you."

"Okay," I said, "I'm going to have to make this right."

"How?"

I handed Dorian the unused railway ticket, and his eyes opened wide.

He'd just had time to put the ticket in his pocket when Prefect Sally Gamboge walked up, bristling with indignation. She had Courtland with her, and they weren't there to add me to their birthday list.

"What are you still doing here, Russett? I thought we agreed you'd take the train out?"

"Circumstances have changed."

She glared at me. "I hope you don't regret that decision," she said coldly.

"Is that a threat, Madam Prefect?"

"Not at all," she replied, "merely an *observation*."

"An observation duly taken on board. I feel it is my duty to report that Miss McMustard has just taken the fifteen forty-three out of the village."

"*What?* Bunty? A walkout? Impossible!" And after telling me she would "deal with me later," Gamboge marched off to find out what had happened to Bunty.

"So," said Courtland once his mother had gone, "it looks like you owe me a ticket. A deal is a deal."

"The deal was I'd get on the train. And I did."

"Sticking up for the Greys can be a costly business," he said, glancing at Dorian. "I hope you've got deep pockets."

"I'm going to make a point of discussing the whole Grey issue next week," I murmured, "in the Council Chamber. I think we might see some changes around here."

Courtland wasn't that impressed with my bravado.

"Making plans for next week? How cheerfully optimistic of you."

And he went off to join his mother.

"Here," said Dorian, as soon as Courtland had gone, "have a flapjack. We ran out of syrup, so I used cod-liver oil."

"Crumbly," I said after taking a bite, "and a bit fishy."

We both stood on the far side of the street and looked across into the window of the Fallen Man.

"Now that we've got two tickets, we'll certainly take the Colorman up on his offer," murmured Dorian. "We'll be off on the Sunday train, straight after Imogen's Ishihara."

There was a pause.

"Eddie?"

"Yes?"

"Why didn't you take the train? You're almost certainly going to disappear off into the Outfield tomorrow. And I know you can't possibly want to marry Violet."

"Do you want to know the real, honest, totally truthful answer?"

He nodded.

"Because there's someone else here in East Carmine. Someone hopelessly unsuitable. It's all a really bad idea and will lead to trouble of the worst sort. But no matter what, every minute in her presence makes my life a minute more complete."

"Yes," he said, looking across at Imogen, "I know exactly what you mean."

We stood there for some moments in silence.

"Another flapjack?"

"No, thanks."

I wrote several letters after I'd returned home. One to Constance, explaining that it was always my intention to marry her, and that we had both been the victim of an up-color Gazump. I wrote one to my father, telling him how much I loved him, and then one to Fenton, apologizing about the rabbit and enclosing a five-merit piece as compensation. I placed all the letters in my top drawer, to be found when my room was cleared out, then went downstairs to make supper. I made more than was necessary, and on two dishes, to make it easier for the Apocryphal man and his Extra.

There were periodic knocks on the door, and every time, my heart jumped as I thought it might be Jane come to tell me that she had changed her mind and would be coming with me to High Saffron. It wasn't. It was residents who wanted me to do something for them in High Saffron. Like look for Floyd Pinken, who had vanished there a decade previously, or Johnson McKhaki, who had done the same twenty-three years before *that*. "I'll call his name," I said to McKhaki's aged widow, who would certainly have won first prize in a deluded hope contest.

Lucy Ochre came around to wish me well. She had a message from the Greyzone.

"You have a new name: 'He-who-runs-with-scissors.'"

I'd heard of the phrase before, and it referred partly to the "Home

Safety and Sharp Objects" directive in section eight of the Book of Common Sense, but mostly to describe those who didn't care what trouble they caused in the selfish pursuit of their own polluted ideals. It meant you had rejected the simple purity of the rainbow and were thus incompatible with the Word of Munsell. Beyond contempt, in other words, and well overdue for Reboot. From the Greys, a huge accolade.

"An honor like that," I remarked, "is usually bestowed posthumously."

"I think they wanted you to enjoy it, if only for a short while."

"How thoughtful. Who sent the message?"

"The one with the retroussé nose who fights a lot. Have you and she got a thing going?"

"I don't think she's a 'thing' sort of girl."

Lucy agreed with that sentiment, then asked me to take a pendulum with me to conduct a series of harmonic tests on the expedition.

"All my calculations seem to indicate that High Saffron is suffused with musical energy that seems to peak with the ball lightning cycle every thirty-seven days."

I told her that while this was fascinating, I had enough on my plate, and she agreed, gave me a long hug, told me not to come back dead and went away.

"Tommo was right," said Dad when he got in from work, "the deMauves are *seriously* oiled. We got ten grand for you, with two up front."

I had gotten used to being treated as a commodity by now.

"Up front?" I said. "What for?"

"Tommo is an exceptional negotiator. George deMauve told me that he'd sign his daughter over as soon as he sees your Ishihara results. And I'm good for my word. Half the gravy will be yours."

"And what if I don't come back?"

"We'll get you safely back somehow," he said in a quiet voice. "We're just not sure precisely how. How do you want to spend the evening? The Verdi concert?"

"What about Scrabble?" I suggested, thinking I should be in if Jane came calling. Dad agreed even though he didn't much like Scrabble, and went to fetch the board.

The rest of the evening was something of a blur. I can recall the prefects' coming in turns to wish me well, and to give useless snippets of advice that I could happily ignore. Even Sally Gamboge came around for form's sake, but although her mouth uttered fond words, her eyes spoke only venom. The Apocryphal man graciously took the smaller of the dishes, and I had just achieved a triple-word score with *azure* when the dusk warning bell sounded.

"I'm supposed to be meeting Violet," I murmured. "I'd better be off."

"Glad you're coming around to the idea," he said. "She's not half as bad as she appears."

But instead of going to see Violet, which was what I'd implied, I went to hide in the broom closet, which was what I'd meant.

So that's where I was when Violet was looking all over the village for me. It was warm and comfortable, and quite against my own expectations, I fell fast asleep, only to wake when the lights-out warning bell sounded two hours later.

I trod silently up to bed and had just changed into my pajamas when the world once more plunged into blackness. I lay awake for a while, listening to the Morse on the radiator. The gossip was once more about me—how I was either insane or fatally misguided to have volunteered myself. I listened for a while to the gossip channel, acknowledged the words of well-wishers, then turned my ears to the serial, where, as promised, Mrs. Lapis Lazuli had extended the broadcast to finish the chapter of *Renfrew of the Mounties*.

I listened until all the Radtalkers had signed off, then settled down to sleep in the pitch-dark. Before I did so, I crept out of bed and fumbled my way around the bedroom to wedge a chair under the doorknob. There was someone in the village who could see at night, and I didn't want him or her coming into my room.

I didn't know who it was. In fact, I didn't know lots of things. But that would all change, come the following day. I would achieve *enlightenment*, and then, in celebration of this, Jane would have me eaten by a yateveo. But it wouldn't be personal. It would be a *precautionary*.

Wedding Plans

3.6.02.01.025: Licentious behavior between unmarried
partners is strictly prohibited. Fine: five hundred merits.

I awoke with a start to find my bedclothes in disarray. I had slept badly, waking at every tiny sound that might, to my fuddled mind, have been a threat. The room had just been brought back to sightfulness with a glimmer of sunlight on the opposite wall. I checked the bedside clock—it was five in the morning. I rolled out of bed and carefully removed the chair from under the doorknob, quietly opened the door and padded across the landing to the bathroom.

I had a pee and walked back into my bedroom and almost yelled in alarm. Staring at me from outside the window was none other than Violet deMauve. When she saw me jump, she put a finger to her lips and made a gesture for me to raise the sash, which I did, foolishly realizing at that moment that with all my elaborate plans to safeguard myself the night before, I had neglected to note that my window was easily accessible by standing on the back-door porch below.

"What are you doing here?" I whispered. She didn't answer, but simply clambered in, then turned and gave the thumbs-up to her unseen companion below, who took the ladder away. Violet then pulled down the window, jumped noiselessly onto the rug and started to remove her clothes, smiling coyly at me as she did so. I couldn't deny that the fashion in which she did it was alluring. After all, Violet was not the sort of girl for whom anything could be left to chance, so she had doubtless rehearsed this often.

"You had no right to cancel my half promise to Constance."

"That would have been Mother," she said. "Goodness, she is so naughty. But when she has her heart set on her daughter wanting something, she's pretty unstoppable."

"It's not just naughty, it's unforgivable—and rude."

"Tish, Edward. You stood me up last night, and that was very rude. If I weren't so desperately in love with you, I might be offended."

"Listen—"

"I'm not miffed, sweetness. The path of marriage can be rocky, and I am willing to forgive you, as you will surely forgive my mother for telling that beastly Oxblood tramp where to get off."

"I don't want to marry you, Violet."

"Don't be silly, darling. You get to jump up five hues and be Red prefect, I'll eventually be *head* prefect and our strong Purple offspring get to preside over East Carmine's residents forever and ever. What's more, you and I and your father get some folding in our back pockets. And Daddy has jam. It's a win-win-win-win-win situation."

"So what are you doing here, if it's all decided?"

"Father has made an offer depending on your bestowal, but I wanted to make sure you were the one. What do you think?"

She was by now entirely naked. Violet, it seemed, was giving me a private viewing. Naturally enough, I had seen many girls naked, and many had seen me—at swimming, changing rooms, communal showers. If there hadn't been a punch-up at hockeyball, we would doubtless have seen each other in the changing rooms there. But showing one's body to a potential partner in the context of premarriage courtship was quite a different matter. In this instance, Violet would be showing me not just her body, *but her desire for me to see it.* And I, for my part, would be expected to look at it in a way that showed I appreciated the gesture.

I tried not to look at Violet, but it was, I am ashamed to say, difficult. Her postcode had been expertly scarred using a typescript that looked tantalizingly just outside permissibility, and the rest of her was pretty much perfect. It was a difficult situation, and if I hadn't been thinking of how much I wished she were Jane, she might have seen the whole thing as a washout and been gone in a second. As it was, she beamed happily at me, and before I knew it, she had slipped between the sheets.

"Violet!" I said. "What are you doing?"

"I'm just making *sure*. We wouldn't want to get married only to find there had been a frightful mistake, now, would we?"

"The Rules—"

"My father *administers* them, sweetness."

"Then what would your mother say?" I asked, in a feeble attempt to shame her.

"It was her idea."

I looked nervously out the window. "She's not watching, is she?"

"Of course not, sweetness. She said we must make sure that everything is functioning correctly—for dynastic purposes, you understand, and definitely *not* for physical enjoyment."

"Of course," I remarked sarcastically, "perish the thought."

"Stop talking, Eddie, and do as I tell you. It's not the time and place for our first argument, now, is it?"

"Look—"

"*I said no talking.*"

Apparently, I passed muster. Or, rather, as Violet put it, "We can work on your technique." In any event, within no more than ten minutes and with only the minimum of talk—commands from Violet, mostly—we had committed a potential five-hundred-point demerit together. For me, the first time. Violet quickly dressed, kissed me on the forehead, told me she would report to her parents that all was well, then silently lifted the sash, lowered herself to the porch below and jumped to the street with surprising agility. I stared at the ceiling but didn't move, my mind in something of a whirl. It had been *momentarily* pleasant, but I couldn't help feeling a leaden sense of betrayal deep down. Not to myself or the Collective's strict moral code, but to Jane.

We Travel Out

2.3.06.56.067: The consumption of more than 2,500 Mcal per day is forbidden.

I rose, had a bath in the hottest water I could bear and donned my Outdoor Adventure #9s. I left my signet ring, my spot and my merit book with the prewritten letters in the top drawer, then padded quietly down the gloomy staircase. I fumbled for my walking boots, strapped on my gaiters and picked up the knapsack that I had packed the night before. Dad was waiting for me by the door, and although we weren't huggy sort of people, we were this morning. Despite his previous night's optimism, this morning Dad looked like a man who knew he wouldn't be seeing his son again.

The village was quiet and sleepy. Dawn in the summer wasn't the hub of frenetic activity that it was in the winter. In fact, I didn't expect anyone to be up for at least another half hour, and then it would be only the baker, the postmistress and the mole catcher. I made my way to the statue of Our Munsell to wait for Carlos Fandango and the Ford. I didn't have long to wait, for a disheveled figure soon ran around the corner of the town hall. He seemed to be doing up his shoelaces as he ran, which was an impressive sight. It was Tommo, and I frowned. Not only because of who it was, but what he was dressed in—his Outdoor Adventure #9s.

"Hello, Ed!" he said with an uncharacteristic display of cheery purpose. "Ready for the big day? Good morning, Courtland."

I turned to look behind me. It *was* Courtland, and he seemed also to be dressed for adventure. I didn't quite get it. If there was anyone in the village who *shouldn't* be sent to High Saffron, it was Courtland.

"There's been a change of plan," he announced. "Tommo and I are coming with you."

"Does Yewberry know?"

"Not yet."

"The Council will be furious when they find you've volunteered yourself," I remarked suspiciously. "Why the change of heart?"

"The Gamboges have a bit of a public relations problem at present, and I'll need some sort of credibility if I'm going to be Yellow prefect. Besides, I could do with the cash."

He looked pointedly at me. "After all, you never know when demerits might come one's way. Good morning, Violet."

Violet had indeed just appeared. She smiled coyly at me and gave my arm a squeeze. I felt a flush rise to my cheeks, and was glad none of them would be able to see it. But if Courtland going on this trip was a mistake, Violet would be a disaster—and a serious liability. If anything were to happen to the head prefect's daughter, we'd lose every single merit we'd earn. Lower colors had a duty of care to see that those of the very highest hues came to no harm.

"This is utterly, utterly insane," I said.

"Oh, hush, Edward," said Violet, "This is just the sort of merry jaunt that will firmly cement our relationship. Once we bravely face the terrors of the road together and emerge victorious, we can take our places as East Carmine's most celebrated couple."

"There are eighty-three people who might disagree with that plan—if they could still speak."

"You are *such* a whiner," said Courtland. "Just dry up and relax. Where are we meeting Fandango?"

"Right here, but he's late."

In answer, there was the sound of a vehicle approaching, and the Ford rounded the corner from the direction of the flak tower. But it wasn't the sedan; it was East Carmine's second best: the shabby flatbed, but with the heavy crossbow removed. And Fandango wasn't driving, but *Jane*. My heart rose and fell in quick succession. I was glad to see her but didn't want her to know what had happened that morning. If, as Stafford had intimated, Jane actually *did* have feelings for me, doing the youknow with Violet would not go down well, if at all.

320

"Where's Fandango?" asked Tommo.

"Some damn fool tricked Bunty onto the train," replied Jane. "He has to pick her up from Bluetown in the other Ford. Got a problem with that?"

Courtland and Tommo exchanged glances.

"So where's the relief driver?" asked Tommo.

"Clifton called in sick," replied Jane, "and Rosie has a bad foot. George and Sandy were unavailable, so I took over. *Reluctantly.*"

She didn't look at me at all, and I smiled to myself. She'd changed her mind. She was here for me after all.

I took my place in the cab, sandwiched uncomfortably between Jane and Violet while Tommo and Courtland sat in the flatbed. Without a word Jane moved off and took the western road past the flak tower, the silent linoleum factory and the railway station. Within a few minutes we had let ourselves out of the stockgate in the boundary wall, and five hundred yards farther on we stopped just past the Outer Markers and the image of the giraffe. Without anyone speaking, Courtland, Tommo and I took off our ties, carefully rolled them up and placed them in our pockets. Violet removed the bow from the top of her head and used it to tie her hair in a loose ponytail. There wouldn't be any prefects out here, and we could slip them back on before we crossed back again.

We picked up the pace on the smooth roadway and sat in silence. I didn't want to say anything to Violet in case she let the cat out of the bag to Jane, and I didn't want to talk to Jane, because everyone would know that we had some sort of common understanding. But I couldn't sit there and say nothing, so I asked Jane how far it was to Bleak Point.

"Less than an hour, if all goes well."

"How are you, Jane?" said Violet, attempting to be friendly and magnanimous.

"A whole lot better if you'd keep your overhued trap shut."

Violet instinctively opened her mouth to voice objection, but then realized where we were. Beyond the Outer Markers, all the Rules past volume three hundred and eight were null and void. Jane could say what she wanted. Actually, she said what she wanted *inside* the markers. The only difference was that now she wasn't going to be demerited for it.

"Well!" said Violet in a huffy tone. "*That* was uncalled for. What have I ever done to elicit such rudeness?"

"Let's just look at the highlights, shall we?" replied Jane. "When we were five, you pushed me into a muddy puddle and then claimed I'd

hit you. When we were eight, you told Miss Bluebird that I had copied your homework after *you* copied mine. When we were twelve, you
nearly drowned me during water polo because I had bested you. And
when we were fifteen, you deselected me from the Jollity Fair tennis
squad because I was likely to win. The same year you had me demerited
because I failed to curtsy in your presence, even though I didn't know
you were there because I was asleep after a double shift at the factory. In
fact," went on Jane, "you've accounted for almost a third of my demerits
over the years, something I've spent an aggregate five months of my life
working to offset."

"Greys," said Violet, looking at me and rolling her eyes, "always *so*
overdramatic."

"Mind you," she added, "we're not totally ungrateful—the cash you
pay my brother for youknow helps keep food on our table."

I heard Tommo and Courtland stop talking and tune into the
conversation.

"Wow!" I said, pointing at some bouncing goats that were leaping
through the scrubby Outfield in a series of enormous bounds. "Look at
them go!"

But my attempt to get Violet and Jane off topic didn't work.

"There is nothing wrong with wanting to be at one's best for one's
husband," continued Violet, visibly rankled by Jane's indiscretion, "but
now that I am to wed," she said, patting me on the shoulder, "he will
have to ply his wares elsewhere—and good luck to him; he has learned
much from my expertise."

Jane gave a snort of a laugh that, had we been within the Outer
Markers, would have been branded impertinent. Out here it was just
fair banter, one-on-one.

"What are you sniggering at?" Violet demanded.

"That you think you're an expert at youknow. The sorry truth is that
Clifton gave you good feedback only to increase return business. He told
me you were only in it for yourself."

There was an icky silence, and I could tell Jane was enjoying herself.

"Nonsense," replied Violet as her self-denial kicked in after a millisecond of doubt. "I can't think why he would want to lie to you, or why
his moonlighting might be suitable talk for a Grey dinner table. But we
can clear this matter up once and for all. Eddie, darling, tell Jane how
fantastically good I was this morning."

I closed my eyes and felt sick. This wasn't how it was supposed to happen. My only consolation was that I had been thinking of Jane when it happened, which didn't sound like the sort of excuse I should use.

"Well?" said Violet.

"Yes," added Jane, with a mixture of hurt and anger in her voice, "how was it? Do tell."

"Look," I said, turning to Violet, "I'm not here to give you public feedback every time someone criticizes you."

"Is that a fact?" she replied, her shrill voice rising. "Then what *are* you here for? Marriage is a couple mutually joined as one but doing what the higher hue demands. Didn't your mother teach you *anything*?"

"Well," I said, "I'm sure she was *going* to tell me how insanely bossy up-color girls could be, but then she got the Mildew, and it must have slipped her mind."

"*I'm* going to be the wisecracking, acerbic one in *this* marriage," retorted Violet. "You're to be the long-suffering husband who supports his wife with quiet dignity."

"I'm glad we got that small matter cleared up. Shall we make it part of the vows?"

"Don't lip me, Russett. I can make this marriage bossy or five decades of living nightmare. Believe me, you'll prefer bossy."

We fell silent after that as the age-worn Ford crept slowly up the hill with a cacophony of growls and rattles, squeaks and groans. I looked across at Jane, but she was staring ahead, lips pursed. I needed to talk to her about recent events but didn't see how I could. Not alone, anyway.

We had been driving toward the dam complex and had by now reached the top of the first one. The effort had been worth it. A shimmering expanse of water hemmed in by rocky valley walls suddenly appeared to greet us. It was spectacularly lovely yet also surprisingly bleak, as frequent rhododendron-halting fires had reduced the vegetation to nothing more than stunted scrub. The road was suffering, too. Where the Perpetulite ran across rock, it had thinned with malnutrition, and small rocky outcrops now poked through the roadway, requiring us to creep over some of the larger obstructions with care.

The road followed the eastern side of the reservoir, passed the remains of an arched bridge and carried on until it petered out into silted-up marshland, where the reed beds were home to waders, spoonbills and, most gloriously, *flamingos*.

We motored up a short rise where we found a second dam that had been breached long ago and was now once more a valley with a stream running through it. The road twisted and turned and rose, the vegetation became less burned, and pretty soon we were driving across open moorland. We passed a grove of stunted oaks, then two rusted-iron land crawlers, badly eroded by the wind and rain. Then, just when all seemed to be going well, the road ended abruptly in a plume of errant Perpetulitic growth, with six knotted plastoid tendrils halted in their tracks by a series of bronze spikes. The Perpetulite had not taken well to the spalling and had gone into an ugly frenzy of erratic growth. The roadway had lumped up into eruptive bulges, and the white center line had twisted about itself like cream being stirred into coffee.

Jane pulled off the road onto a grassy verge next to a Faraday cage.

"It's called *spalling*," said Tommo, since we were all staring at the panicked manner in which the road had attempted to rejoin with its lost section. "When Perpetulite catches plastoid necrosis, the only way to protect the road system is to amputate and then spike. I don't think it likes it very much."

"Like I give a ratfink what the road thinks," said Violet. "Let's get on with it."

"I leave an hour before nightfall," announced Jane, breaking out the oilcan from the toolbox. "If you're not here, I go home without you. Have fun now, children, and don't squabble."

"You better be here," said Courtland.

"I'll be here," she said, giving him a smile, "but will you?"

She was trying to frighten him, but it didn't seem to be working.

We gathered our knapsacks, and with little ceremony we walked past the spalled Perpetulite and onto the track of the vanished road, which, despite being fully reclaimed as grassy moorland, was still visible as a flatter section of ground. Almost immediately, I made some lame excuse and hurried back to the Ford, which was being assiduously oiled by Jane with the oversize oilcan.

"I thought you were here because you changed your mind."

"I thought so, too," she said without looking at me, "right up until you couldn't resist giving darling Violet your very best. You had me fooled. For a moment there I thought you were actually quite pleasant."

"It was an accident."

"Where did you mean to put it? Her sock?"

"I'm sorry."

"Why should you be sorry?" She took a deep breath. "Whatever it was,

Eddie, it's gone. I don't care any longer. But since I owe you, here's some advice: There's a flak tower three foot-hours away. Don't go beyond it."

"I have to. That's the point of the expedition."

She shrugged, switched on the ignition, hand-cranked the engine, jumped into the driver's seat, and without another look at me, moved off in a cloud of smoke.

I sighed, cursed my own weakness, then ran to catch up with the others.

We stuck to the easily recognized path of the gone-away road, and after a half mile of well-grazed moorland we descended a short hill and entered a forest of mature oak. A few trees had fallen across the road but nothing too dramatic.

"We'd get the Ford along here," said Tommo, who had trotted forward to join me up front.

The road took us around a sweeping curve and then up a slight incline, where, standing forlornly in a sun-dappled glade, we came across a Farmall crawler such as might have been used to assist with logging. This was where the battle to reopen the road had ended thirty years ago, the Farmall abandoned when it was replaced by plow horses as motive power during one of the periodic small stepbacks. Enthusiasm for keeping the road open had seemingly died with it. I made a note in my exercise book.

"So," I said to Tommo as we walked past the crawler and around a bramble thicket to rejoin the track of the old road, "what's going on?"

"Yes, I suppose I should explain."

"Would you?" I asked. "I'd be really very grateful."

"No need to be like that."

"So what are you doing out here? I thought most Cinnabars were cowards."

"Not most, all," he replied with disarming honesty.

"I'm still listening."

"Right. Well, we were talking about your insane mission, and blow me down if Lucy doesn't go all gooey and say how brave and manly you are. And Courtland and I got to thinking that instead of making it a trip of almost certain death and unspeakable horrors, we could invest in a few safeguards to make the trip work to everyone's advantage. We had a brief chat, and here we are: Courtland, Violet, me and yourself."

"And where do the safeguards come into it?"

"You'll see."

We had arrived at a stone house by the side of the road. The interior was a sea of brambles, and there was a beech growing in the corner. Next to the building were the remnants of an outhouse that had collapsed long ago, and beneath the carpet of roof tiles, leaf litter and moss were the remnants of a vehicle. Although anything metallic had rusted or corroded away long ago, the plastic still remained, along with four perished rubber tires and a pair of glass headlights, which looked as though they might have been cast yesterday. A flash of white on the ground caught my eye, and I picked up a sun-bleached molar. It was definitely human, although it looked as though someone had stuck some metal neatly onto the worn surface. I tapped the tooth on my palm, and the metal section dropped out. It was heavy and shiny, so I put it in my pocket.

"Okay," said Courtland, "here will do."

The three of them dispensed with their knapsacks. Violet and Courtland sat down, while Tommo poked in a grassy mound with a stick. Scavenging for color was one of those pursuits that followed you into adulthood.

"We should give it another half hour before a break," I said. "We don't know how long it's going to take to get there."

"We're not resting," said Courtland with a sense of finality. "We've stopped."

Tommo and Violet looked at me, then at Courtland. Tommo had outdone himself again.

"That's the safeguard?" I asked. "Not going to High Saffron at all?"

"The best plans are always the simplest," observed Tommo with a smile. "Let me explain. We're going to rest up for the day, discard all our gear and a shoe or two, rip our clothes and then stagger back into town whimpering incoherently about swans and Riffraff. Everyone's a hero, we get excused from Useful Work for a month, receive seven hundred merits each and clean up on the sweep I've got going back home. There's no risk, we don't have to do squiddly and no one has to walk their feet off—or come back dead."

He found something in the mound of dirt he had been prodding, and held it up. "Guys?"

Courtland shook his head, but Violet nodded.

"Blue," she said in a grumpy tone.

"And what about the report?" I asked. "We don't get a bean unless we actually reach the town."

He shrugged. "We'll claim we reached the outskirts. You can make up something suitably vague: 'pre-Epiphanic ruins, entwined with the roots of mature oaks,' then add a bit about 'vibrant color lying half buried in the leaf mold.' That will do it."

"We could do the same thing next month," said Violet, "and the month after that."

"And without prefects to check up on us," added Courtland, "there's no risk."

"So you're with us on this, right?" said Tommo. "No sense in risking certain death when you can make good money with a little harmless subterfuge."

I stared at them all. Ordinarily I *might* have entertained such an action, especially with two prefects-in-waiting already signed up. With me onboard, there would be three-quarters of East Carmine's future Council in agreement, which would be enough to keep it hidden forever. But it didn't bode well. If this was the level of corruption *before* they were in power, I dreaded to think what it might be like when they took office. Besides, I didn't like being pushed. Not one little bit.

"Why don't you guys just stay here?" I suggested. "I'll walk over there on—"

"We really have to be together on this," said Violet. "We'll be debriefed. They'll see through it."

Courtland got up and walked toward me. I dearly wanted to take a step back, but I thought I'd fare better with him knowing I wasn't frightened of him, so I stood my ground.

"Listen," he said once he was uncomfortably close, "we're not expected back, so if we lose a member no one will be surprised. We can do this with you or without you. Do it our way, and it's a heap of cash and certain life. Do it your way, and it's certain death and no cash."

"Kill me and Violet's dynasty goes all to Blue."

"I think I'm okay in that respect," said Violet, patting her stomach. "If I marry Doug on Sunday night no one will look too carefully at the calendar."

I could feel my heart sink. "Two grand up front," I murmured, suddenly realizing what was going on.

"I'm afraid you're right," said Tommo. "As your father will no doubt attest, I am a fine negotiator. With the High Saffron excursions sporting a one hundred percent fatality rate, he was wise to at least make *something* from you. And he gets a grandson—even if he can't ever tell anyone.

Don't judge him too harshly. It was his best option. And he got deMauve to agree in writing that the boy would be called Eddie."

I didn't know what annoyed me more, being threatened with death or having my own father sell our Chromatic heritage without my knowledge. Dad must have shown Violet the ovulating shade, too. DeMauve had gotten a lot for his money.

"He didn't know about the not-going-to-High-Saffron plan, did he?" I asked.

"No," said Tommo, mustering a shred of decency. "As far as he was concerned, it was simply the deMauves hedging their bets against your disappearance."

It was consolation of sorts. At least I knew my father's actions had been fiscal rather than personal. There was a long pause in which we all stared at one another.

"So what's the deal?" asked Violet, who was growing impatient.

Courtland was bluffing. He wouldn't kill me in front of Violet. She'd have leverage over him at every single future Council meeting and would never keep something this serious under her hat.

"There's no deal. I'm going on."

"You Russetts!" screamed Violet. "So *nauseatingly* self-righteous!" She folded her arms and glared, not at me but at Courtland and Tommo. "Honestly, boys, I thought you said you'd gotten this all sorted out. If I get into trouble over this, I'm going to really make you burn when I'm head prefect."

"We *had* sorted it out," explained Tommo meekly. "We just hadn't thought Russett here would be such a party-pooper-prefect's-pet."

"Then I'm bailing on this monumental farrago," remarked Violet as she came rapidly to a decision. "I think I've just twisted my ankle and am unable to proceed." She looked daggers at me. "And if you commit the discourtesy of surviving so I have to marry you, I will strive to make you unhappy for the rest of my life."

Violet got to her feet and shouldered her bag before turning to face us. "What's our story?"

"Simple," said Courtland, still staring at me. "We stopped here for a break, and you stumbled on the way out on some rubble, then headed back."

"What if Russett blabs that this was all a merit scam?"

"Don't worry," replied Courtland, "he'll come around. Won't you, Eddie?"

"All I want to do is to complete the expedition," I said, staring back at Courtland. "Other than that, I don't give a ratfink's bottom."

"There," said Courtland, "he agrees."

And Violet walked off at a brisk pace without another word.

"This is all very well," said Tommo once we had gathered up our belongings, "but this means *we actually have to go to High Saffron!*"

"What's the matter?" asked Courtland. "Frightened?"

"Too bloody right. I think I might have twisted my ankle, too—or something."

"You're coming with us," said Courtland in a voice that didn't invite contradiction. "You got us into this stupid mess, so you can certainly see it through."

"Right you are," said Tommo without enthusiasm, "overjoyed."

"We're moving out," I said. "The next rest break is in an hour."

I saw Tommo and Courtland exchange glances. If Tommo had gone with Violet, I would have felt disagreeably ill at ease. Courtland was capable of almost anything, but not, I reasoned, with Tommo about. Toady that he was, Tommo could stand to earn serious merits for snitching on Courtland if he tried anything stupid. Even so, I knew I would have to be careful.

Before leaving, I wrote on a sheet of paper torn from my exercise book that Violet had turned back, added the time, signed it and laid it in the middle of the road with four stones stacked in a pyramid on top of it.

We walked out, and I mused to myself that this expedition was much like any other I had been on—full of arguments, and running anything but smoothly.

On to the Flak Tower

3.6.23.12.028: Ovaltine may not be drunk at any time other than before bed.

The going was harder and the road less distinct as we trudged on. It didn't look as though vehicular traffic had moved down this way since the Perpetulite spalled. Much of our time was spent wending our way through thick rhododendron to avoid the occasional yateveo, and trying to keep to the track as best we could. At times the heavy canopy made the forest so dark that it was almost impossible to see. At one point I lost the path of the old road entirely, and only picked it up again once the forest had thinned out and been replaced by open grassy moorland.

I walked with a sense of heightened nervousness, but relaxed as soon as I heard Courtland and Tommo talk about mundanities. Tommo asked him if grass looked yellow to him, and Courtland responded by saying that *all* green looked yellow, since it was the only component of green a Yellow could see. After about half a mile of open ground and a slight incline, we came across the lumpy remnants of a village, the only aboveground feature a stone meetinghouse that was almost consumed by two yew trees. I checked the time and sketched a plan of the village in my notebook. On one side of the crossroads was another deeply rusted land crawler swathed in brambles and coarsened by a heavy overcoat of lichen, its tracks now choked with a profusion of primroses, celandines and meadowsweet. Although similar to the Farmall crawler we had seen

330

earlier, in that they shared the commonality of tracked locomotion, this was considerably larger and more heavily built—the outer shell was fully four inches thick in places. It was also badly damaged. The vehicle looked as though someone had attempted to turn it inside out; the steel was jagged and split like a shattered pot.

"Can we take a break?" asked Courtland.

"Five minutes, then."

I walked across to examine an old mailbox, almost consumed by a mature beech that had grown around it. The small door had split with the force. I opened it easily, and amid the abandoned birds' nests and dry leaf mold I found the remnants of things that had been posted but never collected. A glass pendant, a few coins and a wireless telephone in remarkably good condition.

"Whoah!" said Tommo, pointing in the direction we had just come. "I just saw someone!"

"Claptrap," replied Courtland, with slightly less confidence in his voice than he might have liked. "There's no one out here but us."

"They were just next to that tree over there, peeking over the wall." He pointed at a dilapidated section of wall about thirty yards away, back in the direction from which we had come.

"Are you sure?" I asked.

"Clear as day. Do you think it might be . . . *Riffraff*?"

We all looked at one another. Even Courtland appeared ill at ease, despite his usually brash exterior.

"Only one way to find out," I murmured and sprinted up the road toward the wall and looked over. In the field beyond I saw a couple of alpacas, which stared at me with a bored expression and went back to their grazing. There was no one visible, but the gorse-pecked hill offered an abundance of good hiding places. There might have been a hundred Riffraff for all I knew, and my stomach turned uneasily. I stood there for several minutes listening and staring, and after hearing and seeing nothing, returned to the crossroads.

"Nothing but a couple of alpacas," I reported. "Couldn't it have been them? I mean, no one has reported Riffraff in this area for, what? Twenty years?"

"Thirty," said Tommo, "but then most people who have come this far never came back. And they eat the brains of—"

"Just button it, Tommo, you're not helping," said Courtland.

"I second that," I said. "Shut up, Tommo."

331

"What do we do?" asked Courtland, once we had been standing there doing nothing for a few moments. "The Rules state that if we encounter even a *hint* of Riffraff, we abort."

"I didn't see anything," I said, trying to be positive.

"You and your stupid ideas," Courtland said to Tommo. "And speaking personally, I'm too valuable to the community to be lost on some dumb expedition."

"You agreed to it readily enough last night," replied Tommo defiantly.

"Then why don't you just go home?" I suggested. "No one's stopping you."

But Courtland, arrogant as he was, was no idiot. If he sneaked home early and I returned later on, everyone would know he had chickened out. He wanted the village to know that he was not just the next Yellow prefect, but a selfless resident, willing to risk his life for the good of the village.

"Let's all just calm down," I murmured. "Tommo, are you *positive* it was someone?"

He took a deep breath and looked at both of us in turn, then shrugged. "It *could* have been alpacas," he replied. "In fact, that *must* have been what it was."

"Then I'm going on," I murmured. "What about you two?"

Courtland gave Tommo a slap on the back of the head. "Idiot! Yes, I'm still coming—and so is porridge brains here."

I jotted another note to the effect that Tommo had thought he had seen someone, added the time, tore out the page and left it under a small pile of stones as before. I made a similar note in my log, and we walked on, this time with a more nervous gait and with frequent looks over our shoulders.

After ten minutes or so we reached the top of the hill and entered a grove of beeches. Their heavy canopy was draped with creepers, and the occasional moss-covered fallen trunk blocked our way. Considering that we were less than two hours from the village center, it seemed odd that we were walking in a place almost completely unvisited for five centuries, yet was somewhere I could visit and be back by eleven. If I was so inclined. Being in the Outfield was exciting, but worrying, too. I could feel my heart beating faster, and my ears twitched at every sound.

After twenty minutes more of easy walking across a grassy plain with only giraffe, elk and deer for company, we entered a small spinney near another land crawler, then walked out the other side and came to an abrupt halt.

"Munsell in a *canoe*," whispered Tommo.

"What is this doing here?" said Courtland. "I mean, why would anyone build a pipeline that goes from nowhere to nowhere squared?"

"I don't know."

In front of us was a good-sized oak. But not the usual drab grey variety. This one was bright, univisual purple. The bark, leaves, acorns, branches and even the patch of grass beneath it were full edge-of-gamut magenta. We stared at it for a while, as none of us had seen anything so large bearing such an inappropriate color. This was a chromoclasm—a fracture in the magenta pipe of the CYM color feed, where the dye had soaked up through the soil and stained the surrounding foliage. National Color doesn't like anyone knowing anything about pipeline routes, partly because of the potential for damage by monochrome fundamentalists, and partly because local villages would ask for costly spur lines. But Courtland was right. It didn't make any sense. We weren't on a route that went from anywhere to anywhere, nor was there any way to tell in which direction the pipeline ran. But it looked as though we had found the breach the Colorman had been looking for.

"Good job Violet isn't here," said Tommo. "The brightness would give her a migraine in a flash, and you know how ratty she gets when she's having a headache."

"What's that?"

"What?"

Courtland didn't answer and instead walked into the purple grass and picked up a human femur. It too had been stained magenta. He looked around and found another bone, this time the left half of a pelvis, and tapped them together. They made the dullish thud that fresh bones make, and not the ringing click of the long dead.

"What do you think, Court?"

"Couple of years."

We were all looking around then, to find something that might give a clue as to who it was or where they were from, but the bones had been scattered by animals. We didn't find the skull, but I did find a single brogue, a belt buckle and a celluloid collar. It had a postcode and a name scratched on it: Thomas Emerald. Courtland and Tommo didn't know him.

"A lot of Rebootees were lost out here," said Courtland. "They never stayed long enough for us to learn their names."

"He had three spoons on him," said Tommo, picking them out of the soil and rubbing the magenta mud off so that he could read the codes engraved on the back, "and none of them were his. Do you think the codes are registered to anyone?"

"They'd be worth a small fortune if they've got clear title," said Courtland. "Let me see."

So Tommo handed them over, and Courtland put them in his pocket and grinned avariciously at him.

"Nice one, Court," said Tommo. "Thanks for that."

"Why would he take spoons with him on a toshing trip?" I asked.

"Maybe he didn't," remarked Courtland, with a greedy gleam in his eye. "Maybe he pulled them out of the soil at High Saffron."

We looked at one another and walked on.

We came to a river and, after wading across, walked past the five-arched bridge that had once carried the roadway, now sitting rather pointlessly over a grassy dent. The mutual anxiety we were feeling had momentarily cleared the bad air, and we walked along side by side for a while, talking nervously.

"So," said Tommo with forced bonhomie, "what was Violet like?"

"Exactly as you might imagine."

"Yikes."

Courtland voiced what we were all really thinking about. "Why didn't we find Thomas Emerald's skull?"

We suddenly stopped and looked nervously about, the unspoken horror of having our brains eaten by Riffraff suddenly making us more than jumpy. But no matter how hard we stared, it was simply an empty landscape with trees, wildstock and grassland. And aside from the occasional *pwoing* of a bouncing goat, it was quiet, too—oppressively so. We were utterly alone. At least, we *hoped* we were.

"Okay," said Tommo after I had told everyone to move off, "what do we do if we see a Riffraff?"

"Run," I said.

"Fight," said Courtland.

"You fighting is good," said Tommo. "While they're occupied with you, Ed and I will be activating the 'run like a lunatic' plan."

We passed through a grove of beech trees that had grown over the track in happy profusion, then came across some grass-covered earthworks, a few bramble-filled pits and a deep, grassy ditch that zigzagged away to the left and right of us. We paused for a moment on the edge of the open moorland and stared at the road, which carried on in a straight line until it vanished over the summit. It was the loneliest section of the route, a two-mile stretch without any sort of cover at all. I looked up at the sky to confirm that the likelihood of lightning was low, then set off at a brisk walk.

The course of the road was easily delineated by the flat profile and two low, grassy ridges about thirty feet apart that might once have been walls. The landscape up here was different, as the road had been disrupted by several large pockmarks, some of which had filled with water and might have been natural dew ponds but for their uniform roundness. Here and there we could see rusty scrap and twisted aluminum poking out of the turf like a metallic harvest that no one had troubled to remove, and the wildstock were considerably tamer. As we approached the isolated herds that drifted across the upper pastures, they parted languidly to let us through, with only the mildest sense of curiosity. It portended well, as they spook easily, and Riffraff were known to kill and eat them. I even spotted an antelope I hadn't seen before. It was a dark reddish color with stripes down its front and back legs, the latter doubling as a convenient place to display its bar code. I jotted down as much of its Taxa as I could before it turned away.

We walked like this in silence for a good forty minutes until we encountered the first proper structure we had seen since leaving East Carmine. The flak tower stood in a commanding position at the top of an escarpment that looked down on the broad, fertile valley hiding the remains of High Saffron. Cynics that Courtland and Tommo were, I think even *they* were impressed, and we all stopped to soak up the view.

The Flak Tower

2.5.03.02.005: Generally speaking, if you fiddle with something, it will break. Don't.

Although I had seen the ocean on at least three occasions, I had never witnessed a more beautiful stretch of coastline than greeted my eyes that afternoon. The land was dappled with the shadows of the clouds as they drifted lazily across the sky, the sunnier patches highlighting points of interest better than any tour guide. The town nestled comfortably on either side of a long tidal estuary that led into a bay where several abandoned ships were anchored. The biggest of these was a flat-decked vessel so large that it was now an artificial breakwater, the sloping deck white with the guano of seabirds, and the gently rusting hulk altering the dynamics of the bay so dramatically that the whole area between the ship and the shore had silted in and was now dry land.

Of the town, not much could be seen from where we stood. The remains of the bypass appeared as a circular swathe of different-colored vegetation, and a bridge across the river was still standing. The town itself was hidden within the foliage of thick woodland, from whose canopy only a few buildings protruded. The outlying commercial and residential areas could just be seen as a faint grid pattern of different trees and brush. There seemed to be a road that led out to the east and another to the north, but of the open spaces Yewberry had hoped for, I could see nothing.

"We've still got a good four-hour walk to go," I said, estimating the distance. "Less if we can meet the Saffron end of the spalled Perpetulite. Five minutes' break."

"We'll take ten," said Courtland, and he and Tommo trotted off toward the tower. Scrap found on trips like this could be claimed as personal trove and was worth 50 percent of its value—not a huge sum, unless you'd brought a handy wheelbarrow, but enough for a scone or two at the Fallen Man.

I looked around to make some notes. Easy vehicular access past the looming six-story tower was blocked by a large grassy mound. To one side was a corroded bulldozer, which had sunk a foot into the earth. Behind this was a jumbled collection of boxy-looking vehicles, which were all in the middle stage of rust death and shrouded with nettles, brambles and outcrops of hawthorn and elder. The tower itself was identical to the one at East Carmine, except that it had not been stripped of its narrow bronze window frames. The tower was one of eight that I could see, ringing the town from the highest points all around and, it seemed, connected by a series of steel posts at least twenty feet high and set at fifty-foot intervals. I walked to the first of the high posts and noticed that in places it was still draped with the remains of wire, and that glass insulators similar to those on the telephone poles were bolted to the steel.

I recalled Jane's advice to go no farther than the flak tower, and since she had known with all certainty that the tower was there—something that Yewberry hadn't—it meant that she probably knew what she was talking about. We had done enough for today anyway. I would make detailed notes of this area, and after that we would return, report the magenta tree and continue the expedition another day. No cash and no glory, and quite possibly a disappointed Council. But I like to think I take my role as team leader seriously.

I retraced my steps to the tower, where I could hear Courtland talking to Tommo. The main door was of bronze almost eight inches thick and had seized in the partially open position. I stepped inside and walked down a short corridor, then through an inner door. I had expected it to be dark inside, but it wasn't. Two lightglobes were burning brightly in the interior. One was in Courtland's hand as he searched the debris, and the other was fixed precariously to the ceiling, where Tommo was trying to dislodge it with a stick.

"What's the point?" I said, "They're Leapback. You can't take them back with you."

They ignored me, and I looked around. The room was large, perhaps half the size of the ground floor, with a room off to one side and another bronze door, which partially hid a flight of steps that led upward. Dominating two walls were long sections of steel desks, upon which lay the shattered remains of remote viewers. I found a working shard that had text on it that moved when I drifted my finger across, but nothing like the one I'd seen in Zane's parlor. The floor was covered with dust, rust, broken furniture, scraps of clothing, general rubbish and *bones*—some relatively new, others so old they crumbled to dust between finger and thumb. As I sorted through the debris with my foot I saw several red objects wink at me, and I picked up a crimson button and rubbed it on my shirt.

"Here," said Courtland who had been exploring one of the antechambers. "I've found another of the missing."

I walked across to where Courtland was waiting at a bronze door leading off the main room.

"She's at the back," he said, passing me the lightglobe, "ten years dead, perhaps more."

I walked inside and found myself in what looked like a storeroom. There was only one narrow vertical slit for a window, and the shelves had collapsed so the floor was now covered with rusty tins, the odd jar and a heavy carpeting of dust that kicked up as I walked. But Courtland was right. Lying on the floor was the body of a woman, fully dressed and with skin stretched as tight as parchment across her bones. She had a satchel next to her, and I emptied the hardened leather bag onto the floor. It had about twelve spoons in it, and a large quantity of coins.

"Wow!" said Tommo, reaching forward to collect them. "That'll buy Lucy from Mrs. Ochre."

"I don't get it," I said, mostly to myself. "She's dressed for travel or light leisure, not for outdoor adventure."

I scratched my head. The remains of Thomas Emerald had been wearing a *brogue*. I didn't know where these two had come from, but they weren't from East Carmine, and they certainly weren't part of an expedition.

"We're going back," I told them, searching the woman's clothing for a name tag.

"Going back?" echoed Tommo in surprise. "Lying-that-we-got-to-High-Saffron going back, or aborting-the-mission going back?"

"Aborting. We come back another—"

"But we don't get paid," he interrupted, "at least, not if you insist on being honest and stuff."

"Another time."

"There are spoons there," said Courtland, staring at the pile we had just discovered, "and we've got at least four more hours before we have to turn back. I'm the higher color, so I say we go on."

"You forget yourself," I replied. "There are no spots out here. *I'm* team leader."

"All right," he agreed, swiftly changing tack. "Did you see the ring she was wearing?"

I looked to check her dry and wizened hands, but it was only a ploy, and I heard the door swing shut behind me. Before I could even move, the bolt was thrown.

"Well, now," said Courtland from the other side of the door, "that's for meddling in Yellow business—a present from the Gamboges."

I swallowed hard and tried to sound normal in spite of my anger and indignation. "Open the door, Courtland. This isn't funny."

"On the contrary," he replied with a laugh, "I think it's quite rich. I'll admit that I thought the whole expedition lark was a load of rubbish this morning, but it's grown on me. I quite like the idea of becoming 'the man who brought color back to East Carmine.' But it's the spoons Tommo and I are really interested in. We're going on to High Saffron."

"What if you don't come back?"

There was a pause.

"We wouldn't let you out even if we did. You've been nothing but trouble since the moment you arrived, and I can't see matters improving, especially since your outrageous accusations regarding Travis Canary. No, Eddie my friend, I'm afraid you're staying here for good. We waited and waited but you never returned. Tragic, really, but we did all we could. Violet will be able to squeeze out a tear, and we might even put your name on the departures board."

"Tommo?" I said. "Are you in on this?"

There was a pause, and when he spoke, I could hear the tension in his voice. "You must admit, you could have toed the line a little better, Eddie. It wouldn't have taken much. Double-ordering the Lincoln, for a start."

I swore to myself. It didn't look good. But just then I saw a shape flick past the vertical slit that was my window. My heart fair missed a beat, and I ran to the door, misjudged the distance, and bumped my head painfully against one of the hinge pins.

"Guys!" I shouted while I rubbed my head. "Someone just moved past my window!"

There was a demeritable curse, a scrabble and the sound of something falling over as they made for the exit. I ran to the window and peered out as a few seconds later Courtland heaved into view, closely followed by Tommo. They looked frightened. If I'd made it all up, I'd have been a genius. Sadly, I hadn't.

Tommo cried, "There!" and ran off, closely followed by Courtland. I heard some shouts and a yell, a sharp cry and then silence. I tried to look out of the window, but the flak tower's walls were a yard thick, and all I could see was the rear of the bulldozer, thirty yards away. I rummaged in the dust and debris for a piece of metal to use as a tool to at least attempt an escape, but as I did, I heard the bolt on the door drawn back. I picked up the lightglobe and shone it at the door, and when no one appeared, I gently pushed it open. I stepped into the main room and heard a childish giggle. I turned slowly around. Standing on the steps that led to the upper floors was a young girl aged no more than ten, wearing a much-repaired dress. She had bare feet, expertly plaited hair and a grimy face. I blinked, but she was not a Pooka, and after giving me a cheery wave, she disappeared up the stairs.

Before I could even *begin* to digest what I had just seen, I heard another cry from outside, so I ran out the door and sprinted to the back of the tower. There I found Tommo and Courtland grappling with *Jane,* who, while putting up a good show for herself, would eventually succumb to numbers and greater strength.

Without stopping to think, I kicked Tommo and felt a rib break beneath my toe. He fell away with a cry, and I thumped Courtland as hard as I could, which wasn't that hard, and I hurt my hand. But it gave Jane an opportunity to free herself, and as quick as lightning she had expertly turned Courtland onto his back and held a sharpened potato peeler at his throat.

"Okay, okay," he said, his manner suddenly changing. "Let's just think about what you're doing here." He looked up at me. "Eddie," he said, "we're going to be prefects together. Tell her to lay off."

I was still shaking. I had never been in a fight in my entire life. "Tell her to lay off? You were going to leave me here to starve!"

He gave out a laugh. "You are *so* gullible, Russett. We were just going to let you stew a bit. A *prank*. Isn't that right, Tommo?"

Tommo was on the ground, doubled up in pain. He shook his head, then nodded, then shrugged, then groaned.

"You can have this one on me," growled Jane. "Tell me to spare him and I'll spare him. Bleed him and I'll do that, too."

I answered without hesitation. "Spare him."

She pushed him away and then stood next to me, trembling with anger.

"Perhaps this is how all toshing parties end up," I said sadly. "Maybe there are no Pookas or Mildew or flying monkeys or anything. Just fear and a few too many arguments over spoons."

I took a deep breath.

"Tommo," I said, "you're heading back to Bleak Point, where you'll wait for us until—when's sundown?"

"Eight-thirty."

"Right. You'll wait until seven-thirty precisely, when you'll take Violet and the Ford back into East Carmine. Can you do that?"

Still unable to speak, he simply nodded.

"Go now."

He very gingerly got to his feet and, holding his side, limped off.

"What about us?" asked Jane.

"We're going to High Saffron."

She stared at me for a moment, head to one side. "You may regret it."

"I can't regret this trip any more than I do already."

"I'm coming, too," said Courtland, getting to his feet.

And with this, she seemed to change her mind.

"Okay, then. But we'd better get a move on. It's about a three-hour walk to where the Perpetulite reestablishes itself, and High Saffron is an hour beyond that."

Courtland and I stared at her.

"You've been there before?" I asked.

"Once or twice."

"Will there be spoons?" asked Courtland.

"Oh, yes," she replied with a smile, "there shall *definitely* be spoons."

A Herald Speaks

3.6.12.03.267: Unicycles are not to be ridden backward at excessive speed.

We followed the track of the old road, which zigzagged steeply down the escarpment. Jane and I both insisted that Courtland walk at least twenty paces in front of us, something he said he didn't mind since he wouldn't be able to see our "loathsome faces." He was carrying Tommo's satchel as well as his own, so clearly had high hopes of bringing home some spoils. I had checked the time before we left; we had used up almost half an hour of our contingency.

"So," said Jane, "how did you enjoy meeting your first Riffraff?"

"I owe her my life, and perhaps yours."

"Possibly. Was it the mother or the daughter who let you out?"

"Daughter, I think."

"That would be Martha. They don't call themselves Riffraff, you know."

"What, then?"

"The Digenous."

"What does that mean?"

"I don't know. It's just what they call themselves."

"And what do they call us?"

"Many names, and none of them polite."

At the bottom of the escarpment the road seemed to vanish entirely,

342

until I realized that a watercourse had also considered this the best way to reach the valley floor, and had washed out the roadbed. So we followed the stream, past the rubble of houses, a telephone booth still with flecks of red paint and yet another land crawler, which was now half buried in the streambed, having had the road washed out from beneath it. I'd not seen one before this morning, and now they seemed to be everywhere.

"So what made you change your mind and follow us?" I asked as we negotiated our way around a boulder the size of a garden shed.

"You may have noticed I have a temper," she said, "but when I calmed down, I realized that this world, blighted and imperfect as it is, would be better with you in it."

"That's quite a compliment."

"Savor it," she said. "I don't give them out often."

We reached a gentle rise in the land. The river moved off to its original course on the right, leaving us on the flat, grassy track of the old road and taking us into a beech forest of great maturity. Large slabs of fractured concrete had been lifted by the slow power of root systems, but of any visible scrap color, there was none. Five centuries of accreted leaf mold, soil and vegetation had effectively put it beyond easy reach, and any bizarre notion that color might be lying around on the surface was nothing more than wishful thinking. Opening High Saffron to mining operations was going to be a massive task. DeMauve would have had no choice but to found a satellite village closer to High Saffron and then have Chromatics spend a week at a time sorting the tosh before transporting it back to the railhead at East Carmine. The extraction of hue would be a long time coming and barely worth the effort. But that, I thought, was why High Saffron remained the treasure trove that it was. Untouched and virgin, it would be as rich as any tosh pit, yet discovered.

"Courtland's getting quite far ahead."

"Let him," said Jane and stopped walking. I did the same, and she turned to look at me. "Are you ready to run with scissors?"

"Could I *walk* with them first?"

"No. You're either in or out. Now: Are you ready to run with scissors?"

"I think so."

"There's no 'think' to it. Your life is going to change radically in the next few hours, and I want to make sure that you're not going to do anything stupid. You need to know that there is no one you can trust, no one you can talk to, no one you can rely on, except *me*. We do things my way, or we don't do them at all. And if you try to take matters into your own hands or betray me, I'll be there to make sure that all avenues back to me are permanently silenced. Do you understand how important this is?"

"Yes, but as you've threatened my life several times before, I may be getting blasé about the whole thing."

"Okay, we need to add some trust. I'm going to show you something I've never shown anyone before. Watch carefully."

And she leaned closer. I knew she had lovely eyes, but until now I'd never realized quite *how* lovely. Light in tone, but with a curious corona around the edges. As I watched, the fine pinpoints of her pupils moved, stretched and grew in size. I tried to step away in alarm, but she held me tightly until her empty pupils were almost to her whites, and she had the grotesque, hollow-headed look of the Previous. I shivered. But I didn't look away, and her eyes slowly returned to normal, until with a few rapid blinks, they were back to pinpoints once more.

"That was . . . really creepy."

"Long ago, everyone could do it. And listen, I'm sorry about putting the wheelbarrow in your path—I had to know whether you were one of . . . *them*. After all, you were showing a lot of interest."

"That was because I liked you."

"No one's ever liked me before," she said, "so you'll excuse me for becoming suspicious."

"Jabez liked you."

"Jabez liked my *nose*."

"I like your nose."

"Yes, but you don't *only* like my nose. There's a big difference."

"Whoa!" I said, as what she had told me finally hit home. *"You can see at night?"*

She gave me a smile.

"Quite well, too. On a full moon there's almost enough light to play tennis. I think I'm the only one they don't know about."

"They?"

"The ones who killed Ochre. The ones who arrive after dusk and are gone before dawn."

"Riffraff?"

"Nightseers. Above and beyond the Rules. The last line of defense against attacks upon the Munsell Doctrine."

"How can you be sure they don't know about you?"

"Because I'm *alive*. Are you running with scissors or not?"

"I'm in," I said taking a deep breath. "But *wait*. How does—"

"Soon, Red, soon."

She smiled and kissed me on the cheek. It seemed like a totally natural thing for her to do, and I wasn't shocked or surprised. But the guilt wouldn't go away.

"Violet is very strong-willed," I said quite spontaneously.

"As long as you didn't enjoy it."

"She was very aggressive," I remarked reflectively. "It's not supposed to be like that, is it?"

She shrugged. "I've heard it's supposed to be quite fun."

"Actually," I added, looking down, "it was a harvest for a Purple offspring. Dad showed her the egg shade last night—she's with my child."

Jane raised an eyebrow. "And all this with the collusion of the head prefect?"

"With a one hundred percent fatality rate, I wasn't expected to make it back. I think the plan was for her to lament my loss and then marry Doug as planned. He'd never know it wasn't his son."

She shook her head sadly. "That's Purples for you. Now, listen," she added, rummaging in her bag while I stood there blinking stupidly to myself. "We need to take some precautions, you and I. Try to think of nothing."

She had a compact much like the one Travis had used to keep his lime. She flicked it open, and the color—a rampant Gordini, I think—seemed to come flooding out and fill my vision. My entire left side went immediately numb, then began to burn with the sensation of a million pins and needles.

"Good afternoon!" said a cheery voice. I blinked, for there in front of me was a young man in a tidy grey suit with the splashy paint tin logo of National Color embroidered on the left breast. "Thank you for accessing Gordini Protocol NC7-Z. Please be patient while reconfiguration is in progress."

"I can see someone," I whispered, leaning closer to Jane.

"Just relax. Keep staring at the Gordini and tell me when you hear the big dogs."

"If you suffer any undue discomfort during reconfiguration," continued the young man in a jolly singsong sort of voice, "you may wish to seek assistance with customer services, available on #8." He smiled again. "National Color. Here for *your* convenience. And remember, feedback helps us help you."

And he vanished. I continued to stare at the Gordini, as did Jane. The pins and needles were replaced by the smell of freshly baked bread and

I could hear my twice-widowed aunt Beryl talking about cats, which she never did. And through it all, music and onions.

"Mantovani."

"I get Brahms. Keep staring."

The edge of my vision fringed with all the colors of the rainbow, and then, for a brief and very exciting moment, I could see in full color. It was like the world had been transformed into a color garden—but one that exhibited not the limited CYM palette of National Color, but an infinite variety of hues, delicately complementing and enhancing one another in a complex Chromatic harmony—I could even see the off-gamut violets, a color I had never seen before. The world as it was *meant* to look.

"It's . . . beautiful!"

I then heard the sound of rushing water. My fingers snapped straight and I blinked uncontrollably.

"Got the dogs yet?"

"No, I'm still at blinking."

And then they started up. Terriers yipping and wailing in an annoying fashion as the pathways in my head cross-fired. Light to sound, smell to memory, touch to music, and color to everything.

"Small dogs any good?" I asked.

"Keep at it."

The small dogs were joined by medium-sized dogs, then finally the deep, throaty *woofs* of Great Danes. They were joined by bloodhounds and wolfhounds, and pretty soon my head was full of dogs doing nothing but barking, whining and panting.

"Big dogs."

She snapped the compact shut, and the sound abruptly cut out. I staggered for a moment.

"Steady," she said, holding my elbow.

"What was that?"

"Precautions. A little bit of reconfiguring in the cortex. The big dogs just indicate you're done—like the whistle on a kettle. Make a note of the time. We've got a couple of hours to be safe."

"I saw colors. *Real* colors. And a Pooka."

"He's actually a *Herald*. A lost page from a missing book. He's always there and always says the same thing."

But I wasn't really listening; I had far too many questions.

"You said 'precautions'? And what do you mean, 'We've got a couple of hours'? A couple of hours for what?"

"All in good time, Red. Come on, we better catch up with Courtland."

"The Herald said something about 'Gordini Protocols.' What are *they*?"

"Trust me, Red, all in good time."

We found Courtland waiting for us at a stone meetinghouse that was smothered with heavy ivy and still a creditable two stories high.

"Thought I'd lost you," he said. "Get a load of this!"

He pointed inside the meetinghouse. The roof had vanished long ago, and the floor was covered in a thick carpet of moss. Floating just inside the doorway was an elegant craft about the size of a Ford. It was definitely a vehicle of some sort, but without wheels and constructed entirely of floatie material. Despite a thick layer of lichen and creepers that were draped on it from above, it was still drifting free. A yard-high mark around the inside of the meeting house showed where it had moved about with the air currents, scraping against the walls. The only reason it had not drifted out and eventually made its way to the sea was that the meetinghouse door had partially collapsed, blocking its only escape. I placed my hand on the craft but, even by pulling hard, could make it dip only a small amount.

"At least six hundred negative pounds," murmured Courtland, "spoons, a complete floatie. This place has riches in abundance—am I glad I came!"

I looked at Jane, who said nothing, and we moved off. The road we had been following was soon joined by a second that snaked in from the north. But it wasn't any easier going. If anything, it was worse. The road was covered with the grassed-over lumps of rubble, long-rusted wreckage, stunted trees trying to grow as best they could on the thin soil, and at times impenetrable rhododendron that had to be skirted around, further slowing our progress.

"Where does the Perpetulite start?" asked Courtland.

"About a mile down the way," Jane replied.

I looked at my watch. "We're getting pressed for time. At this rate all we'll manage is a quick look around before we need to head back."

"You won't want any more than that."

After thirty minutes of scrambling over debris, we finally arrived at the Perpetulite. It was a four-lane roadway of perfect grey-black compound, and the bronze pins had been driven in closer together than at Bleak Point, so the spalling was less severe.

"Thank Munsell for that," breathed Courtland, emptying a bootful of earth and sitting on the glossy black central barrier. The roadway even had Perpetulite lampposts of a much more modern design than the iron posts I was used to, and the lightglobes, where still present, were alight.

We walked down the road, which seemed somehow more incongruous here in the depopulated wasteland than at home. There, at least, there was someone to use the road or even see it; here it existed purely for its own sake.

There Shall Be Spoons

2.3.06.56.027: Flowers are not to be picked; they are to be enjoyed by everyone.

As we walked toward the town, the scattered broadleaf forest was replaced by the curved, whiplike branches of the yateveos, and since they always kept the ground beneath them meticulously clear of any brush or vegetation, the verges, side roads and collapsed buildings had a creepy well-manicured look to them. Not that our path was totally maintenance-free and perfection; the Perpetulite's ability to remove debris worked only as far as the curb, so the edges of the road were marked by low banks of grass-covered detritus, a little like piecrusts.

Courtland saw his first spoon ten minutes later. It was by the side of the road, but he didn't pick it up. There was a yateveo looming above, and Jane told him there would be more spoons farther on. Even though the canopy of the carnivorous trees extended almost completely across the roadway and the barbed spines were at tensioned readiness, as long as we kept from yelling and didn't smell of blood, they wouldn't be able to sense us. The root sensors of the yateveo could not break through the tough layer of Perpetulite.

The road entered a circular junction, and we took the route that led to a bridge across the river. The tide was out, and by looking seaward along the silted-in tidal reaches, we could clearly see the large, flat-decked ship that dominated the mouth of the estuary. Even from this distance it was

349

gargantuan; the gulls that wheeled above its superstructure looked like little more than specks.

Fifty yards beyond the bridge we came across a railway track. To the left it continued on toward the coast but looked unused; the way was impeded by trees and thick shrubbery. To the right the tracks curved off into the trees and headed north. We were standing at some kind of station, made entirely of Perpetulite. There were platforms, benches and light stands, but no ticket hall or canteen. It was quiet, too, and as we stood there, a bird fell from the sky and landed at our feet, quite dead.

"Spoons!" exclaimed Courtland, and he was right. Dotted along the side of the road were more of them, in great abundance. There were no yateveos here, so he scooped them up by the handful and poured them into his satchel with a satisfying jangle. But as we moved on he discovered more and, unable to carry them all, he became more selective. By the time we had walked the short distance to the twice-lifesize bronze of Munsell, he was nonchalantly tossing aside spoons that were not perfect and started collecting only the ones that were pristine or had unusual postcodes on the back, or those he described as yellow.

Beyond Munsell's bronze was what looked like an open-air meeting place. It was a flat, circular piazza perhaps a hundred yards in diameter, with a series of ionic columns set about the periphery at fifteen-foot intervals. On top of these was a continuous and gently curved architrave, and decorating this in a long unbroken frieze were animals, human figures and Leapbacked technology, some familiar, some not. We passed slowly through the processional entrance arch and noticed that the columns, floor, panels and even benches and classically styled lamp stands were made entirely of a reddish veined Perpetulite, as though attempting to emulate the more transient marble.

It was, perhaps, the most awe-inspiring construction I had ever laid eyes on. Not just because of the scale or the symmetrical perfection, but the *craftsmanship*. The capitals were finely sculpted with a dramatic flourish, and the delicate sinews of the horses' bodies within the frieze were as finely detailed now as they had been since construction, and would remain so as long as there was oxygen in the air and there were nutrients in the soil.

It was between the columns that the rain-tarnished spoons had gathered. There must have been hundreds of thousands of them—perhaps more. They were heaped right where the swirly-patterned Perpetulite ended and the lawns began, and they lay in a long jumbled mass that was so high I could barely step over them. But oddly, while most were already covered in moss, leaf mold and lichen, the ones facing the piazza were still shiny and new. I walked across to the simple stone monolith that stood in the center of the piazza. It was slender and tall, and it bore a familiar inscription. I sat on one of the benches to look at it:

Apart We Are Together

"What do you think?" asked Jane, sitting down beside me.

"It's certainly impressive, if not a bit disturbing," I replied. "The centerpiece of some long-abandoned town?"

"Actually, this is just the beginning of High Saffron," she said as Courtland whooped with joy over some particularly fine spoon he'd just discovered. "The rest of the town carries on toward the coast. But it's not deserted. Not always. Far from it."

The sun went behind a cloud, and I shivered. The atmosphere in the piazza seemed suddenly oppressive, and I noticed for the first time that there was no wildlife of any sort, not even so much as a butterfly. I lifted my hand from the bench. There was a sharp pain as I left some skin behind, and a droplet of bright red blood splashed on the bench; a second later it began to bubble.

"It's best to keep on the move," said Jane, and we stood up. My foot knocked against a spoon that I hadn't seen, and as I bent to pick it up, I yelled. Lying beneath the surface of the Perpetulite, like a drowned man under ice, was a blank face staring back up at me. His mouth was wide open and his hands palms up. His bones were all perfectly visible within the gentle overlay of soft tissue, and even the herringbone pattern of his jacket was discernible. Like the giraffe I had seen outside East Carmine, the indiscriminate organoplastoid had simply absorbed him as if he were nothing more than rainwater or leaf litter. But as I stared at the apparition in the smooth surface, I noticed that another, more fully digested body was just discernible to his left. And beyond that there was another. And *another*. As I looked around, I saw that the swirling pattern I had assumed was as random as that in linoleum was actually a jumble of semi-digested people, lying in haphazard profusion. The Perpetulite had consumed their tissue, bones, teeth, clothes—and left behind only the indigestible parts, which were simply moved tidily to the side. You didn't take much to Reboot, but tradition dictated that you always took a spoon. And it wasn't just spoons at the curbside. It was buttons, buckles, shoe nails, coins, all stained rust-red from the hemoglobin.

"The Night Train from Cobalt junction," I murmured. "It doesn't go to Emerald City at all, does it?"

"No," said Jane, "it comes right here."

I looked around at the piles of spoons. All those people who had been sent to Reboot because of sedition, unruliness, bad manners or disrespect, or by deceit or accident. They said you were reallocated to another sector once you had been educated. They lied. All the Rebootees ended their days here, except perhaps the few who got away—the woman in the flak tower and Thomas Emerald's remains under the purple tree. Little wonder they had been dressed in Standard Casuals.

"But it's against the Rules," I cried, shocked not just about the murder but about the subterfuge that accompanied it. "The prefects lied to us. It's against everything Munsell stands for."

"Technically speaking, you're wrong," she said, shaking her head. "It's written that the pursuit of Harmony requires sacrifices from all of us. It just doesn't specify what. Hard work, selflessness, Civil Obligation—and sometimes something else. And I'm not sure the prefects actually know anything about this at all. It's Head Office."

I looked around at the spoons and had an idea.

"All these people wouldn't have had their postcodes reallocated, would they?"

"No," she agreed. "Now you know why the Collective is so underpopulated."

"But the Previous numbered eighty million or more! You're not telling me that they were all sent to places like this?"

She looked across at me.

"I don't know what happened to the Previous."

"Does the Apocryphal man know?"

"He might have an idea, but to him it's not emotive—merely history."

I thought for a moment in silence. There was so much unknown, and so much to discover. But right now, I had only questions.

"Why didn't more people attempt to walk out? Why would you just stand here and wait to be absorbed?"

"I wish it were as simple as that. Believe me, Eddie, you don't know the half of it."

She looked up at the sun to gauge the time.

"We need to leave. I'm not going to raise any suspicions by bringing you back after dark."

"You can do that, right?"

"You have no idea how beautiful the night sky is. You can see the stars—bright points of light hanging in a sky of empty blackness."

"I can imagine."

"You can't. No one can. The same can be said of fireflies, glowing in unison on a moonless night."

"*Fireflies?*"

"My point entirely. And there's the moon, too."

"I can see that," I said, "if dimly."

"Not the moon itself," she replied, "but the lights on the unlit side of the crescent. There are other glowing specks adrift in the night, too— pinpoints of light that criss-cross the sky."

And she smiled at me. But it was a tired, relieved smile. She hadn't shared this with anyone.

I walked across to Courtland, who was doing his best to weigh himself down with spoons. He had stuffed both satchels, all his pockets, his boots, and he even had two large handfuls. If he could have stuffed them in his ears, he would have.

"What?"

"We're leaving."

"Suits me. I'll pay either of you twenty merits to carry this satchel for me."

We told him he could carry his ill-gotten gains himself, and we walked out of the piazza. Despite our refusal to work as pack mules, Courtland was ecstatic and talked ceaselessly about his good fortune and how carefully he was going to introduce the spoons, so the market wasn't flooded, and how it would take a month to check the engraved postcodes against the register to see if they had clear title.

"Can't have the prefects asking questions," he said, "even if Mum is one of them."

He jangled and clanked when he walked, and in his intoxicating acquisitiveness, he hadn't once noticed the lost Rebootees beneath his feet.

Courtland

1.1.02.01.159: The Hierarchy shall be respected at all times.

The progress was easy on the Perpetulite, but it slowed when we reached the spalling and the road reverted to thick rhododendron and tussocked lumpiness. Courtland was hampered even more by his load and was soon sweating and blowing like a steam engine. He called a halt as soon as we had reached the place where the road branched.

"I'm going to leave these here," he said, unloading all the cutlery except the ones he was carrying in the satchels. "We could tell Yewberry that we need to come back for a further expedition."

"We're not coming back," said Jane in a quiet voice. "There's nothing here for anyone."

Courtland laughed. "There's enough spoons here to fund an entire color garden; forget the scrap color, East Carmine is in the spoon business, with me at its head. Are you tired, or is it just me?" He sat down heavily on a moss-covered lump of concrete.

"People aren't supposed to come here," said Jane, perching on a fallen tree. "After the wires corroded and the flak towers fell into disuse, the Perpetulite was necrotized to keep visitors away. No one was ever supposed to come back from High Saffron, and no one ever did."

"Until now," said Courtland.

"Yes," repeated Jane, "until now. Tell me, Courtland, when you were pretending to conduct the chair census in the Greyzone yesterday, were you looking for anything in particular?"

"Like what?"

"Unlicensed supernumeraries."

His surprise was genuine. "There's one in East Carmine?"

"There are sixteen," replied Jane cheerfully, "and five of them are blind."

"B-word?" he asked incredulously. "You mean without-sight b-word?"

"Mrs. Olive has been blind for twenty-two years," said Jane, looking at me. "Makes a nonsense of the fear of night, doesn't it?"

"How can someone survive Variant-B Mildew?" asked Courtland, not unreasonably. "I mean, as soon as the sight starts to go, the Rot kicks in, and you're spared the horror of permanent darkness."

"It's not a horror," said Jane, "far from it. Someone remade the night as a barrier to restrict movement, and sightless people who have no fear of the darkness would give the game away."

"Night as a barrier?" asked Courtland. "But why?"

I looked at Jane. I wanted to know, too.

"There used to be places called prisons before the Epiphany, where the demerited were restrained against their will."

"It sounds hideously barbaric," I said.

"Prisons are still with us," she said, "only the walls are constructed of fear, taboo and the unknown."

"But why didn't the sightless catch the Mildew?" I said. "I still don't understand."

"They didn't catch Variant-B for the simple reason that they were safe and comfortable in their attics," explained Jane. "In fact, not one single supernumerary has ever caught the Mildew. And that's quite significant, don't you think?"

I'd heard enough. I wanted it to stay as death on the road at the end of the Night Train, and Head Office quietly feeding the wantonly disruptive to carnivorous trees and an ancient technology. It was enough for today, enough for all week—enough for all time. Enough.

"We've got to get moving," I said in a more forceful tone. "If we're not at Bleak Point by sundown-minus-one, we're going to spend a miserable night in the Faraday cage. Courtland, Jane—we're leaving."

Jane didn't budge, and neither did Courtland.

"I feel a bit odd," he said, "and I can't feel my elbows."

I felt my own elbows, and noticed nothing unusual. I looked at Courtland's fingernails. They had grown a half inch. It could be only one thing.

"The Rot," he said in a quiet voice, tinged not with dread but with sadness and inevitability, "and not a blasted Green Room in sight. What rotten luck. If there's one thing good about curling up, you at least get to Chase the Frog."

"No, no, no," I said, holding my head in my hands. "Don't make the Mildew part of this!" I felt tears well up inside me, and a retching sob as everything came crashing down around me. The yateveos and Perpetulite didn't kill anyone back at High Saffron—they just mopped up the remains.

"It was as I said," murmured Jane. "Everything looks fine, but behind the door there's a fire raging. I'm sorry, but if you and I are going to run side by side with scissors, you're going to have to open that door and feel the heat on your face. Perhaps even burn a little. Scar tissue always heals harder."

"Mildew's not a disease at all, is it?"

She took a deep breath and squeezed my hand. "It's a color. A greeny-red that I call greed. The piazza at High Saffron is made of self-colored Perpetulite."

"But almost everyone gets the Mildew," I said slowly, "and hardly anyone comes down here."

"There's a list," said Jane sadly. "Annex XII. And when you show symptoms of anything on the list, you're shown the Mildew."

It took a moment for what she was saying to hit home, and when it did, I didn't like it.

"Don't leap to judgment," she said hurriedly, guessing what was on my mind. "A swatchman's job is ninety-five percent healing. They're not murderers. Once, I think Annex XII was a list of symptoms that would allow you the option to enter the Green Room. Somewhere along the line it became compulsory. But ask yourself this: Does your father preside over many Mildews?"

"No," I said, considering the matter, "he's always been proud that he hasn't lost a single person to the Rot."

"It's a good sign," said Jane. "It shows that he has a conscience. Robin Ochre worked the system as best he could to avoid having to show anyone the Mildew. He juggled targets, cooked the books and even used misdiagnosis and misdirection to avoid the worst. When that didn't work, he had them pretend to do a walkout and confined them to attics. Anything to avoid the checks-and-balances man from Mutual Audit. We had twenty-six Extras hidden away at one point. Some of them still ended up in the Green Room, but by their own choice. He kept the village entirely Rot-free for seven years. He was an extraordinary man."

"And that's why they killed him?"

She shrugged.

"I'm not sure of the precise reason. All I know is that he was taken from his bed at night, flashed some Sweetdream and then dumped in the Green Room. He never even saw them coming. In the night, you never do."

"Have you ever seen them?"

"No," she replied, "but I'm always on my guard, and check out all newcomers where possible. I don't frighten easy, but they frighten me. There's nothing they won't do to protect the Stasis. Nothing."

"Dad might be staying," I said. "Mrs. Ochre and he have a thing going."

"Then he may need our help. He'll need to know about the Extras."

"And place him in danger?"

"By not enthusiastically embracing the full capabilities of the Mildew, he's already at risk—even if he doesn't know it."

I looked at Courtland, who was now coughing almost continuously. His skin was going waxy, and his ears had become white and brittle. He was dying, and he knew it. I helped him off the slab of concrete and laid him on the soft grass with one of his satchels under his head.

"Why not us?" I asked.

"The Gordini I showed you," she said quietly. "For a couple of hours we're immune to all hues—good or bad."

"But you didn't show it to Courtland," I replied reproachfully. "Your inaction killed him. No one deserves this. Not even him."

She looked at me and sighed.

"You're right. But he couldn't go blabbing about all this into the village. If we're to make a difference here, we have to make hard decisions. And as tough calls go, this one is a doozy. Believe me, you're going to have to do much worse than this—in the pursuit of freedom, the innocents will suffer—and at your hands."

"Perhaps," I said, "but I'm not there yet."

I pulled out the small square of Lincoln that I had taken from Lucy. I was expecting a quick hit when I unfolded it, but nothing happened. Or at least, not to me. To Courtland it was everything, and he sighed with relief when I showed it to him. After a moment or two, his breathing became easier and he stopped panicking. I didn't put the Lincoln away, even when he'd had enough. He carried on staring at it until he became drowsy, confessed that it was Sally who "did Travis in," told me I was a rogue and a cheat and then asked us to tell Melanie that he actually quite liked her, and that it wasn't all about the youknow. He mentioned something about not trusting Tommo, then lost consciousness. I lifted his eyelids to keep the numbing shade flooding into his cortex, and could feel myself shaking. I didn't even like Courtland, he had tried to kill me—and still I felt tears running down my cheeks. Within five minutes the grey tendrils had started to appear on his lips, and as we watched, a cakey substance sprouted from his ears, nostrils and tearducts. I kept his eyes firmly open and bathed in Lincoln, and although not as enjoyable an exit as Sweetdream, it was fairly painless. After ten minutes the growth had filled his lungs, and his breathing became more labored, then stopped entirely. I pressed my finger on his neck and kept it there until his pulse had faded to nothing.

I stood up and walked away to think for a moment.

"Are you okay?" asked Jane. "Don't go all funny on me. I'm out on a limb for you here."

I swallowed my anger and revulsion, and took a deep breath. "Okay," I said, turning to face her, "we can go."

"Not yet, we can't."

She took Courtland's arms and instructed me to take his legs, and we carried him into the forest until we reached a grove of yateveos. She told me to haul him to his feet at the edge of the spread, and we then just let him fall backward. There was a flash of movement, and the tree had him deposited in its trunk within a couple of seconds while Courtland's spoons spilled from his satchel and cascaded to earth with a musical ring.

"I always act out my cover stories for real where possible," said Jane as we walked away. "I'm not going to be caught out by shoddily prepared homework. Come on, it's getting late."

We headed off among the grove of yateveos and followed the narrow strips of safe ground that lay between the highly territorial trees.

"You said the Herald was a lost page from a missing book. What did you mean by that?"

"I was being dramatic. The truth isn't lost or missing—it's right here, in our heads." She tapped her forehead. "We're more complex than you think. Perhaps more complex than you *can* think. There's stuff locked up in our heads—we just can't access it without the correct combination of hues. Pookas, memory sweeps, cross fires, the Mildew, Lincoln, lime and Gordini are only the smallest part of it. There's more. Much more. We've only dipped a toe in the lake."

"How does it work?"

She shook her head. "I have no idea, but I don't think we're the first society to embrace the visible Spectrum as the focal point of our lives. There was another before us. A better one. One that went wrong or was displaced. They left stuff behind. Not just Chromaticology and the Mildew, but complete histories, accessed by nothing more complex than a subtle combination of color."

"The painted ceiling," I said, "Rusty Hill."

"You saw a partial Herald while you were looking at the violets. But not enough of the ceiling is finished to hear her speak. When it is, then we might know more about the Something That Happened. We may even discover the nature of Munsell's Epiphany."

I thought about this for a moment.

"Zane was buying paint that day in Vermillion, wasn't he?"

She nodded. "We need to complete the mural. To even have a hope of defeating Head Office and Chromocentric Hierarchilism, we have to know how it all came about. Ochre stole the swatches to exchange for paint. Zane wrongspotted himself so no questions would or could be asked. I wrangled the Perpetulite to get him around—we even went into neighboring sectors to avoid suspicion."

"Is that why everyone was Mildewed in Rusty Hill?"

"Yes," she said in a quiet voice. "They started to complete the roof, and the workers started to see confused snippets of Heralds. They were reported as Pookas, and the system swung into action to protect itself."

There was a pause.

"So that's what enlightenment feels like," I said in a quiet voice. "You said cozy ignorance was a better place for people like me."

"It still might be. And listen, I want you to know I'm sorry."

I stopped. We were standing on the narrow area of safety between the spreads of two medium-sized yateveos. I had been in this situation before with her, and my heart fell. I thought we'd been getting along. I turned to face her, and she looked at me apologetically.

"Do you have to?" I asked.

"I do. And I'm really, really sorry."

She hooked a leg in mine and expertly heaved me off balance. I landed with a thump, and there was a sound like a whipcrack. I cried out in pain as one vine wrapped around my leg and another took hold of my arm. I felt the sensation of being lifted, and the ground and Jane moved rapidly away from me. I think she waved.

The Way Home

2.6.23.02.935: Residents may not keep pets in their room.

And this is where you find me now. Head down in a yateveo, musing on the events of the past four days and how I could have been so stupid as to deny myself the endless opportunities to avoid this particular destiny. Like most people, I'm not much scared by death, but swans, Reboot, creepy crawlies, my twice-widowed aunt Beryl, social embarrassment and loss most certainly did frighten me. Loss of my father, loss of Jane, but most of all, loss of my potential obligation. Not my *Chromatic* obligation, you understand, but the loss of my obligation to *real* truth and justice, deeper and more powerful than I would find in a thousand Rulebooks. I'd found enlightenment and a sense of purpose, and lost it again. But it *had* been mine, if only for a short while.

It began to darken. Not the darkness that was already within the yateveo, but an *enveloping* darkness, even blacker than the night but without depth or time. This was it. And as far as reporting what death was like, I can use only one word: *colorless*. But oddly, that wasn't quite it. After what could have been anything between a couple of seconds and a century, I saw a dim sliver of light open up in front of me, and I believed, for a moment, that I was about to be reborn. Perhaps to another couple somewhere in another sector, and a long time after a forgotten Edward Russett was lost on a toshing expedition to the middle of nowhere.

But I wasn't being reborn. It was the same old me, and I was flowing out of a split in the tree's digesting bulb, coughing and spluttering. I felt someone place her mouth over my nose and suck out the liquid in a sort of power-assisted nose blow, and after retching up a stomachful of gloop that burned my throat, I managed to open my eyes. The first thing I saw was Jane's face, staring at me with a concerned expression. We were sitting at the base of the trunk, with Jane holding the sharpened potato peeler she had used to slit the bulb. The yateveo was making halfhearted snatches in our direction but doing no damage.

"Phew!" she said, sticking a finger in my ear to clean it out. "You stink."

I retched again and she handed me her water bottle. "Rinse."

I took a swig and spat the foul-tasting liquid from my mouth.

"Were you almost gone in there?" she asked. "It took a while to get into the bulb."

I nodded. "My whole life flashed in front of me. The last four days, anyway—which probably amounts to the same thing."

She gave me a hug. "Oh, I'm so sorry—I should have explained. This is part of our cover story. But, hey, I've come to a big decision: That's the last time I try to kill you."

"Promise?"

"Absolutely. In fact, I may actually try to save your life if the opportunity presents itself. And if I ever threaten you again, you have my permission to give me a good telling-off."

She smiled again. "You can call me by my name, too—and I promise not to thump you. Will you kiss me?"

So we did, there in the dappled shade of the yateveo, covered in digestive gloop and not an hour from the darkest secret of the Collective. It was, as I recall, every bit as good as I thought it might be.

"I may have trouble getting used to the new Jane," I said. "I'm not sure perkiness really suits you."

"It's only when we're together. Broken anything?"

"I think I landed on something. Something the yateveo couldn't digest. Have a look would you?"

Jane had a look and laughed.

"What?"

"You have a spoon or a fork or something embedded in your left buttock."

"Hilarious. Pull it . . . OW!"

"Sorry, what were you saying?"

And we giggled, then guffawed, then burst out laughing. Inappropriate, given the circumstances, but something of a relief.

"Was it really necessary to have me eaten?" I asked.

"That was Courtland we just got killed, pumpkin, not some poor Delta that no one gives a fig about."

"Did you just call me pumpkin?"

She scratched her ear nervously. "Is that okay?"

"I suppose. Listen, you could have had *yourself* eaten."

"What do you think I am, nuts? Okay, here's the story: You get captured by a yateveo, and while Courtland is risking his life to slit the bulb and release you, he is grabbed and deposited in the same tree. But because there is no gloop to break his fall, he breaks his neck. Stone dead in an instant."

"How about that," I said. "Courtland died a hero."

"The best lies to tell," said Jane, "are the ones people *want* to believe."

I was lucky that the tree had been relatively young: The barbs were numerous and quite short, as opposed to the other way around. Despite this, my leg and arm were still painful, and the juices stung in my wounds. I was very glad when we finally reached the stream and I could rinse myself off and wring out my clothes. Once done, we began the long walk back to the base of the escarpment and the flak tower.

We didn't talk for a long time, each of us consumed by our thoughts. It's confusing to suddenly have to reappraise all you know, to rejigger one's outlook in the light of new knowledge, and realize that everything you thought was truth and justice was little more than an elaborate fiction. Most of all, I couldn't help wondering what my mother had suffered that required her to be Mildewed. I was only glad that my father had not been her attendant swatchman.

"Why did they have to kill all the Rebootees?" I asked, finally breaking the silence. "Why not just, well, reeducate them as they claim they do?"

Jane thought for a moment.

"I used to think the most ingenious part of the whole system was how color and mandate were interwoven. The Rules dictate every aspect of our lives, but our devotion to the Spectrum gives them credibility and relevance. But then I got to thinking that perhaps it was all much, much simpler, and that the complexity of the Rules and the strict Chromatic Hierarchy were there to serve a greater master."

"And what's that?"

"Continuous sustainability. A community where everyone has their place, everyone knows their place and works ceaselessly to maintain continuance. If you were to dispassionately consider the principal aim of the society to be longevity rather than fairness, then everything is downgraded to simply a means of attaining that goal. Rather than waiting for a resident to prove themselves disharmonious, the system simply flags them early and sends them off to Reboot as a precaution. If you think about it, the whole notion is quite ingenious."

"I'd be the first to applaud," I said, "without the murder-of-innocents aspect. But once we tell everyone the truth," I continued, "Head Office will have to explain itself. After all, the Rules apply to all, irrespective of hue or position. If the headmaster knows of High Saffron, he can be personally held to account."

"Almost certainly. But Head Office has many defenses. Prefects, Mutual Audit, National Color—and the Nightseers. We'll have to tread carefully and leave no footprints."

"But you do have a plan?"

"We *did,* but without Ochre and Zane I'm not sure where to go. I'm up for Reboot on Monday, but I'll probably just ride the conveyor to a far-off corner of the Collective and join up with the Riffraff or something."

"You'll have seven hundred merits for coming to High Saffron with me," I pointed out, "which only leaves you a hundred short. Dad owes me a thousand, and Tommo has a sweep going. We can bring you up to full residency with that lot."

"It would make more sense to still be around," she mused, and we fell silent for a while as the afternoon was hot, we were in a hurry and it was a lot harder going up the escarpment than coming down.

"So," I said as we finally rounded the last corner and came within sight of the flak tower, "is there *any* good news?"

She looked across at me and smiled. "I think the answer is in loophol-ery. Small changes can be effected by a certain degree of *circumvention.* We'll use the Rules to change the Rules."

"Defiance through compliance?"

She nodded.

"I like the sound of that."

"How do we put High Saffron out of action?" I asked. "I mean, that's got to be the first priority, yes?"

"Maybe not. We need to know what we're up against before we attempt anything."

"But thousands will die if we don't do something!"

"And millions will die if we fail. We can't afford any mistakes, Eddie. How often do you think a Grey with night vision and a potential Red prefect with a conscience find themselves wanting to change things, and together? If we do something rash, or hasty, or ill conceived, we'll simply be silenced. It may take hundreds of years before another attempt against the system is possible. Careless talk about Pookas killed eighteen hundred people in Rusty Hill. The whole of Green Sector South fell to the Mildew one hundred and seventy-six years ago. What do you think happened for them to earn that? Sedition on a grand scale? Or a single word said out of place? One thing we do know about Head Office is that it's not noted for its restraint."

We walked past the flak tower and up to the summit section. We reached the purple tree as the shadows were beginning to lengthen. I'd been walking slower, and we were behind schedule. I only hoped that Tommo would wait for us.

"So what's your plan?" she asked.

I had been thinking about this. "Stay in East Carmine and become Red prefect."

She smiled. "With you on the inside and me on the outside," she said, "we may get to learn something. Formulate a plan. And when the time is right—strike."

"So life carries on as usual?" I asked.

"Life carries on exactly as usual. Same old Chromatic claptrap, dusk until dawn."

I suddenly stopped walking.

"What's up, pumpkin?"

"I can see a snag."

"A big one?"

"Elephant-sized. I'm expected to marry Violet."

"Yes, I was wondering when you'd remember that particular nastiness."

"Jane?"

"Yes?"

"Will you marry me?"

"I thought you were on a promise to Violet?"

"I never agreed anything to anyone."

"Your dad will veto it."

"I can persuade him otherwise. And think: It will brown off the deMauves like nothing else on earth."

"I'm in," said Jane without hesitation. "I'll leave the timing of the announcement up to you."

And we kissed again. It was a warm, indescribably lovely feeling. But it was more than just physical. It was a dialogue between two young people with high ideals and a Big Plan. It was about belonging, secrets, partnership, commitment. It was also a kiss, unlike the last one, that didn't taste of yateveo gloop. And after we stopped, she just stood there, eyes closed.

"Mmm," she said, "that was nice. Listen, why didn't you leg it back home to East Carmine yesterday? I know Violet nixed the whole Constance plan, but you wouldn't have had to risk High Saffron."

"Actually," I said, "it was what Stafford said."

"Oh, yes?" she asked suspiciously. "And what was that?"

"He said that I should 'never underestimate the capacity for romance, no matter what the circumstance.' I think he was referring to you."

"Fathers!" she snorted. "Does yours meddle, too?"

"You're Stafford's daughter? I thought he was a G-8?"

"He is."

"But you're G-23."

She sighed. "The G-code isn't a family name. It's our address."

"I didn't know that. But then," I added, "I never really troubled myself to find out."

"Don't worry," she said, "it's a Chromatic thing. No one troubles themselves with the Greys. And thanks."

"For what?"

"A great first date. I really enjoyed myself."

"For our second date I thought we'd dismantle the entire Collective and replace it with a system run on the principles of fair play, equality and truly harmonious coexistence. What do you say?"

"Teaser!" she replied, and gave me a playful slap on my shoulder.

We ran the last half mile into Bleak Point, for the Model T flatbed was still there. The sun was almost a thumb's width from the tops of the hills—if we drove really fast, we might make it back to the dams before the light went completely. We'd still be stuck out at night, but at least closer.

"At last!" said Tommo as we ran up. "Do you know the time? It's eight o'clock!"

"Thanks for waiting."

"Waiting nothing," replied Violet. "Plank-head Cinnabar doesn't know how to drive."

"Neither do you."

"I am a Purple," Violet replied loftily. "I don't do that sort of thing."

Jane ordered Tommo to hand-start the engine, and after five minutes of fruitless cranking, the motor finally coughed to life. Wasting no time, Jane reversed the car and tore off back toward East Carmine as fast as she could.

Return to East Carmine

6.6.19.61.247: Vulgar mispronunciations of everyday words will not be tolerated.

We drove in silence for the first ten minutes, Jane concentrating on getting us home as quick as possible, but without mishap. I was sitting on the flatbed with Tommo, and Jane and Violet were up in the cab, silently ignoring each other. When Jane and I arrived, Tommo had been sitting in the Faraday cage at the side of the road, with Violet positioned on the Ford's running board facing away from him. She looked beside herself with rage and had doubtless been venting her anger on him for most of the day, which can't have been a huge bundle of laughs, even with someone like Tommo, who deserved it as much as anyone.

It was lucky that it was a clear evening; navigation might still be possible ten or fifteen minutes after sundown. Jane could have driven us all the way home, of course, but she'd told me she would keep her pupils locked tight and suffer the same woeful lack of night sight as the rest of us. We all knew we weren't going to make it; the question was how far we would get. But the other unasked question could not be ignored forever, and it was Tommo who finally asked it. "Where's Courtland?"

"He got taken by a yateveo on the walk back."

"Wow," said Tommo. "But you're okay, right?"

"I'm fine."

"You've no idea how good that makes me feel."

"Well, thanks, Tommo."

"Oh, it's nothing personal," he said, just in case I misconstrued his meaning. "If both of you had been killed, I would have stood to lose a fortune on my sweep. At least this way I get to break even. And listen," he added, "that really hurt when you kicked me."

"And you were going to leave me to starve to death in the flak tower. Do you want to make something of this?"

"No."

"That Tommo is a reptile," said Violet. "If I find myself alone with him again I will feed him poison, and accept the consequences."

"And I'd gladly drink it."

We drove on down the road, on several occasions running dangerously close to the verge as Jane took the sweeping corners recklessly fast. I looked across at the sun, which was just beginning to touch the hilltops. I turned back and Violet caught my eye, smiled, bit her lip and then attempted some repairs.

"Edward, darling," she said, "I'm so sorry about what happened early this morning. It was theft of the most malicious kind. But we were all just so worried that you might not have returned, and the deMauve lineage has much benefit to offer the village. You do understand how important that is, don't you?"

I thought carefully. "I'll forgive you, Violet, as long as you defer the seven hundred merits you should have earned to Jane Grey here."

She consented easily to this without looking at Jane, and I asked Tommo to be my witness, to which he readily agreed.

"You are a dear!" said Violet. "I declare our marriage firmly back on— Mummy and Daddy will be delighted."

"I won't be marrying you, Violet."

"I'm only pretending you have a choice to be polite," she said in a more forceful tone. "In fact, there isn't a choice at all."

"I could be on a promise."

She gave out a short gale of laughter. "No one in the village would dare to offer you a promise while I'm the front-runner," she declaimed haughtily. "That's the advantage of having so many people eager to be your friend."

There was a pause in which she stared at me, and I stared back with an unconcerned look. Then she frowned and glanced at Jane, then at me, and then the penny dropped.

"Oh, no. That is so sad. Please tell me you're joking."

"I'm not joking, Violet."

"I withdraw my pledge of seven hundred merits. Cinnabar, you heard nothing."

"I most certainly did," he replied, their argument—whatever it was—still firmly in his mind.

"Listen here, Russett," said Violet. "If you're after a bit of youknow on the side, I don't mind. In fact, you could definitely do with the practice. I'll even give you the two merits it'll cost you." She winced, expecting to be punched—no doubt her intention—but Jane ignored her and just continued to negotiate the turns of the road as we thundered on toward East Carmine.

"I aim to lead a blameless life from now on," Jane remarked evenly, "tending to my Civil Obligation and my husband."

Violet made a face.

"Even the thought makes me want to vomit. Jane *Russett* sitting at High Table with the rest of the prefects? Have you any idea how shabby and *nouveau couleur* that is?"

Even Tommo was beginning to get concerned.

"Listen," he said to me, "I'm all for this annoying-Violet game. In fact, I wholeheartedly applaud it. But this is some sort of huge scam, right? You're holding out for more cash because she tricked you into a harvest? If that's the case, you need to speak to me to renegotiate. We might up it to twelve grand, but even the deMauves will draw the line eventually."

"Don't see me as you, Tommo. I don't want to marry Violet, I want to marry Jane. I think we should marry who we want. It's as simple as that."

"And what about my marriage fantasy league?" he asked. "Do you have any idea how hard I've worked on that?"

"Dangles to your stupid league," interrupted Violet. "What about our baby? Could you really see it growing up to be Doug's?"

"You tricked me. And if you go public, the deMauves are finished as head prefects. Your family would have to go to Grey and back before they'd be reinstated."

She fell silent, deep in thought. There was truth in what I said. Although my father and I would also get it in the neck for our involvement, the deMauves had far more to lose.

The sun dipped below the horizon as we reached the first of the dams, and with only ten minutes or so of navigable light left, we weren't going to make it home. Or at least, not tonight. It would be a cold and lonely night, huddled in the cab, and not helped by Violet, who would doubtless complain volubly until dawn.

"Hey," said Violet, suddenly changing tack and addressing Jane directly, "would you like to be my friend? I have lots of friends. Some say, in fact, that I have more friends than anyone else in the village."

"I think I can live quite happily without your friendship, Miss Violet."

"Then I'll buy him off you," said Violet impatiently. "How much do you want?"

"He's not for sale. Not at any price."

"I can get you a cushy job at the linoleum factory."

"I'll be the Red prefect's wife," replied Jane coolly. "Why would I want to work there?"

"You're getting above yourself," she remarked, her voice rising. "You are *horribly* arrogant. This is because you think you've got a better nose than me, isn't it?"

Jane turned to look at her.

"I don't think I've got a better nose than you. I *know* I have a better nose than you. If the arbitrary division by which the Collective is split were set by nose quality rather than color vision, I'd be head prefect."

"And," I added, eager to back her up, "if it were run on the basis of who was best at manipulative dishonesty, it would be Tommo."

"If it were run on those who demonstrated the most smug, pompous, and self-satisfied attitude," continued Tommo, eager not to be left out, "you'd both run it jointly."

We traveled on in silence, and as we approached the marshy area where we had seen the flamingos earlier, the light fell abruptly within the valley walls, and Jane slowed to a stop as a wall of impenetrable darkness loomed up in front of us. We could still see the sky, but everything below the line of the ridge was a muddy gloom that seemed to dance and ripple as our eyes attempted to give it some sort of form. I heard Violet swear, then make some comment on how her parents would be sick with worry. But this was as far as we could go without artificial light. Or at least, as far as we were willing to *admit* we could go.

"Tommo," I said, "did you steal one of the lightglobes from the flak tower?"

"I got kicked in the ribs," came a sour voice from the darkness. "My mind was on other matters."

"I think we should sing," said Violet after a pause.

"If you do, I'm taking my chances with the night," retorted Tommo.

And they started to bicker.

"Yewberry gave me three hand flares," I announced as I rummaged in my bag. "Each one will last five minutes. They might get us as far as the closest dam to the village, and within line of sight. They'll be keeping an eye out for us, so at least they'll know we're all right. Who wants to have a crack at it?"

Violet was of the opinion that we should stay where we were and use the flares throughout the night to ward off Pookas, Riffraff and nocturnal biting animals. Jane was for pressing on, and Tommo was past caring one way or the other. I took Jane's and my opinion as a consensus, so fumbled my way to the front of the car, perched myself on the front bumper and lit the first flare. It sputtered into life, and by the meager light that penetrated less than twenty feet ahead, we moved off. It was slow going, and by the time the first one had burned out and I'd started the second, we had reached the broken bridge. I began to think this was a poor idea when the second flare burned out without any end of the reservoir in sight, and when I fired up the third and final one, the tension in the Ford was painfully high.

We were about a minute from the end of the final flare when I spotted a fine white point of light in the distance. It looked at first to be the lamppost, but it couldn't have been this far out, and as we drew closer I could see that it was *another* flare, but this time a large Daylighter, which spread a flickering white light a hundred yards in every direction while giving off a rasping hiss and a pall of dense white smoke. Flares were used sparingly, and only to effect an emergency night extraction of a valuable member of the community. Violet or Courtland, for instance.

We drew level as my hand flare gave out, and we could see that the Daylighter had not long to burn, so we carried on to the next flare, and the next. It was in this manner that we returned to the stockwall gates, past the linoleum factory and into the outfall of the main lamppost, where all the prefects and most of the village were waiting for us.

After the initial relief and cries of joy, Courtland's absence was noted.

Sunday Morning

2.6.02.13.057: Every resident will take the Ishihara test in
his or her twentieth year.

The sun was high when I awoke, and I lay in bed, thinking about the previous night's debriefing, which had carried on until lights-out. My detailed report of the impracticality of mounting any sort of color-scrap extraction plan was met with annoyance and dismay, but not much surprise. To my relief, the Council seemed to be of the same opinion, accepting that since it had been deemed impractical two hundred years ago, when Ford flatheads and tractors were still in abundance, then it was doubly so now.

Violet, and to a lesser extent Tommo, had been severely criticized for risking the loss of their Civil Obligation on such a foolhardy venture, and neither of them spoke of the scam they had planned. It seemed that at least in this they were agreed, if in nothing else. The question then turned to Courtland's loss, and our account of it. It was met with shock, then sadness, then finally a certain degree of acceptance and regretful pride that he had given his own life to save mine. I thanked Mrs. Gamboge in a tearful exchange, and Bunty McMustard was named deputy Yellow prefect.

I made to get up but then realized I didn't have any jobs or tasks to perform, so just lay back on the sheets and ran over the events of the previous day. It would need many more conversations with Jane before I could get all the loose ends straightened, but that's what honeymoons were for. I smiled to myself.

There was a knock, and Dad popped his head around the door. We had not spoken privately since I had returned home, so his collusion in the deMauve succession had not yet been aired.

"I'm sorry about selling your, um, heritage to the deMauves," he said, gazing out of the window, "but I really didn't think you would come back."

"I'll work my way past it," I said, trying to be as honest as I could. "There are bigger things to worry about than the deMauves."

"You're right," he agreed, "and it might not be the best time to tell you, but I'm staying on as permanent swatchman—to carry on Robin Ochre's good work."

"Keeping the village free of Mildew?"

"For as long as I can."

I was about to reveal what I knew, but I decided today would not be the day to tell him. We would bring him slowly into our plans.

"I'm also planning to marry Mrs. Ochre," he added. "She's agreeable, but I wanted to make sure you weren't going to go nuts or anything."

I could think of far worse people to be my mother than the mildly eccentric Mrs. Ochre. And Lucy needed a brother on the Council to enable her to keep studying the harmonics without any problems.

"Sounds like a fine idea, Dad. I've always wanted a sister. But be warned: Tommo wants to marry her."

"Tommo as my son-in-law?" he said, getting all protective. "Not if I have anything to do with it!"

And we both laughed.

"Look here, Eddie," he said, all serious for a moment, "deMauve is spitting blood that you've chosen a Grey over his daughter. Daisy he might have tolerated, but Jane is an insult. The ten grand I'd get for you is important, but if I don't exercise my veto, then I'm planting myself firmly on your side of the divide—and I need to have the Council with me if I'm to be an effective swatchman."

"I love her, Dad," I said after a long pause, "from the moment I first saw that nose of hers. She'll be a Russett and your daughter-in-law and living in this house. You'll get used to it. But more to the point, it's important that residents understand that this can and should be done. A fig to Chromatic betterment; one should go with one's heart—in all things. But I don't expect you to understand. Hue first, love second, right?"

"Not strictly true," he replied, and handed me a worn, red-jacketed merit book.

I took the book and felt the soft cover, then flicked through the pages of merits that my mother had gained through abundant good Civic Work. It was over and above what was demanded of her by the obligations. She had served the Collective diligently, only to be disposed of when the Rules decided she could be of no further use. It made me angry, and I began to tremble.

"Look at the back page, Eddie."

I did as he asked, and recognized her postcode and handwriting. There was also the official stamp that transferred her merits to her husband and, more important, her color-perception ranking.

"Some of us do things we regret, then fix them as best we can afterward," he said in a quiet voice, once I had read and digested the implications. "We're not so different, you and I, although by rights, we should be as different as different could be."

"You'll always be my dad," I said, handing the book back.

"And I won't veto your marriage, or cease to keep a careful eye on you."

We stared at each other for a long time. I didn't really know what to say. I'd always assumed that my mother's ranking was high, but it wasn't. She had been only 23.4 percent Red. With Dad at 50.23 percent it didn't take a math wizard to realize that my 70-plus percent couldn't be anything but purchased parentage. Perhaps most people were. Perhaps that's how it really worked. Dad had not married to enRedden the Russett line, but for a much more noble reason, the same as I hoped to do myself.

"So who was the man who made me?" I asked at length.

He looked at me for a long time and then said in a quiet voice, "Some questions are not easily answered." He looked at his watch. "It's just past nine. You need to be in your formals and ready outside the town hall in half an hour. I'll run you a bath."

I found Tommo talking to Doug outside the town hall. There were still ten minutes to go before we had to file in and wait in the anteroom, and it was customary for those who were due to face the spots to arrive early and chat with parents, friends or residents who had taken their tests the year before. Violet was there, along with Daisy and Imogen, who was looking quite lovely and very nervous. She and Dorian had agreed on terms with the Colorman and were going to elope on the train that afternoon. Of the ten of us, seven had nuptials already agreed—some of them from wrangles going back ten years or more. Tommo's fantasy marriage league may have been something of a joke, but the principle was sound. The day of your Ishihara was the day your life was set. A relief, if you were the sort of person who didn't much care for making decisions, but anathema to those who did.

I saw Violet talking to her family; when she noticed me, she looked quickly away.

"Nervous?" asked Dad.

"A little. How long did it take when you had it done?"

"About twenty minutes. A few minutes to discover my predominant perception, then some fine-tuning to find out the range. They use a lot of test cards to make sure you're telling the truth, so you'll never know whether seeing anything in the dots is good or bad, positive or negative."

Doug wandered over.

"I'm sorry that you're up to marry Violet again," I said. "I'd do anything to help out, except marry her myself."

He shrugged good-naturedly. "I was always expecting it, so the shock wore off long ago."

"Have you heard the rumor?" said Tommo, striding up. "Dorian's going to elope with Imogen on the fifteen forty-three."

"And speaking of marriage," he added, turning to Doug, "hold out for at least three grand from the deMauves. Barring any sleepers, Violet's pretty much in the bag."

"Three grand?" he said in a quivering voice. "I can't ask that much!"

"Believe me," said Tommo, laying a hand on his shoulder, "deMauve will definitely pay that to have his daughter in the Green Dragon's bridal suite by Monday night. I'll negotiate for you if you want—I need the merits after Eddie's little disappointment."

"Would you?" asked Doug. "I'd really appreciate it."

Doug walked off to speak to his family, and I was left alone with Tommo. We were silent for a while. I was going to be a prefect, and I needed Tommo on my side. He could never know what I was up to, but his skills at wily artifice might be an asset.

"How are your ribs?"

"You broke two."

"I'm sorry."

"And I'm sorry about that whole leaving-you-to-starve-to-death deal. It was Courtland."

"I know."

We shook hands and smiled uneasily. The friendship wasn't yet healed, but would be, given time.

"Good morning."

I turned. Jane was dressed in her best Grey formal wear, with her hair plaited and interwoven with wildflowers. She looked quite lovely—radiant, in fact—and was accompanied by her parents, who were grinning like mad. I shook hands with Stafford and was introduced to her mother, who was a small, chirpy-looking woman with only one ear.

"Very pleased to meet you," I said.

"Pardon?" she replied, cupping her hand to her missing ear before bursting into laughter, for it was a joke.

"Mother!" implored Jane. "Please don't embarrass me."

"I'm sorry I was unable to ask you for your daughter first," I said to Jane's parents, "but the conditions of our courtship were somewhat onerous."

A bell sounded.

"You're wanted," said Jane's mother, kissing us both. "Good luck."

We made our way to the Chapter House, where Yewberry was ringing the hand bell. We filed into the anteroom behind the Council Chamber and took a seat, whereupon Yewberry read brief instructions regarding protocol and told us to just relax and enjoy it. At the end he made a lame joke, which wasn't funny, but we laughed to break the tension. All eyes, however, were soon riveted on the door that led to the Council Chamber. You would walk out of this room a youth and enter the village twenty minutes later an adult. You were even allowed to exit the Chapter House by way of the prefects' entrance. It was quite an honor.

Ishihara

6.3.01.01.225: The Ishihara test is final and can be neither reviewed nor retaken.

A t ten o'clock *precisely,* the first person was seen. It was Violet, and she went to the Colorman with a spring in her step. We all sat silently under Yewberry's watchful eye, and after twenty minutes it was Doug's turn. He gave us all a bow before vanishing next door, and after half an hour, Jane was called. She caught my eye as she went in, and gave a half smile. We'd brought books, but none of us read them. For the most part we all just sat and stared blankly into space, shuffling down a place every twenty minutes, so that the next person to go was always sitting nearest the door.

"Edward Russett?"

"Yes?"

"You can go in now."

I got up and entered the Council Chamber, carefully closing the door behind me. There were two people in the room: my erstwhile father-in-law and the Colorman, who was dressed in long robes that had no color in them at all, but were fastened by a long series of buttons that reached from his throat to his feet and shone brightly in the broad beam of light that descended from the skylight.

"Hello, Eddie," said the Colorman in a friendly voice. "Take a seat. Do you have your merit book? I know you've already been verified, but I need to check again."

So I did, and once satisfied that I was who I said I was, he shuffled to get comfortable and cleared his throat. "It's very simple. All you have to do is tell me what you can see in the pictures."

There was a big book on the reading stand in front of me, and deMauve positioned himself on my right, ready to turn the pages. At a signal from the Colorman, he opened the book.

The page was a mass of grey dots, which ranged in size from a period to the width of a pencil. But interspersed within this grey mass were *colored* dots, and they made up a picture.

"What do you see?"

"A swan."

"And in its beak?"

"There's nothing in its beak."

"Quite right. Would you turn to page seven, please, Mr. deMauve?"

There were more dots on this page, but it wasn't a swan, it was a number.

"Twenty-nine," I said.

"Good," said the Colorman. "And what about page eighteen?"

It was the outline of a bouncing goat. And after that, a wavy line, then nothing, then another number. After each answer the Colorman referred to his chart, scribbled a score and gave Mr. deMauve a new page number. After fifteen minutes of this I was shown a chart that carried no numbers, or a picture of any sort—just a mass of differently hued dots. I was about to admit that I couldn't see anything when the number sixteen popped into my head. My conscious mind wasn't seeing the color, but my unconscious mind was. "Sixteen."

"Hmm!" said the Colorman, uttering the first response that gave away any opinion. "Page two hundred and four."

Again, I could see nothing, but felt it was a horse.

"It's a horse."

"Quite right."

We went through twenty more plates, some of which I could sense, and others I couldn't. But I could tell the process was almost done. The Colorman was starting to relax. Finally, after three images in which I could see nothing at all, he added up the score, scribbled in my merit book and stood up.

"Welcome to the Collective, Mr. Russett," he said, shaking my hand. "You have much to contribute and an obligation to fulfill. Do it wisely, do it fairly, do it by the Rules. Remember: Apart, we will always be together."

I turned smartly and walked out of the chamber and into the sun-shine, much relieved. My father was there, waiting to greet me, and a little way away was Jane, sitting on the color garden wall.

"Well?" said Dad, and I opened the book with a thumping heart and trembling fingers.

"Eighty-six-point-seven-percent Red," I said, reading the figures, "and negligible across the Blue and Yellow fields."

"Congratulations."

"Thank you."

He gave me another hug, then said Jane wanted to speak to me. I walked over with something akin to a stupid grin on my face. If I didn't defer my prefectural duties, I would be sworn in just as soon as I did the traditional "knocking on the Council Chamber door." We could make a start, Jane and I, and perhaps even travel to Emerald City on a fact-finding tour of the faculty or something. But as I walked up, my grin was not returned. Quite the opposite, in fact.

"Problems?" I asked, sitting down next to her.

"Only of a personal nature. It won't alter our Grand Plan. It's just that, well . . I turned out twelve percent Yellow."

I laughed. It was only 2 percent above threshold, so was as good as nothing, and for Jane's huge dislike of Yellows, there was the nub of a fine joke about it.

"You're no longer a Grey. That must make you a Primrose, minimum. Has Bunty asked you to spy on anyone yet?"

"Eddie," she said with a serious look that I didn't much like, "there's something else. I've also got fourteen percent Blue."

All of a sudden I wasn't laughing. "Anything else?"

"No."

"Blast!" I yelled so loudly that people nearby looked up and tutted audibly. Raising one's voice showed very poor self-control. "Blast, blast, blast!"

"Hey," she said, taking my hand, "perhaps it's for the best. The Grand Plan's still on, right?"

"How can it be for the best?" I asked. "You're *Green*. We're *complementary*. We can't ever marry and we shouldn't really talk to each other. And now I've got *nothing* to stop my father from insisting on a union with Violet!"

"Eddie," she repeated, "stay focused. I know this is hard, but there are some things bigger than both of us. *Is the Grand Plan still on?*"

I said nothing, and instead stared at the ground with my head in my hands, wondering what kind of bribe it might take to add a few points to Jane's score. It didn't matter even if they had. The Ishihara was never repeated. The test was perfect, the Colorman above reproach. Infallible, in fact. I looked into her eyes, which were blurred with tears. The truly ironic part of this was that once I was married to Violet, we would not be complementary any longer and could talk freely. If deMauve and Violet had wanted to rub our noses in it the cruelest way possible, they could not have planned it better.

"Okay," I said, "the Grand Plan is on. Who knows? Maybe being within the House of deMauve is the best place to be. Purpose first, love second, right?"

"I could always kill Violet. I could make it look like an accident."

"Don't joke about things like that."

"Sorry."

I wanted to kiss her, but people were watching, and fraternizing between complementary colors was not just demeritable but severely taboo. I had a position to maintain, and we had a plan together. We had a future together, too, just not one that would see us married. Or at least, not to each other.

"You have to go now," she whispered, "but leave your window unlatched tonight."

"You're coming in?"

"No, you're coming out. It's time you met some people."

I gave her an imperceptible nod, cleared my throat and stood up.

"Thank you, Miss—?"

"Brunswick."

"Thank you, Miss Brunswick," I said in a loud voice, since a small crowd had gathered to see how the Edward/Jane affair would pan out. "Will you release me from my promise?"

"I shall do so," replied Jane in a formal manner, "and I thank you for your interest."

And we bowed curtly and shook hands. I walked smartly away, and was instantly grabbed by Mrs. Gamboge and tugged unceremoniously away from the crowd.

"Don't think I don't know you killed him," she growled, staring at me angrily. "I'll have my revenge. Not just on you but on that stupid Grey."

"She's Green."

"She'll always be a Grey *within*, Russett. And I'll find proof. Even if I have to walk to High Saffron myself."

"Be my guest," I replied, "but you're wrong. Courtland died trying to save me."

"And that's where your story falls apart. I know my son. He would never have lifted a finger to save you."

It was a very sound argument, and we hadn't thought of it. Jane and I would have to review our lying procedures.

"You disgust me," added Gamboge, "I'll make it my life's work to destroy you."

"Likewise," I said, leaning closer. "I will aggressively pursue the manner of Travis' death. Perhaps we should discuss the timing of Penelope's allocation at Council tomorrow?"

She blinked several times and pursed her lips. But she said nothing more and moved away. The strange thing was, I hadn't even broken a sweat under her attack. Being a prefect was going to be quite enjoyable.

I made my way through the crowd and rejoined my father. "Okay," I said, "we'll do it your way."

The DeMauves

5.6.12.03.026: Open Returns can never be questioned or rescinded.

iolet had scored 28 percent Red and 57 percent Blue, which made her just Purple enough to one day become head prefect. She was delighted when my father got word to her of developments, and quickly broke off with Doug, much to his relief. She was well mannered enough not to comment on Jane's and my misfortune, and we sat side by side on the sofa in the living room of their house, one of the largest on the main square. They had two servants, three Titians and not a spot of synthetic purple anywhere in the house. They had breeding, after all, and the overly ostentatious expression of one's hue was not the done thing at all.

My father was there, and he had been chatting to Mrs. deMauve, who was as delighted and relieved as Violet over the change of circumstances.

"More tea?" said Violet.

"No, thanks."

The door opened, and deMauve walked in. I knew almost immediately that he had bribed the Colorman, as he had the faint smile on his face of someone who had just turned up a winning ace.

"So," he said to my father, "I understand things did not work out as expected?"

My father explained that, due to an "unforeseen incident," his son was once more available, and wondered if deMauve would care to enter his daughter into an arrangement.

"At the same rate?" he asked.

"Yes," said Dad.

"No," said I.

"It seems as though your son has issues with authority," said deMauve, "an ugly trait, and not one we should encourage."

"I would like to work for National Color," I said, "but I need you to endorse my application."

"Absolutely not," replied deMauve crossly. "Yewberry is the worst Red sorter we've ever had, and with High Saffron a washout, we'll need you in the Pavilion to even have a *chance* of meeting scrap-color targets."

"What if I were to make East Carmine the spoon capital of the Collective?"

"We can't make spoons," he replied gruffly. "It's not allowed."

"But what if I can get *around* the Rules? Can you imagine the riches such loopholery might bring to the community?"

DeMauve stared at me. Like it or not, I was an adult now, and at 86 percent, almost an equal.

"Keep talking."

I showed him the utensil that had been embedded in my backside when I was thrown into the yateveo. It wasn't really a spoon, but then it wasn't a fork, either. It had a spoonlike shallow scoop, but with the addition of three tines of a fork. I handed it to deMauve, who stared at it intently.

"I call it a spork," I said.

"How *ingenious*," remarked Violet, who was eager to have the pretense of a strong and supportive marriage, and was resolved to start as she meant to continue. "Whatever made you think of a brilliant name like that?"

"It's engraved on the back."

"Oh."

DeMauve turned the instrument around in his hands. It was mildly corroded from where it had lain inside the tree, but none the worse for that.

"Redundant production-line space at the linoleum factory could churn these out by the thousands," I said. "We'd be on full grid color by next year, and hosting Jollity Fair in three."

The head prefect nodded to himself. "I think you might be right. If the other prefects agree, we will do a trial batch for peer review of Rule Compliance. If it passes, you can have your endorsement to National Color."

The marriage deal was duly completed, and although expected to kiss Violet in front of them all, I didn't, which caused only minor consternation. I was still a good catch, even if the marriage was a sham. The meeting ended with the nuptials fixed for tomorrow at ten, with a week's honeymoon at Purple Regis, paid for by the deMauves. There was also the question of surname, and it was decided that I would abandon the Russett name, but that it would become a middle name for the infant. There were other wrinkles to iron out, but nothing too onerous—or nothing that *seemed* onerous, given that I was marrying Violet.

Sacrifices

1.1.01.01008: All residents are required to make sacrifices for the good of the community.

Half an hour later I walked down to the railway station to see Imogen and Dorian off. Despite a last-minute attempt by Yewberry and deMauve to find something in the Rules to stop them, there was nothing they could do. The couple had made their beds, completed their laundry and even finished homework that had been left over from their schooldays. Bertie Magenta was incandescent with rage, and not just because he was losing Imogen or his evening "on appro." It seemed that he had surrendered his ticket for "safekeeping" and had been told by his father to "work his passage home."

Fandango, too, was outraged, and while a small crowd, variously mixed with well-wishers and outraged parties, stood arguing opposite Imogen and Dorian's compartment, I went to wish the Colorman a safe journey.

"I heard you got deMauve to agree that you could sit the National Color entrance exam. Congratulations."

"As you said," I replied, "a capacity for ingenuity is looked on favorably by National Color."

"It is indeed. I am not involved in training, but I suspect we shall meet again. I like to think of National Color as a close-knit family."

He paused for thought.

"I never did find Ochre's second accomplice," he said. "I would expect you to tell me if any information reaches your ears?"

"I shall."

"Good. Do you want some advice, Edward?"

"I would welcome it."

"Sometimes people dabble in ideological matters that they shouldn't before they follow the one true light."

He said it in a pointed manner, and I felt my skin prickle. He might *suspect* something about Jane and me, and he might be fishing. I was instantly on my guard.

"I'm not sure I understand your meaning."

"Then let me throw some figures at you. Three hundred years ago, upward of ten thousand people were consigned to Reboot per annum. Last year's figure was five hundred and sixty-nine. In another three hundred years, it might be nil. Do you understand?"

I did, of course. He was trying to prove the system to me. I couldn't even show I properly understood.

"Yes, sir," I replied, "it shows that Munsell was right, in all things— except perhaps the spoons."

I laughed, and the Colorman laughed with me.

"Yes," he said, "the spoons."

He nodded in the direction of Imogen and Dorian's compartment.

"A fine couple."

"A happy couple."

"I've instructed them to take the Night Train to Emerald City," he said, fixing me with a steely gaze. "It's more comfortable."

I felt my heart miss a beat.

"But . . . that's the *Reboot* train," I remarked, trying to sound as normal as I could. "Wouldn't it be simpler to send them on the Emerald City Express?"

The Colorman stared at me with seemingly no emotion.

"I've wired instructions for them to be met and sent into the City. There is no risk. Do you have any objections to this plan, Edward?"

He stared at me with, I think, something of a triumphant smile. He had me trapped, and he knew it. If I said nothing, Imogen and Dorian would be sent to High Saffron. If I lodged an objection, he'd know that I was fully aware of what was going on. Jane and I would be finished even before we'd got started.

I took a deep breath, and recalled Jane's words: *The innocents will suffer, and at your hands.* I'd bested Sally Gamboge and deMauve, I was on the Council and even had a chance at infiltrating the notoriously secretive National Color. More, *I knew things no one should ever know.* Jane and I had an outside chance to discover the whole truth and destroy the Collective. Was all that more important than Dorian and Imogen?

"They could go on either train," I said. "I'm just happy for them to get away."

And I smiled. And in that smile, I condemned two people to death. Two innocent people. Two people in *love.* But also in that smile, I might have saved thousands. I also laid the foundation for Jane and myself. We would succeed, if only for Dorian and Imogen, and all the others who left their spoons behind in High Saffron.

The Colorman's face fell. He thought he'd got me.

"Excellent," he said without emotion. "Good day, Mr. Russett. We shall meet again, of that I am certain."

I told him I would look forward to that day, but he was no longer interested. The whistle blew, I wished him a safe journey and the train steamed out of East Carmine.

It took part of me with it.

Acknowledgments

I am hugely indebted to both Hodder and Penguin for affording me the luxury of tackling this novel, a departure from my usual oeuvre that proved rather more difficult to get onto paper than I had anticipated. I trust and hope that the tardiness in its delivery have not tested too harshly a robust relationship. In particular, I would like to thank Carolyn Mays and Jamie Hodder-Williams in the UK, and Molly Stern and Clare Ferraro in the United States, for their patience, guidance and continued faith in my abilities. My thanks also to the many talented individuals in marketing and publicity both sides of the pond, and to Bruce Giffords and Ian Paten for their sterling work in correcting what is my poor grammar and speling.

Huge thanks must also go to Tif Loehnis and Luke Janklow of Janklow and Nesbit for their support and continued efforts on my behalf, and to Dot Vincent and Rebecca Folland for their work developing my considerable foreign readership. My thanks would be incomplete without mention of Eric Simonoff, who for many years oversaw my U.S. interests and without whom my presence on the western side of the Atlantic would not be as strong as it is today.

I would also like to thank Mari Fforde, for help in ways too numerous to mention, from simple research to support, editorial skills and also allowing me continued sleep when Tabitha was teething. My thanks also to Matt McDonell for his valuable insights into what it is like to be colorblind, to Mike Pringle for the "enactment" joke and to Tom, Charlie and Corisande for many valued discussions. I should also mention my immediate family of Maddy, Rosie, Jordy, Alex, Tabitha, Mum, Cress,

Maggy and Stewart for simply being there, and finally my thanks to Milly, who has always believed in me and whose unwavering enthusiasm for walkies kept me well exercised.

Jasper Fforde, July 2009

  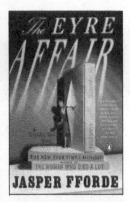